From the Inside Out

SCORNED
JEALOUSY
DYLAN
AUSTIN

S.L. Scott

Dear Kendra,
Where will yours
♡ lead you?
♡ ,S.L. Scott

From the Inside Out

SCORNED
JEALOUSY
DYLAN
AUSTIN

To My Family, With Love

SCORNED

From the Inside Out

Part 1

S.L. Scott

CHAPTER 1

March 12th

I HATE HIM with all my soul and every fiber, muscle, and nerve of my being. Dylan Somers broke me and my heart simultaneously, destroying everything I knew my life to be. Over the course of the next year, my friend Brandon had to put me back together. Piece by piece, he glued me back into a semblance of what I used to be before I knew Dylan, or so I thought. What I didn't realize was he was also bonding himself to me in the process. One night, my friend became my lover. Brandon never should have played that role, especially since I was still too broken to be good for anyone else. So we went back to being friends because I needed a friend more than a lover.

Dylan hasn't seen me since he walked in and sat down in the same restaurant as me. When my hand twitches, I realize I've pulled my phone from my purse, subconsciously to help diffuse the panic attack before it has a chance to hit. I refuse to let his presence overwhelm me or call Brandon every time I start freaking out.

This isn't a restaurant I frequent and being in the same place after all these years is completely coincidental. I've lost my appetite, so I push the plate of food away from me.

I glance over at him and *her*—red hair, red nails, red lips, red shoes, too tight red dress, red clutch perched on the table next to her glass of red wine. Everything about her is cliché and predictable to attract men. I roll my eyes, but then mine meet hers again and I look away. In that glimpse, I caught that her eyes are light colored, maybe blue, *probably* blue.

Mine are hazel—green on a good day, brown on most.

The face I really want to see is turned the other direction with his back to me. Dylan hasn't seen me in three years. It makes me wonder if he ever did, even when we were together. I don't know anymore and I hate to think about that time... the time when it was bad.

Sitting at this table for one, I've forgotten if it was ever good between us, or did I block it out? If I dig deep, really deep past the pain that was inflicted during those last few months we were together, it was blissful and perfect. I felt loved. I felt pretty. I felt whole. We were more good than bad, but now only the scar remains.

Glancing back to their table, her eyes are on me again. Quickly, I dig out a fifty and toss it on the table. That will easily cover my bill, even at an over-priced, too-trendy-to-be-considered-trendy-any-longer establishment on the Upper West Side.

My eyes meet hers one more time and I hope mine don't give anything away. Things like: how I know what he looks like when he falls apart from an orgasm, how he liked for me to touch him *there*, but not go further, deeper, and how when he's upset, his eyes match the skies right before a storm rolls in. I know all these things because I've experienced them with him, so I know him, the real Dylan.

Does she?

I look at him this time, just him, blocking her from my focus. His hair is styled. He always did have great hair, light brown, darker when gelled. I smirk at the thought that he still has great hair despite the hateful curses I wished upon him to go bald. The light starch to his shirt proves he hasn't changed. He insisted on that perfection, but still wanted to be comfortable in his clothes. The large face of his watch gleams under the track lighting above. Dylan Somers was always very confident... or cocky. I'm not sure which anymore. My memories on that specific trait of his has somewhat faded, overtaken by more harmful ones.

He holds too much pain, more than I can endure tonight. I walk through the intimate tables of the dining area. When I pass, she nods to him while smiling as if to tell him silently that I'm watching, as if to tell him, he has an admirer. *I'm not an admirer.* I'm an adversary—the enemy—the person he hates the most in the world if I recall his words correctly.

I push the door open and the cool air hits me. We're on the verge of spring, but it's still chilly, so I wrap my arms around myself and head south.

"Juliette?"

Hearing his voice causes my insides to freeze, but my feet keep moving. I don't respond to that name. Do I even know who Juliette is anymore?

"Juliette? Is that you?"

I hear his footsteps. They quicken but I refuse to respond to careless niceties he feels obligated to dole out.

Why?

Why does he try?

Why does he care?

What does he want?

"Hey!" He shouts from a distance, planting himself in a spot on the sidewalk, not willing to chase me. I roll my eyes because I'm walking in four-inch Prada, so he can easily catch me if he wants. He just doesn't want to. That's his arrogance showing. Everything always came so easy for him, including me back in college.

Rounding another corner, I find safety in the shadows of the building and keep walking. Memories of how bad the ending of us envelops me...

"I hate you," he shouts. "I hate you for making me take this job. I hate you for making me buy that car. I hate this apartment and the furniture. I hate everything I've had to do since moving here for you."

He used to say love, but lately, all I hear is hate. He's used it generously in the last week and more than a few times tonight, five in the last minute. It's ironic he's now using the car and the job he chose against me, both of which he got without talking to me at all. He now blames me for the regret he feels. I guess the saying is true; we hurt the ones we love the most.

My feet keep moving as the flashback continues...

"I hate this life... my life with you," Dylan yells at me.

"Have you met someone else?"

"God damn it, Juliette! This is about us, not anyone else."

He turns his back when he shouts. I can't see his eyes, which makes me question his truthfulness. I'm at a loss here. Do I speak again or is remaining quiet best these days? My phone rings, causing both of us to look over at it. He's not happy about the intrusion, though I'm relieved.

"I have to get that." I walk across the living room and pick it up.

Before I can answer, Dylan says, "Get it. I'm done here anyway." My eyes lift from the number flashing on the screen back to his that are looking down. "We're done." He leaves on that note, walking into the bedroom and leaving me to take my call.

"This is Juliette." I walk out of the apartment to give him the time alone he seems to need right now. Time is needed to cool down so we can talk about what is happening and what I did to upset him.

After many reassurances of my return to work, I hang up the phone with my gallery manager. Dylan's parting words sink in. We're done. Suddenly, I begin to understand that Dylan won't be here when I get home. Is it even home without him? I realize he meant what he said and I'm at a loss... again. I'm losing him. I'm losing my heart. I'm losing my other half. My soul. Everything that matters.

Taking a deep breath, my heart pounding, I move even quicker to get away from him and the memories, and all that ties me to the past. There's no more Dylan and Juliette, there's no point in making a scene on the street.

Finally, I reach my comfort zone. My hand is shaking although I'm standing in front of my own building.

One ring.

Two rings.

Brandon answers, "Hey, Jules, it's kind of late for a social call."

My heart calms and I smile. "You love hearing from me and you know it."

He laughs. "Yes, I do. Anytime, day or night for you."

"Can I come over?"

I hear shuffling. He's looking at the time. I know he is. It's only ten-fifteen. Still early.

"Of course," he replies, always overly concerned about me, "Is everything alright?"

"Buzz me in."

"You're already here?"

"Yes."

"Where's your key?"

"Buzz me in."

The lock releases and the door is opened without further question. He knows when not to push. He's great like that.

I climb the two flights, running out of breath after the rushed walk home. I walk in, setting my purse on the table by the window. I like the view from his apartment because it's the opposite of mine. It gives me a new perspective. He leans against the kitchen archway and watches me. The arch is a comforting design feature in the otherwise modern apartment. "The spare room has fresh sheets *oooor* you can crash in my room," he says like he's joking, but I know he's not.

The offer makes me smile, but just slightly because we haven't been lovers in a long time. "We're better as friends," I gently remind.

He crosses his arms over his chest, and says, "No harm in trying."

His intense dark eyes follow me around the room. His eyes are blue, but so different from Dylan's. His are the deepest oceans and Dylan's the sky above.

The weight of his gaze lays heavy on me, scanning my back as I look out over the street, spotting a pocket view of a lamp in the park. I turn and insist, "I'm tired."

"You know where everything is."

"I do." I breeze past him as if I own the place. In a way I do. It's a second home to me. I have some of my things, my belongings stashed around, in the bathroom, in the bedroom—the guest bedroom. My vitamins reside in the kitchen. Just things, inconsequential things.

I stop in the doorway to the guest room before I disappear for the night. "Thank you."

"You're always welcome here, but next time, use your key."

That makes me smile, a real one, genuine in its roots. "Goodnight, Brandon."

"Sweet dreams, Jules."

Dylan's intrusion into my life tonight has caused an imbalance in my world. My dreams aren't sweet. I'm restless, even at his place, where I used to find solace. Memories of the night he left me flood my dreams...

Reality strikes at the exhibit. I lose my mind and my new client when I breakdown in the back room. I had just sold a painting and pulled it from the collection at the request of the buyer. Behind what I thought were closed doors, I cried. Reflexively, I rub the canvas with my hand in an attempt to wipe the tears away, but the paint smears under my touch. The tips of my long brown hair also leaving their own distinctive mark.

My tears ruined his masterpiece—a piece the artist just painted live in front of potential customers. I'm called unprofessional and careless, and in his fit of rage, the artist refuses to work with me again, my tears costing him a five thousand dollar reward for his time and talent. The loss of the love of my life cost me more. He didn't seem to care about that. Artists can be testy that way. He broke the frame and trashed the painting when the buyer pulled out of the deal, not wanting my common problems splattered on his painting.

When a customer overheard the argument, he reassured, "It will be okay. I promise."

At the time, it was hard to believe his words. They still haunt me because I want to believe, but can't seem to hold onto them.

When I return home late that night, the car is not parked out front and the apartment is bare. Dylan hated that car, he hated the furniture, he hated his life. Yet, he still took it away. He took everything he hated, except for me.

Nothing remains in the place we called home except a twenty-five dollar coffee maker and my clothes dumped on the floor because he took the dresser.

I kick off my shoes and go to make myself a cup of coffee, but he took the beans that I had freshly ground this morning. Now I have a coffeepot with no coffee to go in it. I drop to the floor in the kitchen and fall apart, completely apart, my heart shattering into a million pieces. The gallery breakdown was just the predecessor of what was to come. This is the remains of my life, the end as I know it. In the course of a ten hour absence, my life was packed and moved to another location never to be seen again.

All the love we shared has vanished like Dylan, the coffee, and the dresser.

Was this planned?

For how long?

Movers on the same day?

A storage unit or another apartment waiting for this day?

It seems too organized, premeditated.

I hold the black coffee maker in my arms, cradling myself around it, needing to have something tangible and this is all that is left. This is all I have to show for a life born from love but died from misunderstandings and lies.

CHAPTER 2

March 13th

WANTING TO LEAVE before Brandon rises, I start the coffee pot before I go. It's a small gesture to show my gratitude. I used to love surprising Dylan with breakfast in bed and a hot cup of coffee years ago, but now my damaged side wins out and small gestures seem to be the only kind I'm capable of these days.

OPENING THE INDUSTRIAL back doors, a gust of warm air enters the gallery with me as I walk inside. The first warmth of spring I believe. I should take my lunch down to the park today. I bet the buds of the crabapple trees are blooming. The deep burgundy flowers are my favorite, but I'm sure I'll only see the white. The white are more common in the city. They're blander, more normal, more acceptable, conform more, less vibrant, less life lives in them, cheaper. I leave the doors open, knowing others will soon arrive for work.

My heels clack against the wood slats of the floor as I make my way. My office has a window in the front, facing the street. I don't like sitting in a fishbowl, but it's en vogue, so I deal with it.

We just had the floors redone, but I still see scuff marks as I walk. I usually try to avoid looking at the floor, but then that leads my gaze up and I only notice the marks on the white walls. They have to be white. Stark white highlights the art. This concept seems foreign to those who work here since no one else makes the effort to care like I do. I focus on my office ahead instead, so I don't continue counting all the spots that need retouching, driving me mad.

I call for Frank, but he's not in. It's too early, two hours too early. He'll spend his morning touching up the painted walls. It's been at least a month and completely unacceptable at our gallery's art price point to let that slide another day. Paint is cheap. Talk is cheap. Words are meaningless to me. Actions are everything. A hard lesson to learn, but now it's ingrained.

Holding my chin up, I don't let my emotions show. Emotions are a weakness I've worked hard to suppress the last three years—a detriment to not only my heart, but my job that I had to overcome.

I won't make that mistake again. Now I like predictable, reliable, responsible. Those don't toy with your emotions or wound you. I live according to a plan that was put into action two years ago. It was the only way I could see surviving. If I didn't have to think about things too much, I wouldn't have to think about Dylan. It all made sense at the time. But a black plague of questions shrouds me daily in regards to my plan.

Can plans change?

Should they change?

Does time change them?

Or do we change in time?

I should talk to Brandon about this. He can be very insightful when it comes to my quirks.

The morning flies by with tedious office tasks. I hurry to the park at lunchtime to lull the hour away in the peaceful surroundings. After I find an empty bench, I sit in solitude. While eating, I close my eyes, letting the chirping of the birds fill my ears and feel the breeze against my skin. The shield that usually protects me slips and for a brief moment in time, I feel serene. In times like these I realize how much effort I put into pretending to be normal.

My hand drops to my lap and memories of picnics, playing

Frisbee, laughing all come back. Central Park in the springtime is a sight to behold, an experience to be had, a way to wile the hours away frivolously. I loved lazy Sundays. I loved them with Dylan. I know he loved them with me as well. He just forgot how good it could be, how good we could be together.

I haven't willingly indulged my desire to think about Dylan since seeing him at the restaurant the night before. I'm not strong enough to do that, so I refrain. Every time he wants to make an appearance in my thoughts, I think of *her*, and that puts the façade right back in place. *Her*—with her red everything. *Her*—that had the pleasure of his company last night. I wonder if she asked him who he was chasing and if he told her the truth. I wonder if she went home with him and erased all lingering thoughts he might have had of me.

I wonder so much and won't be privy to answers, so I store these thoughts in that place where I push all my memories of him. I lock them away in the dented and damaged chest that lives in the recesses of my mind. It's dark and dangerous, so I don't venture there often.

However, sometimes I slip and revisit, much to my dismay.

I open my eyes to the laughter of children playing tag nearby. Something that should make me happy makes me sad, and I feel the wall rebuilding itself, brick upon heavy brick.

March 14th

MY ALARM GOES off on time, but today is different. The weight that the date carries is already starting to drag me under. Grabbing my pillow, I bury my face under it. While holding my breath, I pray for the will to make it through the next twenty-four hours in one piece. It would have been wise to take the day off from work. I usually do, but end up there anyway needing to take my mind off other things. Things like wondering.

I *wonder* if we had broken up sooner, would it still hurt as much?

I *wonder* if we hadn't broken up if we'd be married.

Would we have kids?

I *wonder* if he's dating someone else.

I *wonder* why I would even add the word 'else' on the end like that.

Maybe he's married to the woman in red... with kids.

Or maybe it was just a date and he's single and available.

Was he ever available? Truly available?

Yes, he was once. Remembering his smile triggers my own, and how it affected me back then, how it brightened my day and made me anxious to return home to him. Memories run rampant and I hold the pillow over my face even tighter. When I open my eyes, I feel disgusted that I smiled over a memory of Dylan's smile.

Tossing the pillow aside, I roll out of bed, deciding to skip the dramatics, and get ready. A hot shower does little to comfort me and even less than the memory of him did a few minutes before. I dress in a hurry, not taking my time, a dress pulled from the hanger haphazardly. Shoes are taken from the shelf without second guessing, wallet thrown in my work bag because I don't want to take the time to find the 'right' purse for this outfit.

I leave my hair down to dry naturally, letting the waves form how they do when I don't straighten them. When I move into the kitchen, I see the coffee pot, *our* old coffee pot. I don't drink from it. Ever. It doesn't come to life and percolate or provide me with the much needed caffeine to kick my ass into gear. It stands as a monument, a symbol of what used to exist here, representing the lives that used to live between these walls. It sits idly unused next to my $2,000 DeLonghi Coffee Center—my most decadent purchase A.D., After Dylan.

I've used the DeLonghi a total of three times, mainly because I don't have the time to learn how to use it. I'm not home much if I can avoid it. Today is about overcoming the date's history and making a fresh start, so I write a post-it note and stick it to the front of the machine's gleaming stainless steel surface. *Learn to use.*

Since I don't know how to use it, I walk down the steps of the stoop and head west one block. Opening the door to my favorite local bakery and coffee shop, a calm comes over me. Other than the park, this is one of the few places where I allow myself the courtesy to relax and absorb the comfort. Maybe it's the warm wood tones and the soft music playing in the background that eases me. Maybe it's the homemade smells that fill the air. Or maybe it's because my apartment and the gallery lie in stark contrast to the quaint little shop.

"Juliette?"

With my guard down, I'm caught relaxing, so without thinking, I look up. "*Dylan,*" flows from my lips as if it's still allowed to reside there, as if I say it every day.

I think of the name often, but I never say it.

Ever.

And yet... I just did.

CHAPTER 3
Jules
March 14th

"I CAN'T BELIEVE it's you," Dylan says, glancing around as if everyone should be as surprised as him.

I swallow—hard—left without any other words in me. He renders me speechless and that's just not how I ever saw this going when I played this reunion out in my head.

"Was that you the other night?" he asks. "At the restaurant?"

Hmmm... How should I respond? *Yes*, it was, but I avoided you even though I heard you shouting my name, *that* name, down the street. Or maybe, *no*, I have no idea what you're talking about?

The lie is much more appealing right now. "Which restaurant?" My voice betrays my poor acting skills and goes up an octave.

"I could've sworn that was you, but I wasn't sure. You look... you look different."

Good different or *bad different?* Ugh, why do I care?

"I mean, you look really great, Juliette." There's that name again, overshadowing what I think is a compliment. Hearing *that* name makes me cringe and melt all at once. I hate this feeling. I hate how my memory serves me too well and I feel somewhat less of myself just because he's talking to me.

"Bistro down on 72nd," he continues. He's also still staring at me, seeking, searching.

I reply, "I ate there the other night."

He furrows his brow. "So it was you. Why didn't you..." I know what he's going to ask, but he thinks better of it, not finishing. I think he gets the hint that I'm not really open to this conversation. "I'm sorry for bothering you." Rocking back on his heels, he suddenly seems unsure of his own words, thoughts, of what he should do. "I just wanted to say hello."

I angle my head gently to the side to *really* look at him. He looks good—great, in fact. Time has stood still for him. He looks happy, or at least not unhappy, like the last time I saw him before he left me.

Two of his fingers tap down on the table and he says, "I should go. It was really nice to see you again, Juliette." *Cringe.* "Maybe we'll see each other again sometime soon."

"There's a possibility since we've seen each other twice in the last few days when we hadn't seen each other at all over the last three years." I don't know where this comes from as it bursts from my mouth, like stating some weird statistical anomaly. I should have just let it lie and let him walk away.

He seems surprised once again, but this time probably because I've spoken more than four words. When he smiles at me, I feel the first hairline fracture form on my outermost protective layer, my shield, as if alerting me to tread carefully. I still smile, an old reaction to him.

Speaking at a much quicker pace this time, he says, "You really do look fantastic. Life is treating you well."

That's where he'd be wrong.

He glances over his shoulder, seeming to be waiting on someone. I'm sure he is, which causes a dull ache in my heart. When his eyes return to mine, he signals to the large clock over his shoulder. "I've got to run. I have a meeting downtown in twenty and I should've left ten minutes ago."

Maybe that's what he was looking at before. I thought the worst of him and he proved me wrong. I don't apologize or even return the smile this time. I owe him nothing more of myself. He took all of that with him when he left years ago.

"So, yeah, I should get going." He steps backward and has this goofy grin on his face like he actually *is* happy to see me.

I always loved that goofy grin. The small fracture widens every time I feel anything other than scorn for this man. In a small way, I want to test the theory. But not today.

He turns, then rushes out the door and my gaze drops to his coffee he left behind on my table. I stare at it, my granola parfait long forgotten. Picking up the cup, I see droplets of coffee around the hole in the lid and I'm tempted to taste it. I don't know if I want to taste the coffee, or him, or both, but the thought disturbs me and makes me feel stalkerish. I set it back down exactly where he left it, spinning it back to the way it was before it was abandoned.

Tucking my hands under the table, I grasp them together to keep from touching the offensive white to-go cup again. I tilt my head to read the order label stuck crookedly on the side: *Black*. I glance down at my porcelain coffee mug and the black, no fuss coffee that remains and remember the times we shared black coffee together.

The bell chimes and my eyes flash up. His half smile and body language speaks of his embarrassment as he returns. "Forgot my coffee, and I seriously need the caffeine this morning."

I watch as he wraps his fingers around the paper cup. My heart races, remembering how they used to wrap around me, in me, curling, teasing, pleasing... Forcing my eyes up, I watch as he sits down in the opposite chair. He looks nervous once again, uncertain as his eyes search the tabletop for the words he wants to use. After clearing his throat, his voice is deep and hesitant when he says, "I want you to know I'm sorry."

Sorry.

After three years of heartbreak, tears, and numbness, the power of his words is the key, turning the lock on the chest that's buried in the recesses. Tears form in the corner of my eyes and my gaze drops down to the wood grain of the table, unable to look at him with any kind of emotion other than hurt. Waving my hand erratically in front of me, I unknowingly let him off the hook, as if to say *oh, that, that was nothing. No worries.* But my words don't match my actions. "Don't," I say, all emotion that's threatening to come back is gone again in an instant.

When I stand, he stands. His hand gently caresses my upper arm and my eyes follow it. Realizing the act of touching me is unwelcome, he pulls his hand back, and whispers, "I didn't mean to upset you. I just want you to know how I feel."

Struggling from being this close to him, I say, "It's not necessary and you're supposed to be downtown in five minutes." I bolt for the door in a blur of words and excuses. "And I've got to get to work."

The bell chimes my exit, another echoes as he follows me out onto the sidewalk. I know it's him. I can feel his presence, his heat, his concern, his apologetic face searing my back. I rush forward, away from him, but he remains close. Finally his footsteps falter and he says, "I know what today is, Juliette."

Cringe. I stop, not able to take it any longer. With my hands fisting at my sides, I turn around and lose my temper altogether. "Stop calling me Juliette!"

He's stricken with my untamed emotion, his face one of shock and horror, confusion, and still so damn apologetic.

Stepping to the curb, I flail my arm into the air to hail a cab, needing a fast getaway, an escape from him. When the taxi pulls away from the curb, I exhale as the chest is sealed tightly and returned to where it belongs.

CHAPTER 4

Dylan Somers

March 16th

I WANT TO see Juliette again. I can't stop thinking about her. She's a beautiful woman, not a girl anymore. I miss the girl, but I threw her away, thinking the grass was greener. It wasn't.

She's different, on the inside. Changed. Did I do that to her? I hope not.

With my feet resting atop my desk, I have a chewed up pen cap in my mouth as I stare out my corner office window. My cell phone and call button have been silenced, so I'm not disturbed. I let my thoughts drift back to the beginning of the end...

Juliette pulls back from the kiss and whispers that she's tired. It's 2:37 in the morning. My ego takes the hit and I roll away from her, taking it out on her by giving the cold shoulder, by making her feel she's done me wrong. I feel rejected. Excuses, I know, but it's how I start distancing myself, preparing for what's coming.

She rubs my back lovingly and apologizes. The tension eases in my body, but my head holds tight. I slip out from her reach with a groan and pretend to fall asleep.

That's the first time I hear her cry because of me, because of the way I'm hurting her. It's soft and quiet but her pain is apparent. We've never gone to bed angry and we didn't tonight, but somehow in the night, I managed to hurt her and now here we are.

I hate myself. I hate what I'm becoming and yet it's like I have to go after it with full intention. I'm going to break her heart... on purpose and that breaks mine.

I pick at the sandwich in front of me but I'm not hungry. I don't want food. I want coffee, with her, at the coffee shop. The run-in was a fluke, seeing her there—a planned accident, if I told the truth.

I was shocked as hell to find out she kept the apartment. I took a chance and ventured over to the part of the city that still feels like home, even though it hasn't been in three years. I wasn't aware of the date when I woke up this morning. That was just coincidence, but after seeing her two nights earlier, well, *who I thought was her,* I had to verify with my own eyes.

When I googled her, it brought me back to the old apartment. I showed up early because she was always a morning person. I am too now, but I used to be more of a night owl. Today, I got there early and waited, like a stalker. Man, I'm fucked up. I waited knowing how fucked up what I was doing really was, but I couldn't get her off my mind. Now, like then, I can't sleep, but for very different reasons these days...

I can't sleep because of the guilt I carry. I watch Juliette instead. There's just enough light from the bathroom for me to see her face. She has this nightlight that she leaves on in there. She said it made her feel safe at night. I teased her because I didn't understand and thought nightlights were childish. But now I hope she finds comfort in it. Comfort I can't seem to give her anymore. Comfort she's going to need if I keep going in the direction I'm going.

I carefully slide my head onto her pillow and press my nose down so I can smell her hair and her skin. I love her scent. It's inviting, drawing me near, and gives me security.

I'll miss that.

I'll miss her, though I know she won't believe me in the aftermath.

Biggest mistake I ever made was leaving her. Three years later, I've paid a price for that decision. Now I'm paying the debt, chipping away at it little by little as I watch her during an early morning stakeout. She came out of her apartment, and from behind sunglasses I watch, from the safety inside of a small grocer's window. She doesn't see me, but I see her. She is nothing less than stunning but she doesn't look happy, her mouth never deviating from a straight line as she walks down the street.

I miss the neighborhood, the apartment we shared, that coffee shop, the grocer, her... us together. I lost myself the day I walked out of our apartment the last time. It was the opposite back then. I thought I had found myself. I finally had what I thought I wanted—a shortcut to success. I quickly discovered that success comes with a price and I had to pay up.

I took a leap of faith, put everything into storage except my best suits—I had two—and knocked on Hillary's door.

It started out as harmless flirtations in the office, but it grew into something more on New Year's. She lit a fire in me that I hadn't felt... I hadn't felt since I first met Juliette. She made me feel good, like the world was ours to conquer if I'd just accept some fake destiny she laid out before me.

Hillary was a predator and I was her prey, weak to temptation. She smiled when she saw the suits in my hand. She took them from me, hung them on the coat rack that stood by the door and jumped on me, her laughter filling the corridor of her high-rise condo.

We partied—hard. I'm shocked we still had jobs, but she gave me power. Power I had never felt before. I was made a manager within two months.

She took me places and introduced me to people of society— people of wealth, people I discovered were as loyal as conmen. I was the toast of the town one day and when they were through with me, nothing. She came from money and she loved to spend it on me. I thought I wanted all that, that life. I hadn't had money in years.

With Juliette, we had to be careful. We were young and broke because we had just started our careers. She landed an associate sales position at a gallery downtown and I had been accepted into a Manager-in-Training program for a large telecom firm. We felt like real fancy somebodies, living the high life, or so we thought: An apartment in New York City, nice furnishings, take-out three times a week, and a new car. I'd never owned a new car before. It was exciting—ridiculous in Manhattan but exciting.

That car was the start of our downfall though neither of us recognized it at the time. Over time, I resented her for keeping me from a bigger life. Back then, I didn't know how false and fleeting that life was. I hated that new life, the life with Hillary.

My watch beeps twice, alerting me that my lunch hour is over. I swing my feet down and toss the sandwich in the trash. I depress the do not disturb button to allow calls back in and I turn on my cell. My afternoon is swamped with papers and proposals, clients and business calls. I now manage a team of sixteen at an investment firm in the Financial District. I'm making five times the money I made three years ago. One would think I'd made it big by all appearances. *I haven't.* The money doesn't matter to me anymore. I was happier when I didn't have much. I was happier when I had Juliette.

I'm lonely though I'm always surrounded by people. I miss the warmth of her arms, her gentle sighs in the night. I miss the damn nightlight. I miss her, everything about her.

Hillary and I broke up after six months. We ended just as abruptly as we began. It was all fire and passion in that relationship. A tit for a tat. Heated arguments. Heated make-up sex. *It* was never satisfying. *She* was never satisfying. *She* wasn't Juliette. She could never replace her.

My four o'clock invites me out for dinner and drinks. I accept. I always do. It's part of my job. Dinner is on the company, which pleases the clients. We have cocktails with our meal. I have two. They each have three. Then they tell me there's a new bar about six blocks from here—a strip club.

I agree to go because I'm supposed to. I walk, they stumble. I laugh, they crack up. I play the charismatic wingman to their antics, keeping the clients happy. On the way, we pass a party, a gallery holding an event tonight. The painting in the window grabs my attention, causing me to stop and stare.

I love art. I love looking at paintings, in particular. I prefer them to sculptures and such. Juliette was always so passionate about art and loved to talk about how art opened our minds to the endless possibilities. I loved listening to her.

Something inside the gallery draws me to this exhibit and I want to see more. Signaling for the guys to go ahead without me, I tell them I'll meet them there. They're too busy stumbling to care.

Walking around the room, I scan all of the paintings to get a feel for the collection as a whole before going back to the beginning to appreciate them one at a time. That's just how she taught me. The fifth painting captures my attention. I grab a glass of wine as a waiter passes, and stare into the depths and ridges of the oil.

"It's Rusque. He painted it last year while on holiday in Cannes."

Tensing, I don't turn, afraid she'll run away again. Instead, I let her voice blanket me in warmth, familiarity, comfort, and I try to relax like we talk all the time.

"If you look closely," Juliette continues. "You'll see lavender mixed in with the orange, black, and red in the bottom left corner. I really like the unexpected lavender." She pauses and I glance over. She appears to get lost in the painting for a moment before she adds, "It's something soft found within the harsh."

That sounds a lot like how I would describe her after seeing her this morning. I keep that thought to myself though.

She giggles out of nowhere and I turn to look at her, hoping I've elicited the sweet sound. But I see a glass of champagne in her hands and have fond memories of how it always made her laugh. I should have known it wasn't me.

Her back is to me as she moves to the next painting, and I can't pretend to be respectful by restraining myself to quick glances any longer. I look at her, really look at her, watching wholeheartedly, and allowing myself this indulgence. She walks with grace, and refinement, an outer confidence. After placing her glass on a table nearby, she holds her hands behind her back, her delicate fingers wrapped around a small wrist. Her pace is slow, feeling much like an invitation to stay, so I follow.

I can't turn back the clock and appreciate what I had, but I still feel the loss of her every day. Realizing I have nothing left to lose since I already lost her, I take a chance. "I don't know what to call you."

She stands there studying the painting in front of her, no anger gracing her beautiful face like it did this morning. "I go by Jules now." She glances my way and that's all it takes to be utterly captivated by her, just like I was years before.

CHAPTER 5

Dylan

March 16th

"I LIKE JULES," I reply, leaving the words lingering between us.

Juliette turns her head and looks past me. Her eyes widen like she sees someone in the distance, someone she recognizes who makes her smile. "If you'll excuse me," she says, not making eye contact, her gaze planted on my chest. I can see her struggle not to look up before she walks away.

Disappointment and relief covers me equally. I like the time I spent with her, just like this morning at the coffee shop. But it's intense, heavy between us. I'm relieved to have the chance to take a breath and gather my wits back together. She throws me entirely off my game.

That makes me wonder if I'm playing a game with her. I don't mean to. It's not my style anymore. *When did I get game anyway?* Juliette loved that I had no game... when we met. I was popular, but didn't screw with people's heads to get my way.

With Hillary, it was all games. Life was a game to her. People were puppets to be toyed with, their emotions and lives irrelevant. Unlike my family, who are financially secure, coming from money for Hillary taught her not to value anything or anyone. People destroyed in the process were just consequences to the petty game. The first time I met her, I saw the devil in her eyes...

She was there. I think she was waiting for me and I don't normally drink strong cocktails like martinis, so it was easy to lose my better judgment. What happened became a blur in the darkest of corners past the small antiquated payphone booth, hidden from the rest of the party.

Targeted. She had targeted me and knew she would get me eventually. I wasn't strong enough, the liquor loosening my grip on the important things in my life, like Juliette.

Hands firmly wrap around my neck, pulling me toward the dark. My body ruled my mind in its weakened state. It was obvious that fate had already decided, it was obvious what her craving for me did. She was not shy, but like a woman possessed. Maybe obsessed was more appropriate when looking back.

Her lips found mine, but I resisted, turning my head. I'd never been with an aggressive woman before. The sudden stirrings I felt were unexpected. Somehow as she whispered the things she would do to me, for me, I knew. She was not going to take no for an answer. She would be relentless until she broke me.

She brushed across my cock, just on the outside of my pants, but it shamed me that my body wanted more. She couldn't see my anger as I grabbed her wrists and removed them from where only Juliette had been since the day I met her. She couldn't see the guilt that was already washing through me as I spoke of the love I had for my girlfriend. She wouldn't have cared anyway.

Taking advantage of my faltering, she dragged my hand down her body demanding that I touch her. Suddenly I realized that I wanted her. Not as a whole, but on some level, some buried part of me liked her touch, her directness, and the words she spoke in hushed tones in my ear. She had to have me and she wasn't afraid to ask for what she wanted. She wanted to please me. She was eager. I told her no, then Juliette came to mind and I stepped back. She reached for me, started pulling me back to her, but I ran. I ran into the restroom and I threw up.

My stomach rolled as I emptied the contents along with my heart and my life into the toilet, and flushed it all away. I avoided my reflection in the mirror as I washed my hands and my face, trying to bring color back to my cheeks, not wanting to worry Juliette. I scrubbed my mouth clean with paper towels before escaping quickly while making sure she wasn't out there again waiting to pounce. I made it back to my girlfriend just as the clock struck twelve, giving her a closed mouth kiss.

Hugging me tight, she told me how happy she was, how lucky she was that we get to spend another year together. The moment was ruined when I saw Hillary over her shoulder though. She smiled at me like she knew she already had me. I closed my eyes, trying to block her out while I appreciated what I held in my arms.

It was in that moment I decided I would trade Heaven for Hell. I still hate myself for hurting Juliette. I was never dumb, but I was obviously naïve. I see that now.

The very first time I saw her on campus I knew she deserved better than me. I would tell her that, but she would laugh, never believing me. In the end, I proved her wrong.

This morning I saw she doesn't wear a ring on her left hand. I only went there after figuring out what the date was. I took a chance to ease my conscience and tracked her down so I could apologize. It was long overdue. I saw the fear and anger in her eyes though. She felt ambushed, her eyes telling me much more than she did.

Looking back over my shoulder, I see Juliette hug a man in a tailored suit. *Is he deserving?*

The way she embraces him makes me wonder about the nature of their relationship. He touches her with a familiarity that's more personal than professional. He's attracted to her, that much is obvious. They hold each other too long and I feel the beginnings of jealousy. When she looks down instead of resting her chin on his shoulder, I feel a small sense of relief, but should I?

I turn back to the painting before moving to the next one,

needing to stop the crazy thoughts I'm having. I don't want to invade her space, even though I completely want to.

"You have some fucking nerve." I hear a man say from behind me.

I turn around at the crass statement only to be faced with someone that takes me by surprise. "Brandon!" I exclaim. His face is tight, eyes blazing, jaw locked, and his arms crossed over his chest. "How are you?"

"Save the pleasantries, Somers. Why the fuck are you here?"

It's hard to look tough or feel like you can hold your own when you're holding a wine glass. I set it down on a passing tray and cross my arms over my chest. I can see how this is gonna go down. "By that greeting, I guess you've still got a hard on for Juliette."

"Fuck you. You don't know shit about anything, much less me or her."

His eyes flicker in her direction and I follow watching as she pulls a calculator from her pocket and types, showing it to nice-suit-lukewarm-embrace man. When I turn back, I say, "This is over Juliette. You're pissed I'm here... or threatened?"

"It's Jules," he says. "You have no right to call her Juliette."

"But that's her name, and I'm still in the dark as to why she's so insistent on being called Jules now."

"I'm not giving you anything, asshole. Why are you even here? You didn't do enough damage the first go round. You crawling back? What the fuck, dude. She can finally sleep at night... most nights, and here you are slithering back into her life." He pokes me in the chest.

I don't take lightly to the interrogation, but with the tidbits he's dropping out about her, I'll take it a bit longer. Knowing I have the upper hand here, I reply, "It's all coincidental. I stopped in because I liked the paintings. I didn't know she worked here. But why are you here? You two together?" I look back at her briefly, surprised she would date him. He was never her type and definitely not deserving of her. Jealously settles into the pit of my stomach.

"It's none of your business what our relationship is, but the one thing I am that you never were is supportive," he says, pointing at

Juliette. "You don't know what you did to her—"

"I do. I made a huge fucking mistake, but—"

"But nothing, my ass! I bet you money you know what today is and here you are rubbing her nose in it."

Looking down, I sigh. The heaviness of the day is wearing on me. "Look, I know today is the day we broke up. I don't need the reminder. I'm reminded every fucking day I wake up without her," I say, lowering my voice as other patrons start to look at us.

His voice lowers to a menacing degree. "I'm warning you, Somers. Stay away from her!"

"Don't tell me—"

"You two need to leave." Juliette appears, seething with no patience for either of us. "You're starting to cause a scene."

"I'll leave when he does." Brandon stands tall, determined.

She looks at him and I see a slight break in her firm demand. "Don't do this, Brandon. I'll see you later. I promise."

Glancing back at me, I don't get another word from her before she turns around and walks across the gallery.

Brandon looks at me and in a hushed tone, he utters, "Fucker!"

"Asshole!" My back is to him already as I walk out. I debate if I should go home or join my clients at the strip club down the street. Turning back to steal one more glimpse of her through the window, I see her hugging Brandon. It's warm, welcoming. She finds security in him, but I'm still left wondering when the neighbor became more. *Or was he waiting for me to screw up all along?*

Hailing a cab, I decide to head home. I'll send my apologies to the clients tomorrow. I'm in no condition to entertain. After dumping my wallet and phone on the kitchen counter, I brush my teeth and strip down to my boxers. With all the lights out, it feels too dark in here. I walk to the bed and stub my toe on the corner of the frame, and hobble the rest of the way. After climbing in, I check my alarm clock and lay there thinking about Juliette... thinking about *Jules.*

I pull my comforter up to my neck, but it doesn't feel like enough now, so I reach down for the throw that I shouldn't have. It's the one

I stole from Juliette that made Hillary mad. I drag it up the bed and cover my arms, trying to sleep while the feeling warms me from the inside out.

Jules

I KNOCK, KNOWING Brandon will probably be asleep, but he's expecting me. When he opens the door, the smallish smiles on our faces are a giveaway for how tired we are. It's late, so no big greetings are needed. He scratches his head and I can tell he wants to ask me why I didn't use my key. But he doesn't, he just kicks the door open wider.

After brushing my teeth and pulling on my pj's, I slip into his bed, foregoing the guest room. His bed is warm. *He's* warm, but doesn't fill the void and it's better than being alone across the hall.

We don't normally share a bed, but if I'm alone the tears will come, overwhelming my head and heart. The date hasn't changed and he understands that tonight is different. I'm tense, wanting to escape my own body and mind, so tonight I let him hold me. I try to settle my nerves and heavy emotions, thinking I should be happy how the evening played out. Paintings were sold and big commissions were made, giving my paycheck a huge boost. A dedicated buyer bought another, adding to his growing collection, all of which I've sold to him. He's persistent and dresses nicely, wealthy, single, and handsome. He's interested in me, hopeful even. I don't know why he waits for me. He deserves a medal for his patience. I carry too much emotional baggage to burden him with. *Can he not see how damaged I am? How I'm scarred from the inside out?*

CHAPTER 6

Jules

March 23rd

IT'S BEEN JUST over a week since Dylan came by the gallery. When I demanded he leave, I'm not sure if I meant temporarily or forever. A week and three days earlier, I would have meant forever. Now I'm not so sure.

I'm still left wondering what he and Brandon were arguing about. *Maybe me? Knowing them, probably me.* I want to know, but won't ask Brandon even though he would tell me if I did.

I'm caught in flux. The pattern of my days has changed. I used to wake up and listen to the numbing news on TV. It was background, white noise. But lately, I've forgotten to turn on the TV altogether, my mind on Dylan instead.

His tie was loosened at the neck and the top button undone. I could tell he had drinks prior to arriving at the gallery by the size of his pupils, and how soft the lines were around his eyes, relaxed even. *When did he get those lines? Did he always have them or has life given him those?* One thing I know for sure, I liked them more than I should.

He wears his hair shorter, not by much, but I notice the difference. It still wants to break free from the confines of the gel

31

he's using though. I like it a bit wilder.

I see the way he watches me when he thinks I don't notice. I see him—always. His gaze heated my back when I shifted my head down as my buyer, Mr. Barker, embraced me. I saw Dylan out of the corner of my eye and he was staring. *He said he hated me. Those were his parting words. So it makes me wonder if he could feel something other than hate for me now?* His expression would say yes, but knowing him and how heartless he truly is, I'm probably reading too much into it.

That morning in the coffee shop, I noticed he doesn't wear a ring or any identifying marks of having worn one, like a tan line or indentation. I don't think he's married, but I'm left wondering if he's engaged, taken, or single. My bet is engaged. Most women would fall all over him for his looks alone. Add in that he looks like he might have money now...

I really fucking hate that I wonder these things. The lady in red often disturbs any nice thoughts I might be having, so I turn on the TV to distract me.

Brandon knows me too well. He knows I've thought of Dylan, that I still do, but he also knows how to navigate my moods. He's not said anything yet, but it's coming. I can feel it, building like it's on the tip of his tongue. He knows Dylan's gotten to me. He just doesn't know how much.

ANOTHER WORK DAY begins and I go to the gallery. I orchestrate the artists, make sure the bills are paid, the clients checks go through, the paintings delivered. I busy myself within my passion. I'm living my dream.

We used to talk about our dreams all the time. I used to tell Dylan how one day I would run a gallery. I wanted to discover new talent. I lost myself after I lost him, struggling to get back on track. But I never gave up on my career. I was determined to make something in my life work. Sometimes I wonder if him leaving caused me to focus on my job even more and that's why I am where I am. I'm young to hold this position, but the gallery owner was impressed, saw the potential, and took a chance on me despite my age.

I watched as Dylan walked into *my* gallery last week. My insides flipped, but I couldn't run, didn't want to hide. Just like years before, he commands attention even when he's not trying. There is still nothing ordinary about him... It's quite frustrating actually.

He approaches art like I do and the way I view an object or painting. He even prefers paintings like I do. They seem more open, open to interpretation, open for ones own realities to be placed on the artist's vision. Sculptures are more stated. I watched him view the exhibit on that date that I dread each year. I watched him study the art, utilizing what seemed to be the technique I taught him, walking around the room doing a onceover first. The way his body moves—so familiar, and yet somehow different as if life has had no negative effects on him at all. His body has also changed. It's more manly—broader shoulders, sharper jaw line.

I can't speak to the internal changes. I hope there are some. I hope he's different from the person I knew at the end our relationship, but deep down, I also hope he's still the person I loved three years prior.

Dylan showing up twice in the same day has messed with my head again. My thoughts aren't clear, they're fucked up.

He did this. He did this to me.

Why is he back in my life?

Why does he seem to be in every part of my life again? Is it planned or coincidence?

I'm pretty done with all of it, with everything. I'm fucked up because I don't care about anything anymore, least of all myself. I dress the part though. I make a pretty package. I wonder if Dylan still finds me pretty.

I've made a lot of money over the last three years, so I can afford nice things. My shoes are more expensive. So are my clothes, but that's all superficial stuff. I don't spoil myself. I wear my dresses to more than one event even if I'm photographed. I'm not shallow. I just have a few nice things. I deserve them and they make me smile when I wear them.

But I do take cabs. That's where I splurge. Cabs were always a splurge when we were together. We had this change jar...

A taxi fund is set-up next to the phone where our spare change is dropped daily. Dylan hasn't added any in at least a month, but I don't say anything. He's been stressed lately and I don't like to upset him and it feels like a topic that might. But I can't help but wonder if he's buying other stuff with his spare change. Maybe a coffee from Starbucks? Maybe lunch out with his co-workers?

Maybe... I don't know. It hurts to think about this kind of stuff, so I avoid it, pushing down the questions that fight to be asked. Our home is empty without him here. His presence mixed with mine fills it, brings it to life. It's felt lifeless over the last month.

I'm still a saver. Old habit. Brandon says I should quit my job and travel. That's how much I've saved. The art world pays well if you can find the talent like I have. My heart may not be whole, but what remains I've given to the artists I've worked with, those who are willing to put themselves on the line, the ones who are willing to be rejected and still carry on.

How do they do that? How do they carry on, follow their dreams, their passions after rejection? I carried on, but I'm still not whole. I lost myself in the work instead of repairing my insides.

Sitting at the park today, I look up from the book in my lap and smile when I see the ducks are back. It's officially springtime in Manhattan. Seeking the silver lining after a dreary winter, I look around, hoping to see a family. It's hard to hold onto anger for so long, so tightly. It's exhausting really.

Tossing my book in my bag, I gather the trash I've collected from my lunch and stroll back to the gallery. A man in the distance, one walking toward me on the sidewalk, head down, reminds me of

Dylan. Damn him for taking up more space in my head than he deserves.

It's not him though, just someone who reminds me of the Dylan I knew before the break-up.

I need another focus. My next exhibit apparently isn't challenging me enough. I need to get out of the gallery like I used to and go do a studio visit. I'll visit my latest discovery. He lives in the Bronx. It'll be good to get out of the city, so I catch a cab.

An hour later, I slide the huge metal loft door open, the loud music blares. He once told me to come by anytime, day or night. He meant it. He likes me, maybe a little too much. I don't mind his flirtations because he's personable, charming, not sleazy at all. He goes by Jean-Luc, but one time I saw an electric bill on his bar and the bill was addressed to John. I suppose that Jean-Luc works better in the Manhattan art scene, feeding the illusion.

Jean-Luc kisses me on the cheek before pulling me across the loft. He's shirtless with paint splattered across his body—today blue and orange. He wears old black Dickies that hang low, and he never wears underwear. I find that oddly sexy. Jean-Luc is younger than me by a few years and enthusiastic, loves life, passionate about his work. He'd make a good lover. He promised me once, after lots of tequila, that he would be good to me and treat me well. I've imagined the potential several times.

Standing in front of the large windows overlooking a dilapidated manufacturing plant, he finds the realness, the rawness of living here inspirational, wanting to share it with me. I don't argue the lack of safety in the area because he's gifted in his visions.

I spot my picture taped to the window, centered on a pane of glass. The painting next to it is orange; an abstract woman in the center that he claims is me. She's painted blue.

Am I blue?

He explains, "Life is happening whether you embrace it or not. You need to let go of the past, the pain, whatever holds you back from having a bright life. You need to free yourself, your mind, your heart."

It scares me that he might know me better than I thought. But he doesn't know about the love of my life, or the breakup, or my breakdown that ensued. He knows me in the present, what I've given him, which isn't much. I would have chosen black paint, and maybe if I'm in a good mood, charcoal grey. Charcoal grey feels more like the hue of my heart.

I've been hurt and can't seem to let go of the pain. I hate Dylan, but I don't want to hate him anymore. I want to embrace life. But I have questions. Questions like—*Why?*

Why did he leave me that day?

CHAPTER 7
Jules
March 30th

"I HAVEN'T SEEN him since then," I say, dragging a beet through the overly dressed Bibb lettuce on my plate.

"But you want to. I can tell," Brandon responds too confidently, cocky and brazen.

I drop my fork and it crashes against the plate. Probably too dramatic, but I don't care. I gave up the notion of caring years ago. Looking down at my lap, I rearrange the cloth napkin that has been slipping toward the floor because of the slick material of my dress.

He says, "You're avoiding the question."

"You didn't ask a question. You simply stated—"

"The truth."

I cock my head to the side and give him a look he's become accustomed to. "Let's not do this."

"*See?* Still no response." I hear his sarcasm. "Jules, do you want to see Dylan again? How's that for direct?"

"Dylan." I pause as the once familiar name leaves my mouth, no longer having that distinct bad taste it used to summon.

"Yes, Dylan Somers."

I swallow, then distract by taking a long gulp of my iced tea. Looking away, I stare out the crystal clear windows that overlook Central Park.

When I turn back, Brandon has his head down, shaking it. He's disappointed in me, I can tell. His head lifts, his eyes leveling with mine. "You want to see him again. I know you do, but why? Why after what he did? Why would you give him the time of day? He doesn't deserve you. He never did. You're just affected by his looks." He takes a sip of water not expecting me to reply... yet. He knows I will when I'm ready. Unfortunately his rant is not over either. "You're kidding yourself if you think you're special to him, if you think you ever were. No one treats someone the way he did you if they really love them."

"I don't want to keep talking, rehashing this until everything we had is twisted. You don't know how it was. It was... it was only bad at the end, the very end." I struggle to meet Brandon's angry eyes, but I do it despite the tears weighing heavily in the corners of mine. "He loved me. I know he did. And I, I loved him."

He slides his hand across the table and finds mine, taking it and gently squeezing. "Are you looking for closure or something else?" He sighs as if he's exasperated by me. "I don't want you hurt again. I don't want you to end up like you were before."

I hold his hand firmly. "I don't know what I want anymore—"

My hand goes cold. He's on his feet, money hitting the table before I have time to finish my sentence. I watch him leave the restaurant. I should rush after him, but I close my eyes and take a deep breath. Then I make my way out the doors and into the chic waiting lounge by the escalators. "I thought you left me." I hate how weak I sound.

Brandon's eyes lock with mine, the venom oozing before he strikes. "I would never leave you, Jules. I'm not *Dylan*."

I wrap my arms quickly around his middle, resting my cheek on his chest. Some of this is for him, some for me. We often confuse who's supposed to be feeling what and when these days. Some days it makes me want to take a step back and reaffirm my own strengths.

Others, I need him too much, reminding me of how we used to hang out back when I was still Juliette...

Brandon, our neighbor, has invited us to the movies. I've been dying to see it, but Dylan hasn't. I know he's stressing about his monthly quota and money, but we can afford this small luxury. Dylan says, "You go. I'm tired. I've had a long day and I just want to veg out."

"I don't want to go without you—"

"You've been wanting to see that movie for weeks now."

I feel bad, guilty for leaving him alone. "I can stay home, make dinner. We can cuddle."

"No, go. Trust me. I'm in a bad mood anyway."

There's a pause. "Okay, if you're sure," I say.

He's staring at the TV ahead, remote pointed at the screen. "I am. I'll see you when you get home."

"Alright. I love you."

"I love you," he mumbles not looking my way.

I'm pathetic for not letting the pain go, for holding onto it while holding my best friend. Brandon is gonna hate me soon enough because right here, in his arms, I know what I'm going to do and it sucks, but I have to. Even if it hurts him.

DYLAN SPINS AROUND in the large burgundy chair, tossing his headphones on the desk like he just got caught doing something he wasn't supposed to be doing.

Was he? My stomach is unsettled by the thought, my confidence faltering.

He's on his feet, mouth agape, and staring... but only momentarily. I have a strong suspicion he never loses his cool for long. My defenses rise in his presence.

"Julie—" He corrects himself. "Jules, I'm surprised to see you." He stammers and for a brief second, I see the boy I knew through his discomfort, which makes me smile. He also smiles, but his breathing is heavier than it should be. "I wasn't expecting," he starts again, then pauses to run his hands carelessly through his hair like old times, but his fingers stop when he remembers his hair is styled. He's messed it up now. I love that I've thrown him off balance. "I'm just, well, you know, this is unexpected. You visiting me." I glance at one of the chairs in front of his desk. Noticing, he offers, "Come in. Have a seat."

I cross the first five steps of the beige office, analyzing all he's become since our break-up. Apparently he's a big deal around here, judging by the corner office. Maybe the years haven't been as hard as I had wished on him.

I watch him sit back, his hands bracing himself to the arms of the chair. Inwardly, I enjoy that his mind must be going crazy with assumptions as to why I'm visiting him at work.

Detouring to the window, I take a deep breath as the silence lengthens between us, making him more uncomfortable. I can feel his nervous energy from here, it's palpable. Dylan is nothing like he was the other night, the false calm and bravado not crutched by alcohol.

"Jules?" he says, breaking the silence by speaking my name.

"You surprised me at my work, so I'm returning the favor," I reply, turning around and leaning my back against the window sill. I try to maintain control of the situation, pretending I'm comfortable being like this with him again.

"I didn't know you worked at that gallery," he justifies, and I actually believe him. He seemed surprised, but held it together. "I'm sorry if you felt intruded upon."

"No, it's not that." I owe him nothing, so I stop there. I scan his office for photos and see two frames, one on the low console behind him. His parents—happy, all smiles, arms around each other's shoulders. Picture perfect. I miss them. I wonder if he knows that his mother still emails me.

The other frame is smaller and facing away from me. I want to see it, to know who it is, to see the person that has found a place of honor on his desk, but I can't and I won't snoop. I'm not the least concerned about coming off as polite. It's not that at all. It's that in that moment, in this room filled with old, wilting, mixed-up feelings, I'm scared to know the truth about the man Dylan Somers has become. I'm afraid of finding out I was forgotten the same day he left. That would hurt me in new ways and change the memories that were good between us.

Why I decided to torture myself this way, I'll never know. I have nothing to prove to him, so I head for the door without another word. His footsteps are heavy on the carpeted floor behind me. "Jules, wait."

I don't wait and he stops shy of the double doors that separate the reception desk from the offices of importance that lie beyond where we came from. The desk is still abandoned by an employee taking their lunch break, an employee that is the gatekeeper for Dylan. The employee that I never encountered due to off-timing in his or her schedule, the one who would normally keep people like me from visiting.

The elevator button is pressed as the glass door shuts quietly behind me. Stepping inside, I push L, then secure myself in the back corner hoping for a non-stop descent. I'm not that lucky. The elevator doors slide open one floor down.

"Jules?"

"Hello." I smile, pleasantly surprised. Maybe my luck is changing.

CHAPTER 8

Jules

March 30th

AUSTIN BARKER, ONE of my top art buyers, steps into the elevator with me, double checking that the lobby button is highlighted. When he turns back to me, he smiles as if disbelieving his own eyes. A thrill resides there when he looks at me, making my stomach clench in the best of ways. "This is a nice surprise," he says, his smooth but deep voice shooting straight for my heart.

He's not the aggressive type and has proven his patience with me through the years. I've always found him quite charming, and surprised he stayed single. Dark hair highlights his handsome face with his straight nose leading to full lips. His sharp jaw and green eyes are not to be discounted. From the side, I see he's got a small bump at the bridge of his nose that's barely noticeable, but I notice, and I really like the flaw.

I grip the railing behind me and stand more upright. "Yes, a nice surprise," I repeat his words. I'm still shaken from seeing Dylan moments earlier, so I brush my hand down my skirt, needing to be professional in front of a client. My head tilts and I smile before trying again. "It's really good to see you, Austin. Are you in the building on business or do you work here?"

The elevator music fades away as our conversation begins. He smiles, looking down, a bit shy. When his eyes meet mine again, he says, "I'm here on business. My financial group is in the building."

Dylan works in finance.

Turning my attention back to Austin, I ask, "I'll have the paint—" but I'm interrupted by the doors opening.

"Oh, we're here." Austin waves his hand out for me to exit first.

The lobby is busy, but it's New York, which makes it easier to blend into the crowds and lose myself usually. But I'm with Austin and liking the change. We walk together past security and toward the doors. I continue what I started to say before, "The painting should be delivered this week. We'll be calling you to set up a date and time at your convenience."

"It's an interesting piece. I look forward to seeing it hanging in my home."

"I think it's a great addition to your collection."

We step onto the sidewalk and both stop. Looking around, then back at him, I kind of wish we had more time together. I shift and then turn back catching his eyes directed at me. "Jules?" A nervous pause. "Can I give you a lift somewhere?" he asks, referencing a car at the curb. "My car is right over here."

Following his hand, a sleek black car is waiting. A driver stands, opening the door when he sees Austin.

"No, that's fine—"

"I insist," he says, stepping closer, cautiously. "I don't have any more appointments today and no commitments tonight. That's a rare occurrence for me."

I hate taking cabs across town at the beginning of rush hour, but I know it's not just that. I know it's really that I want more time with him. "Alright then."

We slip into the backseat, and as soon as the door closes, the world outside is silenced and it's just the two of us. Looking to me, he asks, "Where to?"

I think for a minute. I could always go back to work. It's early still, only 4:15. I should go to the gallery and get some work done.

That would be the responsible thing to do.

But Austin shifts, interrupting the guilty spiel I'm putting on myself, and says, "I'm going out on a limb here because I'm happy to see you. I know we've... you've kept things professional over the years, but I'd like to spend some more time with you." He laughs lightly, feeling embarrassed. "You know that already though. How about some coffee or—"

After my lunch with Brandon and then my brief meeting with Dylan, which I already regret, I could really use a drink. "Something stronger like a cocktail?" I ask

"Exactly," he laughs. "I know this great bar in my neighborhood. It's a good place to unwind."

Fascinated by the handsome man next to me, I reply, "Sounds perfect." He's most certainly endearing with his shy side, and his persistence reminds me of how many times he's asked me out over the years. He's never brought another woman with him to a show or exhibit he's attended at my gallery. He's charismatic and likes art, but I also catch him watching me, a kindness to his smile.

"Great!" His zeal is flattering. He directs the driver and off we go.

Austin has money—the paintings, the chauffeured driven car, his apartment in Tribeca. I take a deep breath. I had inklings before, but now to hang out with him, to see the life he leads outside the gallery... it's a lot to take in. My deep breath doesn't go unnoticed.

"Are you alright, Jules?"

His concern is evident. "I'm fine. I just haven't done..." I say, waving my hand between us, "...this in a while."

"*This?* Oh." He understands I'm referring to us, being together much like a date. "I don't want you to feel uncomfortable. If you want to go, you can tell me and Henry will take you home. There's no pressure. Just two friends having a drink together for the first time."

His sweet nature makes me smile, putting me at ease. "Thank you, but I'm just being silly. I want to be here, with you. Anyway, it's not our first date. It's about our seventh, I would say."

The car pulls to the curb and he opens the door before the driver has a chance. Leaning down, he offers me a hand as I slide across the slick leather. When I set my hand in his, his hold tightens and our eyes meet. His are stunning, an innocence of hope residing there. Maybe that's what happy looks like. It's been too long since I've seen happy this close. His hand goes to my lower back, gentle guidance, care. Laughing so effortlessly, he says, "Yes, I suppose you're right. Just treat this like, like when we're at the gallery. Now, let's get that drink."

It's a pub. The man who is more than well-off financially takes me to a pub. "A pub?" I question.

"Not just any pub," he starts, holding the door open for me. "McKeown's. It's an institution and holds its own amongst the trendy bars that have overtaken the City."

We enter and I immediately realize it's also a sports bar. The walls are light, the furnishings are wood, not pretentious, TV's all around. A different game is showing on each, but I don't look twice to find out which ones or even the sport they're highlighting. Austin takes the lead, weaving through the tables. It's crowded and loud and not where I expected to be taken, but I think I might like him even better for picking this place. After finding a small table in the back corner, he starts to loosen his tie. "Do you mind if I take this noose off?"

With a laugh, I reply, "Of course not."

Leaving it to hang down loosely around his neck, he then undoes the two top buttons of his shirt. Staring, I find the dip at the base of his neck strangely erotic. I swallow hard, forcing myself to look away before I start to fixate on the smooth skin of his collarbone that I just got a peek off. Too late. I'm totally staring until we're rudely interrupted... A waitress approaches. She eyes him with a smile.

He looks to me. "What would you like to drink?"

"Maybe a beer since the place kind of calls for it."

"I love a girl who'll drink a beer," he says, eyes twinkling.

"You choose which kind though. I'm not a beer connoisseur."

"Two Guinness." He swivels in his chair toward me. "It's a solid beer, heavy. Too much?"

"I think I'll manage." I lean back in the chair, feeling the weight of the day start to lift away.

"I'm glad I ran into you."

Our drinks arrive, wordlessly. The waitress has set her sights on someone else, Austin not reciprocating the way she wants. I like that he doesn't. I shouldn't like it as much as I do, *but I do.*

We both take a sip, our eyes meeting once over the edge of the pint glass. My cheeks heat and I try to play it off by saying, "I'm glad we did too."

"Cheers." He leans forward on his elbows tapping his glass against mine.

AUSTIN HAS ME in stitches and it feels good to laugh this hard. We continue on a second beer as he tells me about some crazy deals he's had to sort out in other countries when he didn't speak the same language. There's a lot of hand gesturing and facial expressions. He's completely captivating. I giggle, feeling much like a schoolgirl when her crush says hi for the first time.

"You're beautiful when you laugh." He slaps his forehead. "I mean you're always beautiful but especially when you laugh. I think I should stop drinking. Your lovely company mixed with alcohol is going to my head, jumbling my words. I hate to cut the night early, but we should probably go before I completely screw this up."

"You're not screwing up, not at all." The smile falls from my face and I lean my elbow on the bar, tilting my head, feeling lighter altogether. "You're doing quite the opposite, in fact."

"You're standards are too low, Ms. Weston."

"Eh," I tease, "it's fun to slum it every now and again."

"Ouch!" He chuckles, then adds, "Well, you've got my number. Feel free to call me the next time you want to slum it."

"I will." The air turns. It's been nice, manageable between us, fun. But now, I want to kiss him and that makes me doubt myself. I know he likes me, but in *that* way... or just in a conquer kind of way. The man is attractive, stunningly so. He can get women without a problem, and probably dates models. Though over drinks and from what I know of him from the past, he's never come off in a way that would make me think he's shallow, not at all. Quite the opposite actually; his relaxed nature eases my uptight personality and makes me want to stay with him longer.

I wonder if he saw how my mind was warring inside because he says, "Before we go, we should talk about the painting since I've got your undivided attention." He smiles, his calm contagious.

"You can have my undivided attention anytime you want, but concerning the painting, I'm free on Friday." I smirk, enjoying his flirtations. I run my finger around the rim of the glass, feeling a little flirty myself.

"How can I persuade you to hand deliver it?"

I look up, my walls coming down. "Dinner would be lovely."

"You're lovely. Dinner it is. If you don't mind, I could really use your keen eye to find the right spot to hang the Rusque."

"I'd be honored."

With his most bold move, he takes my hand in his, a foreign but very welcome touch. "I don't cook, but I'm a damn good heater-upper."

I deserve someone good in my life. "I bet you are."

With a small smile in place, he asks, "I can order in or would you prefer to eat out?"

"Order in and I'll bring the wine."

"Sounds like a date."

"Yes, it does."

Bringing my hand to his mouth and placing the most gentle kiss on the top of it, I watch as his lips touch my skin. He then stands, encouraging me up. "I should really get going, even though I don't want to. I have a meeting in the morning that I need to prepare for tonight."

"Of course. I'm sorry for keeping you." I pull my hand back.

"I didn't mean it like that, Jules. I'm sorry. I like being here with you. I'd prefer to stay all night, but... I can't."

"No, no. It's alright. I have some things I should take care of tonight as well and we have Friday to look forward to."

He stands and with a big grin on his face, he confirms, "Yes, Friday."

With my hand still in his, I stand up, my body pressing against his strong one. In a whisper, I say, "Thank you. This was unexpected and fun. I'm glad I came."

"Thank you. I'm glad you did as well." A shared few seconds between us and then he continues holding my hand as he leads me through the crowded bar and out to his car. "Please let me drop you off. I'd feel better seeing you safely home."

"I'm thinking the gallery if it's not out of your way."

"You're a workaholic, Ms. Weston."

"I have a feeling you're familiar with that disease."

"Too familiar for my own liking. I need a real life again." He looks at me as the door opens.

"We all do, but I hope you find what you're looking for." I slide into the car.

He gets in next to me and with a confident smile, says, "Things are starting to look up."

CHAPTER 9

Jules

April 1st

"I'M SORRY. I was foolish for walking out."

"Don't, Brandon. Let's just make up and move on."

"I shouldn't have said those things to you, Jules."

I huff in annoyance. "You can say those things because you care about me. Friends tell each other what they think."

"Oh trust me, I thought those and more, but I shouldn't have said them."

"I thought you were coming over here to apologize. That's what the message said. So why am I here trying to make you feel better about something that not only do you not need to apologize for, but you also don't need to feel bad about?" I look up.

Brandon's looking out my office window, mulling my words. "That was a mouthful."

"You're a handful. Let's call it even and move on, okay?"

He smiles. "Yeah, I'd like that."

"Sit down. You're making me all anxious and stuff pacing around like that."

He does. "It's like being in a fishbowl, this window is so big."

I sigh, following his gaze onto the street. "I know. I hate it."

"Move to the back office."

"Can't. This space was designed to give that feeling even at the expense of the Art Director."

"You're snarky today."

"I'm snarky every day."

"Especially today though. What's up?" he asks. "You're hiding something."

I keep my head bent toward the papers on my desk, but lift my eyes only to be met by his eager ones. "I went for a drink with a client yesterday."

"That Austin guy, right?"

"Yes, how'd you know?"

"It was inevitable. He's been chasing you for too long. You've been holding off for too long... See? Inevitable."

"I had a good time. We had a couple of drinks and it was fun."

Brandon leans forward, resting his forearms on my desk. "You deserve happy." I look back down, pretending to be busier than I am. "Jules? You should allow yourself this happiness. I can see it in your eyes, there's something different, a lightness. Your mouth wants to smile, but you work so hard to hide it, fighting it. Just give in."

As we stretch into a zone I'm not quite comfortable in, I detract. "I saw Dylan."

"What? When?" Brandon's tone changes, the harshness felt in a small vibration across the glass of my desktop as his hand starts tapping.

I stand up. Walking over to the filing cabinet in the corner, I duck my head to avoid his judgment. I shouldn't have told him, but there's no point in lying about it now. "Yesterday, I went to see Dylan. When I was leaving I ran into Austin in the elevator."

"You what? Why'd you go see him? What happened? What'd you say? What'd he say?"

I turn around, leaning my shoulder on the tall cabinet. "Not much. I doubt we even exchanged twenty words the whole conversation. He was surprised to say the least."

"I bet." Brandon looks away. "I'm glad something good came out of it. The drinks with Austin." He's letting me off the hook, so I nod. When he stands, he adds, "I should get back."

I walk him out. We hug goodbye, not saying the word, not needing to.

April 2nd

THE SUN SETS and the sidewalk outside my window is empty. People are already home or have arrived to their after work destination while I remain at my desk. The day was long, but it will be longer. I never mind putting in extra hours since I don't have anything to return to at home.

Just a few days have passed since the exhibit, enough time to allow the worry, the stress to set in. I look over at the painting that's cushioned in bubble wrap and covered in a protective outer layer of brown paper. It's leaning against my wall and has Barker written on the outside.

I call my two interns in to load it onto the truck. When they don't answer the back phone, I decide to hunt them down, but find Dylan instead. He's standing in the middle of the gallery eyeing a Chihuly vase. I can tell he wants to touch it, maybe hold it, but he restrains himself. I understand the desire. I wanted to do the same when I first saw it.

It's stunning.

He's stunning.

Annoyingly so, and more than he was back then. My hate isn't as strong as it once was, not even matching the emotions I felt a few weeks ago. Does this feeling lead to *like* one day or will I be living with a lighter version of this hate forever? I'm disconcerted by my kinder thoughts toward him and spin to return to my office, hoping to remain unseen.

"Jules?"

I stop, but don't turn around while taking a deep breath before releasing a shaky exhale.

He's in my gallery, so I must play nice, I must play hostess. It's my job and there are other visitors, witnesses around. Instead of avoiding him like I want to, I turn with purpose as if I intended to speak to him the whole time. "This Chihuly is quite remarkable," I start, sticking to my role. "I haven't seen those shades accomplished this eloquently before. And we've had a few Chihuly's over the years."

He's not buying my act. I can see it in his eyes. I worry he still knows me too well. He plays along with my game. "It's interesting. Pretty."

Novice description. There's no deep emotion evoked when something's called interesting or pretty.

I start to turn back around, since I have nothing more to say, but apparently he does, "Wait. Please. Can you spare a few minutes?"

The interns provide a happy diversion. They're sloppily dressed, which is unacceptable, but when I look at my watch, they don't have time to change. I lead them into the office and point at the painting, reminding them of the delicate nature of the piece they're handling.

Stepping into the doorway, I reply, "Only a minute." I sigh as if he's interrupting my important business of avoiding him.

He's cautious in his expression, realizing that him needing to speak with me is not a mutual desire. In thought, he eyes the wood floor beneath his feet, drawing my gaze down with him. His shoes are Gucci, easily identifiable in design. I look him over as I scan back up to see his face. His suit is tailored to fit... in all the right ways. He's too handsome to be such a bastard, his looks wasted because of his lack of soul.

Catching me appreciating the physical package he presents, his smile turns hubristic and I shrug, silently admitting my act. Owning it, I cross my arms over my chest and raise my chin a bit. I look him directly in the eyes and wait for him to say his peace.

"I don't know why I'm here," he says. "It's as if I was already here before my reasoning kicked in. I know you don't want to see me. The other day at my office, I could tell. I could also tell how much I've hurt you, the pain I've caused. But ever since I saw you..." He runs his hand through his hair, then gets this determined look on his face.

I grip the doorway not sure if I want this conversation to continue, but the silence holds me captive. His eyes hold me prisoner. I'm statue still when he steps closer. My breath caught in my chest. I grip harder, my fingers curling around the casing.

"I should go," he says, then rushes out the open front doors.

My fingers release and I push off the wall, running after him. "Wait!"

Suddenly being face to face with him like this, I'm not sure what to say. He waits for me to speak this time, for me to say something. Expectations I falsely gave him when I chased him down. I have nothing left to say, nothing except, "You didn't finish. What were you going to say?" I shift uncomfortably, keeping five feet between us. "Ever since you saw me? What, Dylan?"

His face contorts and this time I see the pain in his eyes when he replies, "I can't stop thinking about you."

My response is automatic, not rehearsed. "You must."

"I tried. *I'm trying,* but I'm failing—miserably."

"Why?"

"Because I can't stop."

"You left! And you're trying to not think about me?" My anger peaks. "Fuck you!" Years of pent up emotion building and releasing together. "You're all I've thought about for 3 years." I turn abruptly and go inside, grab my purse from under my desk, and march straight toward the back door. The severe click of my heels against the polished floors exposes everyone in the room to my mood. I yell for the evening manager to lock up, then quickly escape out back, slipping into the waiting van. I have a short ten minute ride to pull my shit back together before this delivery, before my date with Austin begins.

CHAPTER 10

Jules

April 2nd

THE ELEVATOR DEPOSITS us right into Austin's apartment—the penthouse.

He isn't there when the shiny silver doors open in front of us, but then he is, rounding a corner with a gorgeous smile and warm greetings, welcoming and surprisingly, bare foot. So casually dressed and so sexy. He kisses me on the cheek as his hands hold my shoulders, professional, yet I feel the tingling of something more developing.

I wonder if he does.

I have staff with me, so I must behave. He winks at me before greeting them. I stand and wait for instructions. He's the client. He should make the decisions.

"How about setting it over there against that wall? I haven't quite decided and would like to get Ms. Weston's professional opinion on how to best highlight the painting."

After setting the painting down, the interns look to me, so I thank them before walking them to the elevator with a reminder to drive safe and that we have an employee meeting on Monday morning. They leave and we're alone. Austin's turned on some music, classic rock. Another pleasant discovery about this charming man.

"Wine? *Or...*" He jogs into the kitchen and comes back out just as quickly to show me. "I found this great Gossett champagne. My wine guy pulled it from the reserves for me."

He has a wine guy. I'm impressed. His excitement is contagious and I smile, relaxing. "The champagne. We should celebrate."

"We can drink to the Rusque finding a home." On a mission to open the bottle, he goes back into the kitchen. "Make yourself at home, Jules." His voice travels from the confines of the other room.

I study his décor—clean, neutral palette, highlighting the artwork. I like that. I used to be more eclectic, warmer in my taste... back when I was with Dylan. I had a much more carefree style. Over the years, I've learned that clutter is confining and never replaced any of the knick knacks he took the day he left me.

Looking at the walls, a large painting hangs above the couch. It seems to be the one piece I didn't sell him.

Handing me a glass of champagne, he says, "I picked that up in Europe four years ago. It caught my eye and I had to have it. Do you like it?"

"It's lovely," I reply, studying the bright colors up top that fade to a gradient mix with the muted base tones. "It's a great find. I've not seen anything like that here. It's unique in its composition."

"That's exactly how I felt when I saw it, but could never put it into words so perfectly." Tapping the fluted crystal against mine, he toasts, "To new friends and amazing art."

"To amazing friends and new art," I add, the crystal chiming between us.

We sip, then he says, "Let me show you around and you can help me find a place to hang the new one."

Most of the paintings he's purchased from me hang gallery style down the long and wide hallway. He says, "I had it designed this way to showcase the paintings."

"It's an art lovers' dream. Have you had your place photographed professionally?"

"Once, last year," he looks down, seeming self-conscious. "It was silly really, a local publication."

We stop in his bedroom and I see the Cirie I sold him three years ago on Valentine's Day. "That's more powerful than I remember," I note, staring at it hanging above his headboard.

He stands there, analytical, before saying, "The deep burgundy blending into the more subtle red, but stopping before it turns pink. I can feel the passion behind it. Cirie knew when to stop. It's not feminine—"

"Or masculine," I say, interrupting, "just beautiful."

I hear him whisper behind me, "Yes, so beautiful."

I glance over my shoulder.

His eyes are on me.

I blink and turn back to face the painting. "Yes, it's pure passion. Above the bed is the perfect place for it to hang."

He steps closer, silently admiring... the painting or me, I'm not sure. His fingers brush against my elbow. His voice comes out lower, "Come with me. I'll show you where I was thinking the Rusque could go."

Liking his touch when his hands are on me, I follow him into another room sticking close. Much like Austin, his office is breathtaking. The room is identical to his bedroom with two full walls of windows, but this room has no curtains to block the world out. He stands back, leaning against the door as I explore the room. The other two walls are white and bare, needing something, craving something vibrant.

"I think the painting should go right here. It feels right." I turn around abruptly and ask in all seriousness, "Do you use this room?"

"All the time."

I release my relief through an exhale. "Good. I would hate for that piece to be abandoned in some room that's never used, where it would never be seen."

"So would I. Your passion for art is very sexy."

"Art is sexy."

"Indeed."

I sip then gulp my drink, eyeing him, admiring his lean and fit figure. "It must be hard to date a tycoon," I joke, the bubbles going to my head. "The world is at your feet, literally right outside the window and down thirty-seven flights."

"I've never dated a tycoon," he retorts. "So I wouldn't know."

I laugh and he smiles at the sound. Sipping my drink, each bubble bursts in my mouth. I walk to a window and look out. "It's a long way to fall."

"No further than Heaven and you survived that." Laughing out loud, I try to contain the roll of my eyes that wants to escape from his corny comment. "I'm sorry. I always wanted to know what it was like to say one of those awful pick-up lines and you gave me the perfect set up."

"I think you've been carrying that around in your back pocket for about fifteen years too long," I tease.

He grins. "Maybe longer. I've been interested in girls for a long time now, Jules."

"I just bet you have." I punctuate my words with a wink.

Standing in front of him, the silliness between us alters into something more, something with depth and it scares me. I swallow hard, trying to change it back by asking, "Do you believe in love at first sight, Austin, or should I walk by again?" Together, we laugh this time from my bad pickup line. Walking past him, I bump his hip with mine playfully, then with my smirk still in place, I say, "Now feed me, I'm hungry."

Following behind, he says, "If I knew you better I'd..." but catches himself and stops.

I lean against the wall between two bold, modern paintings, a bit breathless, a lot playful. "You'd what? What would you do if we knew each other better?"

His feet stop in front of mine and a roguish smile plays on his lips. "If we knew each other better, I would have slapped your ass for that pun."

"Consider us good friends then, but let's skip the ass slap, even as appealing as that sounds..." His eyebrow arches, his body leans forward, one hand stationed above my head. Our breathing picks up, but also deepens, both of us wanting more. I finish by saying, "... And just kiss me."

His hand is on my neck, sliding upward over my jaw, caressing my cheek. "You are a fascinating woman, Ms. Weston." His lips press against mine. They're soft, yet purposeful. Full and wonderful. My eyes are closed, enjoying, savoring, wanting more. He pulls back and our eyes slowly open. The tip of his finger glides along my bottom lip. Leaning in again for a quick, sweet kiss, he says, "You said something about being hungry—"

"Yes, starving." In more ways than one right now. My body craving him more than food.

He takes my hand and we walk back to the kitchen. "Rao's?" I ask when I see the bags on the counter.

"I like it. It's impossible to get into the restaurant as you know, but I have kitchen connections and get take-out every couple of months."

"You went to a lot of effort for tonight."

"You're worth it," he replies not understanding how much it means that someone thinks I'm worth the effort. He starts unpacking the bags. "Hope you like spaghetti and meatballs. I got the house salad and dessert." He raises his eyebrows up and down when he says dessert. It's really quite cute.

He's quite cute.

"I love Italian."

I LEAN FORWARD with a straight face, and say, "You must be tired because you've been running through my dreams all night." I can't hold a straight face any longer. "That line is so bad, but I remember a time that I actually thought that was clever."

He laughs, struggling to keep his full mouth closed. His hand covers it, just in case. He's all manners and etiquette. "You've got to stop, Jules. My stomach hurts from laughing so hard."

"You sure it wasn't from the large meatball you stole from my plate?" I'm kidding with him. It's fun to eat so casually in his living room. It's easy to feel happy around him. I need easy. I need happy. I need more laughter in my life. It's been too long. Smiling feels good. Laughing feels freeing. "Okay," I say, "I've finished my pasta. You finished my meatballs. Let's dig into dessert."

"You're my kind of girl," he replies, starting to stand.

I read his comment two ways and it makes me feel good. "No, let me. You've been serving me all night. Let me serve dessert."

"No, you're my guest."

"Nope, you just sit there and enjoy the view." I shake my ass, then walk into the kitchen. Peeking back out, I ask, "That wasn't too forward, was it?"

The candle he lit on the coffee table earlier reflects in his eyes, or maybe that's something else. "No, I liked it a lot."

Opening the refrigerator, I spot the container of dessert. "Austin, I *looooovvvveee* Tiramisu," I call from the kitchen. I bring the container out with two spoons in hand, no dishes. I sit down on the floor on the other side of the table from him. He smiles. "No plates?"

"I didn't want to make a bigger mess than necessary. You know how to share, don't you?"

"I do. Just forget all about the meatball stealing."

"Already forgiven and forgotten."

He digs in and then leans across. "You should try mine."

"We're eating the same thing."

"I don't know," he says, eyeing his spoon. "Mine tastes so much better. You should really try it and let me know."

I grin, leaning forward. Feeling flirtatious, I close my eyes and wrap my lips around the spoon seductively. When I'm finished, I open my eyes and catch him licking the spoon I just took my bite from.

With a contented sigh, I say, "I think you're right. I think yours is better."

"I'm not positive, but now I'm thinking it might not be the

dessert. It might just be me."

I'll happily play along. "Come here then and let me taste you. You know, just to figure out if it's you or the dessert."

He crawls on his knees around the table, no hesitation, his body hovering over mine. My stomach tightens in anticipation as I rise up onto my knees. I want this. I close my eyes and let his kiss take me away.

AN HOUR LATER, my dress is a mess. I frantically straighten it along with my wild hair in the bathroom.

When I walk out, I blush, not being able to look him in the eyes. This behavior is so unlike me and if we wouldn't have stopped when we did... my mouth dries, knowing it's time for me to go home.

My tongue runs over my bottom lip—a lip that's swollen from kissing—his wonderful and erotic kisses. "I should go," I say, wanting to avoid any major awkwardness. "Thank you for dinner and dessert..." I wave my hand around, definitely making it more awkward. "... And everything else." Oh God this is embarrassing. Hopefully I'm not blowing it after such a great night.

"You're a beautiful woman, but I think you're pretty damn cute when you get embarrassed, Jules." He takes me gently by the arm, halting my retreating body. "By the way, you have no reason to be embarrassed."

"It's been a long time. I don't know what came over me." I talk to our feet, avoiding his eyes altogether.

He pulls me to him, wrapping his arms around me, comforting me. "You were turned on. I was too," he says, lifting my chin up against my will until I relax and look him in the eyes. "You can still see how much you turn me on." He glances down between us then back up again. I don't need to look. I can feel how turned on he is. "Do you want to talk about it? I don't want you leaving here feeling bad about what we did or regretting it. I liked it too much for that. I like *you* too much for that."

"I don't want to talk about it, not tonight. I'm tired and that will take too long. I won't regret it. It was amazing. You are amazing."

"Then let's talk about me and how inflated my ego is now that I gave you an orgasm from second base." He chuckles, the sound is refreshing and when I start to laugh, I feel the weight of a long carried burden beginning to lift from my shoulders. He adds, "I haven't made out like that since I was in college."

I hit his chest in jest and reprimand lightly, "You are so bad."

"I can't have you taking things like tonight too seriously. We have enough problems in life. We don't need to add embarrassed over having an amazing time with a handsome man to the list."

"Stop it!" I playfully reply, squirming in his arms. "Next time I'll resist just so I can deflate some of that ego of yours."

Gripping me tighter, not wanting to let me escape, he takes me by the waist and swivels me. After kissing me lightly on the head, he says, "Never. I don't want you to ever hold back. You don't have to with me. Outside of our apartments you can be who you need to be to feel comfortable enough to face reality, but in here, I want the real you—the you I saw tonight. The you that laughs, and recites cheesy pick-up lines, and spontaneously orgasms when a guy grabs your boobs. That's the you I want when it's just the two of us." He kisses me on the corner of the mouth. "Now please tell me that I get to spend more time with this you sometime soon."

I nod, wanting this, wanting to spend more time with him because I like this me too. I like the me I am with him.

"Yes, I want that." I wrap my arms around his neck and pull him slowly down to me. "I'd like that a lot." *Kiss.* "Even the spontaneous orgasming part." *Kiss.* "Especially the spontaneous orgasming part." *Kiss.*

I step back from him, grabbing my purse and head for the elevator. "I hate to orgasm and go, but I have an early morning meeting."

"I think your embarrassment is now called bragging. Ms. Braggy

Braggerton, how's Sunday night for you? Can you fit me in?"

I glance down at his erection that's straining against his pants, then back up and reply, "That remains to be seen... or should I say felt, but I'm free that evening. My place. I'll text you directions." The elevator doors open and I step in.

"I'm too much of a gentleman to reply to that, but I want you to know that I think you're pretty damn fantastic." He leans his shoulder against the door that is trying to close on him.

"Also," he says, stepping back, but I finish his sentence, "I owe you one."

I see him fist-pump just as the doors close. I laugh aloud because I'm happy, because no one is around to judge me, or take away how perfect this night was.

CHAPTER 11

April 15th

"I'M SORRY," AUSTIN says, "I didn't expect it would be this long until I saw you again. I've had some words with my corporate accountants over this last minute tax bullshit."

"Don't worry about it. I've been busy anyway." I fist his shirt in my hands and pull him closer. "I'll forgive you on one condition."

Our lips meet.

Not shy.

Possessive.

Reciprocal.

Smiles interrupt before we go too far. The newness of the relationship is exciting. "That was the condition," I say, "so we're all good here."

His hands go to my sides and he whispers, "I missed you if that matters."

"It matters a lot."

More kisses from him. More giggles from me.

"Show me around your place." He walks away, letting his fingers linger on my hip as he passes. Studying the room, he turns. "You just have the one piece?"

I follow his gaze to the painting that hangs above my couch. "Yeah."

"I thought you'd have an apartment full of art, putting mine to shame."

Although I could have bought all the pieces he did, I don't treat myself that way. *A touchy subject. A complicated one too.*

"I apologize." Worry graces his face, his forehead wrinkling as he approaches. "I didn't mean to insinuate that this one isn't enough—"

"I know. It's okay, Austin. You didn't offend me. This painting is the only one that struck me enough to hang it."

He kisses the side of my head, his hand finding my waist again before he turns to stand in front of it. "It's an extraordinary piece. The streaks making it unique. Was water used on it?"

"Something like that."

"Oil, not acrylic?"

"Yes."

"I can give you a tour, but it will consist of: here's the living room, this way to the bedroom, and the bathroom right through there, and then we'd be back in the kitchen."

He must have noticed the lack of furniture, the lack of décor, the lack of life because he asks, "I like it, Jules. Have you lived here long?"

"Yes, a while now and thank you, but you're being too kind. I know it's small, but it is what it is and about all I can manage to maintain with the amount of hours I put in at the gallery."

"It's great. Now," he says, rubbing his hands together. "How can I help with dinner?"

I laugh because like him, I ordered food. "You can help me unpack the bag. Hope you like spicy. I ordered Thai."

Thirty minutes later, he sets his plate down on the counter. "That was great. I haven't had Thai in a few months, maybe a year. Thank you."

"My pleasure." I clear the plates, putting them in a sink of soapy water, and offer him another beer.

We ate standing up in the kitchen. Austin makes himself more comfortable by moving to the couch. With a devious grin, he says, "You know I always crave something sweet after eating something spicy. Can I treat you to an ice cream?"

"Make it a froyo and you got yourself a deal."

He stands and stretches. "Froyo it is."

The night is warm, no sweater needed, but I stand close to him anyway. "Oh my God! This is unf!"

"*Unf?*" he repeats.

I lick my spoon clean and see him smile at me. "Yes, unf! It's orgasmic."

He laughs and I blush, but I love saying what I want around him. He takes everything in stride and has a great sense of humor.

"Speaking of," I start to say, but rise up on my toes and kiss him instead of finishing with words.

His lips are cold from the frozen yogurt and he tastes of berries. His free hand finds the back of my head, holding me to him, both of us wanting more. Our chilled tongues heat quickly once they touch, mingle, and slide. A moan escapes as I forget about my dessert and savor him instead.

Although I don't, he must have remembered where we are because he stops with a gentle smile on his face and whispers. "You make me want to do things to you, Ms. Weston, but not on a New York street."

I toss the rest of my frozen treat into the garbage and take his hand. "Yeah, I think we're done here. Let's go back."

He tosses his own container and we start walking. We don't talk on the way back, anticipation building with our pace. As soon as I lock the deadbolt, he's on me, pinning me against the door with his body, his mouth on my neck, hands in my hair. My right leg lifts seemingly of its own accord balancing against his hip. His hand grips my thigh, holding it up while sliding down.

Breathless and with his eyes closed, he leans his forehead against mine. "You are driving me crazy, Jules. I feel out of control around you." He takes a deep breath. "I'm not used to that."

"You do the same to me," I say with a breathy pant. "I haven't felt like this in a long time."

"And I thought I was special," he teases.

Leaning my head back against the door with a thud, I laugh. "You know what I mean."

"I know exactly what you mean." Looking me in the eyes, a more serious tone takes over. "You all right with this?"

"I am. Look, I find you attractive, *extremely* attractive and, well..." My body heats against his, wanting him. "You turn me on probably more than I should admit to. You have beautiful eyes," I say because they are and the way they look at me makes me weak in the knees.

He bites down on his bottom lip, gazing down at me, then says, "You have beautiful everything, Jules." He kisses me.

This is the moment. The moment I need to decide if I'm going to take this further. He's made his feelings clear, but am I ready for more...

Further.

Further emotionally.

Further physically.

Further into a relationship with this man who seems to be perfect—a perfect man who is interested in me for some reason despite being broken. *Does he not see that? Is it not as obvious on the outside? Have I become that good of an actress?*

He'll find out and when he does I'll lose him. But maybe...

Maybe he can heal me.

Maybe that's why we seem to work right now.

Maybe he needs me just as much.

Maybe he's broken on the inside too.

He sighs, touching my cheek. "Hey there, where'd you disappear to?"

I look down, ashamed that I got lost in the muss of thoughts clouding my brain instead of appreciating what's right here, what's tangible and real, loving and giving. I slide my hand up his neck to his cheek and look at him. His small smile shows his concern, despite trying to mask it. "I'm sorry," I reply.

"Jules, we can slow down if that's what worries you."

I like the way his hands feel on me, gentle, patient, but firm.

Strong. I lean forward tucking myself against him, resting my cheek on his chest and close my eyes.

Inhale.

Exhale.

Inhale.

Exhale.

"I like you, Austin. Definitely more than I should—"

"Why shouldn't you? Tell me. Are we moving too fast?"

"We messed around on our first date, but it took us three years to have a drink. So it's fast in some ways and not in others, but I like it. You make me feel and I haven't felt anything in a long time. It's nice."

"You haven't had feelings for anyone in a long time?"

"Yes... and no. I've not felt anything at all for years. I've been numb."

"You were hurt." He guesses right.

I drop back against the door, not ready to face him, staring at the space that has developed between us when all I want is his warmth again, his hands all over me. Instead, he tucks them into his pockets, the exact opposite of what I want. "I was, but I've been hurting myself ever since." I take him by the arm and walk to the couch.

I deserve to be happy, I repeat, hoping one day I truly believe it. But for now, I convince myself that I'm good enough for this great guy. I swallow hard, then say, "It may sound strange, but I want this, you, what's happening between us. I like it and I don't want it to stop. I don't want to do this slow and careful. I just want to continue enjoying this."

He laughs, the weight of the conversation lifting. "I do too. I like what we're sharing. I've not been in a real relationship in a few years, not one that was good and honest. I think we may be good for each other because this, this is as honest as it gets. Our cards are down—"

"Our walls are down."

A soft smile covers his face. "Let's just enjoy *this*."

"Just have fun?"

"Just have fun discovering what *this* is."

"I want that," I say, hope seeping in.

He kisses me. Hard. Topples me over and I want it, this, him. A kiss is not enough. I need more. I want more. I want all of him.

Will he?

Should we?

I block those questions out of my mind, living in the here, the now, with him, with perfection and green eyes and dark hair with soft waves, strong arms, hard abs, hard... other parts—hard *and* large other parts.

I grind up. He grinds down. He moans, and like a drug fix, it sends me straight to my happy, freeing place. My skirt is pushed up to my hips as he slides between my legs. Light wool pants and a pair of boxers can't hide his arousal.

I moan because I'm so fucking hot for him right now, especially when his hand touches me... Right. There. I practically rip the fabric belt of my dress open, my body exposed in the quick movement.

AFTER CATCHING OUR breath, he says, "I'm sorry. I hope I wasn't too rough."

"You weren't." I reach up, soothing, comforting him. "Did it feel good?"

"Too good, but I didn't mean to... you know, I didn't want it to happen like that on a couch. I got carried away. I don't sleep around as much as the gossip columns say." He sits back on his knees. "I would have preferred to romance you."

I cut off his need to apologize, "Austin, it was fun and it felt good. You felt good."

He lies down, squashing me, but I love it. A calm washes over us and we exhale, sinking further into the cushions of the couch. "I like this. What we have going here," he says earnestly.

Snuggling closer, I hope he feels the same satisfaction that I do. I whisper just in case he doesn't, "I do too."

"I'm going to Europe for two weeks on Thursday."

With my eyes closed, I say, "I have a show that will keep me busy."

He kisses my temple. "Don't miss me too much."

With a gentle laugh, I roll onto my side and wrap my right arm over his stomach. After placing a soft kiss on his chest, I reassure, "I'll miss you. More than you know. You're already starting to feel like a habit I can't break after just two dates."

"You're just in it for the fantastic orgasms I give you."

"Might be," I joke back.

This is nice.

This is easy.

Easy is good.

... And then I think of Dylan.

JEALOUSY
From the Inside Out
Part 2

S.L. Scott

CHAPTER 1
Jules
April 18th

MY PHONE FLASHES with a missed call as soon as I turn it back on. I had turned it off while visiting with Jean-Luc, wanting to check on his progress for his upcoming show in two months.

"You look different, beautiful Jules." Jean-Luc is very intuitive. I've always liked that about him. He noticed the change in me as soon as I walked into his loft.

"How so?" I ask whimsically, a small smile forming on my lips as I walk around the large space.

"Your aura has shifted. You seem happy."

I laugh, then scoff at the notion. "These windows need to be cleaned. You need to let some sunshine in."

His body warms my backside, his chest to my back. The smell of oil-based paint mixed with a hint of cleaner and his sweat, fills the air around us, stronger than my perfume. The rough skin of his hand runs down my arm. His lips are at my ear as he presses his bare chest against my shoulders, only a tiny dress strap between us. "I like you better sullen and hard to get. Aloof is sexy when you do it."

"I never purposely act aloof. Sullen maybe, mainly miserable. That's what I was going for. I guess I failed. I'm reevaluating my whole emo image as we speak," I deadpan. It's easier to play along with his dramatics. He's an amazing painter when he's riled up.

"Emo," he repeats, chuckling, his breath hitting my neck. "Yes, emo and sunshine don't go well together."

"Changing."

"Don't," he whispers. "Don't let someone change you, who you are. You're perfect, always, delicate and perfect to me."

I turn slowly around, our chests now touching, no professional space remaining between us. I lean forward toward his ear, cheek to cheek, and whisper, "We're perfect as we are. Let's not change this, the distance we keep works better than the reality ever could." I kiss him lightly on the cheek, then take a step back. "Thank you for accepting me how I am."

Backing away from me with a smirk on his face and a paintbrush in hand, he points it accusingly in my direction. "You've met someone. Tell me, Jules, does he let you have your quiet moments? Does he let you thrive in your sadness and love you regardless?"

I roll my eyes. "You're such an artist. Not everything has to be so extreme. Sometimes things happen that mess with the flow and then you come to realize that everything flows better than it did before the change."

"So I'm right. Just tell me he's opposite of me. Lie to me if you have to. You're good at lying. Convince me that my hope being dashed is purely because he offered you something I couldn't."

"He's nothing like you." I tell him the truth, though it would be easy to fall for Jean-Luc if I let myself. He's very sexy in his own way. He has great eyes, or maybe it's just the way he looks at me that I find so appealing. "He won't destroy me or drag me to the dark places to wallow, the places you like to frequent."

He's painting, his back to me, solid black on the canvas. He glances at me over his shoulder as if he's studying me for the lies, or the truth, to see if he can figure me out. He's always seen me clearer *than most. We're similar, or were. I'm not sure today. "Stay true to your heart, beautiful Jules."*

I nod, but he doesn't see.

I listen to my voicemail in the back of the taxi while returning to the city from the borough where Jean-Luc lives. Hearing Austin's voice makes me smile. "I'm in Paris. Six hours separates us by plane. Five hours on the clock. I don't like it," Austin says with a laugh. "I want to be on the same continent. I don't know." He sounds embarrassed for admitting his feelings. "I just want to be near you again. Feel free to put out a restraining order on me for this fucked up stalker sounding voicemail." I laugh to myself as I continue listening to him. "I miss you. Is it too early in our relationship to say that? You know, I'm just gonna hang up now. It'll be safer for the both of us if I do. We'll talk soon. Call me or I can call you again or email, text, pigeon carrier. This is why I need to hang up now. I suck at this. Goodbye, Jules."

I disconnect, smiling and hold the phone to my chest. He's so sweet and funny. He warms me on the inside, not from embarrassment or lust, but from happiness, pure unadulterated happiness.

When I return to the gallery, I find a bouquet of gerbera daisies in all different colors arranged in a vase that I recognize instantly as a Boda. The purple and orange colors of the vase are beautiful and highlight the flowers. The glass appears to flow boundless, which always intrigued me about the artist. Austin sure knows how to woo a woman.

Smiling, I anxiously pull the card and read: *I missed you. I still miss you.*

I call him, not caring about the cost of the call or the late hour in France. I just want to talk to him. He always makes me smile and it grows when he answers, "Bonjour, Mademoiselle Weston. This is a pleasant surprise."

"Bonjour, Monsieur."

"Tres bien, Jules."

"Austin, I miss you too. This is all so crazy and fast and—"

"But right, so right."

"Yes, this feels so right," I add. "The flowers are beautiful, the vase is stunning. I've always loved Boda. Thank you so much."

"What?"

"The flowers," I repeat, but the line crackles, the connection dodgy. Damn distance. I speak louder to make sure he can hear me. "Thank you. I love it. You don't have to send me expensive gifts though."

"Jules—"

"How long will you be gone again? I want to see you. We can video chat." I drop my voice down to a whisper, so the other employees can't hear me. "You know, private video." I giggle, my happiness making me silly.

He doesn't. Instead I'm greeted with silence, except for the crackling line binding us together.

"Austin, can you hear me?"

"Yeah, private video chat sounds good." He lets out a breath that's heard loud and clear. "We should do that. But I think you should know that I didn't send the flowers."

A knock at the door draws my eyes up from my desk. A delivery man, holding a pale pink box wrapped in black ribbon, stands there. "Hold on, Austin. I have a delivery I need to sign for." After signing his order, I take the box to my desk and pick the phone back up, holding it to my ear.

"The gift is from me, Jules, not the flowers."

When I look down at the pink box in front of me, I lift the lid. Agent Provocateur is scrolled across the top of the box. I slip the lid off the box and stare down at a black lace over soft pink bra and panty set.

Austin, his voice low on the other end of the call, asks, "Jules?"

"I'm here."

"You got the box?"

"I got it," I reply, nodding. I drag my finger over the luxurious material. "They're beautiful."

"I hope you like it. I thought they would be beautiful on you."

The box is from me, not the flowers. My hands start to shake as Austin's words replay—*the box is from me, not the flowers.*

"Thank you. The gift... it's very thoughtful."

"Thoughtful? I can't say I was really going for thoughtful, but I guess I'll take it."

I sigh, disappointed in myself. He deserves a better response. "I'm sorry. Sexy. It's really sexy. You shouldn't have."

"Believe me, it was purely selfish."

Smiling, I laugh. "Okay, then feel free to be selfish any time you like." I look back at the flowers still confused by the note. Austin is speaking, his mood lightened, but his words don't register as it becomes clear who the flowers are from. *Dylan.* My eyes move to where the card resides. Dylan missed me... Dylan misses me now? So over the last three years *Dylan* missed me?

"Jules?" Austin sounds worried. "I need to return to dinner. I'm in a meeting."

"I'm sorry." My mind refocused. "Thank you for the lingerie. It's very pretty."

"I thought it would look stunning on you." I can hear his smile return, even if just slightly.

"Thank you."

"Au revoir, Jules. I'll call you soon."

"Au revoir." As soon as he hangs up, I set the phone down on the desk, my hand starting to shake as I reach for the note again. My stomach rolls and I feel sick.

Weak.

Ambushed.

I want to throw this vase. I want to see it shatter into a million pieces, this time the vase instead of my heart. Running my finger along the smooth hand-blown glass, I try to appreciate the feel. Shaking my head, I realize I could never destroy something so beautiful, something so fragile. I'm left with questions that I'm not sure I'll get answers to.

Questions like why did he send these? Why is he back, invading a life that was created in the aftermath of him? What do these flowers mean? What did he mean when he said he can't stop thinking about me no matter how hard he tries? Why is he trying so hard? Does he remember the good between us? *Sometimes I do.*

Now I've hurt Austin. I could hear it in his voice and I hate that more than Dylan.

I pick the panties up. They're silky, light as a feather with such fine detailing. They're sexy and naughty, innocent, and pretty. They're perfect, as if Austin knows what I would pick out for myself.

I take the box and go home, leaving the vase to be dealt with another day, tomorrow perhaps.

Within an hour, red wine is poured and I have a bath running. I sink in, letting the hot water engulf my body up to my neck. Lots on my mind, but I let it fade, choosing to picture Austin instead—remembering how he touches me, and then his face as he comes undone.

My hand is underwater, my fingers stroking gently, then rougher, more determined. My mouth drops open as I work myself over, letting my mind wander around the planes of a memory I shouldn't be remembering. Like his laughter in my ears. The feel of his hair. I let go, going with all the things I shouldn't be remembering because I realize it's Dylan, not Austin I'm thinking of.

I reach forward and grab the bar of soap, wanting to scrub my body, needing to wash away this memory and the pleasure it brought me.

JUST LIKE AUSTIN, the lingerie is a perfect fit. Lying on the bed, I admire the caress of the silk over my breasts and the fine detail of the lace straps. I put my arms above me and twist—hips to the side just slightly, breasts pressed together, and then I push the button. I take a few more pictures before I decide on the one I like best. After quickly typing out a message, I send it.

I crawl under the covers, setting my phone down on the base that sits on the night table. But before I have a chance to close my eyes, I receive a return text. *I can't wait to see you dressed like that in person. I've been thinking of you all night.*

I type back: *You're up late.*

My phone dings: *Can't sleep.*

My fingers are in motion, typing again: *Can I call you?* This time my phone rings, making me smile. "Hi," I answer.

"Hi."

"Austin, I'm sorry about earlier. I just assumed—"

"Sounds like I have competition, Jules."

"You don't."

"We're new. We haven't talked as much as we should have. I get it. I might not be the only one you're seeing."

"You are. Please don't think I'm dating anyone else. I'm not. My best friend is a guy, but it's not romantic."

"I'm gonna be honest with you. I'm afraid the word exclusive will scare you. I'm not seeing anyone else and I don't want to. We can move at your pace, but I need you to set that pace."

"Exclusive doesn't scare me with you, Austin. Misunderstandings do."

He sighs. "I agree. Misunderstandings can be a problem. Jules, I told you before that I'd be honest with you." His voice strains a bit, sounding uncomfortable. "I've been lied to and used many times. I won't, I can't do that again."

I take a deep breath, closing my eyes in the dark room, and holding the phone to my ear. "I don't want that either."

He chuckles lightly. "It's funny that we're having this conversation when thousands of miles and a large ocean separate us."

"I like that we can talk like this, even with the distance."

He whispers, "So do I." The weight of the conversation lifts. "You look better than I imagined in that set too and I have a pretty damn good imagination."

I laugh this time. "Oh I know you do."

We talk for another twenty minutes, our more responsible sides eventually winning out at the late hour. After a short but sweet goodbye we hang up, all doubts and hesitations settled as we move forward as a couple.

CHAPTER 2

Dylan

April 19th

"WHAT DO YOU not understand about do not disturb, Tricia?" The words are out of my mouth before I can stop them, my irritation peaking, then dumping it all on her.

She sits there wordless, anger in her own eyes, but smart enough not to say anything back. I turn away from her, others watching this play out. I close my eyes knowing the source of my real annoyance is not my longtime secretary, but the messed up emotions fucking with my head. Immediately spinning around, I apologize to her. Loud enough to where the others can hear because she deserves that respect and I deserve to look like the ass I'm acting like. I lower my voice then. "Please hold my calls for the next hour. I have a meeting on the forty-seventh floor."

"Yes, sir." She calls me sir when she's mad at me. She normally calls me Dylan.

I ride down the elevator and am greeted by the Junior Vice President of Finances. She takes me into the meeting, and the door closes.

TRICIA SMILES, GREETING me when I arrive back at my office three hours later. She hands me my messages, then tells me she sent about a dozen more to my voicemail.

I walk in and drop the messages on my desk before walking to the window, pulling at my tie until it's untied. I toss it onto my desk along with the papers I left hours ago. I cross my arms and stare out at the vast city before me, my mind not into work right now, my mind is on Juliette instead. She's becoming an occupational hazard lately.

I hear a light knock, but don't turn around. I know who it is. "Dylan." Tricia is hesitant. She can read my body language. I'm not happy, though I should be after that meeting. "This package arrived for you while you were gone. I'll just set it here." She sets it on the bureau by the door and closes the door quietly, leaving me alone with the package.

Turning around, my concentration is broken. The box is large. I walk over and rip the tape at the top that's keeping it sealed shut. Checking the top left corner, there's no return address. I remove several sheets of tissue paper and lots of packing peanuts fall to the floor. It's heavy and bubble wrapped. I pull it all the way out, then unroll it. I only get about half way before it's revealed—*the vase*. The vase I sent Juli— Jules with the flowers.

My anger flares again, flames flicking in my chest. "God damn it!"

This woman has caused me nothing but trouble for over a month now. If I was honest with myself, which I'm not, it's been years, but as I said, I'm not that honest with myself to admit that... yet.

I walk over and grab my keys from my desk, then lift my jacket from the coat rack by the door, slipping it on. I pick the vase back up, knocking all the protective packaging to the floor, and walk out. "I'll be gone the rest of the afternoon, Tricia."

Her eyes are wide, darting down to the vase in my hands then back up. I've never left early. I've never even left on time. I always work late, so I understand her shocked expression. "Yes, Dylan. Have a good evening."

"Thank you. You can go ahead and leave now too if you want."

I hear a quiet and happy, 'Thank you,' as I walk out the company doors to the bank of elevators. I hail a cab, which at this hour is a breeze, and head across town.

The cab driver pulls over a few doors down from the gallery. I pay him and walk, no, more like storm with purpose toward the large artsy entrance. I swing open the door and look around. There's no one in sight, so I glance to the left. Jules' office door is open, but no one is in there.

Then I hear her. Her voice chimes through the barren white-walled space. The smell of paint is heavy in the air, drop-cloths down on the floor. The moment of pause is making me rethink my purpose and I stop, unsure if I should be here. The earlier passion I felt is fading until I see her again. She riles me up like no other. With her phone in hand, her eyes go wide. "Dylan?" she says, surprised.

Our eyes only meet for a brief second before she glances down at my hands and sees the vase. She looks away. Turning her back to me, she goes into her office. *Dismissing me.*

I follow her inside and find her rummaging through papers on a table near the door. With her back still to me, she asks, "What are you doing here?" Her tone holds haste, distaste altogether.

And I miss the reverence it once held. I charge forward setting the vase down on the glass desk top, momentarily forgetting I'm handling something of value, something precious. She jumps, startled, maybe scared. It's a blaring reminder of how I mishandled her. She was precious and valuable, but I didn't treat her that way. But my irritation wins out. Looking her in the eyes, my voice is stern, my mouth tight. "I gave this to you as a gift. It's rude to return a gift."

She eyes the vase, concerned, giving me a peek at the Juliette I once knew. She wants to touch it. I can tell, but restrains herself. When her eyes finally meet mine, she says, "I don't want your gifts. I don't want anything from you. I don't want you in my life at al—"

"Enough!" I yell, too loud to be appropriate for the workplace. I've become irrational. "I've had enough of this bullshit, Juliette."

Her eyes flash with anger, anger I haven't seen in too long, in too many years. *Passion.* I thought she was weak at the end of our relationship, but she was always passionate. I was just blinded by my own ego to notice anymore.

Her hands are on her hips in defiance as she glares at me. Pointing at me accusingly, with her teeth clamped together, she strikes back. "You've had enough?" Her voice goes up a notch, seething as her hands fist at her sides. "You've had enough! Fuck you, Dylan! Get out of my office and get out of my gallery!"

I stare at her, my heart skipping a beat or three or five.

Thump.

Thump.

Skip.

Thump.

Thump.

Skip.

I'm mad. I'm fucking offended. But I'm impressed too. Juliette Weston is so fucking infuriating and smart not to take my shit, not to put up with anything involving me, but this situation is frustrating.

Very.

Fucking.

Frustrating!

"Leave," she starts again, her arms hanging at her sides, not defeated, but resolved. "Please."

I feel the shift in the air. I step forward. She steps back. I don't know what I'm doing, but I move forward again. Throwing all the past away, like it doesn't exist, I reach out and grasp her hip... and she doesn't move this time.

Our eyes never leave each others as I gently squeeze, knowing she'll only allow this for so long. She moves, turning rapidly and escaping behind her desk, putting the security of furniture between us. "You need to leave," she says, her voice is softer, her gaze falling from mine as she sits down in her chair.

My insides are twisted, fucked up, my emotions are all over the fucking place because of that woman. Wordlessly, I go, making it into the main hall of the gallery before she's there, behind me, calling to me. "You forgot your vase."

My anger returns when I look back at her. "I want you to have it. Keep it." My words may be terse, but my desires are true.

There's no anger in her eyes though as she holds the vase cradled in her arms, protecting it. Only questions remain. That's all I see when I look at her, the emptiness from lack of answers. I wish I could give her everything she needs, but I can't. I can't fill the blackness I've instilled in her heart. I can only alter it into something beautiful again. And right now that means leaving, because she wants me to.

I wish I could stay and see her passion again. I'm ready for her wrath. If we can get it out and over with, we might be able to do something other than hurt each other. We're caught in a cycle. Wonder if she sees that, if she feels it like I do. Hate binds us to the past and we're stuck in an unwanted emotion. But there's more to us than hate. There's something profoundly deeper.

I don't just know it, I feel it. I feel it morphing inside of me. I see it morphing inside of her when I look deep into her beautiful brown eyes.

CHAPTER 3
Jules
April 29th

THE VASE CATCHES the light and I look over at it by the window, my legs crossed under my desk, the end of a pen between my teeth—a bad habit I picked up from Dylan years ago.

I don't keep flowers in the vase he gave me because they take away from the beauty already there, the artistry in form. I should have insisted he take it back, but I love it too much. When he brought it back, I was happy to see it. Secretly, I was happy to see *him* again too.

Irritated for having that thought *or feeling,* I toss the pen down, watching as it skids across the surface of the desk. I'm not sure how to classify this emotion since I don't allow myself to dwell on such novelties and irresponsibilities.

STARTING WITH THE opener I've rehearsed, I say, "Please don't judge me, okay?"

Brandon stops, the bottle opener in hand, the cork halfway removed. He tilts his head like he knows what's coming, but I don't think he does. I'd be getting more than a raised eyebrow if he did.

Confessing, I add, "I've been thinking about *him* lately."

"*Jesus*, Jules. Talk about a masochist."

"I like the way I don't even have to say his name and you know exactly who I'm talking about." My dry humor is wearing on him tonight.

He must be tired. Tending to the wine again, his eyes focus on the bottle instead of me. He's disappointed, but doesn't want to say it. Then he explains, "If you were talking about Austin or someone else you wouldn't have to preface that statement with 'Please don't judge me'." The cork gives and the wine is poured.

I walk closer to get a glass, and reply, "True."

He turns and leans against the counter, crossing his legs at the ankles. "Lay it on me. That's what we're doing right? You want to talk about Dylan?"

"Talk might be too strong of a word. Maybe mention works better."

After rolling his eyes, a small smile appears. "Okay, whatever."

We stay silent for a few seconds, then I finally give in. "Fine." He looks down, away from me, disapproving of the topic, but I continue, "I saw him last week. He was... a complete mess. It was fun to see, actually." I giggle, which makes him laugh.

"You're so weird sometimes," he says.

"You knew that coming into this relationship, so no running out on me now." I narrow my eyes, teasing him.

"I'm not going anywhere. Are you?" His eyebrows rise up, waiting.

I know he's referring to me moving in with Austin, although he doesn't say it. I sit on the couch, leaning on the arm.

"You're avoiding," he remarks.

An assumption on his part. "I'm thinking."

"It shouldn't be that hard to answer," he says, settling in at the other end of the couch, legs spread wide, his arm across the back, hogging more than half. I don't mind though. He drinks his wine while watching me.

I close my eyes and reply, "That would be presumptuous of me at this stage."

"Would it? Seems like you and Austin are moving pretty fast."

"And?"

"And, well, I don't want to see you hurt."

Sitting up, I look him directly in the eyes. My mood softens. Brandon does that. He still calms me. "I'm not going anywhere... yet."

"I knew you'd throw in a yet. A yet to you is like a hall pass. You can do whatever damn well pleases you because you haven't committed one way or the other."

"I hate you."

"You love me." He smirks.

"I do love you. I just hate that you know me so well."

"Inside and out."

"Ewwww! Don't say that." I laugh, hard.

"You went there, not me. Mind in the gutter much?"

"All the time."

"That's my girl."

"Brandon?"

"Yeah?"

"Start the damn movie."

"Happily. My favorite part is coming up."

"I'm Sally," I call out.

"You're always Sally. I want to have the orgasm."

"I'm the girl. The girl always gets to play Sally. You're definitely more Harry."

"Fine. I'll be your Harry."

SATURDAY MORNINGS SHOULD be lazier. I wish I could sleep in like I could in college, but my body is too programmed. Rolling over, I try to go back to sleep, but twenty minutes later, I'm up and showered. I throw on my yoga pants and a T-shirt, grab some money, and my keys.

The coffee shop is empty on Saturday mornings, especially at this early hour. It's only me and two other people, who obviously can't sleep in either. I decide today is about change. I'll try new things, so I order a frou-frou coffee just to see if I like it any better these days. When I taste it, I quickly decide it's not my favorite. It's overly sweet and doesn't seem to give me the same kick that my usual black coffee does.

I sit and drink it anyway over the next fifteen minutes, watching customers come and go. Then I see Dylan—and he sees me.

Awkward.

Uncomfortable.

I should leave but that would seem rude. *Whoa! Since when did I start caring how I seem to him?*

The debate warring in his head is obvious by the way he shifts as he glances between me and the coffee counter. Surprisingly, I win this round, but I wonder by how much.

"Hi," Dylan says tentatively, no smile, testing the waters.

"Hi." I look down and he walks away.

The barista flirts with him. That brings back so many memories, so many naïve dreams of us that I once held onto so tightly. I'm free of such frivolous notions now. *Wiser.*

Completely distracted by him, I watch his exchange with the barista. He's friendly to her, smiling. *I wonder if he's flirting?* We didn't flirt much, we didn't have to. We were a couple the minute we met. I don't tell the story that way because it felt like it evolved over those first few months, but it didn't. There was no other—just me, just him, us, a couple.

I determine he's not flirting, just being polite, not overly, but appropriately so. When he turns back to me, his expression is more controlled and he slowly walks over. He sits down at a table near mine, but we don't talk.

As he plays on his phone, I can hear the Words with Friends bubbly sounds projected, his move accepted. Makes me wonder who his friends are these days. *Do I know them?*

Turning to the window, I notice how empty the street is. Empty—a lot like the feeling between us now. I steal a glimpse back at him and then look down at the untouched scone in front of me. I thought I wanted it, but I don't.

"Do you play?" he asks, drawing my attention.

I glance at his phone displaying the game on the screen, then up to his eyes. "Are you trying to make casual conversation, Dylan?"

Leaning forward, he puts his elbows down on the table and scrubs his hands over his face, frustrated. "How about I'm trying, period?" He snaps.

"If it's for my benefit, you don't need to."

"Why not?"

I don't face him, not feeling strong enough to do that just yet. I sip my coffee, hoping to find some strength in the weak brew, but reply, "Because we're both here at the same time doesn't mean we need to talk."

"What if I want to talk to you?"

"I don't owe you anything." I stand up, taking the scone and my mug with me. I put the mug in the dish bin and toss the scone in the trash on my way out the door.

"Jules?"

Here we go again. "You don't take a hint, do you?"

He laughs, catching up and walking beside me like he has the right to do so. "Hints aren't needed. You've been more than obvious about how you feel about me. But I have things that I want to say."

I stop, crossing my arms and look at him. "You have some nerve showing up here. You think because we ran into each other at a restaurant that suddenly what? We need to be best friends? Boyfriend? Girlfriend? What are you doing? Why are you here? Did you come to the coffee shop because you knew I would be here? I don't understand this sudden interest in me? What are you doing, Dylan?"

He looks deep into my eyes, exactly where I've tried so hard to keep him from going. No one is allowed to that place inside me anymore, especially not him. I instantly drop my gaze to his shoes. They're casual sneakers, but nice.

"Jules, I've said before. I don't know why I'm here. I just want to be near you. You're on my mind, fucking with me."

"I'm fucking with you?" I walk away too annoyed to stay and listen to any of this bullshit.

"Jules."

"No. Don't!" I yell over my shoulder.

He doesn't... and when he doesn't I start questioning his motives, sincerity, everything he's been trying to tell me. His words are hard to believe when his actions mean the opposite. I stop on the corner and look back. He still stands there watching me. I throw my arms in the air and scream not caring that it's still early in the morning. "What? What do you want, Dylan?"

He runs as if I called him to me. I didn't. I just want answers, but he seems to want answers to questions we don't even have yet. Confusing. And fucked up. He's messing with my mind, too. I wonder if he realizes or if he's doing it on purpose. He grabs my wrists as if we know each other these days. His thumbs graze over the underside of my wrists, my lifeline pulsing beneath his touch. I want to pull away, but I can't. I like his touch too much.

"What do you want from me?" I whisper scared to see what he's feeling but dare to look into his eyes anyway.

He doesn't waste the opportunity. "I want us to start over."

"Start *what* over?" My tone is harsh, incredulous.

"Friends. We can start as friends."

Glancing to the street, then back, I state, "We were never friends, Dylan."

"We were. You were my best friend, Jules."

The tears start coming, building in my chest, and seeping into my eyes. "You were my best friend too," I admit, weakened by the moment, by the feel of his skin on mine.

Tears fall between us. When I look down, I attempt to close my eyes before another falls, but one falls too quick. But that one isn't mine. It's his.

I look up, needing to see that he feels something, that maybe I meant something to him or even mean something now. Maybe I'm beyond repair, my emotions permanently damaged, but when I look up, I don't see the person I hated for years. I see the person I once knew standing before me, caressing my wrists and my heart starts to race, so I drop a confession of my own, "I have a boyfriend, Dylan."

My wrists are dropped. The last of his tears are wiped away onto the back of his sleeve. "Since when?"

After wiping away my own weakness, I stand strong once again, my heart and emotions closed off just as fast as his. "Since none of your business."

"You're impossible, *Juliette!*" His voice and words sickened with hate as he uses my full name.

I strike back not willing to let him hurt me again. "I hate you, Dylan. I hate you so much." Anger causes tears to fill my eyes again and my face heats.

"You're so far removed from the person you once were that I don't even recognize you anymore," he says, "you've lost your soul—"

"I didn't lose it! You stole it just like everything else you stole from me. You took it with you that day. And if I'm such a horrible person, then why do you keep coming around? I mean, who does that? Who keeps going where they're unwanted? It's insane."

"Call me what you want, but at least I feel."

"Fuck you."

"No, Juliette, fuck you." He turns his back and leaves.

I scream in fury at the frustrating man. "You're a bastard, Dylan Somers."

He laughs. "Yes, baby. You're not telling me anything I don't know already."

"Don't you ever call me baby again and stop calling me Juliette! You have no right—"

He's suddenly in front of me, towering over me. "I have rights. I used to make love to you. I have a lot of fucking rights that come along with that."

"No, you don—"

He grabs me and kisses me. Hard on the lips. Holding my face between his hands, so I can't escape. The kiss is a surprise, but the feelings we're sharing so familiar... and wanted... welcomed. Then I remember Austin. Dylan is not him. Dylan is not mine to kiss any longer. I shove him on the chest, our lips separating from the abrupt interruption.

My arm flies through the air, but is caught before my hand makes contact with his cheek.

Toe-to-toe, his eyes narrow on me. "You will not slap me for something that I could feel you wanted just as much."

I give him one last hard look before I yank my arm from his tight grip. No words. No words can capture how I truly feel about him right now. And hate and anger have been overused, so I turn and walk away. By the time I reach the corner, I'm running and this time, I hear nothing behind me except a car backfiring in the distance.

Seeking comfort from my bed, I snuggle on my side, squeezing a pillow as my mind reels. Despite how restless I am, I don't give up on trying to sleep until ten o'clock at night. By midnight, I'm wandering the apartment because my brain is in overdrive. This place holds so many memories—good and bad.

A small circular crystal prism hangs from the window. During the day it catches the light and sends a rainbow of color across the nearby wall and the painting above the couch.

Dylan gave this to me.

At first, I thought he only left me the coffeepot. But a month later, in the back of the closet on the floor, I found it. The string was broken. He didn't see it or choose not to take it. I don't know which, but I'm glad I have it some days, others not so much because it carries a heavier weight than its own with it. Most nights it's just a clear ball of glass and it's more bearable to be around. Tonight it means more.

After retrieving my phone from the nightstand, I discover I missed Austin's call while I paced in the living room. He left a message that makes me smile and feel warm inside. Those are the feelings I want. They come with certainty and I like knowing what to expect. I like him. I call him because regardless of the time. He said, anytime—day or night.

My relationship with him is good. We're healthy together. There's a comfort in Austin I desperately need.

Dylan only causes heartache.

CHAPTER 4
Jules
September 9th

TIME PASSED QUICKER than usual. Summer was a blur of work and romance, art and Austin. We spent five days in Paris back in June. It was amazing. I'd been once before a few years ago, but I was in no state to appreciate it back then. It was a work trip that I extended by a few days to enjoy the museums, the history, the art.

But I didn't. My head was there, but the cavern in my chest still held empty heartbeats. The real ones only beating for a lost love.

The trip with Austin was different, incredible in so many ways. He would give me the world if he could. He's that sweet and kind, loving and generous. But he's worldly too, smart, and charming. He talks of taking the next step. I'm not sure if he means moving in together or getting engaged. And I'm not sure how I feel about either of those yet.

Austin: *I'm sending the car for you. My meeting is running long. I'm sorry.*

Me: *You'll still be there at 8?*

Austin: *I won't be late.*

Me: *I look forward to seeing you later, sexy.*

Austin: *Sexy? I like that. Btw - I have a surprise for your birthday. Prepare to be showered.*

Me: *Literally showered? Is that my present.*

Austin: *lol. I like that idea.*

Me: *Glad you're amused. I'm disappointed I have to wait through dinner to get my present.*

Austin: *You won't be. I promise. Oh, and yes I will now literally be showering you. Hope you have plenty of hot water. I have plans while I'm in there.*

Me: *Aren't you in a meeting right now?*

Austin: *Yep.*

Me: *How does the owner of a huge international company get away with saying 'yep'?*

Austin: *Like you said, I'm the owner.*

Me: *I need to get ready for a fabulous dinner with my boyfriend. He's taking me to this bistro downtown that is impossible to get reservations to.*

Austin: *He sounds connected. Is he a keeper?*

Me: *A total keeper.*

A few minutes pass before I receive another text.

Austin: *Just got asked a question and I had no idea what they were talking about. I guess I need to pay attention but these financial strategists are so boring.*

Me: *Glad I'm not in finance then.*

Austin: *Me too. I'll see you tonight, beautiful.*

Me: *Bye, Charmer.*

I set my phone down on the bathroom counter to finish getting ready. I find it hard to apply makeup properly when smiling so big.

I ARRIVE AT Le Bonne Vie five minutes early and have just enough time to check my lipstick in the bathroom before returning to the waiting area.

"Hi there. Sorry I kept you waiting," Austin greets, smiling, admiring. He kisses me lightly on the cheek.

"Hi there yourself. I haven't been here long, so no worries."

With his hands on my waist, his expression changes. "I have some bad news. Two of my business associates have to join us tonight."

"What? It's my birthday, Austin."

"I know. We just need to get some contracts signed, then they'll be off. I didn't want to keep you waiting any longer, so I told them to meet me here. Just one drink and they'll be gone."

"That's fine. One drink doesn't ruin our plans."

"Mr. Barker, your table is ready." The hostess guides him,

walking too close to him in my opinion.

He sits next to me, two empty chairs across. After looking over his shoulder, he nudges. "They're here. Thanks for understanding." Austin stands as they approach. "Jacqueline Rosen," he starts the introductions.

I stand and shake her hand, "Jules Weston."

"So nice to meet you, Ms. Weston. I've heard lovely things about you from Mr. Barker, such as it's your birthday. Happy Birthday." She hands me an envelope. "I hope you don't mind the last minute wrapping."

Her face, she looks familiar, but I can't place her right away. I look down at the gift and say, "You got me a present? You didn't have to do that."

She waves it off like it's nothing.

I peek inside the envelope just as Austin says, "Ah, here we go. Jules Weston this is Dylan Somers."

My gaze flashes up as the envelope slips from my fingers to the floor.

"Ms. Weston." Dylan smiles as his voice coats my body. When my eyes meet his, I see the same surprise I feel inside.

I glance back to Jacqueline and the picture completes in my head. *Dylan, Jacqueline, the restaurant.* She was all in red just like tonight. I find myself staring at her before my eyes work their way back to Dylan, shocked he's with her... still.

Austin touches my elbow and asks, "Are you alright, honey?"

I glance to him. "Yes, I'm fine. I apologize." I reach my hand forward and Dylan takes it. "Nice to meet you, Mr. Somers."

"The pleasure is all mine."

My heart races just from seeing him again, hearing his smooth voice that enunciates with confidence. The touch of his skin against mine sends warmth streaking through my veins and I wonder if I affect him the same way.

We all sit down, Dylan taking the chair across from me, and our eyes meeting again. "Happy birthday, Ms. Weston."

Austin retrieves the envelope and hands it to me. Trying to act like my Ex being here doesn't affect me, I look inside. "The Red Door," I say, looking at the gift certificate. "That's so kind. Thank you."

Jacqueline leans across the table, caddy-corner, as if we're old pals. "I was there last month for an entire day. I joke that they were going to have to kick me out. That spa does everything first class. You have to try their chamomile herbal hydrating facial. Wonders. It does complete wonders." She laughs, Dylan and Austin chuckle lightly, humoring her. "Of course, you're naturally beautiful, but some of us have to work a little harder."

She's fishing.

Austin's caught because he's polite like that. "I'm sure you have no trouble turning heads." He has a natural ability to make everyone feel good while making it clear to me that he didn't include himself in that group of heads turning, which makes me smile.

I lean forward and tell her, "Thank you again. I look forward to using it."

We order cocktails and Dylan and I continue not looking at each other. I wonder if he's avoiding me as much as I am him. When I dare to finally peek in his direction, the old anger that lived inside of me for so long is not quite like it should be. It's not there at all in fact, *which worries me.*

Jacqueline puts her hands on Dylan a lot. I eye her fingers touching him, pretending to be nothing but a friendly touch, but I can tell it means more to her. When I look up at her face, I wonder if they're dating. I want to ask so badly, so damn curious. While anyone can tell Austin and I are together, the two of them are not as obvious.

I bet Dylan doesn't even remember that I saw them together at the restaurant all those months ago. If they're dating then why is she touching my boyfriend right now? I watch as she reaches across and taps his hand lightly to get his attention. Everything about her annoys me. Her thick, long red hair is a nuisance the way it drapes over her dinner plate, almost knocking over a water glass as she talks to him.

Our cocktails are served. "Thank God," I say out loud though I meant to keep that inside. Austin gives me a questioning look.

Dylan chuckles, making me feel a little less crazy and I smile. He understands the relief needed right now. Jacqueline turns to him, hands on his arm—always with the touching—and says, "Dylan, the contracts." He pulls an envelope from his inside suit pocket, along with a pen he sets down in front of Austin. Jacqueline leans across and starts to explain, "Dylan went over the documentation twice..."

"You're an accountant?" I ask, speaking to him directly as Austin and Jacqueline discuss the details.

"No." Dylan shakes his head, a tinge of happy making his blue eyes sparkle in the restaurant.

I look to my left. Austin is reading the contract as Jacqueline continues explaining the major points, but she stops suddenly and says, "The food smells wonderful. Have you eaten here before, Jules?"

My eyes go toward the sound of my name. "No, this is our first time here."

"I meant to tell you that I love your dress. It's a *wow* dress. Just what a birthday dress should be."

"Thank you," I reply. "I wanted something special."

Austin leans over, sliding his hand behind my back and pulling me closer. "I was going to tell you in private but since we're on the subject, you look incredible." He kisses me lightly, appropriately for a dinner. Then he whispers into my ear, "You make me want to skip dinner altogether."

"Stunning," Dylan adds unabashedly.

Everyone stops talking. Austin sits back in his chair, his hand immediately on my thigh. He tilts his head, surprised like everyone else by Dylan's compliment. Jacqueline appears confused by his vocal nicety.

Maybe it's the alcohol, but Dylan doesn't seem to care. His eyes directly on mine, ignoring the others. He clears his throat and looks down before turning to Austin. "We should let you get back to your celebration."

"Yes, well," Austin replies, "everything looks to be in order and how we discussed." He starts signing the paperwork, directing his attention back down to the documents in front of him.

Just as he hands them back to Jacqueline, I don't know what overcomes me. Without thinking about the repercussions, I suggest, "You should join us. As you said, this is a celebration. Stay for dinner."

Jacqueline jumps at the opportunity. "I'd love to try this place. I've heard it's spectacular."

"Thank you," Dylan adds, "that's very kind. But only if you're positive we're not intruding."

I know what Dylan's doing. I can see right through his act. He wants me to plead, wanting to hear how much I want him to stay. I'm in a good mood, so I oblige. "No intrusion at all," I say, "Please. Stay."

I feel Austin's hand on my thigh, warming me as he rubs gently. "Great, let's order then. I'm starved. That meeting went on about two hours too long."

Jacqueline points out, "The meeting was only two hours long."

"That's my point." Austin raises his eyebrows and smiles.

Over dinner, Jacqueline is working Austin hard. He seems interested in a lot of what she has to say but challenges her on some of those ideas as well. I like that for some reason.

Dylan clears his throat, and asks, "Discovered any new talents I should know about in the art world?"

That he's talking to me over dinner is a bizarre concept, not wholly welcome, but not completely unwanted either. I look down for a moment, unsure how to proceed. *How much of myself am I willing to give him?* Since art is my professional world, it's a topic I'm comfortable sharing with him. "Yes, we held an artist named Jean-Luc's exhibit over the summer. He has another one coming up in a week. He's talented, *so* talented. His next show is called Body Affair."

He glances over to Austin who is deep in a business conversation with Jacqueline, neither of them listening to ours. He replies, "Sounds risqué."

"One can only hope," I reply, bringing my martini glass to my lips and taking more than a polite sip. Looking into Dylan's eyes, I venture into dangerous territory. "What do you do, Mr. Somers?"

"I'd prefer if you called me Dylan."

"Alright, *Dylan*."

"I work in investments. Austin's corporation is a client of the company. Jacqueline is leading his financial team and they brought me in to guide their fund growth."

"Sounds intriguing to hold so much power over all that money. Do you like power?" My eyebrow quirks up involuntarily.

"What man or woman doesn't want power?"

"It's nice to have power, but sometimes at home, in private, it feels good to let someone else take the lead for a while."

"Only a powerful woman can say that."

"I think power means different things in my world than in yours. You, Dylan, seem to be someone who needs it. I don't need power. I just need to know I've done the best I can."

He drinks, three long gulps and I watch his Adams apple as he swallows, remembering how I used to... I shake my head. I shouldn't think those thoughts about him anymore.

There's a welcome interruption from the waiter. "Miss, your plate."

"That looks good. Let me know if you need help with it," Austin says lightheartedly, eyeing my food.

I giggle, momentarily forgetting about Dylan and the redhead.

"How long have the two of you been dating, Jules?" Jacqueline asks as if we're going to be friends.

I'm not the one she cares to impress at the table. I'm just someone she'll use to get what she wants, which is Austin's attention, so I reply tensely, "I'm not sure actually."

I look to Austin who quickly covers for me. "Five months. It's been really great." He grabs my hand, bringing it to the tabletop between us, not showy, but in a casual way. Our fingers are intertwined and as he continues, I look across the table at Dylan. His eyes are on our hands and scanning up slowly until they meet mine, then I face Austin. "... I've learned so much about art since we've been together. Jules and I went to Paris over the summer—"

"Oh I love Paris," Jacqueline says, her hand settling on Dylan's forearm. "Have you been to Paris, Dylan?"

"No." He looks to me again and I'm hoping it's not obvious, that *we're* not obvious. We once dreamed of going to Paris together. "I'm waiting," he says, "to go when I find the right tour guide."

"You can hire one," Austin adds innocently.

"I can show you the sights," Jacqueline offers. Something in her tone pisses me off. It's more than just a friendly offer and her damn hand is still on his forearm.

Dylan laughs, loud and deep, then says, "I meant I want to go with someone I'm in a committed relationship with."

Jacqueline laughs, a bit embarrassed as she should be for being so available. She says, "Seeing me at work a couple of times a week isn't committed?" She squeezes his arm again. The minute caress starting to bother me. "I'm teasing you, Dylan. Yes, going to the most romantic city in the world does make you want to bring someone you love."

Dylan is placating her, being polite and smiling, but I'm not amused at all.

BY THE TIME dessert is served, the mood is light like the conversation again. "Please don't make me eat this alone." I say, pushing the dessert forward to the center of the table.

"I thought you'd devour your birthday treat." Austin says, "Jules doesn't consider it dessert unless it has chocolate in it."

After taking a bite, I savor the rich cake in my mouth, then amend his statement. "It's true. Though I do love a great crème brulee these days and I wouldn't say no to cheesecake."

"I couldn't agree more on the chocolate. Do you mind if I try your dessert?" Dylan asks, picking up one of the four spoons delivered with the dish.

"No, not at all." And for some reason, I don't. I blame the olive-sullied vodka I've been drinking.

Everyone at the table watches as Dylan reaches across and scoops the cake and fudge with his spoon. Normally, one would eat from the side closest, but he doesn't. He takes his bite from the exact place where I took mine. My heart speeds up and my eyes widen watching him open his mouth slowly, insinuatingly dragging the spoon from between his lips. I assume this reaction is from the rich chocolate I just inhaled, but I have a feeling it's not.

Jacqueline and Austin return to their conversation about team dynamics, but we don't join them. We're not talking at all, just watching each other. My chest seems to be heaving a bit more than it should and my body heats. I can feel Dylan's gaze heavy on me, so I close my eyes and try to regain my composure.

"I'll take care of the check. It's my girl's birthday dinner, after all." Austin's voice brings me back and I open my eyes to find Dylan's narrowed at him, irritated.

"Was it good?" I ask Dylan, trying to redirect his glare from Austin.

He looks over, directly into my eyes, a small arrogant smile appearing. "The best I ever had."

Austin speaks, not aware of the current conversation I'm having. "I wanted to give you your present over dessert. Hope you don't mind an audience."

Eye contact is held a beat or two longer before I turn to see Austin's sweet smile. "Okay," I reply. He sets a Tiffany's box in front of me. It's too small and it feels like the thermostat has been turned up a few degrees. The box is way too small to be a necklace or bracelet. *Racing heart.* My breathing shallows.

Oh my God! No, he's not doing this.

Not here.

Not now.

Not in a restaurant.

Not in front of Dylan, my boyfriend... ex-boyfriend. Ex. Ex. Ex.

"Open it," Austin encourages.

With shaking hands, I pull the Tiffany blue lid off. A velvet box resides inside, a box the perfect size for a ring.

Thump. Thump. Thump.

As soon as I take the box in hand, Austin stands suddenly and I feel dizzy. *He wouldn't do this now, not after only five months.* Would he?

When he leans down, Dylan jumps up and shouts, "Wait!" There's panic in his eyes. The same panic I feel, but for the same reasons?

Austin stands back up pulling his phone from his pocket while dropping the napkin that he just retrieved from the floor onto his chair. "I'm sorry, I have to take this," he says, tapping his phone. "You can open it if you want, honey." He walks away from the table.

My heart beats to a dull thud now, calming.

"Open it. I'm dying to see what he got you," Jacqueline says, leaning closer.

Dylan remains standing. Nervous, panicked.

"What, Dylan?" She questions.

I lift the hinged lid. *Earrings.* Oh thank God!

Mimicking my inner dialogue, Dylan says, "Thank God!"

Again Jacqueline stares at him confused. "You're acting so strange tonight. Are you all right?"

I understand his behavior. All too well.

"Sorry," Austin says, returning to the table. "That was Japan. They work opposite hours and I wanted to get that call out of the way so we could enjoy the rest of our night. Do you like the earrings? They're classic and beautiful just like you." Austin picks my hand up from the table and kisses it. "Happy birthday, Jules."

I exhale. The pressure finally off my lungs.

"They're beautiful. Thank you, Austin. The sapphires are breathtaking and vibrant."

"I thought you'd like something with color."

"I do, very much. That was very thoughtful. Thank you," I say, leaning in and kissing him.

I feel his hands on me, gently urging for more, but I don't ever forget we have an audience. I blush when we part and my gaze slowly makes its way over the earrings and across the table to briefly meet Dylan's. The earrings actually remind me of his eyes—*breathtaking and vibrant.*

After dinner, we stop on the sidewalk, everything feeling awkward since I opened my present.

"You and Jules should take the first cab," Jacqueline offers. "Since we invaded your private party and all."

"No, it's fine," Austin says. "We have a car, you and Dylan should take it."

Dylan steps forward, and says, "Jacqueline, you can have the first cab. We live in opposite directions."

"You're not together?" I ask before thinking. "I just assumed. I know it was a business meeting but—"

"No, we're not together," Dylan quickly clarifies. "We're just business associates."

Austin takes my hand. "I should have told you. I apologize. Jacqueline is Dylan's boss."

Jacqueline looks uncomfortable by the conversation.

Looking at her, I say, "I apologize." When I look to Dylan, he's smiling, knowing exactly what I was doing.

He reassures her to end the night on a good note, "Jacqueline is a great catch though."

She turns to him, smiling, not blushing. I bet she hasn't blushed in years. She's more experienced that way.

Our car pulls to the curb and I can see something in Dylan's expression change, but I don't have enough time to pinpoint it. Austin ushers me forward, then we stop and turn around. He shakes Dylan's hand, tells him he's glad he's on the team, and that he's been impressed with his work ethic.

Dylan was always a hard worker, at least when I knew him before. There's something comforting in the fact that he still is, that maybe he didn't change completely.

Jacqueline shakes my hand. I thank her for the gift and promise to get that facial she was raving about. She turns to my boyfriend, shaking hands and holding it, laughing about some inside joke, her other hand on his bicep. Not professional, too comfortable, not just flirtatiousness, but blatant passes in my opinion. Austin takes it in stride. He's used to women finding him attractive. He's gorgeous. Her passes don't pass, but are stopped as he pulls me closer, his own blatant show that he's taken.

I look to Dylan, awkwardness straddling the air between us. The wall of tension that has divided us for so long begins rebuilding again.

With a sigh, Dylan looks down the street then back to me. "It was nice to spend your birthday with you. Thank you for including us." He takes my hand just as Austin releases it to wait at the open door, Jacqueline still talking his ear off, distracting him.

I shake it, though that wasn't the original intention when he took it. "Yes, thank you for joining us." The words aren't right between us. They're for show, not what we feel inside, not truly.

His blue eyes search mine needing more from me, needing what I need from him right now—more. More time, more talking, more of everything.

"I hope to see you again," he adds, his voice quieter, more private as his thumb rubs over my knuckles, reminding me of the gentle bond we once shared.

"Me too." I say, but before I turn away from him for what feels like the last time, I add, "Goodbye, Dylan."

"Goodbye Jules."

CHAPTER 5

Dylan

September 9th

WHAT A FUCKING night! It's like the first time I ever saw her, reliving that moment all over again. She was gorgeous, engaging, and the center of attention. There's no turning back for me. I know what I want, even at the expense of Austin and the damage he can do to my career. It's ironic. I gave up Juliette for my career three years ago and now I'm willing to sacrifice my career to get her back.

The cab drops me off three blocks down at the park near my building. I'm so excited that I run to the center near the pond, not caring if I mess up my shoes, and let it out. I yell in triumph. The smile hasn't left my face since I left the restaurant. I fist pump in the air. *Jules*. It's all because of Jules. Laughing out loud to an empty park seems much more sane when you're high off life.

I haven't felt this good since... well, since we were dating. I run back to my apartment, adrenaline driving me forward as my mind tries to erase all the years that didn't include her. Everything else that happened is just a blur now except for Jules. She remains crystal clear in my mind, tonight refreshing that fading memory of her lips on mine.

Finally, I can breathe. I didn't realize the pressure that remained from our fight last April. The last five months were utter hell. I've tried hard to forget her, but it didn't work. I worked eighty hour weeks. I got a promotion, but all those hours were just a distraction. I took up racquetball. Fun, but not fulfilling. It was a filler of time, not my mind. My thoughts always came back to her.

I run up the stairs taking them two at a time and burst into my place. Stripping my suit off, I drop my clothes as I rush to the bathroom and start the shower. Invincible. I feel invincible.

All because of her.

She looked so fucking gorgeous in that dress.

I step under the spray.

Her body even more incredible.

I scrub my body with soap, drenching my head in the process.

Once I set my eyes on Jules, I couldn't take them off her.

She's not officially taken. *Thank God.* I freaked when I thought Barker was going to propose, but he didn't.

I wash my hair.

His mistake. I won't make that same mistake twice. I now know what I've been missing. She looked edible tonight in that dress and fuck hot shoes. I wanted to drag her into the bathroom and fuck her like I used to. I wonder if she remembers how we used to fuck.

I grab my dick... Leaning forward, my palm goes flat against the tile as my other hand continues.

"Jules!" I call her name while coming hard.

September 10th

MY KNOCK ALERTS her to my presence, though the door is open.

Jacqueline looks up and smiles. "Hey Dylan, come on in and shut the door."

"You summoned," I reply, sitting down in front of her desk.

"I thought we should talk about dinner last night," she says, her smile faltering a bit.

"I had a good time. Did you?"

She stands, brushing her hair behind her shoulders. Walking around the desk, she leans against it in front of me, very close. I know she wants me. She's not subtle, except when it comes to the details. I think that was obvious to Jules last night while Jacqueline was hitting on her boyfriend.

"How do you think it went overall?" She lengthens her legs out and crosses them at the ankles. The action puts her knees between my legs. *Obvious.*

I sit up straighter, putting just a little distance between us. "I think it went well and I think the client had a good time."

She remarks, "Jules was offish, don't you think?"

"No, not really."

"I didn't get a good vibe from her. Like with the gift. Do you think she really liked it or was just saying that?"

I chuckle, surprised I'm having this conversation right now, a conversation about Jules *and her boyfriend.* This is really fucked up. "I think she reacted normal to receiving a gift from a total stranger who was trying to suck up to her boyfriend."

"Dylan!"

"It's true and you know it."

She stands, offended by my accusation. Apparently calling her out hurts her feelings. "We may be friends, but soften the delivery next time."

"Sorry," I say, shrugging. "But I do think you got an appropriate reaction from her. Do I think she's cold? Um, she wasn't last night. I thought she was quite charming actually. We had great conversation over dinner."

Twirling her hair around a finger, she says, "She seemed attached, too attached, like really clingy to Austin considering they've only been together for five months. Don't you think?" I'm starting to get pissed. I don't want to talk about Jules and Austin. I should leave. I stand, but she steps forward. "Don't go yet."

My tone is terse, more than I mean, but I'm over this conversation. "I thought dinner went well—"

"I think we should invite them out again. You know, double."

"That makes no sense. You and I are not dating."

"I just need a little more time with her and I know we can become good friends."

"Why do you want this so bad, Jacqueline? Are you trying to be chummy with her to get to Austin? Save yourself the trouble. I saw how he looked at her, how he touched her." My voice involuntarily rises. "For fuck's sake, I thought he was proposing last night. He's in love with her."

Jacqueline walks back around her desk and sits in her large leather chair, crossing her arms over her chest, and smirking. "Well, well, Mr. Somers, unless I'm completely mistaken, that sounds like jealousy I hear in your voice?"

I shift uncomfortably. "This is pointless. You're trying to get a man that only cares for one woman—"

"But who does that woman care for? You two sure did seem caught up in some intimate conversati—"

"That's because you effectively blocked us out of yours while making the moves on Austin. I was being polite to his date, so she didn't have to watch that play out."

I turn toward the door, reaching it in four long strides.

"So no double then?" she asks to my back.

I laugh, then leave.

September 30th

I ENTER THE gallery behind a small group, blending in while looking around for Jules. I don't see her, but realize she'll be busy tonight anyway. I walk into the other room. The lights are dimmed low, spotlights focused on the walls. I take a glass of red from the wine table. Standing off to the side, I look over the space.

Jules is here. I see her, like a breathtaking angel in white tonight.

Her legs are bare, the short dress showing her figure. *Fucking gorgeous.*

I watch her as she laughs, then excuses herself from a couple she's been chatting with. She hasn't seen me, but walks with purpose before getting sidetracked by a large painting. Stopping. Staring. I always loved watching her admire art. Even from over here, I can tell she's let her mind drift somewhere else. *Transported.*

I take a few steps closer just as a man comes up behind her. He has his hands on her waist, but she doesn't react like his touch is unwelcome or unfamiliar. He's not Austin or Brandon, but she knows him. I move even closer, emotions spinning in my chest. He whispers in her ear and she smiles, amused, tilting her head slightly away from him. He doesn't notice, but I do. Maybe she doesn't welcome him as much as he wants.

There's something in her body language that tells me he's flirting and she's enjoying it, but nothing has ever happened. Maybe it's in *his* body language—he's trying too hard to be seductive. It doesn't come natural to him. He wants her. That much is clear, but he's barely legal looking. Jules Weston needs a man.

I move closer until I'm near, not wanting to invade her space. She turns, then our eyes connect.

She whispers to him, both of them wandering over after. With a smile on her face, she says, "Dylan," as if it's of no surprise that I'm here. We knew we'd see each other again when we said goodbye on her birthday.

"Jules." I greet with a smile of my own. "You look beautiful."

"Thank you. You came to the show?"

"I wanted to see the paintings you mentioned the other night."

While touching the other guy on the shoulder, she says, "This is Jean-Luc, the artist."

This guy is the artist? Of course he is. He hasn't had real passion but tries to capture it in his paintings. He doesn't shake my offered hand. Yep, I called it. He's immature.

Dropping my hand to my side, I look back to Jules who's giggling. She always said artists were temperamental. She reaches forward and grabs my wrist unexpectedly, pulling me closer. "Have you seen this one yet?" She's referring to the painting of the naked woman on the wall in front of me.

Jean-Luc is talking to some woman who flirts with him. His hands are on her just as they were on Jules minutes before. I'm relieved to find out he does that to everyone.

"It's okay, but it lacks sincerity. It's superficial stuff," I note, glancing down at her. "Nothing real about the woman is exposed, just her flesh. Her eyes say nothing. A woman's eyes always say more than her lips ever could."

She's staring at me, my eyes, my face, my mouth. Her eyes overtly lingering on my mouth, then she shifts. "That's an incredibly sexy observation."

I lean a little closer. When her eyes finally meet mine again, I whisper, "Do you want me to tell you what your eyes are saying right now?"

She blinks rapidly, then I feel her breath against my cheek paused to say something.

"That's a painting of Jules." I jerk up to see Jean-Luc referencing to the painting again.

I think my skepticism is showing when I ask, "That's Jules?"

"Yes. I painted it about 5 months ago. She's stunning and her body... I let my imagination run wild."

With sarcasm, I add, "That's why it lacks emotion. You painted for you not—"

"Dylan. Stop." Jules takes my hand and pulls me away. I'd go with her willingly but I like her hand on mine too much. She drags me a few feet away... away from the 'artist.' "Dylan, please don't upset him. He's very talented and very sensitive."

"He needs a dose of reality."

She rolls her eyes but I see the smile in the corners of her mouth. "It's abstract and you, my friend, are going to be thrown out of here with that attitude. It's Jean-Luc's night." Her tone is playful, not threatening.

Nudging her, I ask with a smirk, "So I'm your friend now?"

Looking up at me, she tilts her head. "That's all you got from that?"

"That's all that matters," I say, more serious than I intend. I don't want to scare her, but she's all that matters. That's the truth.

"Oh, Dylan," she sighs, looking around the gallery.

It's getting busier, more crowded. She'll have to leave me soon, so I need to act fast. "Say it, Jules."

With her arms crossed in defiance, she says, "No."

She's such a tease. "Come *ooonnnn...* say it. Just for me. No one else has to hear."

"I don't know what you want from me."

"You're playing games."

"Fine." She leans in really close, lifts up on her toes and whispers, "You win. We're friends."

"Was that so hard?" I poke her playfully in the side, much like I used to when we were a couple. The ease between us right now is not lost either. I see it in her eyes. Jules is smiling from the inside out.

I reach into my pocket and pull the small box out, presenting it on my palm. "It was rude of me to not have a gift for you on your birthday. I thought I'd make up for it." I step half a foot closer, almost touching, but not.

She reaches tentatively for the box and I try to lighten the mood. "I'm sure it's quite intimidating after seeing how you reacted to Austin's small present."

An instant comeback slips from her lips, "If you thought *I* looked worried, you should have seen *your* face."

There's my girl—all spark and moxie. We laugh as she takes the box and opens it like she has a point to prove. Her expression becomes more serious, so I say, "You always loved that one we had years ago."

She looks up, holding the prism by the string. Her eyes are watery now. I didn't mean to make her cry. "Dylan, I—"

"Hey, that's just like the one in your apartment," Austin says, taking to her side and kissing her cheek. "Sorry I'm late. Traffic was brutal from the downtown. Dylan, good to see you." We shake hands.

No matter how much his presence bothers me, he just gave me way more than I expected. She still has it. She has the gift I gave her for Christmas back in college.

Austin is his usual polite self, and asks me, "Did you come for the art or the beautiful company?"

Watching as his arm snakes around her waist, I answer honestly, "The company, of course."

She places the prism back in the box and closes the lid. Turning, she kisses Austin, a nice greeting but she could've done better. I remember some very heated kisses when she'd greet me. With a smile, she says, "Hi, I'm glad you're here."

"So that's like the one you have hanging in your window, right?" He smiles between us, oblivious that he's interrupting anything.

"Yes." Jules' answer is abrupt and she keeps her eyes averted.

Facing me, Austin adds, "That was very kind of you. I know Jules loves those. It will be cool to see this one hanging next to her other one."

I cut in. "I felt bad for showing up empty-handed on her birthday, so I thought I'd I'd bring a token tonight."

Her expression changes when she says, "You didn't have to do that."

"Yes, I did."

"You didn't know it was my birthday." Her voice holds steady, but I see the pain in her eyes that I might have actually forgotten the date of her birth. But I can't reply with Austin standing here and she knows it. She says, "I'm just kidding, Dylan. Of course, you wouldn't know."

I smile, keeping up the charade for her sake and because Austin's a good guy. He almost makes me feel bad for thinking about her, for dreaming of her, for jerking off with Jules on my mind, and for deciding she will be mine again.

Almost, but I don't...

Jules has to work, leaving me and her boyfriend alone. Austin invites me to have a beer with him sometime before he leaves to make a business call. I should go and would rather say goodbye in private. Before I find Jules though, Brandon finds me first, and asks, "You're really doing this, aren't you?"

I reply, "Doing what, Brandon?" Exasperated, I look to my side not actually giving him my full attention.

"Jules? You're going to pursue her, aren't you?" Our eyes meet and the truth is there. He knows without me confirming.

"Austin treats her the way she deserves, so don't ruin it with lousy intentions."

"How do you know my intentions are lousy or less genuine than his?"

"I don't." He sighs. "That's what worries me."

I narrow my eyes, my brow furrowing. "You really care about her, don't you?"

"You know I do." He bites the inside of his cheek in thought, looking out over the crowd. "But we're better as friends," he states bluntly.

Good to know.

Any weakness he was about to reveal is quickly covered when Austin approaches. They greet each other like old friends. Maybe they are.

"Have you seen the painting?" I ask, needing a reprieve from the weight of judgment from Brandon.

We turn, standing side by side by side, Brandon, me, and then Austin. Our heads all tilting to the right, arms crossed over our chests, staring straight ahead—all looking the same, all in love with the same woman.

"Well that's a sight I never thought I'd see," Jules says from behind us, giggling.

We look over our shoulders and see her smiling. She doesn't realize her slip. I should hate that she might be hurt when Austin finds out about us, our past, but I can't because I'll be there to comfort her, like I should've been all along.

"The painting is of Jules," I say, seeing Austin and Brandon swiftly turn back around to see the bold work of art.

Austin spins back to look at her. "Really? That's you?"

Jules nods.

"When did you pose for it?" His voice is concerned and on edge.

"She didn't," I intercept the conversation.

Brandon hasn't taken his eyes off the painting.

"But you said—" Austin starts to question.

"Look at the eyes," I add. "There's nothing there, no depth."

Jules puts a comforting hand on his arm. "Look closely. You *know* it's not my body if you really look. It's all from his imagination."

Brandon has finally tuned into the conversation. He's listening, but remains quiet.

I know that's not her body just by looking at it. There's no mole three inches below her left breast. Her nipples are more pink than brown. She also has a scar on her right thigh from a water-skiing rope burn she got when she was twelve.

She leans closer to Austin and whispers while pointing to her ribs on the painting, "No mole."

Austin shakes his head not understanding. He doesn't know. He doesn't fucking know about her mole. He doesn't know her body at all. I step back, needing the space as anger courses through me. He's careless.

When her eyes meet mine, she knows I know her body. I know that mole. I've kissed that mole. I've savored that mole. I've come on that mole. I've made her come just by appreciating her body with my mouth while circling that mole with my tongue.

Jules looks down, and I have a feeling that she remembers just like I do. Sadness comes over her face and I take a step back, not wanting her to feel bad she's with a guy who doesn't realize she has a mole three inches below her left breast, the guy who claims to love her. I eye Brandon. He knows. He knows about the mole, but stays quiet. And I'm left with the realization that Jules did sleep with Brandon. For some reason, I'm not surprised, but what does surprise me is that she's not with him now.

It's obvious. He was the rebound. Poor sap. It doesn't feel like a victory winning this way but I'll take what I can get right now. One day, she'll see that I'm the one she's meant to be with... again.

She walks me to the door, her hand on my forearm. "Thank you for the gift." Looking around, she seems uncomfortable. "That was very thoughtful of you."

"I'm always thinking of you."

"Dylan, please."

I drop it, letting it go, letting her go... for now. "I'll see you soon, Jules."

With a soft smile in place, she says, "Okay. I'll see you soon, Dylan."

CHAPTER 6

Dylan

October 2nd

THE BREEZE CARRIES the scent of her hair and I inhale. Relaxing, I sit down on a bench facing the city at the edge of the park.

"Why are you sitting behind me?" Jules asks, knowing I'm here.

"What?" I ask. She'll never believe it was a coincidence. "*Jules?* What are you doing here?"

She turns, smiling, the sun reflecting in her eyes, making them shine. "I'm having lunch like I do almost every day here. What are you doing here, Dylan?"

"I come here, too," I reply, "quite often." I'm putting on my best I'm-still-so-shocked-to-see-you face. "This is such a coincidence."

"You work like thirty blocks south of here. You can't even make it here on your lunch hour, much less back again."

"I'm allotted longer lunches and I like this park."

She's silent for a moment, then laughs.

I smile at the sound, then ask, "You buying it?"

"Nope."

"I didn't think so." I drape my arm across the back of the bench, turning to face her more fully. "Whatcha having for lunch?" I ask, peering over the bench down at her lap.

"Something incredibly glamorous and gourmet. Tuna salad."

"Man, I miss your tuna."

"Dylan!" she scolds playfully.

Since the birthday dinner, everything seems to have gone from angry to easy between us. "You're a perv, Jules."

She shrugs. "Eh, what's new?"

So much that we aren't able to talk about yet, so I keep it light for now. "So I have turkey and avocado on ciabatta. You wanna share?"

"You haven't changed. Yeah, I'll trade you half of mine. Turkey and avocado sounds good."

I hand her half of my sandwich and she hands me half of hers. I quickly take a bite of the tuna. "I missed this. You always made the best tuna salad."

She doesn't say anything, but smiles while looking down. She's so beautiful. We chat a little and eat our lunch, the silence between us okay at times.

Eventually I have to ask because I've become obsessed with these thoughts, "Did you think of me over the last three years?"

She turns away and I can't see her face. It's unsettling, but then she says, "Every day."

"Me too." I want to be honest with her. "You never left my thoughts."

This time she holds my gaze, searching my eyes. "Dylan." It's a tone, a warning to stop. "I can't do this."

"Because I hurt you?"

"You hurting me is the *exact* reason I want to have this talk, but it's not appropriate to talk about that when I have a boyfriend."

"Austin," I say, reminding myself..

"Yes, Austin," she repeats. "I don't want to hurt or betray him."

"You betrayed him when you acted like we were strangers on your birthday, Jules. You did that," I point out. "I played along to protect you. Why'd you lie?"

She stands, crumbling a napkin in her hand as she fists it tightly. Her eyes search the surroundings. Turning her head, she looks at my lap, my chest, my chin, not my eyes—everywhere but in my eyes. "I need to get back."

She starts to go, to leave, but I stand. I'm immediately by her side, not touching, but close. It's painful not to touch her. "Don't go... please."

She stops, her gaze slowly sliding up my body. When it lands on my eyes, we stare momentarily before she asks, "What are you really doing here, Dylan?"

"I wanted to see you." *I ache for you.*

"I like that you're here." She pauses to look around the park like someone is watching us. "But this is too much. I'm in a relationship. We can't do this. You said friends."

"You did too."

"I didn't mean it. I didn't think we could actually *be* friends." She tilts her head suddenly and looks like the girl I saw in the quad that day so many years ago, young and bright-eyed, sun shining behind her. "Is being friends really possible?"

"Just live in the here and now with me."

Stepping closer, then even closer, she presses her palm flat against my chest and lifts up on her tiptoes. Her lips graze my cheek, and she whispers, "Help me, okay?"

I nod, closing my eyes, savoring the feel of her soft lips on my skin again. At that, she turns and walks off, leaving me dazed.

When I was working on Austin's financial forecast earlier, I realized how good his company is looking. He's a smart businessman as well as a nice guy. For some reason, maybe because he's a good guy, I don't want him as a casualty despite my pursuit of his girlfriend.

I return to the park every day at lunch for the rest of the week. Technically I'm skipping work for the two and a half hours it takes to get across the city, but I make up for it by staying late. I'm also starting to understand more of the pain I caused Jules when I left her. She doesn't talk about it much, but stuff occasionally slips out. One thing she never mentions is the time right after I left. I never bring it up either, thinking it's best. She's still fragile, as if she'll break if she talks about it, faltering when we get too close to the topic. So I change the subject quickly not wanting to cause her any more pain.

Today is Friday, the end of the work week. As we get up to leave the park, I'm feeling a disappointment slip over me when I realize I won't get to have lunch with her tomorrow. I don't have an excuse to see her. It remains an unspoken emotion as I walk her back to the gallery. Hesitating before she goes inside, I hold the door open longer than usual. Standing in front of me, she looks down, then angles up and whispers, "It's been a good week."

"The best." It's all I can say right now, my heart starting to throb as she takes one more step inside.

"I'll see you Monday?"

"I wouldn't miss it for anything."

"Have a nice weekend, Dylan."

"You too, Jules."

She flashes me a small smile before going inside.

I watch through the glass as she retreats into her office. My breathing is strained without her near, so I step forward needing her just one more time, just one more hit to my heart to help me through the long days ahead without her.

From the sidewalk, I knock on her window, her eyes going wide. Putting my hand flat against the glass, she rises from her chair while I wait, hope teetering on devastation.

Standing in front of me, glass dividing us, she slowly places her hand flat against the window, against mine. My forehead drops forward as does hers, our eyes closing together. The glass is cool but starts to heat with her near, our bodies so close.

Sneaking a peek, she turns her cheek, pressing it against the glass and I kiss it. *Innocent.*

She turns to see the remains of the kiss that I gave. Her lips press against the glass on the opposite side of where mine were and that's when I know for sure. She feels this just as much as I do. It's real. What we're sharing is real.

She steps back and waves goodbye, her words muffled through

the thick glass, her face smiling, "Go, Dylan. I have work to do." She laughs and so do I as I back away with a small salute.

"Bye," I mouth then jog away, feeling on top of the world. I always want to feel this good. While hailing a cab, I grin ear to ear, thinking that things are progressing nicely.

Now, what excuse can I come up with to see her over the weekend? Hmmm...

CHAPTER 7

Dylan

October 7th

I FEEL LIKE I've taken two steps forward, one step back.

Hours. It's taking me hours to get to Jules' front door. I spent the first half of today working even though it's Saturday to take my mind off her. I made a few calls to my family because I hadn't checked in with them lately. My mom answered on the third ring. "Hello?"

"Mom?"

"Dylan, how are you, sweetheart?"

"I'm okay. How are you?"

"Keeping busy. I'm going to the flower show later. I'll be dragging your father."

"Bet he'll love that," I joke.

She laughs. "He's a good sport. We might go to lunch afterwards. I'll let him pick the restaurant to make up for it. So how's your social life? How's the Big Apple treating my son?"

"I've been working a lot."

"No fun?" she asks.

"I've gone to some art exhibits."

"There are some nice galleries there. Maybe next time I'm there, we can visit a few."

"I can take you to Jules'." I say it before I think twice.

"Jules' gallery? Are you talking again?"

I pause, careful what I say next. "I ran into her at one of the exhibits."

"Oh," she says. "How did that go?"

"Okay."

"She emailed me a few months ago and said she had—"

I hold the phone tighter to my ear, thinking I just heard her wrong. "Wait, back up. She emailed you?"

"We email every now and again."

"Since when?"

Now she pauses and I readjust at my desk, anxious for her answer. Then she replies with a lilt to her voice, "We've never stopped, Dylan. It's not much, but every 2 or 3 months one of us will email and the other will reply. I'm sorry. I hope that doesn't hurt your feelings."

"No," I say, still surprised. "I'm glad. I know the breakup was hard on everyone. I'm sorry I let you down."

"No, honey, it's not that. I just missed her. People change. You changed and felt the need to move on. I wasn't judging you for your decision."

"Mom, I have regrets—technically two. One, when I left Jules, and the other, for not groveling at her feet to take me back. I knew what I did was wrong even that first night. Everything was different." I remember how odd it was the toothbrush next to mine was bright pink instead of green, red satin sheets, instead of cotton. The woman next to me was Hillary, not Juliette. I threw up three times that night, claiming I had food poisoning.

I didn't. *I had heart poisoning.*

My mom sighs, bringing me back to my phone call. She sounds sad. Apparently in the emails, Jules writes in general terms, never giving away too much but enough to keep the connection alive. It makes me wonder why she does it, why she keeps it going? And why did I not know about this until now?

Jules hasn't mentioned Austin to her and I don't either. I don't know what to think of her secrets. Maybe she doesn't tell her simply because she's talking to *my* mom. But if he's a part of her life, what appears to be a big part, why not tell her?

I think I know why. Jules doesn't want to destroy my mother's dreams. She's kind like that, the daughter my mom always wanted. Maybe, just maybe, Jules holds onto that dream too. When I hang up the phone, I get up and leave.

And here I am. Finally, I'm in front of our old apartment, now just her apartment. I raise my hand three different times to knock, but don't all three times.

I wait.

I listen.

I can hear that she's home.

I raise my hand and do it this time. *Knock. Knock. Knock.*

"One moment," she calls from behind the wood barrier.

My hands are sweating and I pull at my collar needing more air. This landing is suddenly stifling. The building key still works. I question if the apartment key that resides on my keychain still will. I kept it, but like most things pertaining to our past together, I don't allow myself to dwell on it too much.

Jules is laughing when the door swings wide open. With her wallet in hand, her smile falls as shock takes over. "Dylan?"

Not the reaction I was hoping for. "Hi," I reply.

"What are you doing here?" Her tone is harsh, it hurts to hear.

"I wanted to talk to you, to see y—"

She cuts me off. "You shouldn't be here."

"Sweetheart, is that the food?" My eyes are redirected over her shoulder before she has a chance to pull the door closed enough to block him. "Dylan?" Austin questions from our bedroom, *her* bedroom now.

My mind races as I look back to my dream girl. I'd failed to notice the man's button down shirt that drapes over her body, too big for her frame. *Austin's shirt.* She didn't even bother buttoning most of the buttons, just enough to get by to answer the door. Her hair is loose, not styled, messy even. Gorgeous.

Fuck.

Fuck.

Fuck.

"Dylan?" Austin questions as he approaches. "What are you doing here?"

I'm reeling. I can't think. My eyes meet Jules', which show her concern over the situation.

I lie for both of our sakes. "Your office said I could find you here," I reply, acting nonchalant.

Opening the door wider, he looks at me then to her and says, "You should get dressed."

She goes without another word, but peeks back twice while walking into the bedroom.

"Come in," he offers. "I apologize for my appearance. We weren't expecting company."

We. He fucking said 'We.'

I hate him. I hate him for being where I should be right now. My home.

"Something to drink?" He's not shy standing there in his boxers like he doesn't give a damn that he's fucking with my life.

I reply, "Yes," because I want to prolong my time here as much as possible, not quite sure why I want to torture myself. He goes into the kitchen as I look around the place, catching a glimpse of Jules through the crack of the bedroom door.

"Beer?" he calls from the kitchen.

"Yes, that's good."

I stare, not able to take my eyes off of her naked form. It may be just a sliver of a view, a mere peek, but it's the most erotic thing I've ever seen. My body tightens... until Austin draws my attention back to him and then I'm instantly soft.

"Here you go," he says, handing me a bottle. "I'll go get dressed then we can talk." He looks at me suspiciously before disappearing into the bedroom, closing the door harder than necessary.

The apartment is cold in contrast to how I remember it when we lived here together. There's no life, no love living here now. It's not representative of Juliette at all. Maybe it is of Jules these days though.

"Austin," her voice catches my attention as she walks into the living room. "I'd like a glass of wine if you don't mind."

Excuses to get us alone. I read right through it. Austin nods, acquiescing to her request so easily. I hate him for being so good. Does he have any faults at all?

Through gritted teeth, she whisper-yells at me, "What are you doing here?"

Truth. "I wanted to see you."

"What are you going to tell Austin?" Her eyebrows are pinched together, not seeming to grasp my needs at all.

"I don't know."

"You better figure out fast bec—"

"Here you go, Jules." Austin's back and hands her a glass of wine. He's having a beer.

"Thank you," she says, smiling at him.

I start talking, hoping to find some semblance of an acceptable excuse. My job is on the line as well as my future time with Jules if I don't. "I found an investment I think you should jump on. A little company out of Los Angeles, unknown, but solid."

Austin looks relaxed, but interested. "And this couldn't wait until Monday?"

Jules sits down on the couch as he stands eye-to-eye questioning me.

Feeling like I can pull this off, I continue, "I called your office to see if you wanted to grab a beer. I know you mentioned leaving town soon and wanted to present this opportunity before you leave."

"Wait. What?" She asks, looking at him. "When are you leaving?"

A knock on the door saves him momentarily. "That's probably the food," he says, "I'll get it."

Her face falls as she turns to look out the window. With the glass to her lips, she tilts her head back and takes a long drink. As if she needs to explain, she says, "He travels a lot."

The travel seems to have become an issue between them, an

irritation, and a tidbit I pocket for later. She walks to the window and I follow. The prisms, both of them, that I gave her dangle from the top of the sill, catching the light.

I tap them just as she whispers, "You shouldn't be here."

"Why?" I ask. I know why, but I need her to say it.

Her glare is answer enough but she follows it up with words anyway. "You've crossed a line. I don't understand why but I can assume—"

"Hey honey," Austin says, shutting the door behind him. He walks into the kitchen and sets the bag on the counter, then returns. "I'm gonna go down to the pub around the corner and grab a beer with Dylan. Is that alright?"

Now she turns her glare at him. "That's fine," she replies though her tone is anything but fine. One last glance at me, then she goes into the kitchen and starts taking the food out of the bag. "I'll just eat and watch a movie."

Like a peeping Tom, I watch as he comes up behind her, wrapping his arms around her waist, and kissing her neck. I should look away, but I don't, needing the reminder that he's the enemy.

"You sure?" he asks.

She shrugs out from under his grasp and moves away. "Just go. You know where I'll be."

"Don't be mad."

She doesn't respond but I can tell she's struggling to hold her tongue.

Austin comes back into the living room. "So you got time to grab a beer or two?"

Jules follows him into the living room, wine still in hand, but freshly topped off.

"Yeah, I've got time." *This should be interesting.*

An evil look is sent my way and I smirk. No matter how much it pisses her off, I need to do this. Jacqueline and her scheme to befriend her comes to mind. Is that what I'm doing? Am I using him to get information on her? *Hell yes.* There's no denying it. I gulp down the distaste that's formed in my mouth and head for the door.

Austin's using me to get out of an argument over a travel issue, so she can't be mad at me this time.

"Bye, Jules," I say, "good to see you again."

"Yeah, okay." She turns her back and heads for the kitchen again.

"Bye hon," Austin adds.

No response. Shit, he's in trouble.

"Let's go." As we walk down the stairs, he says, "She's pissed. I'm giving her time to cool down."

"Yeah, she's very passionate."

He stops and looks back at me, narrowing his eyes for a second before carrying on. "I hadn't told her I was leaving in a week. I'll be gone for another three weeks. Asia."

"Three weeks, huh?"

"Yeah, I just wish I didn't have to leave her. We're kind of at a pivotal stage in our relationship."

My ears perk up as my intentions sour toward him. "Yeah?"

"Some decisions are going to have to be made."

I walk at a casual pace beside him feeling everything but casual and absorbing every detail he's willing to share, so I offer, "We can talk about it over a pitcher. First round's on me."

CHAPTER 8

Dylan

October 8th

"I'M GONNA HIT the head."

"I've got this round, so go ahead," I say, watching as Austin weaves through the tall-topped tables of the bar.

The waitress flirts, but doesn't catch my eye. She's a dime a dozen. Jules is special. When she returns with beer and ice cold mugs, she also delivers a rank basket of old popcorn. This time she doesn't flirt, catching on I'm not interested.

"So what'd I miss?" Brandon slams his hand down on the table, causing me to jump.

"Fuck, dude!" I look to my side, pissed.

He's smirking. "Jules bribed me to come down here and keep an eye on you two."

"Oh did she now?" I ask, "What's she so worried about?"

"Try that bullshit somewhere else. You have some major balls coming here with Austin."

"Well," I shrug. "He invited me. What could I say?"

"Maybe that you used to fuck his girlfriend or dated her for what, like two years?"

"More than three."

"Yeah, okay man. Are you gonna tell him?"

"I can't. We have a working relationship. His account has become one of my top priorities." Truthfully, I don't even know if I care about the job anymore. I just want Jules. I've started over before. I can do it again with her by my side, under me, on top... I'm in way too deep.

Brandon scans the bar. "Shit. You're really screwing the pooch here."

"Can you come up with anymore clichés to use tonight? Big balls, screwing the pooch."

"I'll try. Here comes boyfriend number three. You don't hear that every day."

I laugh out loud. *Fuck, we're numbered at this point?* He's right though. "This is pretty pathetic."

"What's pathetic?" Austin sits down. "Hey Brandon, good to see you. You guys know each other?"

"Yeah," I say, "we met at the exhibit." *More lies.*

Austin nods. "Oh right," he says, then pauses. "Brandon, you staying?"

"Yep, let me grab a mug from the bar." Brandon walks away and I glance up at the football scores. Texas vs. Oklahoma—a big game rivalry.

Austin leans in and whispers, "What do you think about Brandon? Jules is really close to him, considers him her best friend. Do you find that weird?"

I lean over. "Let the woman have her friends. It will be better in the long run if she has a life outside of yours."

Fuck! I just gave him relationship advice on how to hold onto Jules. I'm an idiot.

Agreeing, he says, "I can see that."

Brandon returns with a glass and three shots. "Down the hatch, men." I roll my eyes at his abuse of common phrases. We set the empty glasses down. I turn my attention to the large screen hanging over the bar and the blonde bartender who has been keeping her eye on me since I sat down. Brandon announces, "OU has the lead. They have home field advantage."

"Not for long. Texas can take'em. They have the determination to win," I say, watching the screen.

"You wanna bet?" he asks.

"I'll put fifty on Texas." I look Brandon in the eyes, suddenly feeling like we're wagering on more than the game.

"Deal."

"I'm a baseball guy," Austin interjects.

We both look at him. *Loser.* Needing to get this conversation back on track, I ask, "So Asia for three weeks, huh?"

"Yeah," Austin says. "My company had built a strong connection over the last four years, but it's not a viable source anymore. They've changed leadership and owners and it's a mess. I need to go and sort shit out before it blows up completely."

Brandon gives him no reprieve. "And Jules? Didn't you promise her that you wouldn't have any more long trips until the New Year?"

Austin drinks his beer, setting it down and wiping away some of the sweat running down the outside of the glass. "Guess she talked to you about it."

"We're close," Brandon replies.

"Apparently." Austin sounds a little defensive. It's good to see him shaken up. "But yes, I did promise her that, which is why she's pissed." He looks at Brandon and then me, and asks, "Can I ask you something man to man here? I don't want this getting back to her, but maybe you know where her head's at on this."

Brandon nods. He drains the last of his beer as does Austin.

A different waitress sets another round of shots in front of us. "These are compliments of the bartender and myself, gentlemen." She balances her tray on her hip, hand on Austin's shoulder. "You guys meeting anyone else here tonight?"

Brandon smiles. "I'm not, Austin's taken and I'm not sure about him," he says, pointing at me.

Everyone is still staring at me, waiting.

Finally Austin asks, "You and Jacqueline seem to have a good rapport."

"Work rapport. That's it. We're strictly co-workers."

The waitress winks at me, sliding her hand across the back of Austin's shoulders and resting her body against my arm. "So you're single?"

"Yeah, I am," I reply, glaring at the table. I hate that answer, more and more with each passing day. It makes me want to bolt, to run to Jules and tell her everything. Confess every sin and then my darkest secrets. But I can't, so I pick up my shot instead and down it.

Brandon winks and placates her. "Thanks. We're just going to get back to our sports talk." She walks away, leaving him with a wink and a smile.

As I take a gulp of beer, Austin doesn't miss a beat and asks Brandon, "Is Jules a traditional girl? I mean, I'm ready... well, I want her to move in with me—"

The beer lodges itself down the wrong pipe and I choke on it, hacking and coughing. Austin whacks me on the back to help. "Wow," I manage, my throat raw from the coughing, my heart aching over the reality. "That's a big step. I thought you hadn't been together that long."

"You must be a commitment-phobe, Dylan. I'm not. That's why my business is as successful as it is. I see something good and I act. Why sit around and wait for someone else to steal your idea or worse, *steal your girl*? Know what I mean?"

Irritated, I ask, "Women are like acquisitions to you?"

"No." Austin laughs loudly. "Just why sit around when you know it's right." I grab my beer as he continues, "I'm thinking of asking her to marry me, which is why I'm wondering if she'd rather do the whole move-in thing first."

I spew my beer all over the table, droplets flying, my heart leaving my chest.

"What the fuck, Somers?" Austin jumps from his stool.

Brandon practically rolls off his barstool he's laughing so hard. Easy for him to laugh. He has no shot in hell with Jules.

"I, I... I, fuck, sorry," I say, standing while waving the waitress over to bring towels to wipe up the mess.

"Dude, it's fine. Settle down," Brandon adds, snickering.

Another minute or two and a wipe down of the table and we're sitting around again like nothing happened. But my heart is still racing as my mind goes into overdrive. "I think she's more of a traditional girl," I speak up though I wasn't asked. "I don't see Jules wanting to skip a step." I need to say something to discourage this marriage idea. "You should take things slow."

"Maybe I should since I don't know if she even wants to get married," Austin says, looking at me.

"Maybe you're not ready for the next step then," Brandon speaks up.

Austin looks down, turning his mug around on the table. "I need to talk to her. I think if we lived together the travel thing wouldn't be such a big deal. We'd see each other more when I'm home."

The waitress sets down three more shots. "These are from the ladies in the corner booth."

We all lean back and see four women waving at us. We laugh, send a wave their way, then take the shots. Austin makes a face, then says, "Fuck that'll put hair on your ass." *Amateur.*

Brandon cracks up before correcting him. "I think the saying is it will put hair on your chest."

"I'm a real man," Austin says, sitting up. "I already have hair on my chest."

Brandon looks around, Austin and I realizing he's the kind of guy who shaves his chest by his reaction. "Oh shit, man," I joke, pointing at him.

"The girls love it, so suck it." He's defensive, but still laughing.

Austin looks for the waitress. "Do they serve food here?"

I respond, "I'll go see if they have anything." The more I drink, the more devious I become. With just a few drinks in him, he's sharing so much. Wondering how much he can handle, I decide to put him to the test. With another round of shots in hand, I return to the table. "Drink up, ladies. There's no food. Liquid dinner tonight."

Brandon elbows him. "I'll bet ya twenty that I finish first."

"You're on," Austin replies before grabbing his shot glass and downing it.

I laugh as he sways on his stool. The man definitely cannot handle his liquor. Thirty minutes later, Austin is practically asleep on the table while Brandon and I argue over the game again.

Texas took the lead in the third quarter and he just can't come to terms that the home field advantage makes no difference when you're heart is in it. Much like life.

"We should probably get him back to Jules," Brandon says, poking Austin and only receiving a groan in return.

Shaking my head at the sad sight before me, I say, "She's gonna be pissed."

"Yeah, at him," he laughs.

Standing up, I laugh too, even if I do sway a bit myself.

Austin's heavy, about my size, but dense with muscle. The dude works out and it's a bitch to get him back to Jules' building. When we do, we bang on the door. Jules answers dressed only in a skimpy top and sleep shorts. She used to dress like that when we were together, when she was mine. She covers her mouth, gasping at the site of Austin, lagging, hanging between me and Brandon.

"You got him drunk!" She looks between me and Brandon, equally angry at us both.

"He got himself drunk, Jules," Brandon pipes up, slurring.

"You're gonna pay for this, Brandon. No banana bread for you."

"You promised," he complains as we drag Austin inside and dump him on the couch per Jules' request.

She crosses her arms in defiance. "He can sleep out here since he got drunk on what was supposed to be our night together."

The prisms catch my eye and I walk to the window. With a gentle tap to the prisms, I watch as they swing back and forth. Jules is behind me griping at Brandon, holding him responsible. She has expectations of him, of their friendship, but none of me. The door clicks closed, but I don't look back. Brandon's gone and the apartment is quiet.

I gulp, not able to hide in the silence that fills the air behind me.

Her fingers slide over my shoulder, her palm coming to rest there as she whispers, "Dylan." When I turn my head, she's standing close, her body pressing lightly against the back of my arm. "We should talk."

I'm buzzed, but attempt to pretend I'm not. "Yes, we should." When she doesn't continue, I add, "But not tonight. Maybe next week." I'm thinking it would be best not to have this conversation in the state I'm in.

Jules' hand slides down to my forearm. I love her touch and it makes me want to kiss her. My eyes drop quickly to her pert nipples, teasing me under the thin cotton of her top. I let my gaze linger before tracing up her body until I see the beauty of her face again. Her lips, wanting, waiting. Her eyes, urging me to kiss her.

I made the mistake of kissing her when she didn't want me to before and paid the price by not seeing her for six months. *Am I willing to risk it again?*

She makes the decision for us both and kisses me. Grabbing me by the neck and pulling me down to meet her in the middle of the space previously dividing us. My hands hold her waist and our tongues meet.

Heaven.

I pull her closer, but then she pulls away. Tears fill her eyes and she whispers, "No." When she looks back up at me, she adds, "Go."

"No," I respond, not willing to give her up. *Not now. Not ever. Instead, I step forward.*

She stumbles backwards. The word 'No' escaping from her mouth over and over again. "You need to go, Dylan."

Protesting, I say, "You can feel what this is—"

Her leg is grabbed from behind. From the couch, Austin mumbles, "Babe, lay with me." His eyes focused on her, then following her glare to me. "What are you doing here, Somers?" He sits up, tries to, but he's wasted, sloppy.

"I got you here. I brought you back." I refuse to call this place his home, so I stay with the safe word of 'here.' "You're drunk."

"Oh, yeah." He grabs his head. "I need to go to bed."

Jules steps away from him, his hand dropping to the floor. Her voice is clear and concise. "Lay back down because you're not sleeping with me. You can earn your way back into the bedroom." Firm, hands on hips, and completely sexy. She glances at me, then back to him.

He grabs her hand pulling her down onto his lap. "Live with me, Jules."

What? He's drunk. He's talking crazy shit. She'll never accept a drunken offer like that. He kisses her quickly before she can speak. Sneaky. Leaning back away from him, she looks into his eyes, and asks, "You're serious, aren't you? No, Austin. Don't ask me like this. Not when you're drunk."

He pulls her down on top of him as he lays back, his strength evident over her small frame. "I love you, Jules. I want to come home to you every night, every business trip, to you."

I'm forgotten as she leans toward him, listening. I become a spy in the middle of a most intimate moment. My mind is blank, shocked, so I stare, horrified with no valid argument other than I love her more than him.

He kisses her again and she starts to relax. I see her body caving into his.

"No!" *Oh shit, did I say that out loud?* They both turn and look at me surprised by the outburst. I break the bubble, the moment that seemed to be turning in Austin's favor.

His tone is harsh when he says, "Dylan, leave."

I'm an intruder to him. *What am I to Jules?* She looks at me, then her gaze drops quickly with a slight nod of her head.

Without knowing what else I can do, I walk. I'm losing her. I can feel it. I can see it, but why? He's the one who got drunk. He chose to go out tonight instead of staying here with her. He even chose Asia over her. *Is it not obvious?* I would never do that to her.

"I'll give you the world, Jules," I hear him whisper as my hand goes to the doorknob.

I leave. Staying will only make me look bad in her eyes. I have time. He's leaving. He's stupidly leaving her alone for three weeks. I can do a lot in three weeks.

"Dylan?"

I spin around to her voice calling my name. She shuts the door behind her and we're alone in the hall.

"Dylan, we still need to talk—"

"Another time."

"It can't be another time. I thought it could wait, but it can't. We don't have that kind of time." When she walks closer, her steps are tentative. "I know you thought there could be more, but there can't. We've had our time and that time has passed."

My head is shaking as I try to stop her words before they come out. "No, we can talk later. Please. Please let's talk on Monday at the park."

"It won't change on Monday. I'm sorry. I don't mean to hurt you."

"No." I grab her hand. "Don't close the door on us, Jules. Please, just give us—"

"Dylan, *you* closed the door on us. I was there. I remember. I lived through the pain while you did whatever it was you needed to do for you. I can't help that you now regret that decision. But I'm not angry anymore. I finally found someone good. *Austin* is a good for me."

"You just kissed me in there?" My voice is deep, hard, threatening.

"I kissed you to see. I thought it would give me answers. It didn't. It made things fuzzier, dirtier. I made a mistake."

I tighten my mouth, the words much grittier. "You felt it. I know you did. That spark that always existed between us is still there."

She steps back, pressing her hands against the door as if she's scared, as if she needs the solid wood for support. "I said yes." Her body is calm, watching for my reaction to the bombshell. "I'm going to move in with him."

"No! Dammit! No."

Slipping from my reach, she's too far, so I stretch further to grab hold of her, but she eludes me. "It's over, Dylan. *For good*. Final.

Please leave me alone. You need to move on with your life."

"Please Jules," I feel the warm wetness hit my eyes. "Don't rush into a decision that could ruin—"

"I've been ruined for years. Austin is an incredible and patient man that wants me even with all my baggage and damaged insides."

"I want you!"

"Well, you can't have me! You had me and threw me away and for what?" Her voice rises loudly, too loud for the hall. "For what? Why *did* you leave me? Or should I ask *who* did you leave me for?" She crosses her arms over her chest, fury surging. "Tell me. Tell me you didn't leave me for someone. Lie to me just like you did back then."

I can't speak. I'll lose her for good if I confess, but I know I've lost her already. I can see it in her eyes.

"Tell me, Dylan," she demands, stomping her foot while her hands fist by her sides. "You owe me this. Tell me why you left. The reasons you gave me are bullshit and you know it." Rushing forward, her fists are flying. "Tell me! Tell me! Tell me!"

My chest takes each hit, knowing I deserve this. My feet stumble back, but I catch my balance against the railing. "I left you for Hillary." It needed to come out. *Shit! Why? I want to puke.*

She stops immediately. Her face contorts with pain. Horrified and confused, as if I'm the one who hit her. *I did.* I hit her in the heart.

Rocking back on her heels, her voice is low, possessed. "You left me for that whore?"

I'm already pleading before she finishes, "It was nothing. Please believe me, Jules. She meant nothing to me—"

Her face turns cold, her eyes shut down, any doorway into her heart I had managed to open now slams closed. "You left me for someone who meant nothing to you. What does that make me then? It makes me less than nothing. After three years of giving you everything I had, everything I was, all my love was less than nothing to you." Swatting my hands off of her, she says, "Don't touch me. Don't talk to me. Don't come see me anymore. *Don't.* Just don't ever again." She slips quietly back into our apartment, *her* apartment, and slams the door closed.

I should have groveled. Dropping to my knees, the harsh hit of reality has finally come full circle, taking me down with it. My flaws. My weaknesses. Exposed and out for her to judge, to hate me. I want to forget them, change them, erase them, but I can't. Honesty is a tricky thing. I could've lied. I should have lied.

Stumbling down the stairs, I shove the door to the street wide open. The chill of the October night air covers my face, sobering me.

Reality sucks.

I should've lied.

I couldn't though.

Not to her.

Not ever again.

The secret I protected Jules from all this time is now the same reason she hates me.

I know I've lost her.

Forever.

CHAPTER 9

Jules

October 20th

TWELVE DAYS.

Twelve nights.

Some restless. Some spent crying. Sometimes no sleeping at all.

Twelve long days since I saw Dylan, since I told him not to come see me anymore, not to talk to me, not to do anything regarding me.

I'm glad Austin's gone. He's gone for three weeks while I pack. The time apart gives me time to think, to sort through my stuff, sort through my thoughts, my desires, my visions of my future. Sort through Dylan's words, his actions in the past, and in the present.

Sitting at the bottom of my closet, I throw stuff carelessly into boxes labeled: donate, keep, and trash. After hours of cleaning, the trash box only holds three things—two prisms and a coffeemaker— the three things that tie me to Dylan.

At least I thought that was what tied me to him. They're not.

My heart does. My feelings. My memories—good and bad anchor me to him like a weight. I wish I could trash those. I wish I could toss my heart out or donate it to someone who deserves to live a happily ever after.

I started to believe I deserved to again. Austin made me believe I did. But I was telling myself lies, trying to convince myself of an alternate reality. The problem is that no matter what happens or how many years pass, I can't seem to rid myself of Dylan whether I have those three things in my possession or not.

I unfurl my body from the ball I've been in, wipe the tears away, and go to the trash box. Despite my shaking hand and ravaged heart, I can't throw the stuff away. My logical side thinks it will make life easier if I do, but the truth is it won't.

For the sake of my sanity, I compromise. I leave the coffeemaker and take the prisms, dropping them into the keep box.

IT'S LATE. I lay in bed in the dark with the phone pressed to my ear. The curtains are still open allowing light from the outside in. Austin's voice is deep, tired as he speaks. "The deal is going better than expected. The clients have been reassured. I hope you understand why I had to come."

"You needed to fly to China and meet them face-to-face. You're very charming and a skilled businessman. I had no doubt you would repair relations."

"Thank you," he whispers. "How are you, love?"

I smile from the sweet nickname. "I'm okay. Tired from packing."

Speaking of repairing relations... "Do you have any regrets, Jules... about saying yes?"

He must sense my distance tonight. He'd be right. I am distant, for all intents and purposes, but something deep inside is holding me back when all I want to do is move forward.

"Moving in together is a big step." I haven't lived with anyone since Dylan, not officially. "I don't have regret saying yes to you, Austin. I'm just nervous to be leaving here. I've called it home for six years." And I'm nervous to leave the last remaining piece of Dylan and Juliette. When I move, I should try to leave the memories here as well.

October 28th - Moving Day

MOVING SUCKS. MOVING sucks even when you've paid people to move your stuff. I've already done the hard part, the emotional part of packing and figuring out what part of this life I'm moving into the new one. These guys are lifting, carrying, doing the physical part, but the psychological aspect is far more trying.

Just when I think I've got this, that I've made the right decision, doubts inevitably seep into my psyche, making me question everything all over again. The last four weeks have been torture. I'm ready to just be done with it all: all the doubts, all the debate, all the second guessing, all of it. I'm ready to just move in and start moving forward.

I'm paid up for the apartment through the end of the month. The landlord hasn't rented it out yet and our deposit from six years ago holds it through November. For some reason, I like having the safety net.

I don't supervise the movers. I spend every last second I can in the now empty place, trusting them to handle it all. Sitting atop a suitcase, the only thing left here, I look around. The painting also remains hanging on the wall. I'm undecided what I should do with it.

Maybe it should go. Maybe it should stay. It feels so a part of this place, of me, of who I am and what my life has been for almost four years now.

Austin doesn't know its history—its true meaning in my life. It represents *our* downfall. Morbid, but I was grasping for that connection back then. All I had left of him was a coffeemaker. It wasn't enough. I needed more. I brought the discarded painting home so I had a memory from when he left me. Unbeknownst to me, it also kept the pain alive, the destruction of something that was everything in my world, everything that *was* my world. Dylan was my world, so I held onto it.

I know that logically I should leave it, but it transformed over the years from something negative to something more... something that gave me hope. Something that showed I was stronger than all of the bad, that I was someone without him. I survived the devastation.

It's pouring outside, typical for October. Not a great month to move weather-wise, but the weather doesn't matter because I've been given a new chance at a happy ending. Austin will give that to me.

I take a big breath and look around once last time before walking to the window. My footsteps echo through the empty apartment. Looking down to the street below, the moving truck pulls out into traffic as Austin stands on the sidewalk, umbrella in hand, directing them.

He flew back from China a week early, so he could help. Deep down I think he was worried I'd back out. I don't know. Maybe I would have. Maybe I wouldn't. I'm just in neutral right now, going with the flow. This seems to be the right direction, but I guess I'll never know until I do it. Dylan is gone from my life again, so it seems to be the only direction left.

Austin sees me from the street, looking up and waving. He risks the rain to smile at me, then nods asking me to come down. I take a moment longer, alone, here in this place, closing my eyes, I inhale. I expect the air to be stale. But it's lively, sparking all my memories and bringing them to life.

It makes me wonder how different the air will be at his place when I move in, my new residence... my new home. That feels awkward to say. I release a staggered breath and open my eyes again. *Dylan.*

I see Dylan running down the street. I watch with a vested interest. Austin doesn't see him, but Dylan must call his name because he turns around. He smiles even though I know this isn't a polite social call.

Dylan's soaked from the rain, his hands moving in overtime as he says something to Austin. Much like the anxiety I feel beginning to overwhelm me, I see Austin tense as well, obvious even from up here.

What is Dylan doing here?

What is he saying to him?

I run. I run out the door, not bothering to close it behind me, down the steps, bursting through the entrance, hit by the cold rain, and immediately soaked. Austin rushes over, standing protectively in front of me, his arm tucking me behind his back, the umbrella over our heads.

I know before anything is said. I know why Dylan's here even before he calls my name, pleading. "Jules!"

...And my heart leaps from my chest.

CHAPTER 10
Jules
October 28th

DYLAN IS DESPERATE, his eyes locked on mine.

"What are you doing here?" I ask, my voice is harsh though my insides are soft for him, wanting to reach out. I want to comfort him from the pain and calm his turmoil. I want to wipe that expression of loss from his face.

When he comes closer, Austin pulls me to his side, his arm tightening around my waist. Threatening him, Austin says, "Don't come near her. I'm warning you, Somers. Don't make this worse. Don't put Jules in the middle of whatever this is."

Dylan stops to laugh, a tinge maniacally. *"Caught in the middle?"* he asks. "Fuck! She's not in the middle, man. She's all of it. My whole world—the outside, the inside, the middle. My. Fucking. Everything!"

"Dylan," comes out more as a sigh, my weaker side giving into him.

Austin doesn't look at me, afraid to take his eyes off of him, but says, "Jules, he's dangerous. Go back inside and call the police."

Dylan doesn't scare me. "He won't hurt me."

"Jules, don't trust him. Look, Dylan, I don't know what's going on or why you're at my girlfriends' apartment, but you need to leave right now."

"I need to talk to you," he says, staring into my eyes, and ignoring Austin altogether. His voice is loud, shouting above the rain that pummels the ground all around us. "Please, Jules. I'm begging you."

Shaking my head, I reply, "My decision is made, Dylan."

"What the fuck is going on here?" Austin is losing his patience and he releases me. "Jules?" He turns to me, knowing he's missing a key piece of the puzzle. "Tell me what's going on."

I look from Dylan to him, his beautiful eyes pleading and worried, seeing the truth in mine. I can't hide it from him any longer. "I need to talk to him, Austin. Please wait in the car."

"No." He demands, "I won't leave you to talk to this psychopath. He's acting irrational. It isn't safe for you to be alone with him."

"*Please*," I beg, tears filling my eyes. "Just let me talk to him in private. It won't take long. I promise. Trust me. You have to trust me on this."

"I think this is a huge mistake."

"Please, Austin."

After a stern pause, he nods, trusting me and conceding to my request. He's an amazing man. Leaning in, he whispers, "Keep your distance. I'll be close if you need me."

"Thank you."

He leaves me the umbrella and dashes through the rain to hop inside the waiting vehicle.

Dylan doesn't waste another second. "I screwed up so many times, so many times, Jules. I'm sorry. I hate what I did to you. I never really understood the repercussions of my actions until I saw the pain in your eyes when I told you... when I told you the truth." He steps closer and I stay, raising the umbrella up for him to come under. "I saw what I did to you. I can't take back what happened, but I can tell you that no one comes close to what you mean to me. No one can replace you. No one is you."

I raise my hand up to make him stop. "No more, Dylan, please." When I look into his eyes, the blue is a sad foggy color of loss. He now knows. I can see in the depths of his soul that he realizes what he did to destroy us, that what he did destroyed me. "I believe you. I see your pain. It's eating at your soul like it did mine, but it's too late for us. *You're* too late. When I needed you, you weren't there for me. Fate may have thrown you back into my life or me into yours, but it's not destiny. We make our decisions, our own choices, and I've made mine." The tears fall down my cheeks, regret filling my heart.

He drops his head down as he closes his eyes. "Please. I'm begging you to give me another chance. I won't screw up again. I promise to—"

Touching his cheek, I feel the scruff from his unshaven face. He looks up and I see the dark circles under his eyes. I step closer, wanting to hold and comfort him, but keep a distance between us. "You can't make promises that you don't know you can keep—"

"I loved you." His words are adamant, full strength, full belief in what he's saying. "I love you still. I was tainted and a stupid twenty-three year old."

"You're only twenty-seven now. Has that much really changed, Dylan?"

"Everything has changed. My life is only a life when you're in it. Please don't go with him. Don't move in. Don't give up on us or the possibility of what we can be. I know you feel something for me. I can feel it now. I see it in your eyes."

I look away, trying to block out his pleas. "I need to go. Austin's waiting for me."

"No!" Dylan's hand runs anxiously through his wet hair. "What do I have to do to prove that I love you, to show how sorry I am? Tell me and I'll do it. Anything."

My thoughts are jumbling, so I close my eyes briefly to clear them, but it doesn't work. The tears are already flowing. My heart is breaking, aching, and the words just come out. "You could have left me some damn coffee!"

"What? What does that mean?" I walk around him and head for the car, but he grabs my arm. "Jules, don't leave. Don't leave me for him."

I turn back around on that comment. "Is that what this is about? Is this about winning for you? My fucking heart is on the line and torn in two and you just want to win?" My anger wells inside, firing me up, and I shove him in the chest, then I hit him, pounding his chest as I shout, "I hate you. I hate that you're doing this to me. I'm just a game to you, a toy for you to fuck around with. I hate you, Dylan Somers."

Grabbing my flailing arms, he stills me abruptly. "Those are lies. You're lying to yourself, so you can walk away from your true feelings. You were never a game to me. You aren't a toy. You're my heart, my soul, fuck this."

He kisses me... *And I let him.*

One Woman. Two Endings.

For Dylan, continue reading.

For Austin, turn to page 271.

DYLAN

From the Inside Out

Part 3

S.L. Scott

CHAPTER 1

Dylan

October 28th

IT HAPPENED SO fast. I'm here, putting my heart fully on the line and hoping not to be rejected. I kiss her. I can't resist the temptation any longer. It's the only way I can show Jules how much I love her. Then she kisses me back.

The blow to my chest sends me backward and she's ripped from my arms. *Austin.* I'd forgotten about Austin. I don't care about him. Jules is all that matters, so when I see Austin's driver is manhandling her, I run to save her. I'm blindsided by a punch to the face, which knocks me to the side, stumbling to find balance.

Despite the pain, I only think of Jules. I need her. I need to help her, to make Austin understand. I straighten back up, seeing I'm going to have to get through him to get to her. "Austin, I love her," I warn.

Through gritted teeth and narrowed eyes, he yells, "You barely know her!"

This won't be easy. "She *loves* me."

His laugh is humorless, more threatening. "You're deranged, Dylan!"

When Jules cries out, "Pleas—" I punch him. I take the cheap shot when he's not looking, but it's the only shot I've got. "Dylan! Noooo!"

Austin falls to his knees, but I know he's strong and will fight back. I want him to. This situation coming to blows once and for all.

He shouts, "Get in the car, Jules." Without warning he lands on his feet and lands a punch square on my cheek sending me to the ground. The blood comes, my lip busted as I debate if I should fight, feeling this battle was lost almost four years ago when I walked out on Jules. When I look up, Austin continues, his anger taking over. "Fight. Damn it!"

I lay back, my face pulsing with pain from being pummeled as the rain falls down. The throbbing reminds me of the devastation I caused. I'm deserving of everything I get, karma finally collecting her dues.

The grey clouds above calm my insides as they blow over the city. Austin yells something, but my mind is on Jules. She's gotten into the car of her own free will. The battle is over. Austin wins. "Get up," he yells.

When I look over at him, I say, "Finally."

"What are you talking about?"

She should have a good man in her life. Austin is good and can give her the beautiful life she deserves. "Treat her well."

"What are you talking about?" He asks with confusion on his face. "Fuck this!"

He's gone, the car door slammed shut. The loud sound knocks me to my senses. This is it. For real. I've lost her...

I sit up, then I'm on my feet running after the car. I can't give up. I can't live without Jules. The black car is gone before I reach it, escaping down a side street. Austin may be the better choice on paper, but I'm the better man for her. I just need the chance to show her. I run faster, but I stop in the middle of the alley when the love of my life leaves with the wrong man. Leaning against the stone building, I try to catch my breath.

My mind is crazed with ideas. I know where he lives. I can go after her. Hailing a cab, I get in as soon as one pulls over. "Where to, Mac?"

"97..." The fact that she went on her own accord stops me from finishing the sentence. I pause.

The driver asks, "Hey, where to?"

I decide not to give Austin's address and tell him mine instead.

I'm tired of inventing excuses to make myself feel better for what I did. I just need to face the reality of the situation. I fucked up. I threw away the best part of me... No amount of excuses or apologies is gonna change the fact that I hurt Jules and I can't seem to make it right. I've tried, but I finally realize there has to be two willing participants. She knows how I feel about her. I can keep barging into her life, but that just messes up the happiness she's found. I'll always love her and that means I need to put her happiness before mine... for once. It's always been about me and what I wanted. She deserves happiness, even if it's not with me.

When I get home, I lay back on the couch with an icepack on my face, thinking about the day and our kiss. Closing my eyes, I accept that the kiss would be the last time I ever feel her lips against mine again. She was giving me a final kiss goodbye.

October 29th

A POUNDING ON my door wakes me from my sleep. I don't remember falling asleep on the couch. The knocking continues, which wipes away any dreams I might have been having. I hurry to stop the noise that's reverberating in my head. One large bolt and a sliding lock undone and it's open. Jules is standing there.

Small.

Wet.

Crying.

Head dropped. I hope not in shame. I'm the one who should be ashamed.

"I, uh," she starts, looking around, over her shoulder. I can tell she's thinking about leaving.

I quickly offer, "Come in." I wait, praying she will. Slowly she steps into my place. I've never made the mistake of calling it a home. *It's not.* She's not living here, so it's not home for me. "I'm sorry," I say, staring at her. Her head is down again as the words escape me, desperate to get out, to be heard. "And you're here and all wet."

Shivering, she says, "It's storming outside. I didn't have an umbrella." She finally looks me in the eyes, though I spot the fear. I hate the thought that she might be scared of me.

"I'll put your clothes in the dryer and get you something to wear."

Gentle fingers wrap around my wrist and she stops me. "Dylan, your face, it's bruised and swollen. Are you alright?"

I'd forgotten about my face, dismissing the dull ache in comparison to the heartache I'm feeling. Touching my right cheek, it doesn't feel as swollen as it was earlier, though it's tender. Jules was ripped away, stolen from me as Austin hit me. I let him, taking each blow, hoping it would knock some sense into me. Looking at her now, I don't know if it did. I just want to hold her, touch her, and wipe her tears away. I don't. "I'm fine."

Staring into my eyes, some other emotion takes hold of her. She leans up and kisses my neck. My hands go to her waist, holding her, never wanting to let go. My eyes drop closed, and she whispers, "I'm sorry, too."

Surprised, I open my eyes again and look down at her, daring to seek the truth in her hazels. *It's there.* Everything I felt in the kiss is prevalent in her eyes now. I kiss her again, cupping her face, and leaning down to show her how she should be kissed. Every time. With feeling and love, passion and conviction.

Her arms encircle my neck and she lifts up on her tiptoes, deepening the connection. I prolong it, worried that if I stop and we talk that she'll leave me and my heart can't take that. So I kiss her over and over, my hands loving the feel of her body against mine, enjoying every kiss she's willing to give whether this be the first of many or the last of them all. I'll take what I can get.

She backs away, worn down and says, "I can't do this anymore."

"What?" A stupid reply, but I'm frightened of what she'll say next.

"I can't fight this anymore. The world is conspiring against me and when I try to gain some perspective, I realize how lucky I am to have these two men in my life, wanting me." Her back is turned toward me, but hearing about Austin still feels like a punch to the gut. I used to be the only man in her life, the only one who mattered.

I fucked everything up.

"What happened with Austin?" I sit on the arm of the couch, watching her as she walks to the windows and gazes out into the darkness. With a glance to the clock, it's just past midnight, though it feels like everything just happened minutes ago.

She turns, and looks at me. "I won't go into details, but I'm here, so you should know that we broke up. It would be disrespectful to be here if we hadn't."

My heart expands with hope upon hearing that, but I try to keep my expression neutral for her sake.

With her arms crossed over her chest, she asks, "Why should I trust you, Dylan?"

"Because you know we're more than just a few years of the past to recollect one day. We're more than that. We're each other's destiny." I walk closer with caution.

"You throw around the word destiny so easily, like it's true and there's nothing else to believe in. You're so sure *now*," she says, wrapping her arms around herself. "But I was sure *then* and it didn't matter. You changed the course we were on, altering everything forever, Dylan. Can't you see that? Can you see how this is all on you? I've hurt a man I love tonight because you decided to take fate back into your own hands and alter our lives again."

"It was selfish, but I realized what I had—"

"I knew what we had!" she shouts, angry. Looking down at the rug beneath her feet, she takes a deep breath. "I didn't need to fuck someone else to appreciate what I had." Her eyes dart to mine, burning with intensity. "What do you want from me? I need to know and I need your complete honesty. You didn't give it to me then, but I need it now."

"I want a second chance." My response is too fast and I'm afraid it doesn't come off as sincere.

"That's asking so much of me. What if I do give you that and then you realize I'm not the one again? I'm not what you want? What if you meet someone else and want to be with her? These are the things you can't predict. I had four years to think about it, to figure out that no matter how solid the surface is, it doesn't mean the foundation isn't crumbling beneath."

"I understand you might not be able to forgive me or offer me that second chance. It almost makes more sense for you not to." I sigh, feeling hopeless. "But I need you to know that I wasn't living the high life in those years. I worked a lot and very hard. I didn't go out much. I don't have any real friends. I have a lot of co-workers and acquaintances. I didn't date much, despite what you might think. I couldn't." I walk even closer, touching the back of her hand with my finger, rubbing softly, lightly. "I fucked everything up, Jules, but I didn't realize that my life would remain fucked because you weren't in it. I let my pride tell me to leave you be. I'd hurt you enough until I saw you again that night at the restaurant. That was destiny—"

She rolls her eyes. "That means I'm destined to be with half of Manhattan—"

"Please hear me out," I say, taking her hand and she lets me, looking down at them joined. "I know this sounds crazy but I knew that day was coming. I'd been dreading March 14th for months. The date haunts me, a constant reminder of my biggest failure. It was a few days prior and I worked until eight-thirty, then Jacqueline came by and invited me to a late dinner. I was happy to avoid my place. If I'd gone straight home that night, I would have been drinking until I passed out like I had every day so far that week. Turns out, I did it anyway. You consume me. You have for years, but then when I saw you, I just... I couldn't believe it. You'd been on my mind and then there you were all beautiful and, God, better than I remember." I kiss her hand. "Destiny brought us back together and I'm willing to put myself out there for you. I need you to know that I love you. I never stopped. I hurt you, but I love you, Jules. I'm sorry for the pain I caused." I run my hands through my hair knowing I'm word-vomiting, but still do it. "I'm even sorry for Austin getting fucked over in this mess, but I'm not sorry for pursuing you. I'm not sorry for loving you. I'm not sorry for handing my heart over for you to crush this time. I'm not sorry that you're standing here right now because I made you think twice about me and I made you question what you want for you. I'm sorry for so many other things, but I'm just not fucking sorry at all for any of that."

She kisses me. Her lips are on mine and I close my eyes as my mind catches up with my body. My hands take hold of her hips and I tilt my head down and over for a better angle. Our tongues meet as do our hips. Finally, she's kissing me and I'm kissing her. The shock wears off quickly and I let passion take over just as she has. Her hands smooth over my chest and around my back, down my sides, not stopping, the pace, practically frantic. She's pushing me backward and I know where this is going, realizing what we're about to do. I grab her hands and pull back enough to look her in the eyes. "Jules?"

"Shhh, please. I need this. I need you right now. We were always so good this way, Dylan. Please."

Her voice is so soft, pleading and as I look deep within her eyes, I can see she really does want this, but to give her an out that she might need, I say, "This won't fix things."

A small smile crosses her face. "I know... and I want it anyway."

"It may complicate things even more," I rationalize.

"I don't care." Lifting up, she touches my face, bringing me closer and kissing me again.

I shouldn't.

I know I shouldn't.

How can I not though?

How can I resist her?

I can't. I'm too weak to say no. "Not here." I pull her down the hall and into my bedroom.

She shoves me against the back of the door and tugs at my shirt. "I want this off."

I toss it into the darkness of the room while her hands are on my belt, frenzied. It's quickly undone and on the floor. Pulling her shirt and bra off, she bares her breasts, and presses them against my chest. I want to feel them, grab them, squeeze them, lick them, bite them, fuck them like I used to. My memories have definitely not done them justice. They are way more perfect than I remember. I touch her shoulders as she kisses down my neck, lowering her body as she lowers her pants.

She stands before me a woman now, not the girl I so stupidly left. Little differences are noticeable, but only because I knew her body so well back then. The freckle three inches below her left breast is still prominent against her smooth skin. Her hips have more curves, but her body has less softness to it. She's tone, thin but more womanly. She's more confident, not hiding in any way from me. It's dark in here but our eyes have adjusted quickly. I can see all of her and she doesn't mind. I think she wants me to see her this way. I think she likes showing me the person she is now.

She's perfect.

Jules pulls me to the bed, a look of desire on her face. Crawling across the bed first, she tempts me with her ass as she moves. Stretched across my mattress, she calls me to her. Willingly, I go, crawling over her body, hovering, purposely not touching, teasing instead.

Her voice is just a whisper, no smile attached when she asks, "How many women have you slept with since we were together?" Her hand comes up, caressing my neck.

I didn't expect that question. I don't know why, but I didn't. "Um, five."

"I've been with two."

"I'm aware." I'm also aware that she's been with Austin more recently. I know he had a trip to China for most of that time, so I'm assuming it's been close to a month or longer since they were last together. I'm in no position to judge. "I don't have a condom," she says. A hint that it's up to me.

I don't know if I do either. *Shit.* I should check my stash. I reach over and look in the top drawer of the nightstand. "I've got one." As I maneuver back over, I ask, "Are you sure about this?"

"Yes," she replies. "I want you."

"I want you too, baby."

CHAPTER 2

Jules

October 29th

HE ROLLS THE condom down his erection, my eyes following his hands. "God, you're sexy," I say, then gasp, clasping my hand over my mouth. I can't believe I just said that out loud. I close my eyes to help block out the embarrassment that colors me and focus on the silence that surrounds us.

"You think I'm sexy?" Dylan asks. I can hear the smugness in his tone as his fingers slide between my thighs, not wasting any time. My eyes pop open, making me forget why I'm beet red and causing me to squirm when he touches me there. *I'm wet.* He smiles. "You want me?"

"You doubt that?"

"I wasn't sure."

Tonight, his words have been honest, so open with me. "Kiss me, Dylan."

He does while his fingers beginning to work their magic. But his lips disappear as he slides down my body, leaving a wet trail of kisses in his wake. From between my legs, he glances up at me. I watch and feel as his mouth picks up where his fingers left off. He always knew exactly how to please me. My back arches into the mattress and I lose myself in the ecstasy.

It all feels too good, engulfing me. With bated breath, I say, "This is fucking torture." The best, most erotic kind, but torture because all I want is him inside of me again. "Dylan, I've masturbated to memories of us. *Please.* I need to feel you inside of me."

"Shit, *you did*? I did too." He pushes my hair away from my face and kisses me unabashedly on the mouth. And then I feel him right *there*... just where I want him.

When we were together, I would masturbate in front of him, *for* him. He would come so hard, just as I came. It was a fun and dirty game we played. His lips go to my neck, nipping and kissing as he pushes in abruptly, forcing a moan from me. He looks up. Our eyes lock as he pulls back out, then pushes back in. His eyes weigh heavy like mine.

"I missed you," I say, but maybe I shouldn't have. It's the truth. *Can telling the truth be wrong?*

"I missed you so much, Jules," he replies, squeezing his eyes shut.

This is intense—the feelings, emotions, sensations, him. Dylan inside me after so long. It's overwhelming, dragging me under. But I don't mind.

This. Right now. This is everything and all that matters.

Almost breathless, I mumble, "You feel so good."

"You feel amazing." His response is quick and wanted.

We fit. We fit so perfectly together in this way. We always did. *Can we fit together again in other ways?* I wonder, but then I don't because I scold myself for thinking instead of enjoying what we're sharing right now.

I find his lips and kiss him, my tongue seeking more, which he so easily gives. "Dylan, Dylan, Dylan," I chant and it feels natural. It's what my body craves, to shout, to scream again in ecstasy as he hits that spot, remembering exactly how I like it.

"Juliette... *Baby.*"

There's a silence that follows, our quiet pants filling the void. My body reacting to him, his words, and the way he calls me Juliette like he used to. I feel the change in him just as he tenses, worried the moment is ruined. He's well aware of the name he called out, but for some reason, this time, I don't mind. "I'm sor—" He starts to say, but I interrupt, "It's okay. Please don't stop. Do this for me."

"I'd do anything for you," he whispers, looking into my eyes as his hips move to a steady rhythm, caressing my soul with every thrust. Breaking the wall down brick by stubborn brick until I feel the exposure, the light invades with love, or something like it. Our bodies are vessels to connect when our souls can't yet. I realize this now. I realize that I might still love him. I still want him, more than just physically. It's wrong, but feels so right, right this second.

His hands are on me, his fingers rubbing in a way that send me into an abyss I've avoided for too long. "Dylan!" Just one word as I sink beneath, drowning in emotions I haven't felt in years.

Dylan grunts, then groans, saying my name and other endearments as he comes. A series of small thrusts push him to a breaking point that makes me feel alive, worthy, forgiving, and meant to be.

Hearts racing.

Sweating.

He rolls over, bringing me with him. As I lay draped across his chest, I listen to his heartbeat—powerful, comforting, his hand rubbing my back, soothing. My lids are heavy as they lift to see the time on the nightstand in the dark bedroom.

1:30 a.m.

I give in, maybe not entirely to Dylan, but to sleep in his arms.

7:04 A.M.

Dylan.

I can feel him.

I can smell him.

I can smell us all around.

Strong and calming, frightening and troublesome.

My eyes open to find I'm curled into his side, my head on his shoulder. My naked body is against the side of his very naked and sexy body. I smile feeling his cock harden under my arm, ready for more. My thigh is over his, his arms around me.

Tilting my head up, I see his face with his eyes still closed. My stomach clenches seeing the bruising, the small cut, speckles of dried blood still visible. His breathing is regular and his lips slightly parted. He's nothing less than beautiful even with the damage.

Fuck, now I want him again.

I should leave, needing time to process what happened between us and what happened between me and Austin.

Austin. I sigh. I shouldn't be in bed with Dylan while thinking of him. It's rude to both of them, so I slip out from under his arm and replace my body with a pillow. Dylan snuggles into it, exhausted. He needs his rest to help heal.

I use the restroom and wash my face, cleaning up as much as I can with a towel. Afterward, I open the door slowly, turning the knob. I shut it behind me quietly and quickly, hoping I don't disturb him.

Sometime in the night, he dried my clothes for me, making me feel cared for. I pull the clothes out of the dryer and slip them on before heading for the door. I'm startled when the coffee pot percolates to life, the timer chiming. I walk into the kitchen tempted to have a cup, but I don't want to steal a mug, although he didn't have the same courtesy. Standing there staring at the coffee maker drags all the emotions I'd been suppressing back to the surface. My eyes burn from the threatening tears and lack of proper sleep.

When I reopen them, I see a letter on the counter near the coffeepot. It's from Dylan's mother. My heart races, remembering how much I miss her, thinking about our emails over the years, that bond still there. I lost more than Dylan when he walked out on me. It makes me wonder with all that's left to resolve, if it's possible to overcome the past to have a future together.

CHAPTER 3
Jules
October 29th

AFTER SLIPPING IN the building door just as a neighbor exits, I trudge up the stairs that lead to my apartment and check the knob, hoping it's unlocked. I can't remember if I locked it or not before I was whisked away so quickly yesterday. When I check, it's locked and I don't have my purse. I hate having to do this, but I walk down the hall to the only other apartment on this floor and knock. While waiting, exhaustion sets in. I slide down the wall to sit.

The door creaks open. Since I woke Brandon up, he looks sleepy. "What are you doing?" he asks.

"I want to sleep, but my apartment is locked and I don't have a key."

He helps me to my feet, then says, "I'll get it."

I watch as he disappears into the kitchen. He's wearing only boxers. We're beyond the necessity to dress for each other, especially at this hour. He returns, handing me a key. "Hey Jules, Austin dropped his key off. Said he had to go to London. You weren't home sooo..."

I take it from him like it's the most foreign object I've ever seen. "Did he say anything?"

"He said he thought you'd want it back. Not much else," he adds, scratching the back of his neck. "Where'd you stay last night?"

Nodding to my right, I reply, "I'm gonna go."

He knows not to ask too many questions, but he still offers, "I'm here... you know the drill. If you need me or anything."

"Thanks."

I turn back to my apartment, walking slowly toward it, wondering what I'm going to find in there if anything. I hear Brandon's door shut behind me just as I stick the key in, my hand shaking.

When I open the door, I see all my belongings have been returned. The haul of a small moving truck sits in the middle of my living room. The big furniture pieces back in their rightful places which means he directed the movers to do so. My heart aches, but I step closer to the pile of boxes stacked in the middle. I see the painting hanging on the wall, my suitcase and purse where I left them.

My life has been whittled down to an apartment of stuff, most of which I don't even care about, things that don't mean a thing to me anymore.

Looking around again, I notice a note on top of my purse. Bending down, I read it.

Jules,
I love you.
Austin

Sitting down on the couch, I fall to the side, closing my eyes to stop the tears that are welling. Finally, I give into the crushing emotions I've managed to keep at bay and do what I should have done yesterday instead of sleeping with Dylan. I cry.

I've hurt Austin. He's the man who would have given me the world, but I hurt him and then... *then I slept with Dylan.* Grabbing a pillow, I hold onto it, squeezing it to me and willing this endless sequence of pain Dylan and I started to end.

The door clicks as it's opened. I know who it is, so I don't bother hiding my emotions or even looking up. "Jules?" The couch dips next to my head. Brandon's voice is soft, whispering near my ear as his hand touches my cheek, revealing my tears. "Come here," he says. I lift my head up and lay it back down on his lap. "It'll be alright. I promise, Jules. It'll be alright."

"I wish this would all go away."

"I know. It will look different after you get some rest." He strokes my back and I find safety in my closest friend.

I must've dozed off. When I wake, I sit up, my body sore and my heart still broken, but I think of Dylan and a small smile involuntarily appears.

"So, what's the deal?" Brandon asks. "What's really going on?"

Looking over at him, I sigh and decide to tell the truth because it would take too much energy to lie, energy I don't have. "Austin and I broke up." I wait for the comment—a reprimand, or scolding. A judgment even.

But nothing like that comes. Instead, he says, "I figured as much when he returned your stuff and gave me the key to give back."

"And I slept with Dylan."

Once again, I wait for him to comment, a voiced disappointment. But that doesn't come either. He looks at me and asks, "Are you back together?"

"No. I don't know. Maybe."

His brow furrows and I can see the judgment caught in the lines of his forehead. "What are you doing, Jules?"

"Everything is moving too fast. I don't know what I'm doing anymore, my life is spinning out of control."

"Then get off the merry-go-round. This all started when Dylan came back into your life. What if he hadn't? Would you be living with Austin right now?"

"Brandon, please."

"I'm not gonna pressure you one way or the other. But here's what I know. I don't like to see you hurt, but this time, I think you need to figure this one out on your own."

With a heavy exhale, I reply, "Yeah, I'm coming to that same conclusion."

He stands, adjusting his shorts at the waist. "You know you're never really alone though, right?"

I stand to walk him out. "Thanks for being my friend when I need it most." I hug him, throwing myself into his arms and trying to show how important he is in my life through the embrace.

Brandon kisses my head and holds me, then turns and goes. He looks back when I say, "Hey Brandon, thank you and... and... I love you."

"I love you too, girl."

He's the closest thing to family I have in the city and even though I'd love for him to come take charge and tell me what I should do, he's right, he can't rescue me this time. I'm going to have to save myself.

CHAPTER 4

Dylan

October 29th

I KEEP CALLING, but she won't answer. I know she's probably sleeping because she sure as damn didn't get much sleep last night.

My mind is still fucked sideways over the fact that we had sex. When I woke up, Jules was gone. Her clothes and her... gone, her absence felt before I opened my eyes. She might as well have stabbed me because it felt the same at that point.

I lay there, thinking. That's when I smell her all over—the pillow, the sheets, my skin. The air in my room altered to accommodate her presence. Now, lack thereof. I don't regret what we did. Not at all, but hell if I don't feel like I took advantage of the situation. *Did I screw up the potential for a second chance?* I hope not.

I should have been here to listen, to answer her questions, but I couldn't. She was so tempting, like she always was, always *will* be to me—my weakness. Seeing her last night was like the first time I ever saw her, but the need was different. Back then, I was determined to talk to her, to know her, to kiss her. Last night I was desperate for her forgiveness or forgetfulness, and a second chance.

I got more than I expected because I got all of her—her mind, her body, her soul by the time we ended up in bed. I could feel her need for me, her own desperation as our souls reconnected. I wonder if she recognizes what really happened. It wasn't just sex. It never was with us. But waking up alone... maybe the daylight scared her, the reality of what happened yesterday.

Fuck! I grab my stomach sitting up in bed. I hope she didn't go back to him. I hope she didn't realize he's the better man.

He is.

Even I know that, but I'm the better man *for her.*

An hour later, I'm taking a cab to Jules' apartment. I slog up the stairs, my shoes feeling like weights as I walk. *What if she rejects me?* Last night might have been it for us, but after feeling her... being that close again, I have to try.

When I knock, there's no answer. Two more raps on the door and still no answer. I press my ear to the door like the fucking low life stalker I am and listen. *Nothing.*

I return twice over the next few hours before heading home, her decision not to see me again, obvious at this point.

Come Monday morning, I'm sitting at my desk and still in shock that Austin didn't have me fired. At least not yet. I sit idly by waiting for it to happen, but it never does.

Not today.

Not the next day.

Not even the day after that.

I'm still working here, moving up the ladder, but I removed myself from his account. Jacqueline is disappointed when I tell her. She questions, "I think the bruises on your face might have something to do with this. What did you do, Dylan?"

I remain silent, not wanting to lead her on in any way. I never have. I'm not starting now.

"You like her, don't you? You like his girlfriend, Jules." She laughs, flipping her hair over her shoulder, then says, "Holy shit! Austin did this to you." She drops the papers in her hands as she stares at me with her mouth wide open. "You make it so obvious, so now you've piqued my curiosity. Why'd she pick Austin over you?"

Shaking my head, I stare out the window of her large office. I don't have the answer to that. I don't even know if she chose Austin, but she didn't choose me. That is glaringly apparent. I walk to the door as she calls to me, "Dylan? It's her loss. I think you're a great guy."

"Thanks." I leave, not wanting to discuss this with anyone, but especially not at work. Trying to escape the office that seems to confine my thoughts to the past, I go to the park every day, hoping to see her, but she doesn't come.

I try not to go by the gallery, but I've been and watched her from afar. Through the office window, I see her. She often seems to be staring at the vase I gave her, touching it, examining it. Sometimes she looks out the window as if she's looking for someone. I hope she's looking for me, but I hide. I don't want to be a distraction to her, to cause her anymore pain. I tried to force my way back in once, twice, and it backfired. If we're supposed to be together, we will.

November 29th

IT'S BEEN A month. My mind still wanders and wonders, so today is the last day I knock on her door. The last time I'll go to the park. The last time I'll bother her.

She doesn't answer. Brandon comes out unexpectedly though. "Hey man," he says, eyeing me warily. "She's not home."

"Yeah, I gathered."

"So you've been coming here, what every day?"

"Most days."

"She's been working a lot, not home much."

"You don't have to find excuses, Brandon. I know she's avoiding me."

"She told me what happened."

I'm curious what she told him. I cross my arms over my chest defensively; worried that what she told him might hurt me more than her blatant avoidance. "What?"

"That you two were together that night." He looks just as uncomfortable as I feel right now. "I think what she feels for you scares her. Like me, she needs to know you won't hurt her again."

"Never."

He takes my response and mulls it over, gauging me momentarily. "She's not with Austin. They broke up. She's running on autopilot these days thanks to you."

"So am I."

"You look like shit." He shifts, stepping back into his apartment, grabbing his phone from a table by the door. "Give me your number. Maybe we can talk over a pitcher sometime." Jules' best friend is offering to tell me what she can't. It's an opportunity and a death sentence all in one.

I give him my number and ask, "Why are you doing this?"

"Because as much as I want to help her through this, I can't this time. It's something she's going to have to do on her own when she's ready." He shakes my hand, which seems oddly out of place, but strangely appropriate. "She's not ready, Dylan."

"She's stubborn. More than she used to be."

He laughs dryly. "Yes, that she is." He steps back into the doorway to his apartment. "She's still that same girl from years ago, the one you were with. She's just more protective of her heart now. Give her some time."

"How much do you think she needs?"

He shakes his head, laughing vacantly. "I don't know. I don't want her to hurt at all. I know you don't either. Let's grab that beer in the new year if you haven't heard from her."

"Okay."

I walk away from her building feeling the same emptiness I've felt for a month. In reality, I've felt it for years, but deep inside, an inkling of hope remains. Finally, I might have someone else on my side, someone on her side that cares about her enough to know that I just might be the guy she should be with.

CHAPTER 5

Jules

December 30th

THERE'S SOMETHING FUNNY about hate. It seems to be the only emotion you can't hold onto. I used to think it was happiness. It's not. It's hate. It slips through your fingers before you're aware it's gone and you find yourself feeling something else, something new, something different. It manipulates itself. You think you can rely on the emotion like you once did so readily, so easily, but it changes.

It may be numbness that carries you forward now. Or, maybe it's an emptiness that suddenly exists in your belly, in your chest, in your heart. Or maybe you find yourself feeling the opposite and catch yourself smiling at something you hadn't noticed before.

Hate is funny like that.

I tried to hold onto it.

I tried to hate Dylan again.

I tried to hate him for making my life complicated when it seemed... not complicated. When it seemed obvious which way I should go. I tried to control the hate, bring it forth again, summoning it. To own it. Possess it. But it turned, altered from within. It left without my permission. Just like Dylan had years earlier, drifting out of my life without my consent.

Months after I went to Dylan's apartment, I continue to work long hours, trying to block him from my mind. He lingers... in my mind, sometimes even outside my apartment. I know he's there even when he doesn't knock. I can feel him, his hand, his heart just on the other side of the three inches of wood that separates us.

Something inside me won't let him in. Maybe it's a deep-seeded emotion that seems to dwell inside, overpowering my weaker ones, scolding me for wanting him again.

Maybe.

By mid-afternoon, work is tedious, which is unusual. I love my work, but it's not what I need right now. I need to feel something different. *I'm craving a new emotion.*

Tired of punishing myself, I leave. I grab my wallet out of my bag and shove it in my coat pocket. I tell my assistant, Sergio, I'm going to check on Jean-Luc's showcase. I'm determined to distract myself and my pesky heart that longs to be somewhere else, that longs to be with Dylan.

I hail a cab and slip inside. The drive is uninteresting. The view of the working city is uninspiring in browns, winter grays, and dirty whites. I knock even though he tells me I can walk in every time I visit. It's not my home and I don't like to intrude though my unannounced visit may be considered an intrusion in and of itself. It's not to him though.

He answers with a joint hanging from the corner of his mouth as his smile widens and he ushers me in. He sets it down on the nearest window sill of the large loft, then returns to hold me by the face. He's never touched me like this before and though it might be considered too much, too close for some, I'm not worried. I know where we stand. He cares about me, but he doesn't love me, not like Dylan does. He's comforting in some ways though that are different and easy.

"You want a hit?" Jean-Luc asks hesitantly, seemingly unsure if what he's asking is appropriate.

Taking the joint in hand, I inhale while closing my eyes and let it infiltrate my being, taking over for a while. Doubts and pain, regret, and everything but numbness flood my mind, overpowering me with loss. I want to let go. I cough which turns into hacking since I've never smoked pot before. When the coughing ceases, I smile, feeling lighter already. Maybe I should be a bad girl. Maybe that would suit me better.

I know this is a manufactured diversion. The marijuana has created this façade of a feeling. I decline another hit, knowing it would be better to feel nothing than something false.

I walk the room, gazing at his latest works, thinking about the differences in style from his earlier pieces. Jean-Luc is established on the scene and his work needs to evolve as much as his reputation has.

Higher expectations.

Costlier price tags.

Progress in the movement.

I'm not seeing it in these, which worries me.

"I've missed your pretty face, Jules."

I glance, he smiles—ruefully.

I return to the third painting propped against a chest of drawers and critique, "This one needs a response to the question it poses."

"That's the point. There is no response, no right answer to give. This is art."

"Art has a purpose or you couldn't set it apart from a drawing done by a child. You had a point, a motive when you painted it. What was it? I need to see that motive or I'm left empty. That's not a reaction you want when you use such bold colors."

"I'm the new generation of standards. They love me, Jules." His hands go into the air, expressive, overly-dramatic, "I'm Jean-Luc, damn it! I don't have to have a point or motive. I just have to paint my name at the bottom."

"Anyone can paint. Greatness is born from desire and your desires are following a different path right now."

He walks closer, his hand running the length of my arm. "You're too uptight today."

"Arrogance is unattractive, even in art."

Sidetracking the conversation, he says, "Maybe you need something stronger." He holds up a bottle of vodka. He's right. The drink will give me a new perspective, then I will look at the paintings and reassess. I nod, relaxing on the couch that faces an easel and the back of a large blank white canvas. He presents the glass. "It's the afternoon, so I thought we could start with something lighter."

My eyebrows go up that vodka is considered lighter. I sip after a quick tap of my glass to his, the burn rushing my system and easing me.

Sitting back, I close my eyes, lost in memories. I find Dylan frequenting my thoughts again. I don't regret making love with him that night. I can't. It felt right. He felt right. Still does, but I can't go back into something blindly. I did that the first time and caused more harm than good. I believe I've given Austin another chance to find true love, something that I couldn't give him. I loved him, but not the way he deserves.

I know I'm hurting Dylan as well, but maybe that's how it has to be for now. Maybe time will give me a new outlook that alcohol hasn't.

I've been alone a lot lately. Brandon has a girlfriend now who surprised him with a ski trip for Christmas. I think she wanted him away from me, but that's just my opinion.

It's fine because he has earned more than a lifetime of happiness from his good deeds as a best friend. It's just... his girlfriend is a model. I've met her four times and I can tell she already wants to marry him, even after just two months. I'm not jealous. I'm bitter. And happy for him.

My mind is fucked.

I shouldn't be allowed near people when I'm like this, when I'm past hate and leading back into feelings this intense. These feelings hurt.

Painful emotionally.

Physically painful to my body.

I sit down on Jean-Luc's couch, sloppy already, my mind going fuzzy. He joins me. The straight alcohol hitting me harder than expected. I look down at the glass and it's empty, but then he's refilling it. *When did I drink the whole glass?* I should stop. I lean back, closing my eyes, hoping to disappear for awhile.

He whispers what I want to hear as I fade away...

"Beautiful."

"Smart."

"Sexy."

"Is this okay?"

I open my eyes as his hand slides up my thigh to the top of my legs. My skirt is up, revealing too much for his eyes, more than I want to show him. "No," I murmur, then watch as he stands, moving slowly to the easel.

He takes his shirt off. "I'm going to paint you, Jules." His pants drop down, no underwear, and I watch silently. "I paint best in the nude. Do you want to be naked with me? Let me paint you bare, my beauty."

His words cautionary, but intriguing. My better judgment gone just like the men I've loved who have loved me the most. He comes closer, setting the paintbrush down on the coffee table in front of me. Confident, he reaches for the strap of my blouse. My body and mind move like quicksand, unable to save myself. He whispers of freeing the demons that live within. He promises to put them in the girl in the painting and let them reside there instead, liberating me from the burdens of feeding their egos. He promises to paint me broken, so I can be whole again.

His words are therapeutic when you're mind plays tricks on you.

After standing, he walks to the easel that seems to be waiting to be filled with my image. I don't grant him the permission he seeks because I'm too tired. Twisting onto my side, I find comfort in holding myself, eyes closing, unaware if it's been five minutes or five hours. I lose track of time...

Of Dylan...

Of myself.

While he paints.

CHAPTER 6

Dylan

December 31st

"MR. SOMERS," TRICIA calls quietly, peeking her head into the conference room.

I look up, surprised by the interruption. She knows how important this early morning meeting is. Twelve men. Eight women. Eyes all on me as I smile, excuse myself, and hurry over. I shut the door quietly behind me, questioning her. "Tricia, you know I'm not to be disturbed. What is it?"

"There's a Mr. Paine on the phone. He says it's an emergency. He tried your cell, but obviously you didn't answer."

"I don't know a Mr. Paine."

As my mind tumbles through names and faces, everyone I know, it finally registers—*Brandon Paine?* "Which line?"

My heart starts pounding in my chest. There's only one reason he would call me—*Jules.* Something's wrong. I can feel it. It's seven-fifteen in the morning. Not exactly time for a social call.

She replies, "Line ten."

"Can I take it up here?"

"Sure. Just press the red button and you'll be connected."

I dash to a cubicle where someone else sits but hasn't shown up to work yet. "Brandon?"

"Dylan?"

"What's going on?"

"She just called me. Jules just called me and she needs help."

"Where is she?"

"Some building down in the Bronx."

"Call me on my cell in ten minutes. I'm heading out the door now. I'm in the financial district. It will take me a while to get there." I don't think I even hang the phone up. I think I just toss it and run.

Tricia calls after me, "Dylan?"

"Tell them I have an emergency," I shout over my shoulder while running for the elevator.

The adrenaline makes me want to run the whole way, down forty-six flights, but the elevator will be faster. I step inside and press the lobby button. The tranquil music is in polar opposite of how I feel.

I run out and straight for the line of cabs dropping people off at the curb, people arriving for work. "The Bronx," I demand.

The cabbie looks at me in the mirror, eyebrows raised. "That's gonna be a big fare from here."

"I don't care. Just start the meter and drive."

"The Bronx is a big place."

"I'll have an address in a few minutes. Drive, it's an emergency."

"Okay," he says, closing his mouth and pulling into traffic.

I'm holding my phone, willing it to ring when it lights up. "Where am I going?" I ask.

"Calm down, Dylan. I think she's fine. I just texted you the address. I just need to have back-up—"

"Why do you need back up?" Shifting, I'm anxious as shit to get to her and he now tells me he needs me as back up. "What the fuck? Give me her number, Brandon."

He rambles it off and I hang up after telling him I'll call him back. I give the address to the driver in the meantime.

It rings three times before Jules answers and when she finally does, my heart drops into the pit of my stomach. "Hello?" Her voice is weak. She sounds drowsy.

"Jules? It's me... Dylan."

"Dylan? *Dylan...*" She trails off as if falling asleep, then says, "Dylan, come get me."

"I'm coming. I'll be there soon, baby. Just hang on. I'll be there soon. Are you all right? Are you hurt?"

"I'm... fine. I just can't seem to stay awake. I'm so... tired."

"I'm coming." My voice cracks, my concern taking over. I've never heard her like this. Something's wrong. "Can you stay on the phone with me?"

Silence.

"Jules, are you there?"

Silence.

"Jules?"

"Fucking answer me, Jules!" I shout, but there's no reply. If I listen carefully I can hear her breathing into the phone. Despite wanting to stay on, I hang up, and call Brandon. "Why does she sound like that?"

"I don't know. She wouldn't say. *Couldn't* might be more accurate."

I run my hand nervously through my hair. "What's going on?"

"I honestly don't know." He's not hiding the edge to his tone. "I just got back to the city last night. She called me and sounded like what you heard. It's that guy Jean-Luc's place. I don't know what I'm walking into."

"I appreciate you calling me. I should be there in a half hour. I'll meet you out front. Wait for me."

Thirty minutes.

Thirty minutes of torture.

Jules. All I can think of is her. The worst scenarios playing out in my mind.

As soon as I arrive, I swipe my credit card through the machine and jump out of the cab not waiting for a receipt. When I turn around, Brandon is running toward me from the corner, his cab pulling away from the curb.

Brandon doesn't say anything but walks past me and buzzes the landlord. When he speaks to him, it's firm, words like 'cops' and other threats being tossed around.

The door is buzzed open.

Even though the building is in a crap location, I can tell these lofts are expensive once I enter. I still can't let my guard down.

Brandon takes the stairs two at a time and I follow. He says, "Third door. Apartment C."

When we reached Jean-Luc's door, it's cracked open. Brandon stalls, gripping the large steel handle. He looks at me and I've never seen him so serious. Pissed yes, but his expression stresses me even more. "Get her out of here as fast as you can."

I nod, but he already knows Jules is my only priority.

As he slides the door the rest of the way open, we enter. It's quiet except for music softly playing in the far corner.

We're greeted by something unexpected—a painting of her. Dark long hair, waves over her shoulders. Creamy skin. My eyes search for clues of authenticity. Her eyes are closed, so nothing to confirm my suspicions from them. Landing on the mole, it's there, painted exactly where it is on her body.

Fucker!

He painted her nude. For his sake, she better have been a willing subject. We walk around it, one on either side of the large canvas and there she is asleep on the couch, phone lying by her cheek. A blanket covers her, her coat draped over the arm of the couch. I kneel down and whisper. "Jules? Wake up. Jules."

Her lids lift just slightly and a small smile appears. "Dylan," she whispers, her voice is scratchy as she reaches for my cheek. "What took you so long?"

"I was across the city. I'm sorry."

"I don't mean today."

Sighing, I reply, "I got lost, but I'm here now." My lips land on her forehead and I take a second to compose myself, my heart jumping out of my chest and straight into hers.

I hear shuffling behind me and turn to see Brandon looking at a bottle on the side table. "Sleeping pills." He picks up an empty bottle, and adds, "Vodka."

Turning back to Jules, her sweet smile makes me want to kiss her, but I resist knowing this isn't the time. "Are you hurt? Did he hurt you?"

"No. I'm not hurt. I'm tired and a little sick to my stomach."

"Did you take a sleeping pill?" She shakes her head, so I say, "Jean-Luc painted you. Is that why you're here?"

I watch as she looks down, noticing she's only in her bra and panties. She sits up, the blanket covering her as she reaches for her clothes. Her voice starts to tremble as do her hands. "Dylan..." She looks into my eyes and I see she's scared. "He didn't hurt me, but... I was dressed."

"Where is he?" I ask.

"I want to leave," she says, her voice gathering strength. "Let's just leave."

"Did he do anything to you?"

"Dylan," she snaps. "He wouldn't hurt me." Her conviction wanes. "But I know he wanted to paint me. I remember him saying that before I fell asleep."

Brandon stops pacing, and says, "I'm gonna kill this guy." His hands fisted, his face as tense as his arms.

I feel the same but I focus on Jules. "We should call the police," I say to him.

"No!" Her hand goes out to stop me. "I remember him talking to me about putting my demons on the canvas or something like that. I might have told him he could. I can't remember now."

Brandon stops and asks, "How much did you have to drink?"

"I don't know." She puts her feet on the floor and says, "I want to get dressed." She stands there waiting until we both turn around. Right when I turn my back on her, I feel her hand on my arm. "Dylan. Please don't hate me."

Looking back, I say, "I could never hate you." Wishing I could take away her pain and regret, I stroke her cheek. "I tried. Trust me, I've tried."

"I've tried too, but I couldn't because I think I love you too much."

"There's that *too much* again." I lean back, looking directly into her eyes. I can tell the drug has worn off for the most part. "Get dressed. I want to get you out of here."

I take her coat and hold it out, shielding her to give some semblance of privacy.

"Jules, get dressed before this asshole returns or I guarantee I will fucking crush his hands so he never paints again," Brandon snarls from the front door.

I would do more than crush his hands.

Unsteady on her feet at first, she grabs a hold of my arm and slips her shirt and skirt on. I help her with her coat, then we walk to the door. "Get the painting, Brandon," I say when we pass.

She looks between us before turning around. A sharp intake of air is heard when she sees the canvas. "That's me." There's disappointment to her tone as if she's given up something she wanted to hold onto.

I pull her out the door, not wanting to be here any longer. The elevator is large and industrial in nature, so the painting fits. Jules stares at it, intrigued, her fingertips sliding cautiously over the bumpy, dried paint. "It's good. Accurate. He even caught the tears."

"Why were you crying?" I ask, looking at the streaks down her painted face.

"I always cry in my sleep." She states this so matter of fact, as if everyone does that. Her response makes a lump form in my throat as a thousand more questions enter my mind.

Out on the sidewalk, I hear a harsh cracking. When I turn around, I see the broken frame on the ground. Brandon is rolling the loose canvas up as she slides into the taxi.

"Do we need to go to a hospital?" I ask, wrapping my arm around her shoulders when I get in.

Brandon is getting in when she replies, "No, he didn't hurt me."

She glances at me. "He didn't touch me either. I promise." Her voice is just a whisper on the last part as she buries her head into the nook of my neck and closes her eyes.

CHAPTER 7

Dylan

December 31st

JULES FALLS ASLEEP in my arms on the cab ride to her apartment. When we arrive, she insists she's fine and can walk on her own. I stifle a smile because I've grown to like her stubbornness. Actually, I like everything I've discovered about the new Jules. It's more authentically her, not for me, or who anyone else wants her to be. She's created her own life and I respect that.

Brandon follows us into our... *her* apartment and leans on a stack of boxes. "So, what do you want me to do with this painting?" He holds the rolled canvas up in his hand, careful not to let it fall open.

Jules turns from within the confines of the bedroom and tilts her head, leaning against the doorframe. "Just leave it."

"I'm gonna go," he says to me, his eyes then meeting hers.

She has her coat off and is unzipping her skirt when she stops and walks back into the living room. Her voice is soft, caring, grateful, "Brandon, I don't know how to thank you for being there, for being my friend when I needed you most." Her hands are on him, one on the chest, one on his arm.

I should be jealous by the intimate touch, but I'm not because I know where the intimacy between the two of them begins and ends.

He hugs her and whispers, "You don't have to thank me, just don't pull that disappearing crap again."

"I won't. I'm sorry," she says.

Brandon leaves, leaving us alone. I've made myself at home on the couch, watching her.

"I think I want a nap. Will you sleep with me, Dylan?"

"Sleep?"

She smiles and the laceration in my heart starts to heal. With a hand on her hip, she says, "Yes, sleep. *Only* sleep."

I stand and walk into the bedroom with a shrug. "I can nap." I find myself following Jules room to room not wanting to be too far, feeling very protective of her. She pulled a new toothbrush out of a moving box in the living room, handed it to me, and then we ended up in the bathroom, brushing our teeth together. Watching each other in the reflection of the mirror, I feel at home and yet, a little nervous. Our eyes take in the other, reticent but right.

I use the restroom in private after she does, then go into the bedroom. The curtains have been pulled. It's bright outside, but the drapes do a good job of blocking out most of the light. She's on the left side of the bed. We haven't spoken in a few minutes and the weight of the world seems to be heavy between us. I walk over and slide under the covers, dressed only in boxers, hoping she doesn't mind me taking off my undershirt. I'm lying on my back and she immediately scoots closer. Lifting my arm, she takes up residence there without words, without questions, without hesitation. Just like old times.

Draping her arm across my chest, she closes her eyes and I kiss her before closing mine. Our breaths even, steady and slow, syncing together.

Three hours. I wake up three hours later, surprised, considering I wasn't tired. That's a lie. I'm always tired. I don't sleep well these days, haven't in a long time... Not since that night at my apartment.

I'm still holding Jules, wrapped around the back of her. I close my eyes again and push my nose into her hair. Silky. Tropical in scent.

I smile, and she whispers, "Hi."

"You're awake?"

"Your sniffing woke me up," she says flatly, but I can tell she's just teasing.

I lean up on my elbow to lean over her. When she turns onto her back, she's under me, and I say, "Hi."

A sweet stroke on my cheek, down my neck, and over my shoulder and she's smiling too. "I'm glad you're here."

"I am too." I want to tell her more, but save it for a conversation out of bed, not wanting to ruin this.

Her voice is still coarse with sleep when she asks, "Will you spend the day with me?"

"I thought I was."

She laughs lightly, looking down. When her eyes meet mine again, she asks, "Will you go somewhere with me?"

"Anywhere."

Moving quickly from bed, she says, "Well, come on. The day is a wasting."

While she dresses, I go into the bathroom. She didn't mention my boner. What a relief. It's going down, but it was obvious when I was pressed against her.

Finishing before her, I go into the kitchen, needing a cup of coffee. She has this amazing coffee maker on the counter too. It looks expensive, but doesn't seem to have been used much. I pull the ground coffee from the freezer, old habits of both of ours, and start messing with it.

"That thing is too complicated," Jules says, walking in behind me. "I'll buy you a coffee down the street if you want one."

"I'd like to figure this one out. Do you mind waiting?"

"Have at it. I've had it for years and can't really figure it out."

I laugh while messing with a lever on the side. I think that's the steamer. I get a glass of water and fill the tank, switching the machine on, then twist two knobs adjusting the levels. She hands me a mug and I place it under the spout I think the coffee will come out. I flip the lever backward and steam rushes out of a metal tube, then I twist it again. "I hear brewing!" I announce proudly.

She leans in closer, listening carefully. "So do I!" The molten liquid sputters a few times before draining into the mug. "It's working," she says, laughing.

When the cup is three-fourths full, I stop the press and pull the mug out. "Voila," I say, presenting it.

"I'm so impressed, Dylan."

Shrugging, I reply, "Eh, it was nothing."

"You should have the first cup since you got it to work."

"No, I insist. It's your fancy machine and coffee. Try it and let me know what you think."

Bringing it to her lips, she blows before sipping. First it's her nose, then her eyes. Her face contorts, struggling to swallow what's in her mouth. Maybe I should have tried it first.

"Um, yeah, I'll buy you a coffee down the street." She grabs my hand and pulls me toward the door. "Get your jacket." With a wry smile in place, she asks, "Do you want to go by your place and change clothes?"

"I'd like to get out of this suit. And just so you know, I'm going to master that machine."

"I have no doubt you will, Dylan. You were always very good at conquering anything you put your mind to." She breaks away and looks down the hall, shifting uncomfortably. When she looks back at me, she whispers, "I need to take this slow, okay?"

I nod. I want fast, but I'll do slow. *For her.*

After a visit to my place, I'm in clean clothes and we're on the subway heading to a restaurant near the gallery. "So you recommend this place?"

"Do you trust me?" she asks.

Tilting my head, I narrow my eyes at her. "With my heart."

Leaning her head on my shoulder, she smiles again. That's four that I've counted since we woke up and I love every one of them. I move my hand to her lap and she places hers on top of mine, our fingers fold together, entwining. A rough start to the day brings an unexpected, but happy ending.

CHAPTER 8

Dylan

December 31st

AFTER DINNER, WE walk outside and I finally say what I've wanted to say all day, "He left you there. The door was wide open."

"Jean-Luc wouldn't have hurt me. He probably went to his friends place. He lives across the hall. He wouldn't leave me to be attacked or anything like that."

"I don't want him coming near you again." I close my eyes trying to rid myself of what I saw— the painting, the feelings.

I feel her hand soothe over my back and look, meeting her soft gaze. "I wasn't thinking," she says, shaking her head as if scolding herself. "I went there for work... But I knew deep down that he wanted more. He always has. Dylan, I hate to admit how weak I was, but I wanted to feel wanted without pain and baggage. I wanted simple. He's simple in his affections." She scoffs under her breath. "He's very open with his wants. I went over there hoping to feel like my old self, needing the attention."

She takes a deep breath, closing her eyes, steeling herself for what's to come and I feel my nerves heighten. With a hand on my arm, she starts to turn, then wraps her arms around me. As I hold her, she speaks to my chest, but I hear her, "My old self after you. I wanted to return to the life where I was in control and hated you. I can't though. I... my heart." She sighs, then goes quiet.

"What I did was wrong, Jules. Fucking wrong on so many levels, but I'm here now. I've been here, trying to make up for even a portion of the pain I caused. But now, I need to know how you really feel." I hold her tighter; both of us unable to look at the other while these words come out. "I'm not asking for a life with you. Though you know I want one. I'm asking you for today, for right now. That's all. One day—"

"One day," she repeats.

In that moment of silence between us, I pray once more that she gives me this request.

"Okay." She takes a step back, releasing me, which feels all wrong. Her arms go into the air, as she continues, "I shouldn't. I don't owe you anything, much less another chance, but like you, I'm fucking selfish, Dylan." With a shrug, she says, "I like the way I feel when I'm with you more than when I'm not. I know this is unfair. Judge me if you must, but this is me being honest with you now. *We* are not going to be fixed overnight or even over months. It's going to take a long time for me to trust you again, but I'm starting to, even if just a little. I deserve to be happy and what sucks is, even after what you did to me four years ago, you make me feel like I can be happy again, like there just might be a silver lining to this whole mess."

Her arms flop to her sides exasperated. Taking her hand, I rub my thumb over the back of it. "I know what you mean. I understand that you want to convince yourself I'm the bad guy, and I was, but I'm not anymore." I pull her to me, my mouth to her ear, my arm around her shoulders and whisper, "I've never stopped loving you. Ever. Just let me show you. Give what you can give. I'm not asking for more than that."

Her hands slide around to my back and up, holding me tight. Her lips are on mine, hushing the words that don't need to be spoken. Words like 'please trust me' and 'I'm sorry,' 'I love you,' and 'thank you.'

We have time to share those. This is about acknowledging that we will try, at the very least, we will try and maybe one day we can move beyond *least* into something *more*.

I hear her take a slow, drawn breath, then whisper, "Okay."

Tilting my head to the side, I look down so I can see her face. When she looks up, for the first time since I saw her almost a year ago at that restaurant, her eyes are clear, not bogged down with the heaviness of the past.

"What?" she asks, feeling self-conscious.

I'm momentarily stunned by her beauty. Running my hand along her cheek, I let my fingers twist into her hair before moving down to give her a kiss. I find myself gripping her tighter, holding her closer, afraid she'll disappear, like this might not be real.

"Dylan?" Her voice is soft. "It's alright. We have today." She laughs gently, looking down. "Probably tomorrow too."

"I'm hoping by tonight there will be no probably's in the equation."

"So am I."

I savor her words, then ask, "Can I take you somewhere now?"

Her smile grows. "Yes. Is it a surprise?"

"Of sorts."

Two train hops later, we're walking down Atlantic Avenue in Brooklyn. I can see her curiosity peaking and I'm nervous again. I take her hand and go to the office to check in.

"Mr. Somers, good to see you again."

"You too, Joey. How have you been?"

"Can't complain," he replies, looking between us. Curious, I'm sure. I've never brought anyone with me before. He grins as if he's suddenly in on a secret. "Have a good day."

"You too," I call over my shoulder as we walk down the corridor and up the stairs, down another long hallway to the very end. The last unit on the right.

"What's this?" she asks, her nerves showing through her tentative tone.

I unlock the mini garage door and as I lift it up, I grip her hand tighter with my other. "I need to show you this."

The door settles and I glance to her and then back to the ten by fifteen storage unit. Her mouth drops open as she tries to free her hand, but I remain holding it, gripping harder, afraid she'll leave me. *'Please don't hate me,'* I chant over and over in my head as she takes in the stuff before us.

Stepping forward, she stops, then murmurs, "Dylan." I can hear her gulp before she takes another step. "Dylan, this is—"

"It's our stuff. All of it. It's all here. Everything I took from you is here," I whisper, releasing her hand, knowing I have to. I feel the tears form in my eyes when I see her shoulders shake and hear her trembling breath.

She looks at me over your shoulder, then turns back and sits on the couch like she might need the support. When her eyes meet mine, for a brief second, I'm stunned. "You've had this all along?"

"Yes. I couldn't throw it away. I couldn't... I couldn't be around it on a daily basis. It was us."

"No, it was just our stuff, not us."

"The guy at the front desk knew you when you walked in. How long have you had it here?"

"Since the day I moved it from the apartment."

Her eyes search mine as her eyebrows dip in curiosity, piecing it together. "How often do you come here?"

I stand still, frozen to the spot, my eyes locked with hers. "One or twice a month, at least."

"And at the most?"

"Four or five times a month."

Walking to a box, she lifts the flap. Then she leans her forehead against it and starts crying. I know what's in that box. There's a reason that box is the one closest to the couch.

"The photo albums," she says, looking back at me once more. "Why, Dylan?"

"I needed you. I couldn't live life without you—"

"You had me, but *you* chose to leave."

"I know. It's the biggest mistake of my life. I regret it every minute of every day. I know a million apologies won't make it right, but it doesn't mean I ever stopped loving you, Jules."

Reaching for her, she swings her arms protectively in front of her body. "Stop!" She looks down again.

"I shouldn't have taken it. I don't even have a good excuse for taking it. At the time, I think I wanted anything to do with us out of sight, so I could move on. But the bill would come for another year on this storage unit and I would pay it, knowing I could never get rid of it."

"Your sad reasoning hurt me, hurt my soul and now I'm here face to face with everything I never thought I'd see again. I'm gonna need a minute to process this."

Sitting down on the couch, in the spot I usually sit in when I visit, I watch as she starts digging through boxes until she seems to find what she's looking for—her jewelry box. She then sits down on the couch and lifts the lid. A small gasp escapes before her hand covers her mouth. Slowly, she lifts a necklace up in front of her. I gave it to her back in college. She says, "I never thought I'd see this again. What did Hillary say about this?"

It's my turn to scoff. "Hillary knew I had the stuff, but she never knew where or what I had. She never came here. I never brought her. I didn't want her near here or you."

"Why'd you come here?" she asks, setting the necklace back into the velvet lined wood box.

I was hoping she'd put it on, but I know that's too much to ask. Leaning back, I roll my head to the side to look at her pretty face. "Sometimes I would bring a bottle of Jack and take shots while staring at the boxes. A few times, I fell asleep on the couch—"

"I used to love taking naps on this couch."

I smile because she does. "You're letting me off, aren't you?"

"No. I hate that you took all of this away, but it's stuff. I had to reconcile with that years ago because I didn't think I'd ever see it again." She turns onto her side, tucking her legs up under her and adds, "I think it would have been very hard to live with this and know you were still gone. All of these reminders..."

Something catches her eyes and she sits up suddenly. I've been found out as I spot the picture frame of us at Myrtle Beach one summer we visited my family. That's the picture I set up on top of the box in the corner. I would stare at it for hours wondering how I could have thrown our relationship away like I did.

She steps over another box to retrieve it. Running her fingers along the broken glass, she looks back at me questioning. I answer despite the nonverbal request, "I was upset. I'd been drinking."

Jules lowers the frame, defeated, and asks, "Why didn't you ever call me, Dylan?"

"I," I start but stall, my words jumbling in my head, making me feel stupid. "I thought you hated me."

"It's strange, but I never considered the fact that maybe you were feeling the same way I was. So much pain. The difference is that I did hate you, but I think you hated yourself more."

I nod, knowing she sees me much clearer than I thought.

CHAPTER 9
Jules
December 31st

As I STARE at the broken picture frame, I have an epiphany. *Dylan's suffered too.* He's still suffering, just like I am. I turn around and see him leaning forward, resting his arms on his knees, his face covered by his hands. Seeing how broken he is, I sit down next to him.

Broken, just like me.

So much needless pain. That's what I used to think. But now I don't think it was needless. I think it was necessary in some twisted fucked up way. I rub his back, leaning my head against his shoulder. His breathing is harsh, stubbornly unsteady. "Dylan, it's okay. *It's okay.*"

He looks up at me, unsure of what I mean.

Taking his face between my hands, I kiss his forehead, then his nose. I kiss a tear away on his left cheek, and his lips. This isn't about sex. This is about forgiveness, comfort, love. I love him and even though I may not be able to totally forgive or tell him how much I care about him, I *can* comfort him. This is something I can do for him and something I want to do.

Selfishly, it's also for me.

I deepen the innocent kiss and when my tongue enters his

mouth, he adjusts so we're in a more comfortable position. Not knowing fully where this inner urge is coming from, I shift on top and straddle him. Dylan's hands go to my hips and a slow, low moan comes from his mouth right into mine, causing me to react the same.

In one whispered word, he pulls back, being so careful with me, questioning, "Jules?"

Wanting to confide, I want to tell him everything, like how my heart skips a beat every time I see him, how he makes me feel safe though he hurt me and I shouldn't. I want to tell him I think he's even more handsome with age. And yet, when he smiles, he looks like his younger version, the man I knew and loved so passionately. I want to tell him how scared I am to trust him and of getting my heart ripped apart again.

I want to tell him so much but the words don't come, kisses do. The way his arms slide up my body and hold me to him, I feel all the words he wants to say.

Running my fingers into his hair, I pull him closer and kiss him, taking all the bad and flipping it around to create a perfect moment. A quick spin and I'm pinned underneath him, the cushions of our old couch soft beneath me. He's between my legs, pressing into me in a way that makes me want him in ways that aren't proper in a storage unit.

A small grind against me and my head goes back, mouth agape, eyes closed as he sucks on my neck. Right now, in this moment, I realize it wouldn't matter if we were in the middle of Times Square. I want this. I want him. Not just because I'm horny. *Or lonely. Or desperate.* But because Dylan Somers does things to me that no one else ever has. *Or ever could.*

Irrational thoughts cloud my mind as our breathing exaggerates and I feel his erection against me.

"Jules," he sighs, painfully so. Pushing himself up, looking away, he closes his eyes and shakes his head, shamed. "I'm sorry."

"Why?" I ask, "I'm not." I want him— wholly, flawed and all, just like he wants me with my flaws—flaws that we earned over the years apart. Flaws that make us who we are now. Flaws that have defined us just like how he has defined me, and I him.

"I feel like I'm taking advantage of yo—"

"You're not. I want you, Dylan." I sit up, not begging, but wanting to be understood. I look into his eyes, and I see the hint of a spark returning. "You're letting the bad take over the good. Don't. We deserve good, babe..." Before I can stop myself, it slips out just like old times. *Babe*. I wait for his reaction, not sure where his head's at with us, hoping we're on the same page.

He clears his throat, then smiles. "You really mean that, don't you?"

"About the good?"

"Yes."

"We should go, Jules. I don't want to do this with you in a dirty storage unit. You deserve better."

"You're right, I do," I say not because of the storage unit, but because I deserve to be treated better than our past. "It's time to go." Straightening my clothes, I look around at our stuff, our old life together, and my heart starts to hurt.

Taking my hand, he leads me back into the hallway before sliding the garage door back in place and securing the lock. Holding the key in front of me, he says, "Here. This is for you."

Taking the key from him, I ask, "What do you mean?"

"A couple of weeks ago, I signed over the contracts into your name. It's yours and paid for, for another full year. It's always been rightfully yours. I'm sorry I took it."

I stand there staring at him. Closing my hand around it, I grip the key tightly, pain surging from the teeth digging into my skin. "It's mine?"

"I'll also pay to have it moved to another facility or to your apartment or a donation center if you want to get rid of some of it. I owe you."

Thinking about the key, the unit, and his offer, I take his hand and we walk down the hallway together, down the stairs, following the other corridor until we see Joey at the front desk. "Joey, this is Jules Weston. She has the key to the unit. It's in her name now, so help her out if she ever needs any."

"Nice to make your acquaintance, Ms. Weston."

I can't resist friendly smile. "You too, Joey, and you can call me Jules."

"Will do. Goodnight and Happy New Year."

"Happy New Year," Dylan replies while opening the door for me.

Something about his comment makes me wonder what the date is, but a cab is driving by, so I concentrate on waving it down instead. He doesn't stop, so we start walking toward the closest train station. We're quiet for a moment. The cold wind picks up and I wrap my arms around myself to fend it off. "Why'd you show me this place? Why give it to me after all these years?"

Dylan grins while looking around, but I can see the protectiveness in the way he scans our surroundings. "Um," he starts, "I'd been meaning to send you the key for a couple of years, but I thought you might throw it all away and I didn't want that." He peeks over at me before moving closer and putting his arm around my shoulders. The warmth feels nice. "I knew I had to give everything back eventually. I just hoped for better circumstances."

"Is this a better circumstance?"

"Even if we only have today, it's better than the last four years of my life."

"It doesn't erase what happened between us."

"I know. It wasn't about that. It was about you having a say in the matter. A say that I originally took away."

Tinges of anger well inside, but I push the emotion down. "I deserved a say, but that wouldn't have changed your mind. You would have still left, even if I had begged. As we walk up the steps to the platform, I stop, stalling, and ask, "Would it have made a difference if I had begged, Dylan? Begged you to stay?" I've wanted to ask that for so long. Just releasing the words lifts a bit of the burden from my soul that I've carried around for so long.

Taking two steps down and standing in front of me, eye-level, he holds me by the elbows. "I want to tell you it wouldn't have. I don't want you to feel one iota of guilt because of something you did or didn't do back then. I had made up my mind. I was careless. I'm the only one to blame here, Jules."

In his words, I find truth. I *didn't* try. I didn't try to stop him. I let him go. I let him go without a fight, like I didn't love him at all.

"I loved you," I demand. "I loved you so much. You were a part me in every sense of who I was. That may have been wrong, but it's the truth. I'm sorry I didn't fight for us." He closes his eyes as I cup his face, and say, "I need you to know how much I loved you."

He grabs me, eyes wide, taking my breath away when he suddenly embraces me. "Please don't apologize. It makes me feel like shit. *You* never have to apologize." A sharp intake of breath and then he continues, "You deserve better, then and now, Jules" Looking away from me, he whispers, "You deserve someone like Austin and I ruined that for you. I've ruined your happiness twice."

"You didn't ruin my happiness with Austin. I loved him," I whisper while people walk by staring at us. They don't matter though. They only exist beyond our world, our bubble. "But I wasn't *in* love with him. I wouldn't have married him, Dylan. I never loved him or anyone like I've loved you."

He looks up, and although he's not smiling, his eyes are clearer, the truth seeping in, and he says, "I don't want to lose you, but you have a choice at the end of today—to love me or destroy me. It's completely up to you and if you pick the latter, I won't blame you."

"I don't want to destroy you. Even when I hated you, I loved you deep down. I know that or I wouldn't be here with you now."

He releases a deep breath—both of us feeling a weight lift a little more from our heavy hearts. I relax as he walks, guiding me to the train that just arrived. When we step on, there's only one seat available. He leads me to it, but I don't want to sit there alone. I need to be close to him. I have him sit and then I settle onto his lap, my arms going around him and kissing his temple.

Something is different between us. The lies and truths that kept us apart for so long are bringing us back together and I feel a hint of forgiveness filling me. I breathe it in, needing it as much as my need for Dylan.

At each stop, more people exit, leaving open seats. I notice a lot of them are dressed up—suits, party dresses, to the nines, but don't give it a second thought because I'm with him, healing. Feeling tired, I turn sideways, bring my knees up and let him hold me as I rest my head on his shoulder. "I'm so tired."

"Emotionally exhausted," he adds, sounding just as tired.

I smile. "Exactly."

"Are you hungry?"

"Yeah."

"I am too. Do you want to go out or do you want take-out?"

"Can we go to your place?" I ask, not wanting to face my apartment. There are too many memories and boxes, not enough life, to support us being there right now.

"Yes. Do you want to stop by your apartment and grab anything for the night?"

I nod.

He asks, "How about something spicy like Thai?"

"How about something comforting like Italian?"

"I can always eat Italian."

"Formaggios," we say in unison.

My head pops up to look at him and we laugh. I say, "You always did like that place."

"So did you. I can run down there and grab our order while you get an overnight bag packed."

"That sounds very efficient."

He smirks and I laugh. Reminiscing, he says, "I've missed Formaggios living so far away."

"Is that all you missed living so far away?" Lifting my eyes, I dare to look into the deep blues of his.

His lips part as he stares back. "I missed *you*, Baby. Is that what you want to hear?"

"I want to hear the truth."

His arms tighten around me and he kisses me. "Like you said earlier, you always were, and *are* still a part of me. I missed this. I missed you."

They're words that have consequences, but he says them anyway. He says what he feels because it's what I need to hear and I'm warmed from the inside out.

CHAPTER 10

Dylan

December 31st

I LEAN MY hands on the counter and catch my reflection in the mirror behind the bar. A smile appears, one I can't hide, one that knows I'm a lucky bastard.

The bartender tells me it will be another fifteen minutes for my food, so I order a beer. I need to take the edge off. My nerves are frayed from the last few days. I need to calm the fuck down.

It's funny how nervous I am to spend time with a girl that I spent years with before. But we're different.

I'm different.

Jules is different.

We're who we are now, not naïve like we were back then. I won't screw us up this time. I promise I won't fuck this up. I grab the order and walk the three blocks back to her place. Right when I arrive at the front door, she comes out. "Perfect timing," she says, "I'm all ready."

In the cab over to my apartment, she says, "The food smells good. I'm starving."

What I love is that she's sitting right next to me even though there's plenty of room on the other side of her. I take a chance and put my arm around her shoulders... *and she lets me.*

"I'M SO FULL," I say, rubbing my stomach while leaning back to relieve the pressure on my belt.

"So am I," she replies, exhaling. "I'd like more wine. Do you mind if I get it?"

"No, go right ahead. Please make yourself at home."

She was standing from the table when the last part of what I said makes her hesitate. *Home.* Then she whispers, "Thank you," before going into the kitchen.

"I'm glad you're here."

Simple.

The truth.

Plain.

Honest.

With the wine bottle in hand, she tops our glasses off. After setting it down, she stands next to me, then slides onto my lap sideways similar to how we sat on the train. She kisses my forehead, then says, "I want," kissing my temple, "to be here," my cheek and finally my lips, "with you."

She tugs me even closer. "I want you," she adds, just a whisper in my ear, her hand over my heart and I wonder if she realizes where her hand landed.

Fireworks.

We look toward the large window in the living room, the dark sky lights up. Jules rushes from my lap before I can stop her with excitement on her face. "It's New Years Eve," she proclaims as if she just realized, looking at the clock. "It's not midnight yet?"

"Pre-fireworks at eleven-thirty to get everyone in the spirit. The ball drops at midnight."

"Turn on the TV. I want to watch."

After turning the TV on, it blares nonsense about New Years past. I watch her instead. She's much more interesting.

"Jules?"

"Yeah," she responds so naturally, still watching the TV, as if we do this all the time.

We don't. It feels good though. "I missed you so much," I say.

When she looks back at me, her smile falters. Just a bit, but I see it. She comes back over, standing in front of me, arm reaching forward, offering to help me off the couch. I take her hand and stand when she says, "Come with me, babe."

It's an offer I can't refuse.

She leads me into the bedroom and strips her top off, revealing the most innocent of white cotton bras. For some reason I like that it's not lingerie, or lace, or satin. It's pure, innocent, and sweetness all in one.

I pull my own shirt over my head, following the silent instructions her eyes give. We don't stand there long before she moves closer, hands on my chest, fingers in the light hair she finds there. When her eyes meet mine, she says, "I love a man with chest hair."

Resting my hands on her ribs, I notice now while remembering then how small she really is. Delicate in so many ways but strong in others.

I lean down and kiss her. She returns the kiss with equal passion. But I have questions and I need answers before this goes any further. "Hey, pretty girl, what's going on between us?"

With a shy smile, she says, "I was trying to seduce you, but I don't think I'm doing a very good job of it."

I grin, lightly chuckling. "You don't have to try. I'm yours already, but are you sure? A lot has happened in the last twenty-four hours."

"I don't want you to make me forget or to replace any bad memories. I just want to be with you because you make me happy. You make me feel things I haven't felt in years."

"If we do this, there's no sneaking out of the house in the

morning. I didn't like waking up and finding you gone, Jules."

"One day at a time, remember," she murmurs against my neck while kissing me there.

I pull away, stepping back, leaving her alone in front of me. I have to or she'll end me completely. "I can't do that."

"But our talk earlier?"

"I know. I know what I'm saying is the opposite, but when you're here, whether watching TV or talking, eating take-out, or almost naked, I realize I don't want you for a day. I want you for always." I take another step back, my body hitting the wall behind me, putting more distance between us, needing to think clearly. Looking down at my belt buckle that's hanging open, remnants of what might have been, reminds me of what I might be losing by saying this. "If you need more time or..." I finally connect with her eyes. "...to leave, I'll understand. There's just no doubt in my mind. I won't need months of dating to know what I have. I know right now. I know I want you." I stand up straighter, confident in my desire. "I want you, Jules. Not just physically, but all of you. I want to see you on a normal Sunday morning with that messy bun on top of your hair while you do laundry. I want to see those tight black yoga pants you wear when reading a book or napping on the couch." I take another step forward. "I like when your makeup is smeared after sex. You make me want to make love to you all over again and mess it up even more."

Stepping closer, she reveals her own secrets. "I like watching you sleep in the early morning hours. You look at peace with the world. I like when you cook for me because you always put so much effort into it, which feels like love. I like when you walk on the outside of the sidewalk to protect me from I don't even know what, but I like that you do it."

One more step closer and I continue, "I like when you ask me to move the furniture around just so you can ogle my arms and ass as I do—"

"I do not!" She feigns offense.

"You did. Admit it!"

She grins, guiltily. "Yeah, I might do that. But in my defense, you do have a great ass and fantastic arms to ogle. Still."

My smile remains firmly in place as we close the gap between us. Stroking her cheek, I sigh. "My funny, fantastic, pretty girl. What should I do with you?"

Pressing her cheek against my chest, she also sighs. "I wish I had the answers, Dylan. I don't. I just know," she says, tilting her head up, "that I don't want to screw things up like last time."

Grabbing her face gently between my hands, I make her look me in the eyes. "You did not do anything to screw things up. Baby, please believe me when I say, it was all me and fucked up thoughts of indulgence. If I could take everything back and do it over, I would. Believe me when I tell you that every great memory I have as an adult includes you. You are the best part of me in every sense. Please forgive me. Please love me again, Jules."

Arms tighten. "I do." Just a whisper, but heard.

A kiss binds us together. Our lips stay locked as I back her toward the bed. Undoing my pants is a hassle, but I do it quickly and step out of them. Her bra comes off easily and she sits.

So willing.

So beautiful.

So forgiving.

Leaning forward, she pulls my boxers down, then rises back up and removes her own underwear. She crawls backward onto the bed, her body an open invitation. I maneuver over her, admiring the woman she's become.

Like lightning striking twice, she says, "I love you, Dylan."

The power of her words are the catalyst to held back emotions, the realization that she's thrown me a life jacket in the middle of a sea of uncertainty. The heaviness of the moment starts to take over. "You do?"

She lifts up and kisses me. "I do. I truly do, so much. I always have."

Resting on my forearms, I kiss her hard, needing to own every second of this moment. "I feel like I've waited a lifetime to hear those words. Say it again."

"I love you. I love you. I love you, babe." She giggles, relaxing back down underneath me.

She's beautiful as she smiles with not only her mouth, but her eyes.

"What happened to slow?" I ask, wondering.

"Slow went out the window."

"I love you so much. *So* much." I kiss her again, dropping my weight carefully down and sliding inside. I close my eyes as her heat takes over, clouding my mind with thoughts of love and lust, pain and pleasure. All worth it. Reality is the killer of pleasure. Against the soft skin of her shoulder, I breathe. "I don't have a condom on."

"I know," she whispers. "I'm on the pill. Make love to me."

I detect a hint of desperation in her tone as if I could stop. As if I was strong enough. Lifting my hips, I pull almost completely out, then slowly push back in—deep and slow. The pace is set when she meets me thrust for thrust, frantic. I grip onto her shoulders, plunging deeper, faster, eliciting the sounds of her pleasure.

But five words fill my ears and my heart when she says, "I missed you so much." I cave under the weight of the simple phrase that means the world to me. As I come, my sudden burst sends her spiraling into her own. Mine ceases just in time to catch the end of hers.

"I missed you, Jules," I pant, lowering down again.

I don't want to move, but I know I must, so I shift off of her, feeling the cool air hit me hard. She rolls onto her side, sliding against me and my arm drapes over her, her thigh on top of mine, body curled onto me. "Happy New Year," she says.

I turn to see the clock on the nightstand. 12:06 a.m. And I pray that the old saying that what you do at midnight is what you'll be doing all year long tale is true. I kiss her temple as her racing heart slows, relaxing, and she finds sleep in my arms.

"Happy New Year, Baby."

CHAPTER 11

Jules

January 1st

HIS SCENT IS calming and the absolute best smell to wake up to. I stir, refusing to open my eyes just in case this is all a dream. But the second and third best smells invade my world—coffee and bacon. In no particular order. I open my eyes reluctantly, feeling the empty space next to me, briefly lost in confusion.

I'm here... at Dylan's place... in his bed... naked. Smelling him, bacon, and coffee.

Although I'm not happy about waking up to an empty bed, it's his and by the amazing smells wafting from the kitchen, I know he's near. I smile, not able to hold back. Stretching, I take advantage of the large bed, then pull the sheet over my face, revelling, closing my eyes, and breathing him in even more. That's when I realize I can have the real thing in the kitchen. Not bothering with clothes, I scramble out of bed. Sauntering in, I look around the apartment—he once mentioned that he owned it. He wasn't bragging, but just... I don't know. It kind of hurts that he bought a place. *Without me.* Thinking I would never be here.

Stings.

I still rent. Afraid to truly commit to another apartment,

although let's face it, I'm pretty damn committed now since I'm still living there after six years. I probably should have moved but I couldn't. It was the only tie I had left to Dylan.

After last night, I'm finally honest with myself like I have been with him. I deserve this. I deserve happiness. My heart was always his, even when I fooled myself into thinking it could be someone else's. It couldn't. It was Dylan's all along. He's the only one who can heal me and make my soul whole again.

I round the corner into the kitchen from the hallway, a smile plastered on my face and nothing else. But the smile drops when I see a plate of bacon and scrambled eggs next to the stove, but no Dylan.

"Well good morning to you too. Nice ass by the way."

I spin around, startled and find his eyebrow cocked up high, smirk firmly in place, mug in hand. Suddenly I feel shy, exposed. My hands go to cover, but he sets the mug down and rushes me. "Don't." The word is harsh, demanding, but wanting. "Don't cover up." He takes my wrists in his hands, moving them down, out to the side, holding me open.

Coming closer, he places delicate kisses along my jaw, then up. Gentle turns passionate and heated. His hand slides over my jaw, angling me up before slipping into my hair. His other graces my side and up to squeeze my right breast. "Mmmm," I so eloquently groan.

His cock is hard, pressing against my middle, the thin cotton of his boxers offering no support. I wanted him already just from the teasing. His grip tightens on my hips, fingers pressing as he pushes me onto the wall behind.

He's rough, rougher than before. The heat from our bodies emanating and I lift my leg up. He takes it as I look into his eyes. One slight hip adjustment and he's inside me. Visions of a life grander than a mere sexual encounter frequent my thoughts.

This is it. I feel it bubbling under the surface just like my orgasm. This life. *Our* life. We'll be together, starting fresh, starting over. "I love you, Dylan," I mumble and he thrusts harder.

He makes love to me with words like 'love', 'forever', and 'mine.'

His words penetrate my heart like his body penetrates me, leaving no other option for us, but to wholly love each other.

We give and take, greedily. We come together then we fall apart. Tangled arms and legs, ragged breaths, and pounding hearts.

With a dip of his head, he leans his forehead against mine and says, "You really shouldn't walk around naked."

"If that's what I get every time I walk around naked, you will never find me clothed."

He chuckles and my heart jumps, absorbing the sound, taking it in like fresh air. He sets me down carefully on shaky legs, holding me up until I'm stable. "I was worried you'd change your mind in the light of day."

"About what?" I can't help the slight pang I feel inside, hurt for both of us.

"Us," Dylan whispers in a way that I can tell he's afraid his fears, like mine, will become reality.

"I didn't." I want to say *never* but I can't. I feel it, but I can't say it just yet.

Knowing me as well as he does, he changes the subject. "You hungry?"

"Starved."

MID-MORNING COMES and I've planted myself on the couch, pretending to read a book, but really I'm watching Dylan. I think he knows I am, but he hasn't said anything. He continues watching a sports commentary show. I never minded his obsession with sports. It was something he really enjoyed, though sometimes I thought it frustrated him more. He turns, catching me staring.

I smile, he grins as he rubs my thigh, then turns his attention back to the TV. "This feels weirdly normal," I state easily, comfortable here.

His hand shifts to my knee and he squeezes lightly. "Is it weird or normal?"

"Weirdly normal."

He laughs, but I can tell he's thinking about this more than he's letting on. "Yes, it does feel weirdly normal. Like the old days."

"Yeah, a lot like that."

"How do you feel about that?" He gives me his complete attention.

"I feel okay with it. You?"

"I'm happy. It feels good to be with you like this." Leaning over, he gives me three quick kisses on the mouth.

After another hour passes and the pre-show is in full effect. The weight of the situation has had time to settle into my bones. "Maybe I should go." *This shouldn't feel as good as it does this soon, should it?* Doubts start seeping in. *Is it wrong for us to move this fast?*

Walking with my empty coffee mug into the kitchen, I set it down, then feel his arms around me. His lips at my ear. "Do you want to go or do you want to stay?"

"I want what you want." I don't know why this feels so right, so easy. *Is it too easy?*

Spinning me around, he says, "I want you with me."

"I want that too." I do. I just don't know if I should. *Am I giving in too soon?*

"I can turn the game off. We could go for a walk?" He's trying and I know it's for me because in that moment right then, I see the man I've always loved—open heart, thoughtful, attentive, intuitive.

"I don't want you to miss it. I remember how much you love football."

"It doesn't matter, you do."

There's no hiding my smile when he says such sentiments so freely. I hug him, absorbing all that is him into my senses, allowing myself this happiness because I deserve happiness in its purest form. That's what he is to me. That spiteful hate crept away and left me happy. I don't know when it happened and I don't want to question it. I just want to enjoy this for a while.

"You're lost in thought."

"There's a lot to think about," I say, looking up. I pull back just enough to take him in. Strong jaw, handsome face, meaningful eyes. "I'm gonna go home and change clothes."

Arms tighten around me. "Stay. Wear mine."

I laugh. "Dylan, if I go, I'll return. I promise. I know you're worried. I can see and feel it. I'm worried too. I'm worried that if I step outside this bubble it will pop. That's why I've got to do just that. I need to know this is real."

Taking my hand, holding it against his heart, he pleads, "This is real, Jules. I need you to believe that before you leave."

"I want to," I whisper, not quite understanding why I'm suddenly so emotional. "I'm not running away. I'm just going to change clothes, pick up a few things. I'll be back and if you'll have me, I'll stay the night."

"*If* I'll have you? Are you insane, woman!" He smiles. "There's no if. You're it, always."

Leaning forward again, I just want to be closer though we're pretty close as it is. "I won't be long."

"Okay." He gives in, trusting I'll return.

I leave him watching the game. Dylan seemed content, but I could see the worry in his eyes, by the crease in his forehead. Just outside his building, I walk to the curb, then catch my breath, breathing in the cool January air before I flag down a taxi.

I miss him already.

A KNOCK ON the door startles me. I shove the t-shirt I'm packing into my overnight case before walking across the apartment and answer it.

"Hey there." Brandon greets me with a smile.

"Come in," I say, smiling back and pulling him in by the cuff of his sleeve before closing the door. "How are you?"

"I should be asking you that. How are you?"

I return to my room to continue packing the toiletries. "Better than expected."

"Going somewhere?"

"Dylan's."

"So, all is forgiven and you're moving on and... moving in or what?"

He's not being mean or judgmental, just curious and protective. I understand. "One day at a time. Yesterday was a good day for us. We talked and," I say, shrugging, "I had my questions answered. I don't know. Honestly, I'm not gonna overthink this. I feel more at peace with this decision than I thought I would."

"Jules—"

"Brandon, please." I can't look up at him right now. If I do, I'll cry and I don't want to cry. I just want to continue feeling this happiness that has invaded me wholly. "I know you care about me and you're worried. But, he's changed. I can feel it. It's not just his words. It's everything." I know from how he looks at me and his tentative touches, his firm grips and the way he moves when near. "He's aware of what he's lost, of what he threw away. He's showing me how sorry he is. So please don't take this away from me, not now, not after all I've been through."

He steps closer, bending down so he's eye-level and grins, cheekily. "I was going to say I think Dylan's changed for the better. I think his heart just might be in the right place."

"Really? You support this, *us?*"

"Don't get me wrong, Jules, I'm angry about the past shit he put you through, but... I think it's time we all found some good out of the bad. And honestly, I think he just might be the only one who will ever heal your heart."

I throw my arms around his neck, tears falling carelessly onto his shoulder. "Thank you. Thank you. Thank you, Brandon. You don't know how much that means to me."

"Anything for you. You know that, right?"

I nod, because yes, I do know that.

I WAIT OUTSIDE his door for him to answer. Running feet pad across a wood floor in a rush to answer, and the door flies open.

He's there. Breathless, handsome as ever with a huge smile. "You came back."

"I told you I would." I saunter past him while flashing a confident grin.

"I hoped."

I drop my bag and hug him because I can. I can now hug him as much as I want and I might just take advantage of the fact. "Who won?" I ask, referring to the game.

But he has others ideas. "I did."

I roll my eyes. "Okay, you had me at take-out last night. You can drop the Mr. Charming act now."

"It's not an act, Jules," he replies, slipping his hand into mine and pulling me into the kitchen. "I really am charming."

I burst out laughing. "And so humble, too."

"I never claimed to be humble." He pours me a glass of white wine while chuckling. "I ordered pizza. The salad on the pie version you always liked. Do you still?"

He makes me happy and I like the feeling. "I do." I sip, calming the giddy nerves inside. "How long until it arrives?"

"They're busy because of the game. We've got about forty-five minutes left from their estimate."

"Good." I pull him closer by the t-shirt, fisting it, and holding on tight.

A small smirk plays at the corners of his mouth as he lifts me up so I'm sitting on the counter. My legs are spread and he makes himself at home between them. He's hard. I'm wet, and we haven't even kissed. I stagger for air, feeling lightheaded as he moves forward, his lips seeking mine, his hands already gripping my hips, holding me in place. Just as the fullness of his bottom lip hits mine, he whispers, "I want you. I need you so much. My Jules. *My Juliette.*"

Slipping my tongue between his parted lips, I eat his words, devouring them and his needs. I slide my hand down his chest, not caring that his shirt is stretched out and wrinkled from my tight hold. Down further and over his abs that take work to get and more work to maintain.

Down further to his cock. I palm, feeling his erection. A moan from him to me, savoring the sound, I respond with my own. He pulls his shirt off abruptly, tossing it... somewhere. My lips slide down his neck, taking him in, smiling. "Mmmm," I moan, getting lost in him completely. It's so easy to do, just like old times. Just like our best of times. Our bodies connect through passionate kisses, caressing touches, and sexual stroking.

My arms are up, my shirt is coming off as he tosses it away like he did his own. Dylan kisses the tops of my breasts, his hands sliding up my ribs and appreciating the sides of my breasts. Then he cups them, massaging for both of our pleasure.

A thought occurs, bugging me when I should be oblivious to the world outside. I ask, needing to verify, "This is real between us, it's not just sexual, right?"

His lids are heavy with desire but he stops, surprised by my question. "It's real." His hands hold my face steady as his words are scattered across my skin through a warm breath. I tighten my legs around him not wanting him to leave this spot. "Don't think that." His brow furrows. "*We* are not just about sex. We're more than that. We always were. I thought you were feeling the same way."

"I do. I just needed to make sure. Are we moving too fast?"

"Too fast for what? Too fast for whom?"

"What will I tell my parents?"

Amused, but slightly bewildered by my comment he asks, "So, let me get this straight. We're half naked right now, leading into soon to be completely naked and you want to know if your parents will approve of us or not? I think I just lost my hard-on."

I stroke his cock. "Nope, still hard. Maybe even harder than before. I think you might be into dirty parent talk—" I'm laughing too hard to finish my sentence.

"No, just no. Stop this. I need brain bleach." He squints his eyes and shakes his head around like he's in pain.

Grabbing him by the back of the neck, I pull him closer, both of us smiling. "It feels so good to laugh like this. It's been ages."

"Agreed," he says, stealing a kiss.

"I missed you."

"I missed you too, but luckily you weren't gone too long."

"I mean more than tonight."

There's a silence between us as he stares into my eyes, searching, finding what he needs. "I missed you, Jules... more than just tonight, too."

He kisses the corner of my mouth, lingering a moment. Eventually, he scoops me off the counter and sets me down on my own two feet. I'm slightly disappointed but I know the sexual build-up has passed. "I'll get the plates ready. You go watch the game," I offer.

I bring two plates, napkins and my wine, setting them on the table and settle down on the couch next to him. His hand finds its place on my knee and he smiles letting me know all is okay.

CHAPTER 12

Dylan

February 14th

OVER A MONTH has passed and she's still here. Nothing is taken for granted. Too much time lost. Too much time to make up for.

She still lives at her apartment, but she's here a lot or I'm over at our old place. We took it one day at a time for about two days and then we just gave in completely and placed our trust in each other.

It's late and I decide we need to go to bed. She fell asleep over an hour ago and as much as I love holding her, it's cramped on the couch. I scoot out from under her, turn off the TV, and the lamp before leaning down and picking her up carefully. Her eyes open and a gentle smile appears as she wraps her arms around my neck. "You used to carry me to bed all the time."

"You're still light as a feather. I should feed you better," I tease, aiming to get another smile before bed.

She laughs lightly, still sleepy. "Don't worry. I'm sure I'll put on those love pounds soon enough."

"Love pounds? Yes, let's both pack'em on and just grow old, fat, and be happy together."

Her smile stays as she leans her head on my shoulder. "That sounds like a plan."

After getting ready for bed, she snuggles into my side. "Are you sure you're fine with the no gift thing. I know it's a bit untraditional—"

"I could be lame and say you're my gift this year."

"Yeah, don't say that. It's *sooooo* bad."

I chuckle in the dark room. "Okay, I won't. Are you sure *you're* okay with the no gift idea. I mean it is Valentine's? Only comes once a year."

"I don't need anything—"

"Valentine's isn't about buying something needed—"

"It's about being together and showing how much you care about the person you're with. You do that every day, Dylan. I have everything I want and need." She pokes me in the side, trying to tickle me. "Now all your lameness has rubbed off on me."

"Oh, I almost forgot. Will you be my Valentine, Jules?" I hear the pillow whooshing through the air, but I'm too slow to stop it. It hits me in the face. "Okay, okay," I say, my voice muffled from under the weight of the down pillow. "How about goodnight then?"

"Perfect. Goodnight. Sweet dreams," she says calmly, but I can tell she wants to laugh. She drags the pillow back and repositions herself against me. Minutes pass and I'm starting to doze off when I hear her whisper, "Yes."

With my eyes still closed, I mumble, "Huh?"

"I'll be your Valentine, but only on one condition."

I smile though she can't see me. "What's that?"

"That you'll be mine."

I roll onto my side and hug her closer. "You got yourself a Valentine, sweetness."

I wake up around four in the morning. My eyes squinting in the dark to find the yarn I hid under my alarm clock.

Jules' breathing is steady, solid, deep. She's definitely asleep, but knowing she's a light sleeper, I move slowly, carefully, taking her left hand off me and setting it down very gently. I tie the red yarn around her finger and make a bow before kissing it and going back to sleep.

A SLIGHT SHAKE of the bed and what sounds like crying wakes me. Quickly opening my eyes, I see tears stream down Jules' face as she gazes up at her hand, which she's holding in the air.

"You remembered. I forgot," she says, sniffling.

"I want you to remember too though." Back in college, the red yarn was a promise that one day I'd replace it with a ring. I'm making that same promise again... but this time I'll follow through.

"I'll try." She looks straight into my eyes in the softly lit room, the sun just barely above the horizon.

"One day you'll forget all the bad and remember only the good. I'll give you that. You deserve to remember only happiness. You deserve to have beautiful memories of our life together."

Stroking my cheek, she tries to smile though the heavier emotions are clearly winning. "Our life together has always been beautiful. It's the times without you that are painful."

She's right. We were so good together, even up to the day I left her. Her eyes close as she rests her head on my chest, crying. I rub her head and say, "I wish I could erase—"

"Wishing is pointless. The bad brought us back to the now, so no wishing. Let's just live in our reality, scars, battle wounds, and all that comes with a past apart."

"Okay." I agree because I have to. Wishing won't do either of us any good but I really do wish...

CHAPTER 13

Jules

March 7th

I'M TRYING TO be an active listener at Dylan's work party, but some of these financial conversations are really boring. I smile and play along. Stocks, bonds, and bankruptcies aren't topics that I can easily add anything of value to, especially when I don't understand what they're talking about.

Thank God I don't have to be anything but myself with Dylan. I watch him talk, fascinated by how much he's learned and changed from the boy I once dated. He holds my hand, asking my thoughts, showing me how much he loves me. I've engaged in plenty of chitchat tonight, been called beautiful several times, but is it bad if I'm already ready to leave and spend the rest of the night in bed with him instead?

Bed. That's become my favorite place, my favorite escape from the world. It's been hard to set aside the past, but I've been doing it. If I'm not careful, it tends to catch up with me when we're apart.

The CEO has summoned Dylan to join in another business discussion, so I offer to refresh our drinks at the open bar. He's an asset to the company, a rising star. I see that tonight. Dylan's watches as I walk away. He's always watching me, afraid I'm leaving.

I hate that he feels that way, but I understand it too.

For almost a year after he left, I thought I saw Dylan walking around our neighborhood: at the local grocer, the coffee shop, buying a paper at the drugstore like he used to do. But it was never him. I questioned my sanity when reality hit. I also never dared to bring him up to his mother. I wasn't strong enough to lose that bond or to hear about his great life without me. But I also knew she'd tell me if anything major was going on with him like surgery, marriage, kids. She never had to. Thank God.

I still hate that he left, but now... I'm officially out as his girlfriend to his co-workers. I saw disappointment on some of the women's faces and one of the male law clerks when we walked in, which made me smile inwardly and outwardly.

His assistant Tricia is really sweet, almost too excited to meet me. She used words like 'finally', and 'so happy.' She seems genuinely happy too, not jealous, not conniving. She whispered that since Dylan and I have been together, he's been in a great mood at work and that he's a great boss. I started chuckling because my co-workers at the gallery have said the same thing since our reconciliation.

None of them know this is a reconciliation though. I never went into the gory details with them.

I've seen Jacqueline several times out of the corner of my eye. I haven't run in to her yet. I'm anxious about that, even though I shouldn't be. Truth be told, I've been avoiding her. She knows too much and it makes me uncomfortable. I can only imagine what she thinks of me.

After approaching the bar, I glance back at Dylan. He's discussing something intently, nodding and using his hands to emphasize some point. It appears to be an intense conversation. I hope it's nothing bad, not wanting the good mood ruined.

I order him a beer and another glass of champagne for me. With drinks in hand, I turn, my eyes meeting Austin's, making me halt abruptly. Drops of champagne spill over the edge of the glass, the cold hitting my skin.

He grabs napkins quickly from the bar and dabs my wrist, ridding me of the liquid. "I'm sorry for startling you, Jules."

An automatic response flows from me, "Oh no, it was my fault. I wasn't watching where I was going." I try to smile, to bury the feelings that threaten to come. My heart is pounding too hard in my chest to think logically.

I move forward, unsure if I should stay or go. He moves too, but I'm going to Dylan and he seems to be coming with me, so I stop. I have trouble smiling, my stomach turning from guilt. His expression is kind and in a way, comforts me. He smiles and says, "It's really good to see you. How have you been?" Austin has always been too much of a gentleman, too kind for his own good.

"I'm good. I didn't expect to see you here."

"My company is one of their largest accounts, so they always send us an invitation to their events." Here it comes. I can see it in his eyes. "So you're here with Dylan?"

I look over his shoulder and see the topic of conversation. Dylan's eyes flash to mine and then to Austin before he returns his gaze back to the discussion he seems stuck in. He looks restless, unsettled in his stance. He has nothing to worry about, but I'm not sure he believes that completely yet.

I'm his. I always was. "Yes. I'm here with Dylan."

He nods as if he knew all along. "So it was more serious than I thought."

"It was more serious than I thought too, Austin. I'm sorry. I feel like—"

"You don't need to apologize or explain. I don't feel duped or anything like that. I've spent a lot of time trying to figure out what went wrong. I've been flying to China a lot lately, so I've had plenty of time to think about it on those long flights." He laughs, but there's no humor. "I don't think you knew your own feelings until he was back in the picture. I'm just sorry for the timing. Maybe if... Yeah, I'm not going down that road." He looks around, his real emotions starting to break through his smile. "I don't live my life based on what-if's, so I try not dwell." He leans closer and whispers, "I should tell you, I'm seeing someone too. She's heading this way."

And there she is—long legs, about a foot taller than me, blonde hair, blue eyes. She wraps her arms around his shoulders and kisses him on the cheek. "Did you miss me?"

"I ran into a friend of mine. This is Jules Weston. Jules, Misty Connors."

As I say hello, it doesn't escape me that he didn't respond to her question.

I hear an accent in her greeting, but I can't determine where she's from. She eyes me, assessing me from head to toe. I need to get out of this awkward situation. "I should go and deliver thes—"

"Jules?" Dylan has finally escaped and is here by my side. "Austin," he acknowledges politely, shaking his hand with a smile. Not gloating, but not hiding either.

"Hope you don't mind me monopolizing your date, Dylan. We've been catching up." Austin's voice is tight, bitter feelings toward Dylan still lingering.

Dylan looks from me with concern, but to him with confidence. "Completely understandable when talking to Juliette. I hear your company expansion is going well."

Austin's eyes are on me as he answers him, "Very well indeed. How's the gallery?"

"We've had an expansion of our own and decided to open another gallery in Tribeca. It should open by the fall of next year."

"That's great news. You always had an eye for talent. By the way, I thought about you the other day because I just bought a house in Los Angeles. The office is strong and growing fast out there, so I needed more than just a hotel room when I visit. I could really use your eye for some key pieces to add to my art collection. Some art that would complement the new house. Do you make house calls? Your expenses paid for, of course."

Misty looks bored with us. "I'm getting a drink," she states, turning abruptly and leaving.

Dylan's hand is on my lower back, fingers gripping my waist, holding me close, silently claiming me as his. "I don't think that's appropriate," Dylan replies, surprising me.

He's right. It's not considering our dating history, but I'm still surprised that Dylan made his feelings known like that.

Austin eyes him, annoyed as if intruded upon.

"I'd be happy to send you a list of colleagues in LA who could help you," I interject to keep things civil.

Dylan's name is called. We look to see his boss waving him over again. "Shit," he mumbles.

"It's fine. Go ahead," I say, handing him his drink. "I'll join you in a moment."

"Not longer than a moment though."

"No, not longer," I smile, reassuring.

"Austin, it was good to see you again."

"Likewise, Dylan."

They sound bizarrely sincere.

When he leaves, Austin asks, "Are you happy, Jules?" His tone is somber.

I don't have to think about it because the answer is easy, the answer is obvious. "I am. I hope you are too. Misty seems...you know." I leave it at that, hoping he understands he's worth so much more than arm candy.

"I take it you don't approve?"

"It doesn't matter, does it?"

"Your opinion still matters to me, more than it should."

"In that case, I think she's an airhead who wants to marry money, party, and live the life that you can afford to provide her with." That was probably a bit rough and rude. "I'm sorry. I shouldn't hav—"

Chuckling, he says, "Go ahead and tell me how you really feel. So you surmised all that in the few minutes she was here?"

I may not be in love with him, but I care and I don't want him taken advantage of. "She's not good enough for you."

"I can say the same about Dylan."

"I appreciate your concern, but we're not together for superficial reasons. He values me and respects my career. I think you've underestimated him."

"I most definitely did when *we* were together." He shakes his head, reflecting. "Your birthday dinner... yeah, I feel really stupid that I didn't pick up on any of that."

Stepping forward, I place my hand on his forearm. "I'm sorry, Austin. I'm sorry for hurting you. You didn't deserve it."

I can tell he wants to argue that fact, but it's fruitless and he knows it. Our eyes meet and an understanding seems to be silently reached. That's my cue to leave on somewhat of a good note.

"I should get going." I signal over my shoulder before sipping my champagne.

I start to turn, but he stops me by the elbow. "Please, don't go. Stay."

Looking down at his hand on me, the emotion he put into the gesture has my head spinning until... I'm not. *Clarity.*

"Austin, you can do better. Don't settle for someone who is just a bed warmer. Stay single until you find that someone who warms your heart. Misty's not that girl and I guess I wasn't either."

"He's the one, isn't he?"

"Dylan's always been the one."

He leans forward, kisses my cheek, then whispers in my ear, "Live a happy life. You deserve it."

I stop him before he can leave and whisper, "Thank you. So do you. Don't forget that."

While returning to Dylan's side, I glance over my shoulder and see Austin hold his drink in the air. I raise my glass to him, leaving him with a smile. When I face forward, my eyes meet Dylan's.

He's right. I realize that now. We're ready. I want this. Dylan wants this. No holding back anymore. When I approach, he takes my free hand, brings it to his lips and kisses gently.

The others are too engrossed in themselves and their conversation to pay us any heed, so I lift up on my tiptoes and kiss him on the lips before whispering, "I love you."

He kisses my temple and repeats, "I love you."

CHAPTER 14
Jules
March 13th

I STROKE HIS cheek while he sleeps, remembering tomorrow is that dreaded date—March 14th. I haven't brought it up, not wanting to bring any negativity to all the good we've shared.

"I'm giving you my heart, Dylan. I'm trusting you to take care of it."

A kiss to his forehead and stroke across his cheek wakes him, and he replies, "I will. I promise."

May

I'VE BEEN FEELING very at peace with us. We never did 'slow' very well, but even this might be too fast.

At dinner, Dylan mentions that he hopes to have the whole white picket fence, two kids, marriage package. That makes my heart soar. Looking over at me, he smiles and I can see the love in his eyes.

I think I'm coming around to the same idea of forever.

July

WE VISIT HIS family for a weekend in the Hamptons. It's a casual, relaxing time. Renews the spirit to be away from the city. It seems our troubles are finally in the past.

One afternoon, he builds a sand castle with two little boys staying with their grandparents, friends of his parents visiting for the day. I spend the whole time watching him, wondering if he's feeling the same ticking I'm feeling to have kids.

By the time we go to bed, back in the city, on Sunday night, I've come to the conclusion that I need to stop wondering and start planning.

August

"I WANT TO live together," he states one Sunday afternoon. Football on the flat screen, him lying across the couch with his head in my lap, reading a book.

I look down. He looks up. "Really?" I ask.

His gaze goes back to the TV, attempting nonchalance like this isn't a big deal, but we both know better.

This is a very big deal.

"Yeah," he says, shrugging. "We're together every night anyway. It gets tiring lugging stuff back and forth. I'm sure you're tired of that too."

"Where would you want to live? Here or at my place?"

"I'm not sure. I've thought about it and there are pros and cons to both. I wanted to talk to you first, not just have it all planned out already." He sits up, dropping his feet to the ground and faces me. "You want to move in here?"

I look around the place and say, "I'm home wherever you are, but a new place might be nice. Someplace that's between our two jobs to make the morning commute easier."

"That would be good, but are you ready to move? You've lived there a long time."

"Lived?" I ask, rhetorically. "Hm. I only lived there when you did. And Brandon only has two months left, then he's moving uptown when he returns from his vacation with Cara. Nothing ties me to here anymore."

He kisses me gently, and says, "You're my home too."

September — Dylan

MY PLACE SOLD above asking price within two weeks of putting it on the market. We ended up having a bidding war between three offers and took the highest. Jules' apartment, *our old one*, was left to the landlord to deal with after we paid to get out of her lease.

I was worried about her leaving it behind, leaving it for good. After all, she stayed even after I left, so I know she's attached, but she's reassured me. She told me she was ready and as I watch her direct the movers—so confident, so sure of herself—I let it go, trusting her words, trusting that she's happy about starting our life together somewhere new.

"MARRY ME. I want you to be my wife. I want to be your husband. I want to be married to you forever, always."

She sits upright, grabbing her stomach, maybe I went about this the wrong way. I hope not. Her face is serious, mouth agape. Now she's the one staring at me.

"Dylan?" she says, stunned as she swings her feet toward the floor and leans toward me.

"I haven't done this right. I let my feelings get away from me." Pulling the box from my back pocket, I get into a kneeling position, on one knee and hold her hand. I open the box, then ask, "Jules, I love you with my heart and soul. I will love you way beyond the years of this lifetime. Will you marry me and be my eternity?"

There's no pause or hesitation. Just a flurry of arms wrapping around me, her body pressing against mine. "Oh Dylan, yes. I love you so much too. Yes." *Kiss.* "Yes!" *Kiss.* "Yes!"

October – Jules

WE GOT MARRIED as soon as we could. We didn't want to wait. "It's raining," I remark, pouting a bit.

"That's good luck," my mom says. "Stand up and let me get a picture of you. Say cheese."

"Cheese." Just as the camera snaps, my stomach growls. "Cheese sounds good. I'm hungry."

"You think you can wait until after the ceremony? We've only got five minutes left." My mom sees my frown, then goes to dig something out of her purse and says, "Eat this quickly. Hopefully it will tide you over for a bit."

I happily take the granola bar.

"You look beautiful, Juliette," Dylan's mom says while fluffing my veil.

I'm a whole basket case of emotions today. "You have to say that, Carol, it's my wedding day."

"No, actually, I don't have to say that. I once told Mary Stein that her newborn looked like Winston Churchill."

"No you didn't. You're too nice to hurt someone's feelings like that."

She adjusts the pearl necklace around my neck, her gift to me.

"You're right, but I thought it. I've often wondered if Churchill's mother thought him a cute baby." I burst out laughing. She stands back with my mother at her side and says, "See, now you're smiling. Everything is just as it should be on your wedding day."

Two minutes later, I'm touching up my lipstick and my dad comes in. "I was threatened not to ruin your makeup. So, I'm not going to *ooh* and *ahh* like the women do."

I smile.

But when I stand back up, I see his eyes begin to water. "You'll always be my beautiful princess, Juliette." He turns around to collect himself, which brings tears to my eyes.

I touch his arm and when he turns back, I hug him. "Thank you, Dad."

"We need to get you to that altar before I become a blubbering mess."

"Hey dad, can I ask you something before we go?"

"Sure."

"Why do I feel a little shame, like I'm letting someone down because I took him back? What's everyone gonna think about us, you know, because of the bad breakup and stuff?"

His expression softens. "You know, you shouldn't feel anything but love and happiness on this special day. Dylan's proven to us that he loves you. He made a big mistake, but as for being a couple, everyone has struggles and faces roadblocks in life. It's how you handle them and come out the other side that matters. Anyway, the people who matter most are here to support you, not question your judgment. You know what's best for you."

"Thank you," I say as we hug. He's right. The people we hold most dear in our lives are here to support us, not judge us. "That's just what I needed to hear."

"You ready now?"

"Yes, very."

I catch a glimpse of Dylan standing under the arbor as I pass through the glass conservatory of the botanical gardens. I stop, slightly breathless at the sight.

"You all right, Juliette?"

I look up to my dad and smile to reassure. "Yes, I'm fine."

We continue on, rounding the patio, our eyes lock and the world seems to disappear. All I see is Dylan. Only him. Always him.

Twenty people. That's all that's in attendance.

All that truly matters—their support, love, and friendship keeping us afloat in times of need. I keep my emotions from overwhelming me by focusing on the happy of the moment.

The music begins and I take a deep breath, then we walk.

It's surreal standing here after the journey we've taken to get to this point. I could have never predicted after our breakup that we'd get back together, much less get married one day. My heart knows he's the one... maybe it always did. The best part is he knows as well now. We both had to find out the hard way, but looking back and feeling this happy, I realize there was never another option for us. Our lives were always going to be entangled. Even more so now.

Taking his hands, the minister says a few words, but I don't hear any of them. Looking into Dylan's eyes, I see my eternity in the depth of his brilliant blues and I smile.

"Juliette?"

I respond when I hear my name. "Yes?"

"Your vows," the minister whispers.

I don't need a script and I didn't write anything down. I nod, ready for this. "You once told me you couldn't stay away. I'm so glad you didn't. There's no glory in easy and we have definitely not taken the easy road to get here." His hands tighten around mine as I smile up at him. "I thought I could disappear, move forward without my heart. I was fooling myself. Life began when you returned to me, returning my heart in the process. I love you, Dylan Somers, with all my soul and every fiber, muscle, and nerve of my being. I am forever yours and you mine. I'm honored to call you my husband and looking forward to our eternity together."

Despite tradition, he leans down and kisses my cheek just as I look down, my sentimental side showing in my tear-filled eyes.

Glancing to the minister, he nods, then Dylan says, "You were always my fair Juliette. You gave me a reason to live, a purpose in life, when I was just trying to survive another day. You guided the way when I was lost. Like the North Star, you led this wayward soul home again. With you by my side, as my wife, I'll never wander and I'll never be lost again. I promise to love and cherish, to obey," he adds with a smirk. "I will honor you every day of this life and forever more into the next. I love you, Juliette."

After a pause, and I release a long held breath, the ministers says, "You may kiss your bride."

Dylan, beaming with pride and love, leans down and kisses me. Like our very first kiss, my knees weaken, but his hands are strong, as he holds me. We're announced as the married couple we are, and make our way up the aisle and out to a side yard. His mother set up a little bistro table for us with orange juice, two chairs, and a few moments of privacy.

Tilting his lips to my ear, Dylan whispers, "I will love you for lifetimes to come." He kisses my cheek.

"I'll love you more."

CHAPTER 15

Dylan

December

SPEECHLESS.

Silent.

Two pink lines.

Three white sticks being waved in the air.

Pregnant.

Pregnant.

Pregnant.

"Pregnant?" I ask like I don't know the meaning of the words.

She nods, confirming, "Yes. A baby, Dylan."

I feel lightheaded.

I need to sit down.

But I need to know more. "How do you feel?"

"I feel good."

Not what I'm looking for though I'm relieved she feels all right. Gauging, I ask, "I'm mean are you happy to be pregnant?"

Tears stream freely as a smile forms, her eyes alight, "I'm happy, babe. I'm really happy."

I reach for her, holding her to me, needing to feel her against me. "You're having a baby," I whisper into her hair.

"*We're* having a baby."

Shit. *I'm* having a baby.

With Jules.

She's having *my* baby.

So many questions race through my head. Too many. I need to sit.

"Come sit with me." I take her hand and pull her with me.

We sit and look at each other. That glow people talk about is ever present. She's already glowing from the inside out. "You're really happy, aren't you?"

She does this bounce of excitement on the cushion, lifting my hand to her mouth and kissing it. "I'm so happy. I really am. I'm with you and I'm having your baby. How can I not be happy? How can I not be thrilled right now? Are you happy about this? About the baby?"

I take a second to try to comprehend the news, but my heart, *fuck*, even my head tells me I don't need that second. "I'm happy. I'm shocked, surprised, but I'm really happy too."

A gentle smile crosses her face as she scoots onto my lap. Her arms surround me and she kisses my temple. "I love you, Dylan." Only a moment passes before she adds, "I want lots of kids with you."

Tonight I kiss her until her lips are swollen, then I kiss her stomach and our baby goodnight. I lay there holding her and thanking God for this second life I've been given.

January

"Stop staring at me."

"I can't help it. You're so beautiful."

"I just threw up twice. I'm pale and pissy and you think I'm beautiful?" She shakes her head and scoffs. "You must really be in love, Mr. Somers."

"I am." I walk closer, sitting on the floor next to the couch where she's lying. She looks tired, dark circles under her eyes and yes, pale, but never more beautiful. "So in love, Mrs. Somers."

WE FINALLY SETTLE into our new home. It took forever to find and we were sick of living in a rental uptown. We move into a townhouse—four bedrooms, an office, a small backyard, exposed brick. She loves it. She loved it the minute she saw it and we bought it.

All the stuff is unpacked. All the stuff we decided to keep from our separate apartments and the storage unit doesn't seem like much when sitting in this large place.

I just paid the movers and I need a beer after being coerced by her feminine wiles to help carry about ten boxes up from the truck. I grab a beer out of the fridge. While drinking, I notice she's not around. I set the beer on the counter behind me and walk through the living room, my steps echoing across the wood floors. I don't call because I think she's upstairs.

I check our room and then the baby's room... I had a feeling. Don't know why I didn't come in here first. There she is. Sitting in the rocker in the corner, arm draped over her stomach protectively, eyes closed, humming.

Content.

I quietly kneel in front of her, trying not to disturb, but wanting to be close. She continues to hum. *Contentment feels good.*

"DYLAN!"

I run. I run so fast into the bedroom where she was napping when she calls for me. She's sitting upright, hand over the small pooch that has formed in at her midsection. "Dylan! He moved. The baby moved."

"What! *Really?*" I sigh, thankful she's safe, that she's all right.

"Yes, hurry. Come here and feel," she replies, smiling and waving me closer. I rush, sitting down next to her. She places my hand on her stomach and shushes me. I smile but don't laugh, waiting, anticipating, but nothing happens. After a minute or two, I'm a bit disappointed, but I don't say so. I don't want to ruin the moment for her though I can see she's a little disappointed too. She starts talking to the baby, then humming, but still nothing. "Maybe he's gone back to sleep."

"You're so sure it's a boy, aren't you?"

"I know it's a boy."

"How?"

"It's just a feeling, but I know it."

"So you'll be happy with a boy?"

"I'm happy with whatever we get, but yes, a boy, someone like you."

She's all heart and soul. I can't hold my smile. This feeling is bigger than that. As I gaze into her eyes, I see forgiveness and love. And I'm rendered speechless.

"Don't cry, babe," she says, wiping one of my tears away. Leaning forward she replaces the tear with a kiss. Lying back, she takes me with her, holding me close, my head on her chest and gently strokes my hair.

I hope one day I'll deserve her, hoping I'm worthy of her kindness and love.

Everything. I will be everything she dreams of, wants, and needs. The baby moves beneath my hand, under my chin. One solid kick that startles me and I lift quickly to watch.

Another good kick and I laugh. "Hello, baby. Hi in there." A double kick and I lose it, laughing. Looking at her, I proclaim, "The baby knows me. He knows my voice, Jules."

Her smile turns gentle. "Well, of course, he does. You're his dad."

"I'm his dad." *Yes, I am his dad.*

May

MY HANDS ARE sweating. Jules is smiling, perfectly content, knowing she's right.

The sonogram technician announces, "It's a boy!"

"You knew!" I say, "You knew all along." I kiss her forehead just as smugness takes over her expression. "Go ahead. I know you want to."

"I told you so," she sing-songs, then laughs, making the technician laugh as well.

A month later, my thoughts are on her as I paint the baby's room the perfect shade of sky blue, the perfect shade according to Jules. She's the artistic visionary, so I do as I'm told. It makes me happy to do these domestic things. Grounds me to our life, a daily reminder of how good I have it.

A muralist shows up a day later to paint a universe across the ceiling, not dark and scary but a lighter, quite impressive one. "A universe of opportunities," Jules says proudly.

The crib, changing table, and rocking chair are in place. Most details yet to come except for two I wasn't aware of. I find her in the chair, rocking slowly back and forth when I arrive home from work one evening. "Hi," I greet, leaning against the doorframe.

She smiles softly in the dim light of the fading day. "I picked the paintings up from the framers today."

"Paintings?"

Her eyes are bright, happy as she stands and picks up two framed pictures while turning them around. I thought these would be great in the baby's room. I laugh aloud when I see them. Great memories come back from our third date so many years ago.

"You kept these?" I ask.

"Actually, *you* kept these. I found them in a box that was brought over from the storage room."

I hold up the kitten paint-by-numbers and smile. "I did a damn fine job on this."

"Yes, you did, but I'm partial to my puppy painting."

I chuckle. "I think they're both pretty fantastic, just like the artists."

"Only you know how to work a compliment for yourself into the conversation while praising others."

With a smirk, I say, "I call it talent."

"Oh you're talented all right." She leans up and kisses me on the lips, lingering a moment to enjoy it. I know why she does this, because I do the same.

Come July, Jules is big. I don't say that out loud, but she is. She's basically waddling into the kitchen and sits down. But I love every pound she's put on, every love pound she's gained for our baby. Looking across the table at her, I ask, "You nervous about having the baby and how life will change?"

"No. What reason would I have to be nervous? I know what I'm getting myself into."

Laughing, I flirt. "Oh baby, you haven't seen anything yet"

She rubs her belly and giggles. "You gonna give me rainbows and unicorns?"

"Yes, and leprechauns too."

"Sounds magical."

"Magically delicious."

"Are you quoting cereal boxes now?" I ask.

"Yep."

"So you are nervous?"

She shrugs, "Kind of nervous and just a little afraid."

"So you're nervous enough that you're quoting cereal slogans, but just know," I say, reaching across and taking her hand. "I'm here for you. You don't ever have to be afraid."

She sits back in her chair and adds, "I miss my abs. Do you think I'll ever get them back?"

Laughing, I reply, "Not if I can get you knocked up a couple more times. But, no worries, baby, you'll always be sexy to me."

"Charmer."

"I try." I even wink for emphasis.

CHAPTER 16
Jules
September 20th

EIGHT HOURS AFTER arriving at the hospital, our beautiful son, Maxwell Peter Somers, is welcomed into our world, forever changing our lives for the better.

I was warned time would fly, told to embrace every day to its fullest and enjoy the little moments with the baby. Everyone was right. My little Max is growing so fast, already a toddler. I watch Max wobble to his dad, happy as can be. I can't believe he's already a year and a half old. I'm lost in thought, finding myself lost in thought a lot these days. I don't reflect too much though. Life is too good in the here and now to dwell on the past.

"Hey, Jules, I've been thinking," Dylan says and I look up. "What do you think about moving closer to our families?"

Surprised, I sit up on the couch. "Leave New York?"

"Yeah. I've been thinking about it lately."

"I'd move back."

"Just like that?"

I nod, "Yes, just like that."

Instead of walking, Max drops to his knees and begins crawling to his jumper swing. Dylan puts him in, securing him before Max starts bouncing happily away. That boy has the strongest thigh muscles from that thing, which makes us smile.

Dylan sits next to me on the couch, his arm wrapping around my shoulders as I continue, "I want more kids too. I want to have another baby or two."

His eyebrows shoot up, but he only says, "Okay."

"And I want to stay home with them. I've missed so much with Max and I'm tired of it. I want to be there for every feeding, laugh, even poop... I want to be there for it all."

"Okay."

"The sooner the better," I say.

"I had no idea... well, I had an idea, but I guess I didn't know you were thinking about moving."

"I've been thinking about it for a while, but I didn't think it was possible because of our jobs. I've been dreaming about living in your parent's neighborhood. I love their home. Is there a way for us to afford that area?"

Dylan chuckles, glancing at Max, then back to me. He gives me a sweet kiss on the temple before he replies, "I've done really well this year and with all of your commissions we can definitely afford that neighborhood. Once we sell this place, we could probably buy a house outright. You can pick out the house of your dreams."

Four months later...

"DYLAN!" MY HANDS are shaking and I need him. He's the only one who can make things right. Make my world right.

"Jules! Where are you?"

"Upstairs," I shout, knowing I won't wake Max because he's with Nana and Papa.

I hear his steps. They're thunderous as he comes up the wood stairs, down the hall, barreling into the doorframe while making the sharp turn into our room. "Jules?"

I hold it up, eye level to him. The stress and fear that covered his face evaporates and he smiles, a hammer in one hand and a white picket in the other, both dropped to the floor with a loud bang.

I'm in the air, his arms around my middle holding me up and he spins, making me squeal in delight.

"You're pregnant."

"Your babies take after their father."

With a smile, he asks, "Great abs?"

"Yeah," I laugh, "Great abs, cute butts, and they are very determined to be a part of my life."

Grabbing me, he flops us onto the bed, rolling gently on top of me. I smile, brushing the hair that has fallen down over his forehead away. "How do you feel?"

Both of his eyebrows shoot to the roof, but his smile gives him away. "The more that ties us together the better." He emphasizes his point by pressing his pelvis against mine.

Staring into his eyes, I say, "Our souls are bound together, our babies are made from that love. We are forever."

He leans down to kiss my neck and I feel that familiar tingle begin, making me squirm beneath his body. I drag my fingers upward through his hair as he whispers, "How much time do we have?"

I know he's referring to when Max will be dropped off, but I feel his love so strongly that I answer from my heart, "An eternity, my love."

"How about I start by making love to you all day then?"

"Sounds like a good way to spend forever."

I kiss him, putting every ounce of passion, every particle of my being into it, into Dylan and realize it's not what's happened in the past. That's done and gone. It's how we spend our future and mine was always meant to be spent with him.

Forever. Always.

SIX YEARS BEFORE
SCORNED...

Dylan Somers

ADVANCED ECONOMICS FOR Business Majors is as boring as it sounds. I look around, analyzing the others who are stuck taking this course too. "Hot girl, row three, eight seats from the right," I say, nudging my buddy.

"Forget it. She dates Hurst."

"Hurst the quarterback?"

"None other."

"Fuck. Is it serious?"

He laughs under his breath. "Serious until she meets you, right?"

"Sounds about right." I'm not overly arrogant. Girls just tend to leave their boyfriends for me. They're always looking—grass is greener and all that. It makes me wonder if anyone truly does consider the repercussions when facing opportunity. "Forget her. It's not worth it," I reply.

"You sure?"

"Yeah. I'm over cliché and she's a walking billboard for it. She's hot, but," I say, ending my thoughts on her.

"Oh man, the great Somers reign is coming to an end?"

"Maybe," I reply, shrugging. "Fuck, I don't know. Maybe if I met the right girl."

"They don't exist from my experience."

I laugh, then joke, "At twenty-one, you're the least experienced guy I know, so that's not saying much."

"Fuck off," he says, laughing.

The professor tells us to stop disrupting or to leave, so we let the conversation die since technically we're supposed to be learning this crap. After class, we walk out into the overcast January day and I ask, "I've got to head over to the English building. Where you going?"

"P.E. I have a training session scheduled. The season is gearing up. Hey, look over there," he says, nodding toward the bottom of the steps.

She's there, the blonde from class, talking to her girlfriends, probably sorority sisters. I've messed around with enough sorority girls to know I don't want to mess around with any more. They're gossipers... and kinkier than you'd think. "Nah, really not interested."

We walk down the steps, but stop at the bottom. I scan the quad, then turn to him. "You want to put in a few more gym hours tonight?"

"Yeah, I need it. I've gotten some holiday flab."

I laugh. I didn't gain any over the holiday break, but it's not easy maintaining a six pack.

"Cool. Seven-thirty."

"Hi, Dylan," a girl's voice interrupts.

I look to the source and it's none other than the blonde who is apparently dating the quarterback of the football team.

My friend nudges me in jest, laughing, and says, "I'll catch ya later."

"Yeah, okay. Whatever man. I'll remember how you abandoned me. Some wing man you are."

She approaches, giving me her best pearly white practiced smile.

"Hey, have we met?" I ask cuz I don't know her name but she sure knows mine.

"No, but I'd wished we had sooner. I'm Brandilynn."

"That's unique."

"I'm a unique kind of girl. Soooo, I heard you're single and might be looking?"

I highly doubt that when she's wearing a shirt that fifty other girls are wearing and she looks exactly like all of them, but I'll play along... for a minute. "I heard Kevin Hurst has a girlfriend named Brandilynn."

"So you've heard of me?" she asks, looking around and lowering her voice to a whisper. "Sometimes he can be a bit unbearable, especially during bowl season."

"So you're looking for a revenge-slash-need-attention-fuck?"

She fingers the collar of my button up and smiles deviously. "And you like to get right to the point I've heard."

I step backward, her hand dropping back to her side. "What about I'm not interested?"

She smirks. "Everyone's interested in me."

"I'm not."

Her expression changes, the anger apparent, her eyes staring me down like I'll change my mind. "We both know what we want. Let's just make this easy and simple. Meet me at my sorority house at seven tonight. We'll grab some dinner and then go back to your place. Tit for tat. Easy."

"Why do I have a feeling that tomorrow Hurst will be banging down my door taking a few swings at me, me breaking his throwing arm, and you rushing to his side, playing the innocent who was taken advantage of?"

"See, we're on the same page."

I almost respect her audacity. *Almost.* Since this scenario has me ending up getting my ass kicked by the football team, I can't commit fully.

"I'm looking for a girl, but you're not it."

"Whatever girl you're looking for doesn't exist, so why not get the next best thing and be the envy of your friends."

This conversation is going nowhere, so I walk off and leave her fuming.

I see a group of guys I know and join the conversation, knowing I have about fifteen minutes left until I need to be in class again. I'm listening to the play by play of the Rose Bowl from one of the guys who went out to Pasadena to watch when I hear a laugh nearby that draws my attention. I look over my shoulder and that's when I see her. My heart skips about five beats until her eyes meet mine, restarting it. Okay, a bit dramatic, but the voices that were once loud around me become muffled, her laugh taking precedence.

"Who's that?" I ask the guy next to me.

"Some chick from my art history class. Hot, smart, and a great ass too."

"Gotta name?"

"No, but I'm gonna ask her out..."

I'm already in motion.

I walk straight toward her, drawn just like the group that encircles her, listening to every word she says. Her eyes are bright despite the clouds. Dark hair that falls over her shoulders, and I imagine the contrast against my sheets.

She watches me, laughing to be polite as one of her friends tells her nothing that will be as important in her life as what's about to happen. I know this because it's the most important thing that has ever happened to me.

I'm nervous for the first time in years. It's quite unsettling and very telling. She unnerves me, which is how I know she's the one I want. "Hi, I'm Dylan Somers," I introduce myself, staring at her, my heart stunned by her beauty.

"Hello. Juliette Weston," she replies, shifting and blushing under my gaze.

Her friends disappear. My friends are long forgotten.

"Will you marry me, Juliette Weston?" Sounds like a pick-up line, but it's not. I'd do it. I can feel my heart pounding, pulling me to her. Our souls attaching, becoming one.

Yes, I'd do it. For her.

She giggles, then quickly replies, "Why don't we start with a first date."

"How many dates until you'll marry me?"

Her sweet smile falters as surprise momentarily takes over, but returns when she realizes I'm not joking. "Let's just see how things go from here."

From here... From this moment on, I was hers and she was always mine.

AUSTIN
From the Inside Out
Part 4

S.L. Scott

CHAPTER 1

Austin

October 28th

THE UMBRELLA GOES flying as I shove Dylan away from Jules and grab her by the waist. I set her down behind me, hoping to protect her. "Henry, get her in the car!"

"Austin!" she screams as Henry tries to pull her to safety.

When I turn back, Dylan's eyes are locked on her as he makes a move to get to her. I punch him, a surprise blow as he's knocked sideways. Recovering, he turns to me, ready to fight. "Austin, I love her."

"You barely know her!"

His hands fist at his sides and his breathing is harsh. "She loves me."

"You're deranged, Dylan!"

Jules' cries are heard over the rain that drenches us. I turn to her as she says, "Pleas--"

A punch to the right side of my face sends me to my knees.

"Dylan! Noooo!" Jules screams.

"Get in the car, Jules." Losing control of my better judgment, my retaliation is quick and I land a hit straight to his left cheek. He falls this time and I hit him again when he looks up. "Fight. Damn it!"

Dylan lays on his back and I hit him one last time. When I back away, his face is bloodied, but his eyes are open staring into the cloudy sky above with his arms wide open--not fighting at all. "Get up," I yell.

He looks at me. Despite the chaos of the scene, he says, "Finally, I got what I deserved."

"What does that mean?"

"Treat her well."

"What are you talking about?" When he doesn't respond again, I say, "Fuck this!" Turning, I go to the car and slide inside. Henry takes off and I look down at my hands, bloodied and sore.

Reaching across the space that divides up, she touches my arm gently with her fingertips. "Austin." Her voice calm, trying to soothe.

The air in the car is stifling. I look over at Jules, confused by what happened back there. We're over, although the words haven't been spoken by either of us... yet. I feel sick to my stomach, hating that I stooped to Dylan's level. Why did he kiss her? He set me up. Made me do it. *Motherfucker*.

"Jules, we need to talk." I despise the anger that coats the words, never thinking I'd taste such an emotion when it came to her.

"You hit him. You hurt him," she says, finally looking in my direction. When her eyes meet mine, I see her pain and tears. "Austin, I don't understand."

"What I don't understand is why you're defending him?"

"I'm not." She adjusts her body, angling her legs toward me. "I've just never seen you act like that—"

"Don't turn this on me like I'm the bad guy. There's obviously something going on between you two."

"You're right. I've lied... or not told you everything. What I have told you is I'm not whole, as a person."

"I love you. I accepted it, you, your hesitation and caution. You're different with me. I thought we had moved past all the other stuff." I lean forward, dropping my head against the back of the front seat. "Do you love me?"

"I love you, Austin."

It relieves me that she doesn't hesitate this time when it matters, but the other hard questions haven't been asked. With Henry in the front seat driving, I decide to finish this conversation when we're alone at my place.

THE ELEVATOR RIDE is silent for thirty-seven floors. When the doors open, she walks into the apartment, but I can see by her body language that she's not feeling at home. This is going a lot different than I thought it would, so I ask, "Are you staying?"

"Am I welcome?"

"Of course."

She walks to the window and stares out, her eyes seeming to fixate on something in the distance. With her back to me, she says, "Dylan and I used to date." My mouth drops open as she continues. "For years. We met in college and moved to New York together."

"You've been in New York for more than six years, Jules." A glutton for punishment, I ask, "What happened?" I sit down on the couch, the adrenaline from earlier draining from my muscles.

"He left me for another woman."

"So he wants you back? That's what this is all about. He wants you back after all these years, after he cheated on you?"

Turning around, she says, "Yes."

My mind goes into overdrive realizing my relationship with Jules is not simple. It never has been, but it's much more complicated than I thought. She's changed since dating me, become more the girl I had a beer with in a pub that first time. That's progress. But now... "Am I losing you?"

Sitting down next to me, she says, "I'm not to be won or lost, Austin. I have my own feelings and wants."

"What do you want then?"

"I want you."

A sense of calm settles my heart and I lay back. "I want you too."

"It's not that simple though."

"No, you kissed him. Do you know how that makes me feel?"

Standing up, she looks conflicted. Her arms hang by her sides, but her body is angled toward the door. She wants to bolt, so I sit up, prepared to hold her, prepared to ask the difficult questions, but she says, "I meant, I want to be with you. I love you, but... I might still love him too."

I drop my head down into my hands. There's a pain that happens when people feel their insides fighting to get out, it's a punch to the gut that sends you to the mat, hoping the hits stop coming. But while you're writhing in the most excruciating pain imaginable, you somehow know that the pain is worth it—the fight that you were hyped up for before you entered the ring. Those highs are balanced with the lows.

I want to hate her, but I love her. I want to tell her to get the fuck out of my apartment, but also tie her to me and keep her here. I want to beg her to stay and pick me. But I won't. I won't because in the end, she's become my insides and like that punch to the gut, the highs I've had with her were bound to find their corresponding lows.

When I look up, I ask, "You might, or you do?"

I'm answered with silence, her apologetic eyes meeting mine. I stand, taking my phone and retrieve a business card from my pocket. I dial the number and bring the phone to my ear. Walking to the window, I can't see the street, but the rain has cleared and there's this sunset that sends light peeking through the adjacent buildings. It's beautiful, something bigger than us, and something bright in the middle of this depressing mess. The guy answers and I say, "This is Austin Barker. Please turn the truck around and return Ms. Weston's belongings to her apartment. I'll have my driver meet you there with the key and payment." When I hang up, I look at Jules.

"Austin?"

"I love you, but I won't be second best."

"You're not." There's a plea to her tone that matches her expression. She comes to me, her fingers fisting my shirt, holding me to her. Tears run down her cheeks. "I was honest with you *because* I love you."

"You were honest with me now. Not these last six months. I think you should stay at your place. It's best before this gets any messier."

"Messier? My life is already a complete mess and you're sending me packing without even talking about this. Austin, I don't want to lose you."

I cup her cheeks not for her, but because I'm selfish and want to touch her in case this is the last chance I get. Wiping her tears away, I lean in holding my cheek to hers, and whisper, "You can call me if you need me, but I can't make any other promises to you." I hear her breath catch. Her body shakes as her soft cries wrack her body, her arms tightening around my back. She knows this is what we need to do, what she needs to do. I don't want to be her fallback. I want to be her everything. But I can't be anything for her until she realizes that and wants to be everything for me as well.

"Henry will drive you home," I say, releasing her.

Her eyes widen when I back away, crossing my arms over my chest to restrain myself from touching her again. Without warning she throws herself against me, hugging me, and whispering through her tears, "I love you. I love you so much, Austin. Please know. Please know I do."

Dropping my arms to my sides, I nod, not returning the embrace. The rest of my pain tries to reveal itself, but it's not good for me to give so much away. "I love you, Jules." Her hands fall away and she walks to the elevator. We've got about thirty seconds left together before the elevator will be here, so I ask, "What happens after you have your heart broken?"

The doors open behind her and she steps inside. After pushing the button, she looks back at me with tears sliding down her cheeks, and says, "You go numb."

The doors close and I'm left alone. A day that was the start of two lives becoming one is ending with both lives being broken.

THERE'S A WHOLE list of women I can call when I want easy, no-strings attached sex. Women who will come if I call. Jules was the only one who made me think twice, made me think about marriage and a family.

From my office, I watched the sunset hours ago. I've been staring at the Rusque ever since. I thought I'd have more time with her, more questions answered, and hoped to be numb by now. She seems to be an expert in damage control, but the loss of emotion seems to have evaded me. Now I'm pissed.

"Fuck!" I throw my glass of whiskey, mad it didn't get me to the wasted state I wanted. I want to call her, to go after her, to know what the fuck she's up to. *Is she with Dylan? Are they back together?*

I'm so fucking stupid—the birthday dinner when he sat across from my girlfriend chatting her up. That time he showed up at her apartment that time with some bullshit excuse that he was there to see me. We had drinks at the bar and he spoke in sports metaphors while listening to me talk about Jules. *Is Brandon in on this too? Does he know about Dylan?* He must. *Fucker.*

I'm the king of the fucking universe and I'm being trumped by the court jester. I go to the bar in the living room and pour myself another drink, wanting to dull my mind and pass out. I didn't realize how much of an impact Jules had on my life until I walk to the window, standing there while my empire crashes down around me because of a woman.

I down my drink, aggravated. I won't give her up. Not that easily. I'll fight for her. I have to. Looking around my penthouse, for the first time since I bought this place four years ago, it feels lifeless.

OCTOBER 29TH

MY PHONE RINGS as the airplane taxis in. Seeing her number on the screen surprises me for some reason. I answer after taking a deep breath. "Hello?"

Jules says, "Hi."

I don't say anything else, needing her to speak first. She finally says, "I'm so sorry." Remaining quiet, I let her continue. "I'm sorry for hurting you and for lying to you about him. I'm sorry for letting things get as far as they did and for not loving you like you deserved."

'Not loving me.' "Jule—"

"Please let me finish." She says, "You're amazing and I love you, so much. I love you in my heart and I miss you. But I'm messed up on the inside, Austin. He did this to me. He broke more than just my heart. I need help."

"Are you seeing him?"

With a sigh, she says, "I haven't since we left. I might need to though, to work through my issues. It's not against you and I hope you don't feel that, but I have questions for him. You don't understand the damage he's caused. I need answers for closure and answers to move on."

"I'm not going to wait for you. When I said I'm here if you need me, I will be, but that doesn't include sitting around hoping you love me one day."

"You once told me you like the person I am when we're together. I like that person too. I want to be that person all the time. I can't do that living in this purgatory."

The door opens and the staircase is pushed up to the side of the plane. The attendant says, "We're all clear to deplane, Mr. Barker."

"Thank you, Louisa."

"Where are you," Jules asks, her nerves showing through her shaky words.

"I just landed in the U.K."

"You left?"

I pull my own punch. "No, Jules. You left." The other end of the line is silent. "I need to go."

"When will you be back?"

"I don't know. I have nothing to come home to."

She whispers, "I'm so sorry."

"So am I. Goodbye." I hang up, not wanting to hear her say the word to me, not ready for it. I gather my papers, then tuck the files and the photo of her back into my briefcase. Shutting it tight, I stand up and exit the plane.

CHAPTER 2
Jules
October 29th

I USED TO think the day Dylan left me was the worst day of my life.

I was naïve.

Yesterday was the worst day of my life. When I left Austin's apartment, I couldn't bear to go back to mine, so I walk into a hotel on Broadway and stayed the night. I didn't eat and I didn't sleep. Instead, I stared out the window at the bright lights and the crowded street below while listening to the occasional sirens.

This morning, standing outside my apartment door, I stare at the wood grain for a minute before I go in. I have no idea what's going to be inside, wondering if my stuff has been returned just like I was. I can assume my belongings are here already. Austin isn't like Dylan. He wouldn't take my stuff to hurt me.

With a shaky hand, I insert the key and turn. Slowly, I open the door and see a moving truck's worth of stuff sitting in the middle of my living room. My life has been whittled down to an apartment of boxes and furniture, most of which I don't even care about. These things don't mean a thing to me. The big furniture pieces are back in their rightful places and old, familiar feelings wash over me. Maybe this apartment is to blame for the long held emotions I've been saddled with for years.

My heart aches as I step closer to the pile of boxes stacked in the middle. The painting is still hanging on the wall, my suitcase and purse where I left them.

There's a note on top of my purse. Bending down, I read it.

> *Jules,*
> *I love you.*
> *Austin*

I drop to my knees, taking the blow of the wood beneath them. Lowering myself into a ball on my side, tucked between the boxes and the suitcase, I cry with one hand gripping my stomach and the note in the other.

I've hurt Austin. He's the man who would give me the world and I hurt him like Dylan hurt me. My stomach rolls, so I ball up tighter, smaller, holding my legs to my chest. *I'm a horrible person.*

I don't hear the click of the door or his footsteps, but I hear Brandon. "Jules?" His voice is soft, whispering near my ear as his hand touches my cheek. Standing back up, he moves some boxes around, the cardboard scraping across the floor, then curls around the back of me. "It'll be alright. I promise. It'll be alright."

"I hurt him, Brandon. He'll never forgive me and I'll never forgive myself."

"Do you love him?"

"Yes."

Brandon gives me and the path of destruction that is my life far too much credit. "That's the first step. You've got something to work for now."

"He left. He went to the U.K."

"Maybe it was business."

"Maybe. But what if it wasn't?"

"You both need time. Take a few days to figure out what you

really want. Don't rush this. Rushing will only hurt people in the process."

"I'm so tired. I just want to sleep and make this nightmare go away."

"Sleep, Jules. For now." He strokes my back as I roll over and snuggle into him, finding safety in my closest friend... My head hits the floor and I wake up an hour later, groggy and with a stiff neck. Lifting my burning eyes open, I see Brandon stretching beside me. "Sorry," he says, "but this floor is hard and uncomfortable. I had to stretch. You should move to the couch or bed."

I sit up, my body sore... all over and I know it's not just from the floor, but the heartache as well.

Looking around, I sigh. The scene before me makes me even sadder.

He asks, "You okay?"

"Not really." I slide over and lean against the foot of the couch, next to him, and stare at the mounds stacked before me. "There's not much to my life is there?" I count. "Thirteen boxes, two suitcases, and some furniture."

"You stopped living a long time ago."

"I see that now, now that all I seem to do is feel. I'm kind of missing the numbness of the past."

"No," he says, wrapping his arm around my shoulders. "You never looked good in numb. Living and emotions are much more flattering on you."

I smile, a real one. One I want to give to him.

"I didn't fight for him like he deserves." I wait for the reprimand, but he doesn't say anything, so I do, "He broke up with me."

He says, "You need to figure out what you want. You're no good for either of them unless you can commit one-hundred percent."

Silence.

Silence.

I might as well confess all of my sins. "I kissed Dylan. Well, he kissed me and then I kissed him and it was in front of Austin."

I hear a whispered, "Shit," then silence again. After stretching his long legs out in front of him, he looks at me and says, "You know, I've been listening to what you've been saying and it seems to be all about Austin. Maybe, just maybe, your heart has finally aligned with your head."

Looking around, I scan the room, avoiding Brandon's eyes altogether. I can't handle seeing the disappointment in someone else's eyes.

"Your heart is telling you what you want, Jules. You're just choosing not to listen."

"I care about them both."

He stands up. "Welcome to your life." Walking to the door, he stops when he reaches for the knob and says, "You know, I've been thinking. Maybe you need to love yourself for a while. If they love you like they say, they'll wait."

"Austin says he won't."

"I don't like to see you hurt, but I really think you need to figure this one out on your own."

"I'm beginning to come to that same conclusion."

Opening the door, he says, "But you know you're never really alone, right?"

Getting up from the floor and slipping onto the couch, I say, "Thank you for always being here, for being my friend when I need it most."

"You're welcome."

He turns and goes, but I run to my door and call after him, "Hey Brandon, thank you and... and... I love you."

"I love you too, girl."

We're friends, but we're family too.

CHAPTER 3
Jules
November 5th

TIME.

I haven't heard from Austin in over a week, and it breaks my heart. *How does he do it? How does he stay strong?* I feel weak and have called him many times, but disconnected before it went through. At night I think about him in the dark, missing the comfort he gave me when he held me, missing him altogether.

Time.

I'm supposed to give him time... or give myself time. I'm not sure anymore. It's too much to take either way. Austin imbedded himself into my heart when I wasn't looking. Until we broke up, I wasn't aware of how deeply. Now I'm stuck with a wounded organ I used to recognize as my heart. It beats differently now that it's beating alone. It's just not the same. I'm not the same.

My breakup with Austin is different than my breakup with Dylan. I thought I would be better at this, having mastered the art of the broken hearted. *I'm not.* Each day feels longer and emptier.

I haven't talked to Dylan though he's tried to talk to me. I don't take his calls or answer when he comes to the door. I'm lacking the motivation I once had to get the answers I thought I needed.

One thing I'm sure of is that I want Austin. I was just too foolish to realize it then. To move on with him, I may not need the answers I thought I did, but I do need closure. That means facing my demons head on. In other words, I need to see Dylan.

Picking up my phone, I call Dylan. He answers, "Jules?"

"I need to see you."

"When?"

I glance over to the clock. "Nine at Romero's down the street from me?"

"I'll be there."

Hanging up, I roll onto my back, my bed feeling like the safest haven I have since I left Austin's apartment. Looking at the clock one more time, I exhale heavily, then get up.

I don't care about pretension or putting on something presentable. I slip into a pair of old jeans and pull on a long sleeve T-shirt. My Wellies work since it's been raining outside and a parka will keep me warm. I grab a knit hat to help stave off the cold front that blew in yesterday. Emotions like my thoughts run rampant as I walk down the street. It's just two blocks but both dread and anxiety fill me, making each step harder to take.

The door to Romero's is opened and a couple comes out. The man stops and holds it as I walk in. Pulling my hands from my pocket, I look around then unbutton my coat. Dylan sits at the bar. His head angles in my direction, the glass of whiskey spinning between his fingers. He slides off the stool, taking the glass with him. Walking toward me, I see his own anxiety through his expression. He empties the glass and sets it down on a table he passes.

Without hesitation he takes my hand in his, bringing it to his mouth and kisses it. I don't want to see his pain or listen to his manipulative ways anymore. We can't be friends. That much is true and I'm tired of being enemies. I don't know where that leaves us, but I do know that he's not healthy for me. I pull my hand slowly from his and turn away. "Don't," I whisper.

"Look at me. Please look at me," he says.

When I do, I see his Adam's apple move as the weight of what's about to happen sets in and he gulps heavily. "We should get a table."

Our eyes lock and he searches mine. His breathing deepens, now well aware that this isn't going to be good or easy. "Okay," he says. "There are some in the back."

The bar is dim, a few lights on the wall and fake candles on a few of the tables. We find a small table with two chairs against the wall near the emergency exit. He pulls my chair out, then sits across from me. Looking over my shoulder, he nods. I glance back and see the waitress coming toward us.

"What would you like?" he asks me.

"Vodka Soda."

"You used to drink whiskey."

I nod. "People change."

"I've changed," he replies.

The waitress interrupts and takes our order, then leaves us alone again. Sitting back in his chair, he looks at me like he's trying to figure me out. It's too late for that though. We both know it... *or he should.*

The tension lingers between us until our drinks arrive, obviously we both need the courage liquor provides before delving into this mess. I take a sip, then say, "We can't be together, Dylan."

"I'm gathering." His voice is somber, resolved is more fitting.

"Why did you do this? Why now after all the years that you had the chance? Why'd you come back to destroy the only happiness I've had?"

"It has nothing to do with Austin. I know you think it's because I'm jealous, and I am. Out of control fucking jealous. But I loved you all along. I love you now. I was just too stupid to act on it before."

I take another sip and watch a man as he passes us, not wanting to see Dylan's pain. There's too much in his eyes—history, love, disappointment, even hints of desperation. I feel the same unfortunately. "We shouldn't have kissed. You had no right to kiss me and I shouldn't have kissed you back. I hurt Austin. You hurt him too. And for what?"

"For us. For everything that fucking matters to me."

"I didn't matter to you three and a half years ago. Why do I matter now? Because you can't have me?"

"No, because you're my soul and I'm lost without you."

"Dylan, no. You aren't lost. You're confused. You're lonely. You're everything I was three years ago, but that's your burden now. Not mine."

"I'm sorry," he says, leaning closer. "I've said it, but you don't seem to believe me. I made a mistake. I'll pay for it twenty times over if you please just give me another chance." He touches my fingers, the ones I have wrapped tightly around my glass.

Lifting my glass to my mouth, his warmth falls away and I drink. When I set my glass down again, I lean forward this time. "We'll never be together again. You made that decision for the both of us when you walked out our door and never came home."

"I'm coming home now."

"It's not your home anymore."

"Is it Austin's?"

"You've convinced yourself that Austin is the enemy. But you're wrong. You're your own worst enemy, Dylan." I finish my drink and set the glass down harshly before standing.

He stands, panic in his eyes. "Don't go yet. Please. Let's talk this out, Jules."

"You make it sound like we're going to work through this to come to a satisfactory conclusion. What would that conclusion be?"

"We'd be together."

I smile, it's small and genuine, but it's one of empathy. I remember feeling that way—when hope turned to desperation. Moving closer, I wrap my arms around his middle and his arms wrap around me, squeezing me. After a few seconds, I back up and say, "You won't see me again. Goodbye, Dylan." Turning on my heel, I walk away from him without looking back.

Outside, it's sprinkling. This time, as I walk away from him, there is no chase or scene out on the sidewalk. I pull my hat down a little so my ears are covered. While walking home, it hits me. I don't need answers from him. They won't change the past. They will only cloud my future with doubt. Each step is quicker than the last until I'm running and smiling, feeling free for the first time since that fateful day.

I run up the stairs and into my apartment. As soon as the door shuts, I'm calling, not caring about the hour or that I'm wet from the rain. I just need to talk to him. While it's ringing, I think about where he is or might be and if he'll hold true to his promise.

... Then my call goes to voicemail. *"This is Austin Barker. Leave a message after the tone. Thanks."*

"Austin, please call me." I hang up just as disappointment sets in. He doesn't call me for a week.

AUSTIN

EIGHT DAYS EARLIER

MY EYES ARE heavy from the alcohol. I've been hanging around the bar all night, not wanting to feel anything. She said numb, but I can't seem to reach that level of devastation. I still want to call her every damn second of every damn day, but I don't. My pride keeps me strong when I feel weak, except the third night in London...

The nightclub is loud, sirens going off and lights swirling overhead. It's cheesy. The music is thumping and I don't recognize the song, which doesn't surprise me since I don't listen to the popular stations. I follow my Director of Expansion in Emerging Markets through the crowd and around the dance floor to the bar. Chip is in his mid-twenties, a Cambridge grad with honors, and judging by the attention he gets, popular with the ladies. I'm no slouch, even next to him, but I'm also not looking. He is. I see the way he scans the room. It's similar to how he takes his job, very seriously.

"Scotch?" he asks, yelling so I can hear.

I nod instead of bothering with a verbal response. When he hands me a drink, we walk to the end of the bar and get seats just as a couple leaves. He says, "The hottest women in the city flock here on Tuesday nights."

Turning to look over my shoulder, I check out all the women on the dance floor. Leggy, blondes, brunettes, a few redheads sprinkled in. Models and some actresses I suspect. They're a unique breed and usually easy to spot. My heart's not into it though.

"You're single man. You want to get laid? You'll have plenty of opportunity tonight."

"How did you know I was single?" I ask.

"Word spreads fast. Office gossip."

I don't know how anyone knows, but there's no point in pretending it's not true. "It's recent." I shift uncomfortably.

His hand grips my shoulder. "Three months ago I broke up with the girl I dated from university. We were together almost four years. I used to think I'd marry her."

"What happened?"

"The job took over, opportunities presented themselves when I went out. I was a geek all through school. But that's changed. It's not about the Captain of the Lacrosse team or the rich royals. Women see money when they see me. I'm not afraid to treat a woman to a fancy dinner or charm her with champagne and flowers. Geek is now cool. Women want money and security. I can provide that, so the tortoise wins, leaving the hare in its wake."

"What happened to the girl?"

He takes a few gulps from his glass and checks out some women walking by before looking at me. "What girl?"

"Your girlfriend from university."

"Oh. Not sure," he shrugs, "We've lost touch."

Lost touch with reality seems more fitting in my opinion. The song changes and some of the dancers leave the floor and head to the bar. Two women approach and stand behind us. One waves at the bartender, but he doesn't see her.

"Can I be of service?" Chip asks. "What would you ladies like to drink?"

They look to each other and smile before the brunette answers, "Two Chocolate Martinis."

Chip lifts up and gets the bartender to come over. He places the order just as the blonde says, "Do you come here often?" Her accent is strong and more Cockney than refined Londoner. She's pretty—straight hair, low-cut top, and really short skirt that doesn't leave much to the imagination. She's beautiful, but typical and unoriginal.

Bottom line is... *she's not Jules.*

I reply, "No, I'm American."

That intrigues her enough to lean closer. "Are you here on vacation or business?"

"Business," I say, not wanting to go into the fact that it's business that could have been done from Manhattan. She doesn't need the dirty details of why I'm really here.

It doesn't take much—three drinks and a few laughs and she's pulling me into a cab with her friend and Chip. We end up at the brunette's flat. I have no recollection of her name. The blonde is Keira and has her hand running up and down my inner thigh. My cock is a traitor, betraying my feelings for Jules.

Chip and the brunette are in the bedroom before the front door shuts. Keira takes her shoes off, complaining that the heels hurt. She's much shorter than I thought, but still taller than Jules. She puts on a seductive smile and says, "Come here, Austin."

I go, but I know I shouldn't. She runs her fingers down my neck and over my shoulders. "Sit down," she says. When I do, she hikes her skirt up the remaining few inches, exposing her pussy, and straddles me. "Touch me." She places my hands on her ass and closes her eyes as she begins a slow gyrate.

The curse—it's impossible to hide an erection. I toss her to the side of me onto the couch and stand up. I run my hand through my hair this time. "I'm sorry. I can't do this."

"What's wrong?"

"It's not you," I start to say as she pulls her skirt back down.

"I'm in love with someone else."

She looks irritated. Folding her arms, she asks, "Then why did you come back with me?"

"I don't know." The truth.

She raises her voice. "I want you to leave."

"I apologize." With that, I leave the flat without saying anything more.

I grab a taxi and head back to my own flat. When I walk inside, I look at the bare walls. I was going to surprise Jules with this place. I bought it for the great wall space, the location, and spectacular windows. I wanted her to fill it with her favorite art and to help me decorate it. I never had a chance to show her though.

After tossing my keys on the table by the door, I go to the fridge. I down half a bottle of water before I lean against the counter wondering what the fuck I'm doing anymore. Everything was perfect and on the right track until Dylan derailed us. *Fucker.*

Pulling my phone from my back pocket, I flip through my photos from the last few months. It only takes seeing five of her to know I'm not over Jules. Not at all. Moving to the couch, I pick up my laptop and log on. It started off as a therapeutic way to get the words down, get them out. An hour later, I look at the letter I wrote to her and never sent, rereading it. I take a deep breath, then save it to my drafts folder again. I close the computer and lie there, wanting to fall asleep before I do something stupid like sending it to her or worse, calling her.

Tonight I'm lucky and fall asleep.

CHAPTER 4

AUSTIN

SHIT. GRABBING MY head, I'm groggy as I look around. I'm on the couch, my laptop on the coffee table in front of me. Memories from the night before come back in fragments— *Chip. The nightclub. Keira. Jules. The email.* Sitting up abruptly, I grab my computer, log on, and check my sent folder. Nothing was sent last night. *Thank God.* I breathe out in relief when I move to the drafts folder. It's still waiting there, challenging me to send it, to end this madness. My rational side hits me full force when the memory of her kissing Dylan comes back.

Closing my computer down, I decide to get up and shower. I'm tense, stressed, and fucking lonely. I miss her and that pisses me off too. I take hold of my cock, needing to find relief under the warm water. It's not the same like when I was with her, but it feels good to release some pressure, in any form. I should probably take up boxing.

I'm in the office an hour later. I don't have any messages from her, but I do from Jacqueline wanting to go over the latest financial reports. It's the middle of the night in America, so I can't talk to her until the afternoon sometime. I get lost in papers and reports, suggestions for tightening up expenditures in the South American markets.

During my late lunch, I stare out the window, eating mindlessly. Food has lost flavor, my motivation for work shifting as well. It used to be easy before Jules came along. I worked. *A lot.* I played. *A little.* I got by, not content, but moving forward, my work dictating my direction. That changed with a chance encounter in an elevator and spending time with her at a pub. For me, she finally broke her own rule of not dating clients, but maybe we were only meant to be for a brief time. Maybe she was right and she's too damaged to love me the way I love her.

My phone rings, and I glance toward it. With half my lunch still untouched on the desk in front of me, I answer and hear, "Austin, good afternoon, it's Jacqueline."

"Hello, how are you?"

"Well, and you?"

Avoiding the question, I say, "I looked over the report you sent. I have few questions."

"Great. Is now a good time to go over it?"

"Yes."

"Before we get started, I wanted to let you know that Dylan Somers has stepped down from your account. His workload and other clients were not permitting him to stay on top of the requirements needed for your company. We want you to have the best team in place, but we agreed for the sake of quality and accountability. On the plus side, I have freed up my client list to focus fully on your account."

"Thank you," I reply, feeling my jaw tighten just from the mere mention of Dylan. "Shall we go over the reports now?"

"Yes..."

I spend the next forty-five minutes looking at financial reports and forecasts for the first quarter of next year with her.

When we're wrapping it up, she asks, "Business keeping you in London for much longer?"

Business? *No.* Personal. *Yes.* "I'll be here another week or so."

"That's too bad. I was hoping we could do lunch or a drink and catch up sooner." My pause must make her anxious because she adds, "Anyway, maybe when you return."

"Oh, um, yeah, maybe when I return," I say. "Thanks for the update and make sure to go over everything with my CFO. We'll be in touch soon, Jacqueline."

"You're welcome. Goodbye."

"Goodbye." When I hang up the call, I lean back in my chair, lifting my feet up onto my desk. The Gherkin building stands spiraling outside my window and I follow the lines. I'm reminded of Jules' body and the times I would run my hand from her breasts down her side to the dip of her waist and over the curvature of her hip. Sex with her was phenomenal. For someone with so many walls built up, she had none when it was the two of us alone. She made me feel something more significant than the sex itself, something I hadn't felt in a long time.

Christina is the only other woman who has done that...

We were young. Too young. Everyone always said that, trying to convince me that our love was meant to burn out. I don't know if I believe them or not, but I try to as if it will justify why things happened the way they did. It's easier not to think of her. The last time I saw her flashes through my head and I stand up abruptly, wanting the image to go away. "Sophie?" I call to my secretary. "Call for my car and cancel my four o'clock."

Rushing out the door, I hear her say, "Yes, Sir," as I pass.

The car is at the curb waiting for me when I reach the sidewalk. I hurry inside and am driven straight home. I waste no time throwing on my workout clothes. I'm on the street running shortly after. It looks like it's going to rain, but I need this release. I run with speed, trying to wear my mind out as much as my body. I reach Hyde Park in record time. I cut down the path and through the park just as the rain begins. No sprinkles today. The heavy drops cover me, coating my outside while I wish it could do the same to my insides as flashes from a once buried memory come back to haunt me...

Christina lay on the bed—perfect and beautiful, like she always looked. She wore the garnet earrings I had given her just that

Christmas. It was her birthstone. She usually wore pastel colors, but she started wearing clothes in the same shade of red just to match the earrings. "I love them, Austin," she said every time she wore them. It was the most expensive jewelry she owned and the most expensive I had bought. Two hundred dollars that I had saved in increments of twenty from each paycheck. It was all I could afford to set aside. We were nineteen and in college, both of us living off loans and part time jobs at the local sandwich shop. Christina was naturally smart, never having to study, which was the opposite of me. I worked for every A I got. She was carefree, but not frivolous, possessing an enthusiasm for life that most would never appreciate. I did though. She brought out the best in me, made me see life in a new way.

She once told me that she saw me doing great things in life and I was naïve enough to think she would be there with me...

I stop at the edge of the water near a bench, bending over to catch my breath that puffs like smoke before me. I sit on the bench, then lie down letting the rain hit my face, drenching me, taking me back, hoping it can save me somehow. Closing my eyes, every drop reminds me of Jules' tears. I should be angrier, but with each day that passes, my anger morphs into a weaker version of itself. She's temptation at its finest. I drape my arm over my eyes and let the pain wash over me.

Opening my mouth, I catch the rain, swallowing before sitting up and taking off again. Weakness is not what Christina or Jules were attracted to, so I refuse to become less of who I am, running home and taking the longer route to push myself.

A WEEK AND a half later, I hadn't given in. I didn't want to. I thought about calling Jules, emailing her, texting her, but I didn't. She didn't either. I've been left to assume she and Dylan are together. And yet, I can't seem to stop thinking about her and what went wrong and when? Sitting at a pub, I watch people—men, women, couples as they come and go, drink, get drunk, go from quiet to loud, the alcohol determining their tone. I finish my second beer, pushing away the fish and chips that remain in the basket in front of me, then look out the window.

"Hello."

Turning, I see a pretty blue-eyed blonde standing there smiling at me. Her accent is clean.

"Hello," I reply.

"Sorry to bother you, but my friends have a bet going." She's flirting.

"Oh really? And what might that be?"

"You're American?"

"Yes." I signal to the seat on the bench next to me. "Would you like to join me?"

"Yes, I would. Thank you." She sits and then tilts her head just slightly to the side.

"So what's this bet about?" I ask.

"If you're single. You don't wear a ring, you're dressed nicely, handsome." I smile as I listen to her continue, "So this may sound silly, but you seem to be a rare breed in London if you are indeed single."

"Are you asking for you or to win the bet?"

She pauses, then smiles. "Both."

"What's at stake?"

"Two hearts and a round of drinks."

"I'm single, but my heart stayed behind," I reply before taking a long pull of beer.

She sits upright and taps my forearm. "Are you always this honest?"

"There's an art to flirting that I'm not very good at. So I err on the side of being direct."

Amused, she giggles, then looks briefly back to her friends who are staring at us. "Honesty can be called a rare breed as well. Are you in London on business or pleasure?"

"Was it for business or pleasure when you bet on me?"

"Touché." Adjusting to sit back, making herself more comfortable, she says, "I've been rude. My name is Louise. No jokes please," she says, holding her hands up in surrender. "It's a family name."

"I would never mock someone's name." A small, but genuine smile shows she believes me. I offer, "Would you like a drink?"

"Yes. A beer would be lovely."

I get the waitress's attention and order a pitcher and two glasses.

When we're alone again, Louise says, "To answer your question, both."

"So I'm both business and pleasure to you?"

With a laugh, she replies, "I take bets very seriously."

"So what do I have to do for you to win?"

"Kiss me."

I do a double take. "Just like that. You walk over here and kiss a single, non ring wearing, nicely dressed, handsome, but total stranger and you win?"

"Yes."

"Okay," I say, moving closer. We look into each other's eyes and I touch her cheek. Her breath shortens and the smile is gone. When I get even closer, her eyes close and I close mine, leaning in. Just before our lips meet, I reopen my eyes and slide back abruptly. "I'm sorry." I gulp. "I can't kiss you." I refuse to betray Jules like she did me.

"You really did leave your heart with someone else." She looks stunned. I'm sure this is a first for her.

"I did. As for the bet, your group's drinks are on me tonight. I'll make sure the waitress knows."

Staring at me a moment longer, I expect a comment rooted from her rejection. But instead, she collects herself and says, "She's a lucky girl." Standing up, she adds, "Thank you for the drinks."

"You're welcome. Have a good night."

Minutes later, I pay my tab and set up Louise and her friend's drinks to be added later, and leave. When I walk into my apartment, I head straight for the shower. As the water pummels down on me, I mentally reprimand myself for being an idiot. I had a beautiful woman hitting on me, making it pretty damn obvious that she was into me, and I think of Jules.

"Turn over." Not asking.

Jules lifts up, her eyes locked on mine, the devil inside them. She likes when I fuck her from behind. I like it, so we both move swiftly. Her long, dark hair drapes over her shoulders revealing the curve of her neck and the enticing line of her back. I push into her, my eyes closing as I let her engulf me body and soul.

This feeling of ecstasy wraps my mind up in all that's her—her hazel eyes that brighten when she sees me, her hair as it tumbles from a style that kept it confined all night, and the way she likes to pleasure me first, then comes when I do. We're great together and I think about attaching myself to her more than sexually. I want her, all of her as my own, wanting to possess her in ways I've never felt before.

As I dry off, I realize I'm fucked up. She has my insides twisted and my mind conflicted. After putting on a pair of boxers, I climb into bed and pick up my phone to look at pictures and check for texts. A missed call takes me by surprise, a voicemail beeping to be heard. After taking a jagged, deep breath, I listen to the message Jules left, "Austin, please call me."

It takes me another week before I finally do.

CHAPTER 5

Jules

WHEN I SEE Austin's name flash on my phone screen, I answer quickly, "Hello?"

"Hi. It's me."

I get up immediately and shut my office door. A bit nervous, I say, whispering, "Austin, I'm so sorry." I try to stop the tremble in my voice. "I want to see you. Where are you?"

"I'm still in London."

Disappointment fills me. Trying to regain my composure, I ask, "How are you?"

There's a short pause, then he says, "I'm okay. Maybe not as good as I should be."

I gulp from hearing his voice. It's deep, somewhat withdrawn. Not the voice I know at all, but I'll happily take what I can get. "Me either, but I guess I deserve it."

"Sometimes I wonder what we deserve and who decides. Just something I've been thinking about lately."

"Yeah, do we choose our own fate or it is predetermined?"

"I get mad at myself for missing you, Jules." His confession hurts mry heart when it should make me feel good.

"I'm mad at myself for so much more."

I hear him sigh into the receiver, making me remember how his breath felt against my skin. He whispers, "Why did you call?"

"I couldn't stop myself any longer."

"Are you dating Dylan?"

"No."

"Do you want to?" he asks.

"No."

"What *do* you want, Jules?"

"You. I want you." I ask, "Are we still a possibility?"

"I don't know anymore. Seems like I went into everything so blindly before, so stupid, too fast."

"You weren't stupid. I let you down, hurt you when you only deserved to be loved."

He interrupts, "You lied to me. You broke my trust. I don't even know if you really loved me."

His voice is clipped, making me feel desperate to hold onto him if only for a few more minutes. "I did. I still do. I'm so sorry, Austin. I can't get back what we had, but I can make promises for any future you might give us."

I hear him shuffle on his end before he says, "I don't want any more promises. I'm coming home tomorrow, maybe we can talk."

"Austin?"

"Yes?"

"Thank you."

"Don't thank me. That makes you grateful to me and I'm not sure if there's anything to be grateful for yet."

I lick my lips, dragging this conversation out, not wanting to hang up, then say, "I'll see you when you get back."

"Take care, okay?"

"You too." He hangs up and I'm left holding the phone to my ear a moment longer, caught up in the fact that he called at all and hoping he calls me again. I have to put my trust in him, something I didn't do before. I've learned my lesson.

It's another four days before I hear from Austin again. Only one before I hear from Dylan asking me to meet him. I refuse the invite. After figuring out that I'm in love with Austin, I'm not wasting any more time or emotion on Dylan. He had his chance years ago and chose someone else. Now's the time for me to prove that I choose Austin. I need to treat him the way I should have all along.

When Austin asks me to meet him on a Saturday afternoon at Strawberry Fields in Central Park, I go without question. I can only guess at the underlying message of this location. I don't see him when I arrive, so I sit down on a hill nearby and watch the tourists taking pictures and leaving memorabilia and flowers on the Imagine design. When I see a man sitting next to me, I know it's Austin without even looking. He says, "Just for a minute, imagine if you had loved me like I imagined you did. Imagine if your ex had not come back. Imagine if you hadn't kissed him and we were living together. We're not though, so what does your life look like now?"

"Imagine a life that feels emptier than it did before, as if that's even possible. Imagine looking up at night and seeing stars that used to shine because you knew they shined for love. Imagine that love is that powerful." I turn to him. "I was wrong. Love isn't powerful. Love is everything. *You're* everything to me, Austin."

"Do you love him?"

"No, but I did. I loved him in a way that I used to think we couldn't live without each other. You know what? I did live. I survived. It may not have been a pretty life with its sharp angles and my sharp edges, but you saw beyond all that. You softened my corners and made me a better version of myself."

He faces forward, wrapping his arms around his legs and watching all the people wandering around the monument. "It took three years to get you to say yes, and sometimes I wonder if I was blind to the obvious all those years. The night we met... was that the night you and Dylan broke up?"

Shifting, I turn and whisper, "Yes."

"All the signs were there, but I saw past your walls—"

"You saw who I was, through the pain, over the walls, and gave me the benefit of the doubt. You saw who I wanted to be."

His hand slides over, his fingers wrapping around mine, and he says, "Maybe..." He pulls his hand away and stands. "Thanks for meeting me. I'm gonna go now."

"What?" I stand. "Austin, please. Don't go."

"You've given me a lot to think about, Jules." He can't seem to look at me, which feels more like a stab to the heart than an avoidance. "Take care."

"You're just walking away?"

"Yes. I am."

I want to yell, 'Just like Dylan,' but I hold my tongue, turn away instead and start walking in the opposite direction. When I reach the sidewalk, I look back. He's gone. I've wounded him deeper than I realized and it makes me question if I'm good enough for him. Referencing our talk about deserving, makes me want Austin to have someone who's deserving of him. And that might not be me.

Taking the scenic route leads me to the gallery instead of home. I go inside. It's during business hours, so I don't need my keys. I walk into my office and see the vase that Dylan gave me. It's such a great representation of our relationship with the mess of colors fading into the other without boundaries. I pick it up and take it to the back. After finding a box, I pack it up; making sure it's protected inside. Within minutes, it's sealed shut, addressed to Dylan's office, and labeled for FedEx pickup on Monday.

The tightening in my chest loosens, my lungs getting much needed air. When I sit behind my desk I feel freer already. It's Saturday, and I don't want to be working. That's a first in years. I push back and leave, deciding to walk home. There's a quickness in my step, an excitement that feels new. It may seem odd when I've freed myself from one man and lost the other, but maybe I should be alone.

Austin loves me. I know he does. He just can't be with me now. I think I finally understand why. We have to do the work, get to know each other on a deeper level, before we come together again. I want to know his history and what made him the man he is today. I don't know any of that. I only know what he's shown me and vice versa. How we got as far as we did surprises me now. With his constant traveling and me burying myself at the gallery, we seem to have missed a few steps along the way.

I hurry home and climb the stairs by two, then knock on Brandon's door. When he doesn't answer, I use my key and let myself in. "Brandon?"

There's silence, then I'm given a delayed answer, "Jules? I'll be right out."

I help myself to a glass of water. Seeing my vitamins on his counter is another reminder of the changes I need to make. I take the two bottles and toss them in the trash, then head to the spare bedroom. Opening the closet door, I grab my robe and the clothes I've left over here. When I walk out, I run right into Brandon.

He asks, "What are you doing here?"

Taken aback by his question, I look at him and frown. "I had a revelation and needed to talk to you."

He glances over his shoulder toward his room, then back. "I have company, Jules."

My hand covers my mouth. "Oh my God!" When I remove it, I whisper, "I'm so sorry. I'll leave."

As I rush to the door, he asks, "What's the revelation?"

With a big smile, I say, "I need to fix myself. You were right. No one else can do it. I'm gonna stand on my own two feet again. You watch." Lowering my voice, I add nodding, "And congrats on the afternoon delight. We'll catch up soon."

He's left laughing. The door shuts and I walk to my apartment with an armful of clothes. After dumping them on the chair in my room, I move into the kitchen and pick up the black coffee maker Dylan left behind when he left me. I dump it in the trash then go to the window where the two prisms hang, reflecting rainbows on the nearby wall. I reach up and untie them from the curtain rod. I kiss each one then toss them in the trash with the coffeemaker.

It's funny how tightly I held onto things that at the end of the day, or technically the end of almost four years, finally hold no power or meaning any longer. I look at the painting hanging on the wall. With purpose, I step up on the couch, and take the painting down. After setting it in the corner of the room, facing out, I turn on

Christina Perri's latest. Seems to fit my mood. I pour myself a glass of pinot noir and return to the living room. Sitting down in front of the painting, I cross my legs and relive all the good times that come to mind with Dylan, then indulge the bad times too, letting them out, releasing them from the chest where I've kept the memories locked up for too long. A tear joins my wine just as I take another sip.

Getting up, I move closer, and run my finger along the peaks and valleys of the dried oil. Then with flat palms, I rub over it before sitting back on my knees. That's when I get the idea and go into the cabinet under the sink in the kitchen and pull out the yellow paint I once bought for that room. I had thoughts of affecting my attitude, hoping the bright color could bring me out of the depression I was trapped in. I never got around to painting the kitchen. I grab a marinating brush from the drawer and go back to the painting. I pop the lid open with a screwdriver and dip the brush in the sunny color. With one bold move, my first stroke is in the middle of the canvas. Seeing the painting in a new light, I'm exhilarated by the freedom and continue painting until it's completely covered.

Standing back, I drink my wine, then stare ahead. The yellow is not me at all. It's bright and happy. The solid color forces the eye to find the ridges of the old paint underneath, covering the tear streaks that once defined it and I smile.

I pour another glass of wine then wait for the paint to dry by lying in the middle of the floor, listening to music and staring at the ceiling. The room goes dark as the sun sets and I roll to my stomach to look at the painting again. The moonlight provides enough light to see it, and I smile. I get up from the floor and go to the bedroom, pleased with the changes I made today. After getting ready, I climb under the covers and text Austin: *I love you, Austin Barker. One day I'll prove I can be the person you deserve.*

Just as I turn out the lamp, my phone lights up simultaneously with a return text from him: *Jules Weston, I look forward to that day.*

With that text I have hope, knowing he's willing to give me another chance to prove my love to him.

... And I will.

CHAPTER 6
Jules

AFTER SPEAKING TO my landlord and getting my lease settled, I decide to focus on getting my life back on track. Bending over into Downward Dog, I try to keep my mind zen. I smile when I think of Austin. He does more for my mindset than yoga ever could. Slowly I change positions, following the guru on TV.

Forty-five minutes later, I'm showered and dressed in a tee and baggy shorts. Standing in front of the DeLonghi Coffee Center, I pull the post-it from the machine. The 'Learn to Use' note has been mocking me for too long. It's time to tame this beast. Flipping through the manual, I find the page with the first step and go through all twenty-six steps until I'm holding a perfectly crafted latte. I've used the machine before but it was just for plain black coffee. Today I was ready for something new, utilizing all the cool features.

Closing my eyes, I take my first sip. A huge sense of satisfaction comes over me. *Delicious.* I set the cup down and take a pic of my latte, proud of this small accomplishment that feels huge right now.

I take my cup into the living room and set it down on the coffee table. Walking to the bright yellow painting in the corner, I pick it up and climb back onto the couch. I hang it on the wall and step back down to admire it. Yes, this is right. It's a new start, one I should have had years earlier. And if I can't have Austin in my life right now, this painting gives me a stronger sense of the old me than I've felt in years. I turn on some music and get to the task of unpacking my boxes. Some of the stuff I toss into the trash since it holds no real meaning anyway.

Two hours. That's all it takes to unload my life and put it back in place. Happy with the results, I decide to go to the grocery store and stock my kitchen, determined to fill this place with the life it once had. This time, my life though.

I spend the next week cooking at home, enjoying the solitude, and rediscovering the person I once was. The gallery has somehow survived despite me only working forty hours this week. Something I didn't even think was possible. I've underestimated the people I've hired for too long and I made it up to them by not only trusting them to run it when I'm not around, but also treat them to lunch on Wednesday. Their surprised and happy faces made it all worthwhile.

It seems to be going well. I'm happy, happy on the inside, which is invigorating, but I didn't see what was coming. I arrived at Jean-Luc unannounced like I always have. I like to surprise him and see how an artist of his talents spends his day.

Jean-Luc slides the large door open and smirks, "You're just in time."

"In time for what?"

"Come in," he says, turning his back to me and walking across the large loft space. He offers me a drink, "Wine or water?"

"Wine. White please."

After dropping my purse and coat down on the couch, I peruse the newest collection. With my hands behind my back, I slowly walk the space, looking for cohesion. "What's the theme?"

He hands me a glass and I take a sip as he pours what looks to be something stronger—maybe Scotch. Approaching silently, I feel his hand slide over my back and down my arm, his fingers tapping lightly. Something that used to feel normal when I was numb is different now, altered under implications and insinuations behind the touch. Turning, I shift away.

"You're ever-changing, Jules."

"Maybe..." I glance back at him.

When our eyes meet, his change, all playfulness gone. "Why do you let the world affect the melancholy? You're divine when the darkness bleeds through. It's what brought us together. You're more beautiful when you're in a state of chaos."

Jean-Luc is deep in his want for the heaviness in life, but I'm trying to outgrow the negativity, so I take a gulp, needing wine to help me keep it light. "Last time it was sullen and aloof. This time chaos. I wasn't chaotic, I was dead inside. There's a difference." Standing in front of a window, I lift up on my toes to see how much of the sunset is visible from here. Disappointed, I lower back down when I find other buildings blocking it.

I spent some time walking around the room, eyeing the rest of the collection. I'm confused by his vision. They're tumultuous. My head starts to hurt, a migraine feeling like it's coming on. "I can't stay long." My temple pulses and I rub it.

"Sleep with me. It's almost too late. Once you move into this so-called bliss others say we find in life, I'll lose you. I don't want to lose you."

When I look at him, I blink, finding it harder to keep my eyes open. "I need to go. I woke up early and I'm tired."

"Stay." He approaches just as the glass slips from my fingers. His hands hold my neck, his thumbs putting pressure on my throat as my feet meld to the floor, trapping me in the spot.

His lips touch my cheek right before my eyes close.

AUSTIN

"So... I'M FREE tonight. Want to grab dinner?" Jacqueline asks while walking out of the conference room.

Looking at my watch, I stall before answering, "Um, I can't. My apologies. I have dinner plans already."

"A rain check then?"

"Yes, a rain check."

"I'll see you next week."

"Next week. Thank you," I reply. Jacqueline detours back down the hall and I go to the bank of elevators. Dylan is standing there, his back to me. I stop, anger instantly filling my chest. He doesn't see me, which gives me a few seconds to play out fifty different scenarios of kicking his ass. He turns back, ending those fantasies. "Austin?"

The doors open and we both step in. I see how nervous he is and he should be. As soon as the doors close, he's trapped. His eyes are wide. "I'm sorry."

"You're sorry? You're fucking sorry?" He nods, smart enough not to talk. "You fucked her up and then came back to do it again. You just couldn't handle the fact that she's moved on. Let me ask you, Dylan. Was it worth it?"

"I don't know anymore. All I know is that my life is shit without her in it."

"But that's about you. Did you ever put her first?"

He pauses and looks up. Shaking his head, he replies, "No. That's why I'm sorry."

"I loved her in spite of the damage you did to her. I made her happy."

The dark circles and bags under his eyes show he's breaking. Slowly, he's falling apart. This *should* make me happy. He says, "When I met her, she was the most beautiful girl I'd ever seen. She was amazing and she loved me... I destroyed that. I'm sorry. If I could take it back, I would." He's a wreck. "I've made so many mistakes, the biggest of them all was leaving her."

"If you loved her, you would have let her be happy, whether it was with you or not." The doors slide open. We stand there looking at each other.

Finally, the stalemate is broken when he walks off and I follow after. Stopping in the middle of the lobby, he turns back to me and says, "I won't bother her again. She's better without me." He reaches out his hand and we shake. "Take care of her. She should have someone good, someone who can love her the way she deserves."

Without any other words, he leaves, but I catch him before he walks through the door. "Hey Dylan, I'm sorry too."

"For what?"

"I'm not really sure. I just thought I should say it."

A slight smile shows. "I always knew you were the better man." He pushes the door wide open and leaves.

I'm left seeing what life looks like without Jules. There's no doubt how much he loves her. She's already left that kind of mark on my heart as well. Pushing down my ego and the pain I've been holding against her, I move to a quieter section of the lobby and call her.

One ring.

Two rings.

Three rings.

Voicemail. 'This is Jules Weston, please leave a message and I'll call you back.'

"Hey, it's me," I start, "I've been thinking about us. I'd like to see you. Call me back."

At my car out front, I tell Henry I'm going to walk, needing to clear my head, wanting to think about things logically. For five blocks I see the car circle around several times. Deciding to play cat and mouse with Henry, I duck inside a deli when he rounds the corner, then hurry up and over two blocks. I backtrack and see the car just as it passes. He waves and I smile. He's very good.

My phone buzzes in my pocket and I keep heading straight up the street so Henry doesn't have to work so hard. Hoping it's Jules, I pull it quickly from my pocket. I don't recognize the number, so I answer, "Austin Barker here."

"Austin, it's Brandon."

Exhaling heavily, irritated just from the sound of his voice. I move against a brick wall, the exterior to a dry cleaner, to take the call. "What do you want?"

"Have you talked to Jules today? Or yesterday?"

"No. I left her a message earlier, but she hasn't called me back."

"I've left her about ten messages. She hasn't returned any of them. She usually calls me back within an hour."

Narrowing my eyes on a pothole in the street, worry creases my forehead. "What are you saying? Are you worried about her?"

"Yes, I'm worried. It's not like her to not call me back."

A sickening starts rolling through my veins, gathering strength. "Have you checked her apartment, her work?"

"I'm stuck in Philly. I won't be back until tonight. I can't get an earlier flight and the trains are on a delay."

"I'll call you back," I say, waving Henry down. I get in and direct him to Jules' place. I call her direct office line, but there's no answer. I call her phone and go to voicemail again. "Call me, Jules. I need to talk to you right away."

I phone the gallery. A man answers, "Des'Arts Gallery. This is Sergio."

"Sergio, this is Austin Barker."

"Hello, Jules isn't here right now."

"Has she been in today?"

"No. She was out visiting artists yesterday, so she left early."

"Who'd she visit?"

His tone changes. "Is something wrong?"

"Yes, she's missing. Who'd she visit?"

"Let me check her schedule. She's really good about listing everything she does gallery related. Hold on." I hear him rushing, probably into her office. "Ummm...ummm. Here it is. Jean-Luc."

Fucking artist bastard. "Give me the address."

I pass the information to Henry, then call Brandon back. "The gallery shows she was visiting Jean-Luc, one of her artists."

"Fucking hell. I'm gonna rent a car and come back."

"I have the address. I'm heading there now."

"Call me as soon as you know anything," he pleads.

"I will," I reply, then hang up. Flexing my hands, the nerves are eating away at my stomach. Not sure what I'm gonna find—hoping it's not like the other time I'd rather forget. I'm starting to freak the fuck out, so I grip my hands together and train my eyes on the passing scenery.

Traffic is flowing miraculously and we're there in thirty minutes. After pulling to the curb in front of the building, Henry turns around and asks, "Do you want me to come with you?"

"No, stay here," I reply, not sure what I'm walking in on. "I think you should leave the car on and be ready just in case..."

He nods once, understanding the gravity of the situation. I get out and eye the old warehouse turned loft building. The neighborhood isn't quite in transition though I know these lofts probably cost a fortune. I walk in the door that's been left ajar with a brick—not a good sign. I go up the stairs to the third floor, then down the wide corridor to the steel door labeled C. I knock firmly and wait, trying to listen for any sounds.

I'm startled when it slides back abruptly. A shirtless guy with a cigarette hanging from the side of his mouth is standing there, eyeing me. I recognize him from when Jules introduced us a few months back at his show. "What?" he asks.

I push past him and see Jules asleep on the couch. Kneeling down beside her, I try to wake her up. "Jules," I whisper. "Wake up. Jules."

"Who are you?" he asks to my back. I ignore him.

Her lids slowly open and she smiles, the one I've seen during so many sunrises at my place. "Austin?" Her eyes close again.

"Jules, it's me. Wake up, Sweetheart."

When she does, she says, "I'm so sleepy though. I want to sleep."

"No, not here."

Her eyes widen and she looks around. Suddenly she sits up and gasps. "Why am I still here?"

From behind me, Jean-Luc says, "I was going to paint you."

Ignoring him, I focus on her. "Do you not remember staying here?"

"No," she says, her voice weak and so unlike the woman I know. "Something's wrong."

"Did you take something?"

"No."

I can tell by her behavior she's taken drugs of some sort. When she doesn't recall... I know she took something. We both look back at Jean-Luc. I stand to my full height, which is about six inches taller than him, and ask, "Did you drug her?"

I hear another gasp from her. She stands, holding her coat to her chest. "You drugged me. You did that. To me. Jean-Luc? Why would you do that?"

"How am I supposed to paint, to find my purpose if you turn on me. We were on this journey together. A team. You understand me. We didn't have to put on pretenses for pretty suits like him. We could be angry and sad, be painted in blue and not feel alone." He stubs his cigarette into an ashtray. "You believe in my art. You believe art is life. What can he do for you? He'll lock you away in his penthouse, carting you around in his private car, showing you an extension of his privileges instead of the real world. Art is created on the ground, not in the sky. It's dirty and grungy, not starched and dry-cleaned."

He's gone too far. "Shut the fuck up," I say, feeling my anger take over. "What drug?"

"I don't have to tell you shit, man!"

Jules steps forward, her arm against mine. Her tone is soft, in opposition of mine, when she says, "Please. Tell me what drug and what happened, Jean-Luc. If you care about me, you'll tell me."

We watch as he roams around his space, searching for something. Finally, he picks up a paintbrush and starts in on a canvas covered in red. "I wouldn't hurt you. You know that." He glances to her quickly. "You know that, Jules."

She drops her head down, runs her hands through her hair, then leaves her hands covering her face. When she moves them away, she's crying. I wrap my arm around her just as she says, "I know you have these grand ideas of how this is all supposed to play out, the masterpiece you're trying to make your life. But our life, like art, is in the eye of the beholder. Just because I've changed my perspective doesn't mean you can force me to stay the way you want me." She puts her coat on, looks up at me unsure, maybe still shaken. When she turns to him again, I see her tears though they don't fall. He hasn't even looked over here since he started painting. Raising her chin, she says, "Your dreams come on the wings of self-indulgence and arrogance, but I'm not your muse, not anymore." Jules walks to the door. "Your show is cancelled."

I stare at him a minute longer, not as forgiving. He looks at me and asks, "What, Suit?"

Trying to keep my voice calm, I ask again, "What did you give her?"

His posture shows his annoyance as he sighs and shrugs. "A sleeping pill. That's all man. Relax. Nothing happened if that's what you're wondering. I watched her sleep. That's all. I watched as her beautiful aura of darkness disappeared from dealing with suits like you."

"You're sick, you know that? You need help."

"No, I need my muse back, but you destroyed her. Her hate was beauty. Her sadness palpable, too tempting to resist. I paint in blues, blacks, and reds, not yellow or white. You turned my beautiful succubus into a seraphim, my inspiration transformed forever."

"You're spewing bullshit and believing it," I reply, pissed. Needing to get to Jules, I start to leave, but stop. "I'm making you a promise, whatever the fuck your name is. If you touched her, at all, in anyway, I'll come for you."

"And do what?" He puts his paintbrush between his teeth.

I turn back around, standing in the doorway. My glare harsh as anger courses through my veins. "I'll make sure you meet that Hell you're so intrigued by."

Leaving him there in his self-important, messed up perspective, I kick the door to the exit on the first floor open and see Jules standing with Henry on the sidewalk. "Get in," I tell her. Without question, she does.

CHAPTER 7

Jules

THE BUILDINGS PASS outside, the occasional homeless person sitting on the sidewalk. The black car stands out in this part of the borough. The dark tint of the windows protects us from eyes peering in, but I feel Austin's weighing heavily on me inside the car. When I look at him, his expression is unexpected and tugs at my heart. I hate seeing the pain I've caused him. I'm just not sure if it's from our breakup or finding me at Jean-Luc's like he did. Feeling small and embarrassed, I whisper, "I'm sorry."

His chest rises and falls with heavy breaths, his blue eyes darker, his gaze directed at me. Scooting closer, he takes my hand in his and brings it to his mouth, kissing it. I move closer, closing the gap between us and replace my hand with my lips. His hands go to the back of my head, holding me to him. So tight. So close. Our tongues meet in an aggressive collision of passion.

He moves away from me abruptly, looking away.

"Austin?"

"Call Brandon."

"Austin?"

Austin's voice is stern, his words clipped. "He's worried. Call him." Leaning his head against the window, I can tell I'm losing him, again.

Pulling my phone from my purse, I see all the missed calls displayed. My stomach drops, feeling sick. Brandon answers on the first ring, "Jules?"

"It's me. I'm okay."

"You're okay?"

"Yes. I'm fine."

"I was worried," he says. "I'm stuck in Philly and couldn't get a hold of you."

"I'm with Austin."

"I called him, Jules. You weren't answering."

Staring out the window as we cross the bridge, I say, "Thank you."

"You're sure you're okay?"

"I am. I'll tell you more when you're home."

His breath starts to even. "I'll be home late tonight."

"I'm tired, Brandon. Can I see you tomorrow?"

"Yeah." He sighs. "I'm glad to hear your voice."

He makes me smile. "It's good to hear your voice too. We'll talk tomorrow. Safe travels."

"Goodbye."

"Bye." I hang up and look over at Austin. I don't say anything, nervous to disrupt his thoughts, which seem intense from his expression.

When he turns, his eyes are as severe as his thoughts seem to be. "I want you to come to my place."

"Are you asking me?"

"No."

"Okay."

I'VE BEEN INSIDE his penthouse for over an hour and he's still sitting in the leather and chrome chair he sat in when we walked in. He's watching me, watching every move I make, so I don't move much. I tried to open up a conversation, but he wouldn't respond. I'm finding this new side to Austin intriguing, challenging, nerve wracking, and while being the subject of his intense stare, I find him sexy.

I readjust on the couch, tucking my legs under me while keeping my eyes fixed on him. His tongue glides over his bottom lip as my tongue slides over my top one. He loosens his tie and starts to unbutton his shirt—three buttons before he stops. I'm disappointed as I look him over, wishing the show would continue.

When I stand up, I take my shoes off. Tired of this strange, yet fascinating game, I go to him. His gaze traces over my body, causing it to react by warming inside. Standing in front of him, his legs are spread and I sit in his lap sideways. When I lean my head on his shoulder, I'm not sure if I want him to hold me to make it all better or to fuck me to make it all go away.

He slips his arms under me and stands. Carrying me into the bedroom, he then lays me down on the bed. Austin removes his jacket, then his shirt, taking his undershirt with it. I silently watch as he undresses the rest of the way, no clothes covering him as he climbs onto the bed next to me. He wraps his arm over me and presses his face into my hair and neck. A warm breath escapes followed by his pain. "I would have done anything for you." With a jagged breath, he adds, "I still will."

I turn my head, my cheek against his. "I know." Moving down until my forehead is pressed to his, I say, "I would do anything to change what happened, to be the person who knew what to do from the beginning."

"We can't change the past, but I'm realizing I can change our fate." His hand slides under my shirt stopping on my waist. His fingers tighten, squeezing me. "I want you in my life, but wanting you makes me feel weak and I spent years overcoming weakness."

"You're not weak for admitting your feelings. You're stronger for following your heart." I kiss his still lips. I kiss him until he responds, his hands pushing my shirt up as his tongue mingles with mine. Our breath comes harder as I lean my head back and his mouth starts covering my neck. My shirt is pushed up exposing my breasts. Austin places kisses over the tops of each just above my bra. My arms are put above my head as his body moves on top of mine. Risking it all, I say, "I love you."

Everything stops—his lips on my skin, his hands that held my arms, and his hips that had found a rhythm between my legs. He tugs the shirt off the rest of the way then takes my arms, laying them at my sides. His expression is more serious as the light from outside the window reflects in his eyes. I'm unsure how this is gonna go. My heart starts racing, feeling a distance flickering to life between us as he slides to the side and onto his back.

"Austin, talk to me. Please." I hate how pathetic I sound, but I can't help it. "Please."

He looks over at me, and says, "I love you. I've loved you since the day I laid eyes on you." There's a truthfulness that could be called vulnerability, but I see it as quite the opposite. I listen to him, falling even deeper in love with him. "I used to wonder what your smile looked like and if I could ever evoke it. I even used to imagine us dancing at the gallery." He chuckles to himself. "Sounds stupid, but it just seemed like something you would like."

I roll onto my side to face him, running my hand down his arm until our fingers entwine. He says, "You weren't a muse like Jean-Luc wanted or something that needed to be fixed like you are for Dylan. You're this force to be reckoned with, all strong and gorgeous, confident, but sensitive and affected." Turning away from me, he looks out the window. "I saw you crying the night we met, in the back. I heard the artist yell at you."

When he looks at me again, I say, "I've always wondered how you found me at the new gallery."

"I stopped by and found out you had been fired. The guy said he'd let me know if you got work and he did." He smiles to himself. "I also paid him a hundred bucks."

"But why did you want to find me?"

"Because, like I said, I've loved you since the day I laid eyes on you."

My mouth crashes down on his as I roll on top of him. My clothes go flying as we both pull at them until I'm freed. Our mouths create a continuum between us as he pushes in and we become one again. Our bodies move with care, taking our time, hands exploring, moans captured and swallowed. Thrusts deepen, my back arching as his fingers elicit, drawing forth my orgasm, his following quickly after.

Short of breath, we lay there on our backs chasing it until it soothes. When he looks at me, I smile, and he says, "There's that smile I worked so hard for."

The seriousness of the situation arises overtaking the ease of our lovemaking. "Where do we stand, Austin?"

"Where we always did—fumbling through this world together, making mistakes, making them right, making love, making a future."

I snuggle into his side, draping my leg over his. "Together?"

He sounds positive when he responds, "Together."

Worry is replaced by happiness and I smile against his chest. "Thank you."

"I can feel how much you love me, Jules. I see it in your eyes, just like I see your remorse. We all make mistakes. You didn't go after him. As much as I would have loved if you had been the one to punch him, our past seems to always fuck with our futures."

Resting my chin on his chest, I turn to see his face. "Tell me about your past, the one that fucked with your future."

It's his turn to smile now. "You want me to make you feel better about your ex, don't you?"

I laugh lightly. "Maybe."

His body moves with laughter, though I don't hear him. Austin goes quiet for a moment, then says, "Her name was Christina. We were high school sweethearts. Sounds cheesy already, right?"

"No. Sounds romantic."

After a kiss to my head, he continues, "Well, after graduation, we both got jobs and went to college. I remember it being hard trying to balance the long days at class and the long nights working while dating someone. It wasn't her fault or anything she did. I wanted to spend time with her, but there was no extra time."

I lay back, resting my head on the pillow next to him and wait for him to go on.

"It sucks to be poor," he says, glancing my way. "We were both broke. Our families were broke, so our futures depended on us to make our dreams come true."

"What were your dreams?" I ask.

"I wanted to travel."

"You do a lot of that. Is it a dream come true?"

He shrugs. "It used to be. Now, it's just business."

"What do you dream of now?"

His arm tightens around me and pulls me to him. "Being settled."

"You say that like my mistakes don't matter, like this could actually work between us."

Tilting his head downward, he looks me in the eyes, "Jules, what you fail to realize is that I never saw your flaws. I saw the woman behind that shield you carry so prominently. That's not a flaw, that's self-preservation." He sighs. "As for all the other shit going on, I almost had sex in London."

I sit upright, turning to look down on him. "What?" The smirk that covers his face and the cocked eyebrow are disarming. "Almost?" I ask quieter, completely jealous.

"I didn't do it, but I could've, several times."

I lay back down. "Now you're just bragging."

"Maybe."

Pulling the sheet over us, I turn to my side, facing him. "Why didn't you?"

"Because no matter how mad I am at you or how much you hurt me by kissing Dylan, having sex with someone else wouldn't have made me feel better. It would make things worse."

"Am I only in your bed now because of the Jean-Luc incident?" I close my eyes, but feel his hand on my cheek, pushing my hair back.

When I open my eyes again, he whispers, "You're here, in my bed, in my apartment, and in my life because these days, you're what my dreams are made of." I feel the truth behind his confession. "I love you, Jules." His words overwhelm me and I scoot closer, letting the tears fall. He holds me even tighter, but says, "You hurt me. Don't hurt me again."

It makes me wonder if I'm capable of not hurting others when all I do is punish myself. The yellow canvas hanging in my apartment comes to mind and I'm reminded that I can be who I want to be. I don't have the baggage tethered to my heart any longer. I know what I want and Austin is my dream come true. "I won't. I love you."

His chest lowers as he releases a long exhale. Rolling us over, his hand goes from my face over my shoulder and covers my breast, stirring my inner desires. I spread my legs allowing him to fall into position. We make love two more times before the sun sets.

STANDING IN FRONT of his elevator, I wait to push the button. "Come with me," I say again.

He leans against the wall, his head fall to the side. "Why do you want me to come?"

"I don't want to leave you."

"Then don't."

Giggling, I push his chest. "I need clean clothes."

"Forget it all. Leave it. We'll start over. Buy you all new stuff."

Grabbing his shirt, I come closer while tugging. One kiss to his chin, then two on his lips, and I say, "I like this idea."

My hips are grabbed and squeezed. "I like you."

"I like you." I swat his hand. "Now let me go or I'll never make it home."

The smile is gone, replaced by sincerity. "I don't want to ever let you go again."

"I'll be back. Tonight, if you don't mind a late night visitor."

His blue eyes shine with the contentment I've always wished for him, the happiness he deserves. "Are we starting over? You staying at your place, me staying at mine with occasional visits back and forth?"

"No, there's no going back. I'm fully invested." I twirl for him. "See? All here. All for you."

"You look good fully invested. But I might need a reminder of how good fully invested *feels*."

I burst out laughing. "You're insatiable and I approve of this."

He takes my hand and starts tugging me back. I drop my coat and purse, leaving them to fall on the floor. Austin stops, spins my back to the bedroom while kissing my neck, and I let him because clean clothes are totally overrated.

CHAPTER 8
Jules

BRANDON ANSWERS AFTER two knocks. The door is left open as he walks into the kitchen. "Come in," he says.

I shut the door and walk inside. "How are you?"

He stops, setting the spoon down, his face is one of annoyance. Resting his hands on the counter in front of him, he glares at me. "How am I? *How are you?*"

"I'm fine."

Tense, he asks, "What happened to you?"

"Do you want me to tell you the truth or a story to make you feel better?"

"Shit, Jules. Don't play games. I was worried. I almost called Dylan."

"You called Austin though."

"I called Austin because I knew I could count on him, no matter what had happened. Now tell *me* what happened."

Walking to his refrigerator, I open the freezer and search. "Do you have any vodka?"

"Must be bad if you need vodka." Moving past me, he says, "It's right here."

"The vodka's for you. I need you calm."

Shaking his head, he rolls his eyes, then shuts the freezer door.

I laugh while moving to the couch. I know I'm not getting out of this that easy, so I settle in for the long haul, also known as an interrogation.

I DON'T KNOW that Brandon feels any better about the Jean-Luc situation, much like I don't, but I do know Jean-Luc didn't touch me. I know he didn't. I find comfort in that and will try to move on from this.

A knock on my door interrupts my packing. I walk over and look through the peephole, spying Austin standing there. He's making faces at me and I laugh, everything feeling lighter today. Swinging the door open, I grab him by the belt loop and pull him inside against me until his lips meet mine. He kicks the door closed and when we part, he says, "I could get used to that kind of greeting."

"I hope so because that's gonna be the standard from now on."

With a smile, I see his eyes go from me to over my shoulder. "That's new," he says.

Following his gaze, I see the yellow painting. "It's not new. I painted over it."

He's shocked. "You painted over it?"

"Yes. I love it now."

He glances between the painting and me several times, then grins. "I love it too. A happy color suits you much better."

"Thank you for saying that. I feel much more yellow than blue these days."

His smile lights up his whole face. "You really mean that, don't you?"

I lean my head on his shoulder and whisper, "When we're together, I'm reminded of who I used to be. I prefer who I am with you."

"You're who you choose to be, Jules." His lips meet mine,

tongues caress tenderly followed by a sigh. "But no matter who that is, I see the real you."

My breath stalls in my chest as I breathe his words into my heart. "Who am I?"

"You're the woman I was born to love."

"Austin," I sigh, my lips against his. "I love you."

He places a kiss on my forehead quickly, then looks me in the eyes again. "I love you, Jules Weston." Moving to stand in front of the painting, he admires it with a smile on his face. "Yes, I prefer yellow too. Good choice."

As I watch him, my heart races. He's always been the one. I was just too caught up in the past instead of the future that stands before me.

"I see the change in you. I see the woman I fell in love with." Holding his hands out, fisted with his wrists together, he says, "You might as well have me arrested now."

"What?" I frown. "For what?"

"For stealing your heart." He laughs. "Don't think I don't see those lovey dovey eyes you're giving me."

I roll my eyes. "Yellow may be my new color, but cheesy looks damn sexy on you. C'mere. I want to show you something." I walk into the kitchen, and ask, "Latte?"

With raised eyebrows, he asks, "Lattes now too?" He rushes to me, grabs my shoulders and squares me to him. "What have you done with Jules?"

Fighting a hardy laugh, I say, "Progress is happening. You might want to stand back."

He kisses my cheek, and says, "No way. I'm gonna be right here next to you for all of this progress. I'm digging this new sunny side perspective." Leaning against the counter, he smiles. "What brought all this on anyway?"

Leaning back against the counter next to him, I reply, "I woke up and saw my life packed and I was without you. I knew that wasn't the life I wanted. Everything I've been holding so tightly to over the years is just stuff. It was easier to grab a hold of these things and what I was missing than to let it continue and be alone. I don't want to live like that anymore. That's not living at all."

He nods. I see the love through his gaze, but he doesn't say it. He doesn't need to. I feel it. Instead, he asks, "You ready to go?"

"Yes. Let me grab my bag from the bed."

"I'll grab it," he offers.

"Thanks." I take a moment to look around the place. With him behind me, I say, "This place may feel more me after all these years, but a lot less like home." Laughing, I lean back on him. "I sound silly."

"You don't sound silly. Sounds like you're growing."

"Growing up, I think."

Taking my hand, we walk out. I turn the key and suddenly it feels very much like the last time I'll be doing this.

Sensing my mood in the car, he asks, "You okay?"

Sliding across the seat next to him, I lean my head on his shoulder and smile. "More than okay. Better than I've been in forever."

His arm wraps over my shoulders and we watch the world go by together, Austin feeling very much like home these days.

THE NEXT TWO weeks are spent between the gallery and Austin's apartment. He doesn't leave town or work late. He cancels dinners to spend time with me. When I have an exhibit, he shows up to support me. Everything is perfect. I'm still not used to how well he treats me, so I decide to show him just how much I appreciate him.

Whispering, I say, "Follow me." Leading him into my office, I shut the door and lock it once he enters. "Leave the lights off. No one can see in here when it's dark."

"Ms. Weston, I have a feeling you're up to no good."

"Is there any other way to be when we're together?"

He chuckles. I plant my mouth firmly to his and kiss him. Sliding my skirt up on the sides, he exposes my bare ass. His hand slides under the silky material and between my legs. His lips cover my neck in sweet sucking kisses as his fingers know exactly where to touch to get me off.

I spread my fingers over his erection, evoking a moan from both of us. Sliding up to the top of his pants, I move my hand inside and down, wanting to feel the warm skin over his hardness. "Fuck," he groans. "Move to the desk."

Removing my hand, I turn and back up until the back of my thighs hit the front of my desk. His eyes are locked on mine until someone laughs loudly from the gallery floor, a reminder we're not alone, a mere wood door separates us from a hundred other patrons. A couple walks by outside the large window, but when I turn back to Austin, it's as if he doesn't see anything but me. His expression is one of want, lust, and possession. He says, "Turn around and bend over."

My lips part from the shock of his demand, but the sexual tension is building as well as my craving to feel him inside me again. I taunt by dragging my skirt up on just one side and smirking at him.

With purpose, he walks steadily to me. Taking my ponytail in one hand, he twists it around his hand then slowly pulls down until I stop resisting and drop my head back. His tongue finds my neck again and slides his teeth lightly up until his lips are against my ear. His words are just breaths against my heated skin, "Turn. Around."

My mouth drops open and I look up at him.

His voice is harsh and demanding. "Now."

I'd love to be sassy and talk back but I'm too hot and bothered to argue. I want this as much as he does. Turning around, I bend over my desk, the glass cold through the thin material of my blouse. I press my cheek down and close my eyes as he caresses my ass several times, teasing me. My breath quickens as he slides down the middle.

The metal of his belt clangs, then the teeth of his zipper. "I love how soft your skin is, Jules, and how wet you get for me."

Squirming, I say, "I'm on fire for you, Austin."

His laugh hits the back of my head, but it's not playful. Instead there's a heaviness to the sound just like the air around us. The weight of him moulds to my body and his cock slides between my legs. More teasing. My weakness for him, my desire voiced. "I want you inside of me, Austin. Please."

"Why does a please from you sound so fucking hot? Say it again."

I hate games, but for him, I'll play. *"Pleeaase."*

Heat. Steel. Silk. Wet. I'm filled, my cheek pressed harder to the glass top as he thrusts back out and in rapidly. Gripping my hips, using them as leverage, he swears. "Fuck! God. Fuck, Jules."

Pressing my palms against the desktop, I lift up, focusing on the chair in front of me. He picks up his pace. Deeper. Harder. Unrelenting and I take it, loving the feel of his power as he takes me.

His hips slam against the back of me, his large cock hitting that spot deep inside that only he presses. A groan of pleasure escapes me every time he thrusts in. He frees his in conjunction with mine. When his hand snakes around my thigh, he touches my clit and the sensation mixed with him inside of me, sends me falling into a darkness where our love lights my way. Two more thrusts punctuate my ecstasy and he's there with me, then we both drop onto the desk. My arms are spread, his on top of mine. He says, "I want you, Jules. I want you with me. I want to wake up to you and fall asleep holding you after making love to you—"

"Or fucking me?"

"Yes, or fucking you. I just want all of you all of the time. Call me greedy, selfish, or whatever, but I'm in love with you." He lifts and helps me up slowly before turning me around. When our eyes meet, he says, "If you'd marry me, I would ask."

I feel the genuineness in his statement. Glancing down, then back up, suddenly feeling vulnerable around him despite what we just did, I say, "Ask me then."

With a slight nod, he smiles softly before kissing me on the lips. "I promise."

As much as I don't want to get hurt, I realize whether he asks me to marry him or not, I'm in too deep to save myself. That's what love is—it's sharing burdens, trusting in a future that isn't guaranteed, and faith that it all works out. Good in concept, but one that can go awry so easily if not safeguarded. So that's what I plan to do. I will safeguard our good and when we fight, I'll keep the faith and trust in him. He deserves that and more. I deserve all of that too.

CHAPTER 9
Jules

BEFORE AUSTIN AND I take that next step in our relationship, I'm surprised in an entirely different way. Returning to my apartment after a week spent at Austin's, I open the door and find a small box, about the size that would fit a ring. But when I lift the lid, there isn't a ring inside. There's a key.

Holding it up, it dangles from a numbered keychain. 27. In the box I find a folded piece of paper. Excited to see what Austin has in store for us, I grab it and read:

> **Here is the key to our life. It's all the belongings and memories that made us and our apartment together a home. If I could change my mistakes and make it better, I would. Believe me. I would. I screwed up, and for hurting you, I apologize. I will always love you, just like you'll always be my sweet Juliette.**
> **Dylan**

The address of a storage unit in the Bronx is listed under his name and I exhale heavily.

The key.

The key to our life.

The key to our stuff.

My stuff?

Dylan's giving me my stuff back after four years. I pull my phone from my pocket and call Austin. "You miss me already?" he asks in that way that I can hear his smile through the phone.

"Yes. Always." My heart races dragging my past into our future, but I need him now. I need him to do this with me. "I have a favor to ask."

"Anything."

"Will you go to the Bronx with me?"

AUSTIN HOLDS THE door open for me and I walk in. "Hi," I say to the man behind the counter who's reading the paper.

The older man looks up and smiles. "Hi. How can I help you?"

Holding the key up, I say, "I have a key to a unit here."

"Number?" He starts typing on his computer.

Austin rests his hand on my shoulder, and I reply, "Twenty-seven."

His eyes leave the screen and meet mine. "Ms. Weston?"

"Yes?"

"Mr. Somers told me I should expect you."

"Yes, he gave me the key."

Austin's hand squeezes gently and I'm not sure if it's a reaction to hearing Dylan's name or in support of me. Either way, I'm grateful he's here, so I cover his with mine.

The man stands up with a clipboard in hand. "He left you more than the key. He left the unit in your name and paid for a year's worth of rent."

"Really?"

"Yes," he says, pointing. "Right here."

While studying the document, I reply, "That was nice."

"Mr. Somers is a good man. I miss our chats now that he's

handed over the unit." He sits back down. "We talked Yankees versus Mets. We may not have agreed on baseball, but seeing you now, I see we agree on women."

Austin cuts off this conversation, obviously uncomfortable with the details of Dylan's feelings toward me. "Austin Barker," he says, introducing himself. "Ms. Weston's boyfriend."

The man shakes it, his expression friendly. "I'm Joey."

Austin asks, "Nice to meet you, Joey. Can you direct us to the unit?"

The man smiles, then points to his left. "Down there. The end unit on the right hand side."

"Thank you," Austin responds and walks ahead of me. When he looks back, his smile is tight. "We should get going. We have a reservation at eight."

I tell Joey, "Thank you," and follow Austin down the hall. The corridor is wide and we pass a loading garage door on the way.

When we reach number twenty-seven, Austin takes the key and unlocks the large padlock, then removes it altogether. Looking at me, he asks, "You ready?"

Standing here now, my nerves start to take over, but I nod anyway. The five foot wide garage-style door is lifted, a light pops on, and my mouth drops open. I was excited. *I thought.* I was prepared. *I thought.*

I wasn't. At. All.

Everything is here—everything from the couch to the dresser to my grandmother's crocheted throw. My eyes can't settle on any one item when there's so much to see. My heart begins to race as I step inside. "I never thought I'd see any of this again." It's like stepping inside a time warp of my life before Austin.

"Why'd he take it?" he asks.

Over my shoulder, I see Austin with his hands still holding the door up. I shake my head. "I don't know really... to hurt me?" Opening a box in the corner, I say, "Maybe if he didn't want our life together anymore, he didn't want me to have it either. I'm not sure I'll ever really know."

The dresser in the corner holds our framed pictures, all set upright on display. I remember we had ten. I used to count them when I was cleaning. I step up on the loveseat and count them now. Nine. Sighing, I realize I can live with nine. A memory of seeing a frame on his desk the one time I visited him at work comes back to me and curious, I wonder if that might be the missing photo. Honestly, it would make me sad if he hadn't keep any mementos at all. I'm not worried what else he took. Suddenly standing here in the middle of all of this stuff, I realize like the coffeemaker and prisms, none of it holds any power over me anymore, just like he doesn't. My future matters more than my past. Austin matters more.

I spend the next hour rifling through everything as Austin sits on the couch watching while giving me the time I need. With a shoebox of college memorabilia in my lap, I rub his leg and say, "You never finished your story about Christina."

His brow furrows as he leans back. "You want to hear about that now?"

"Seems apropos to be amongst the skeletons and ghosts of my past."

He sets a book down on the side table and says, "Our senior year at college, we were so busy making plans for the future that we forgot to live in the present. Cliché, but true."

I set the shoebox down and give him my full attention. "We all do that."

"We worked together. One day, she was late. I kept calling her because I thought they would fire her if she didn't show up soon, but she never answered." He drops his head into his hands and scrubs harshly as if the thought itself is hard to have. "I finished my shift," he sighs, then continues, "apologized for her missing her shift. I made up a story about her going to the health clinic or something. I can't remember now."

Austin is so handsome, one of the most attractive men I've ever seen, but right now in this small space full of mine and my ex's clutter, he's telling me his darkest secret. It's a story that pains him so much that he looks exhausted under the harsh fluorescent light.

The story itself contorts his beautiful features into anguish. "I found her passed out. Something about meds mixing together. That's what her parents told me the doctors told them. It wasn't the meds. It was her. They knew. They thought she would be happier after she graduated. They convinced her of that and in turn, she convinced me. She said she wanted New York and I believed her, so we moved."

Leaning forward, I run my fingers through his hair, then turn his chin toward me. "If this is too much, you don't have to talk about it."

"I want to. You should know." He looks around, then back to me. "You shared your past with me and I should have told you a long time ago."

"There's a difference. My past forced itself on you."

He takes my hand. "I want you to know." Then he stands and walks to the doorway. Leaning on it with his back to me, he says, "She killed herself three months later. In our apartment."

My gasp echoes between the cinderblock walls. "Austin."

"The neighbors found her when they saw the front door open." Turning around, he peeks up at me. "By the time I was called, the police were in my apartment. I was interrogated as I stood next to her body. She still had some color to her face and I remember leaning down and listening for air, feeling for a heartbeat. They had declared her dead an hour earlier, but... yeah..." He sighs and sits on the arm of the couch.

"You're not to blame. You know that right?"

"Logically, yes. But I was there. I saw the changes in her. I thought she just needed more time to acclimate to the city. I found out later that her parents talked her into giving the move a try. They thought the change would be good for her, but she didn't want to be there. She didn't want to be with me."

"You don't know that. You're filling in the blanks to find answers, but those answers aren't necessarily the truth. I know this firsthand. I don't think she would have moved if she didn't love you. I do think she needed help after the first time. Her parents probably know more than they've told you."

"It wouldn't have made a difference if I knew or not. She killed herself. She took pills that were supposed to help her and killed herself instead of talking to me."

"That's on her though, Austin. Not you. You can't shoulder the blame for her decision."

Wanting to make him feel better, wanting to remind him of the good he's had in the past, I ask, "What did she look like? Describe her."

He pauses, looking at me curiously, but eventually concedes. "She was beautiful. Long blonde hair, big blue eyes. When she smiled, everyone smiled. It came from within and she shined. She fell for me before I grew into myself. I was awkward and kind of geeky, but not fully. I was still kind of sexy, so I was told." I smile, imagining him scrawnier but charming.

"Oh, I just bet you were."

He chuckles. "She was Miss Harvest Fest our senior year. Gotta love the Midwest."

Pieces begin falling into place and my smile dissipates. "At the end... she was like me when we met."

No traces of the lighthearted are left. "A little."

"You can't save the world, Austin."

"I wasn't trying to save you. I didn't need to, Jules. You're doing a damn fine job all on your own, just like I knew you would. You're stronger than you think."

I want the happy that we've had back, so I stand up in the middle of the ten by fifteen unit. I do one last turn, scanning everything, then grab my jewelry box, and say, "We can go."

"What are you going to do with everything?"

"Nothing for now."

Eyeing the box in my hands, he asks, "Is that all you want?"

"I think so."

He steps over the arm of the couch and I maneuver my way out. "Wait!" Running back in I grab my grandmother's crocheted throw, then step back out. Pulling the door down, he padlocks it again and we walk back toward the man on duty at the desk. "Goodnight," I say as we pass.

Joey replies, "Goodnight."

In the car, Austin looks over at me, my box, and the blanket. "How are you doing?"

I don't hesitate, being there was easier than I expected. "I'm good. Better than I thought."

"So he gave all your stuff back."

Not a question. Just a statement. "Yep."

"What are you going to do with it?"

Turning sideways on the seat, I shrug. "Not sure yet, but it seems I have a year to decide."

He nods. "You hungry?"

"Starved." I reach over and hold his hand because even though I thought I would be the one crumbling, he seems to need the comfort. "American Bistro?"

"Yes." He kisses the top of my hand and smiles. "I know how much you like it."

"I do. Thank you and thank you for coming here with me."

"No problem."

I can breathe again. Somehow Dylan giving all that stuff back, whether I keep it or not, has eased my lungs. Feeling lighter, I take his hand and kiss the palm. "I love you."

"I love you too."

CHAPTER 10
Jules

ALTHOUGH I KNEW it was coming one day, it wasn't what I expected at all. The day it came, I was blindsided. But first, I should take you back just about a year...

I'm packing my stuff, throwing it into a large purse haphazardly. I don't care. I just need to see Austin. I slip out of the gallery and hail a cab. Traffic sucks. Nothing new, but I'm still frustrated. It takes forty minutes to cross town and get to his office. I pay the cabbie and rush inside. Waving to the receptionist and then to Tony, the Office Manager, I head straight for Austin's office.

Tony calls, "Austin's in a meetin—"

But I already have the door open. "I'm pregnant."

The room goes quiet and five men turn around to stare at me. I shift from one foot to the other, my cheeks flaming with heat, embarrassed. Then I see Austin smile at me. He calmly asks, "You're pregnant?"

I gulp, then nod. "Yes."

He comes out from behind his desk and says, "We're gonna have a baby?"

"We are."

Taking my face in his hands, he whispers, "We're gonna have a baby." He kisses me. When we open our eyes, the office is empty and the door closed. Austin's smile is so big when he asks, "When did you find out?"

"Just before I came over. I took five tests at the gallery."

His hand covers my stomach and rubs gently. "How are you feeling?"

"It's early, so I feel great."

Caressing my cheek, he says, "We're gonna do this, right?"

"I want to."

"I want this baby and I want you. I want to have a family with you."

I moved into his penthouse five months ago. We don't talk about marriage or kids much. We have in the past. We know we're on the same page when it comes to those things, but it didn't seem like we had to rush things. We did that the first time and it didn't turn out so well. So now after almost two years together, we're taking the plunge in a huge way, but I'm not scared. I'm happy. It may not seem ideal to some, out of order from traditional expectations, but this feels right for us. I wrap my arms around his neck and say, "I want you and a family with you too."

Austin wraps his arms around my waist, and says, "We should look at brownstones or a place with a yard."

"I like the penthouse. We can change the guest room into the baby's room."

"What if we have two or three kids?"

Laughing, I say, "You have big plans. Let's just enjoy this one first before we start planning the Barker baseball team."

"Barker baseball team? I could get behind that idea."

"Slow down big boy. First time, soon to be mom, here. You're making me nervous."

He laughs, walking back to his desk. "I'm happy. This is the best news I've ever gotten."

I sit down across the desk from him. "You really are happy, aren't you?"

His grin is ever present. The sparkle in his eyes shows joy. "So happy. When do you go to the doctor?" He types on his keyboard, then turns toward me.

"I don't know. I just wanted to tell you, so I came straight over."

Reaching across the wood desktop, he holds my hand. "I'm here for you. I'd like to go if you want me there."

"I always want you there."

...and he came to every appointment.

THE BIRTH WAS a dream. I couldn't relate to other mothers. I didn't have a twelve hour labor or push for three hours. I had an epidural, so I wasn't in any pain and things progressed quickly. With Austin holding my hand, our sweet boy, Theodore Weston Barker, was born on March 12th.

That evening in the hospital, we all lay on the bed together. When I open my eyes, I see Austin holding the baby. He whispers, "How are you feeling?"

"Tired." I readjust, moving so I can rest my head on his shoulder and watch our son.

Holding the baby closer to me, he asks, "Do you want to hold him? Are you feeling strong enough right now?"

"Yes," I say, taking him into my arms. I kiss Theo's head, then lower him to my chest. I always thought I could be content with my job, that it somehow defined the person I dreamed of being. But I was wrong. *So wrong.* Being here with Austin and holding our baby defines everything that matters most. This little baby represents a love that survived my mistakes and bad judgments, a love that shone through the pain, giving me pure sunshine.

Theodore's blanket loosens and I move to tighten it but feel something hard through the fabric. Investigating further, I find a ring sparkling in the low light of the room. I glance to Austin just as he takes it. In the quiet room at my bedside, he kneels down on one knee and says, "I once made you a promise that I had every intention of keeping. I've loved you from the moment I saw you, your beauty outshining any painting that hangs in any gallery. I spent three years waiting for you to say yes, but would have waited a lifetime."

My voice is soft, the tears inevitable. "Oh Austin."

"You once asked me what my dreams were and I said you. What I didn't tell you is it was really this—I used to dream that one day we'd have a family together. I think you're the most amazing woman and I know you'll be an incredible mother... and wife. Juliette Weston, will you marry me and give me a forever full of dreams come true?"

Tears fall as I lean, hiding my face against his chest while holding our baby between us. "Yes."

I DON'T CRINGE when I hear my name anymore. I'm actually kind of partial to it these days. Austin still calls me Jules, but every now and then I introduce myself as Juliette with a smile on my face.

My apartment has been sublet for years now after I bought it for investment purposes. I recently rented it to a young couple who moved from Nebraska. College sweethearts. Standing by the mailbox on the first floor, I put the new sticker on, replacing the old one that fell off two days earlier. With their new rental agreement in hand, I walk outside, but stop when I see Dylan standing on the sidewalk looking up. When our eyes meet, neither of us rushes to find words. Instead, we hold the moment with a gentle gaze.

Theo is restless though. When he's strapped in the chest carrier, he likes me to keep moving. With a little protest, I look down at him, holding the back of his head and place a kiss there. When I look back at Dylan, he smiles and nods. I can see the toll life has taken on him. He's not a mess. He still has a great head of hair. And he just might be even more handsome with age. But a sadness resides in his blue eyes, a stormy grey taking over. I wonder if it can ever be erased. It's not something I'll dwell on, releasing all that anger a long time ago.

I smile and give him a little wave before walking away. Not running this time. When I reach the corner, I look back, but he's gone and for a brief moment I wonder if I imagined him altogether. The light changes and I cross the street, walking back to the life I deserve, a life that seemed impossible at one time. Austin gave me a second chance, a second chance at a life full of pure love and as he puts it, dreams come true. He's the most generous, caring man I know and I realize before any promises of marriage were ever made, he made me a promise the night we met, the night Dylan broke my heart. Austin was there at the gallery and made me a promise, a promise he kept when he said, "It will be okay."

He's given me more than okay. He's given me amazing.

THE ANSWER WAS always yes. I made Austin a promise that day in the hospital, but today is when that yes becomes a commitment. And I have no fears or worries anymore.

Standing in the middle of the gallery, in front of a small gathering of friends and family, I say, "The story may have changed, but this was how it was always supposed to end." Our hands tighten. "I didn't need a fairy tale, but ended up in the middle of one. Thank you for being strong enough to love me, for showing me that love isn't just about healing, but about creating a new destiny, one *we* determine. You made me fall in love with love again. You made me fall head over heels in love with you along the way. So today, I happily become your wife as you have become my life. I love you, Austin, forever."

The Justice of the Peace says something, but I'm lost in Austin's eyes as he looks into mine. Then Austin says, "Life was predictable, orderly, and completely boring until I met you. You with your tear streaked face, so concerned about a painting when you were hurting so much on the inside. When I looked into your eyes the first time, I saw a future that offered nothing more than passion and fiery outcomes. When you thought you had nothing to give, *you*, my love, gave me something exciting and new. Kissing you was like kissing fire despite the ice. Over the years I watched you fade, then come back to life. You were always the woman you are today. You just forgot for awhile. I'll spend every day reminding you of how you make each day worthwhile and thanking you for our son. I love you, Jules, forever."

With rings on our fingers, we kiss, sealing a destiny that was always meant to be.

SOMETIMES I THINK of Dylan. How can I not? He defined years of my life for so long, but I found that letting go of the past doesn't erase it. Time has a way of lightening the load that once tainted it. And through it all, I can now look back and remember the good times we had. There were more good than bad when I reflect back. From where I sit today though, those memories pale in comparison to the life I've been given, the life I live.

Looking over at the framed quote that sits on my desk, a gentle reminder I keep around, I read silently, "A storm doesn't ask for volunteers." I gave into the hard times willingly. What I didn't realize then is that there were always other options. It just took me some time to see the beacon of light through the dark. Now that I have, I'll hold onto to this life, finding my happiness in the present rather than living in the sorrow of the past.

The End.

A PERSONAL NOTE

THANK YOU FOR taking this journey of emotions from *Scorned* through *Jealousy* and beyond with me. It was a heart-wrenching, nerve-wracking, loving, frustrating, amazing ride with these characters, but I loved every minute. Hope you do too.

As always, thank you to my incredible team of awesome:

Danielle, Flavia, Heather, Irene, Lisa, Marla, Meire

You make everything I do prettier, better, and even more amazing. Thank you for your time and endless support. xo

ABOUT THE AUTHOR

NEW YORK TIMES and USA Bestselling Author, S. L. Scott, was always interested in the arts. She grew up painting, writing poetry and short stories, and wiling her days away lost in a good book and the movies.

With a degree in Journalism, she continued her love of the written word by reading American authors like Salinger and Fitzgerald. She was intrigued by their flawed characters living in picture perfect worlds, but could still debate that the worlds those characters lived in were actually the flawed ones. This dynamic of leaving the reader invested in the words, inspired Scott to start writing with emotion while interjecting an underlying passion into her own stories.

Living in the capital of Texas with her family, Scott loves traveling and avocados, beaches, and cooking with her kids. She's obsessed with epic romances and loves a good plot twist. She dreams of seeing one of her own books made into a movie one day as well as returning to Europe. Her favorite color is blue, but she likens it more toward the sky than the emotion. Her home is filled with the welcoming symbol of the pineapple and finds surfing a challenge though she likes to think she's a pro.

Scott welcomes your notes to sl@slscottauthor.com

Made in the USA
Middletown, DE
20 July 2016